This Rancid Mill

AN ALEX DAMAGE NOVEL

Kyle Decker

Bad Chemicals can be found on Bandcamp at badchemicalsband.bandcamp.com.

This Rancid Mill
Kyle Decker © 2023
This edition © PM Press

ISBN: 978–1–62963–370–1 (paperback)
ISBN: 978–1–62963–686–3 (ebook)
Library of Congress Control Number: 2022942374

Cover design by Drohan DiSanto
Interior design by briandesign

10 9 8 7 6 5 4 3 2 1

PM Press
PO Box 23912
Oakland, CA 94623
www.pmpress.org

Printed in the USA.

1

Pain lingered like a marriage in the last two years before a divorce. Everyone around me still sounded like a drive-through speaker. The bruises would heal, and my hearing would come back, but I had to accept that irreparable damage had been done somewhere. Somewhere in my head, brain cells were reenacting the mosh pit from the night before. I felt like I'd been savagely beaten by riot batons, and it started to come back to me that I had been. Shows that rowdy are often busted up by the cops, and heads get knocked on both sides. This was especially true in the Year of No Lord 1981.

It's been long established, and never disputed, that cops and punks don't much care for each other. I'm pretty sure the Israelis and Palestinians will patch shit up before we do. They hate us. We hate them. But when punks or their shit go missing, they still need a place to turn, and since they can't go to the cops, they come to me. It doesn't pay much, at least in terms of hard currency. But a good reputation goes a long way, and it's easy to keep costs down when everyone wants to buy you a drink or treat you to dinner. Favors for favors. It's enough to keep me out of the gutter and gives me something to do.

Standing at the counter of 7-Eleven, I fumbled my cheap sunglasses back on as I muttered a "Thank you" to the preppy cashier girl through an unlit cigarette hanging from the corner of my mouth. She didn't respond. Not so much as a "Come again." Likely, she didn't want me to. I handed her the plastic wrap from the pack of Lucky Strikes I'd just bought, which she accepted as if it were a soiled diaper.

I stepped out onto the sidewalk and told natural light to go fuck itself. It was a particularly smoggy LA morning. Early summer has a way of weighing down the dense pollution that hangs over the city like scum on top of a stagnant pond. On days like this, you barely have to smoke. Just step outside and take a few deep breaths. My throat hurt, so I tucked my unlit cigarette behind my ear, rolled the new pack up into the sleeve of my T-shirt, and wandered down Santa Monica Boulevard.

It had dawned on me when I woke up that I'd left my jacket at the venue, a place called the Starwood Club, the night before. It wasn't very far, so I decided to swing by and pick it up. The bouncers knew me well enough that they would never let anyone leave with my jacket. Someone would be there this early. Traveling bands would occasionally crash there, sometimes right onstage. It was just a question of whether or not they'd be up yet.

I was half right. People were there. A lot of people. Maybe every punk within driving distance of West Hollywood. The sidewalk was littered with lit candles. Punk girls wiped their running eye makeup with denim sleeves. Some had photos clutched to their chests, but I couldn't see of whom. The boys clenched their jaws. Some were punching walls. The line of mourners ran up and down Santa Monica and Crescent Heights. The marquee stretched over the entrance to the small parking lot and connected to the neighboring building, and its red neon Starwood sign had been dimmed. The marquee still advertised last night's show, and some were taking photos of themselves in front of it. The lot itself was packed nuts to butts. I pushed through the crowd to the door and stepped inside, ignoring the protests of those who had been waiting. Onstage was a sandwich board with a picture of Jerry Rash, lead singer of Bad Chemicals, last night's headliners.

"Jesus fuck," I said, putting together the simple math. "Oh Jesus. Jesus fuck." I decided to have that cigarette after all.

A girl was onstage. She had a face like Debbie Harry, shoulder-length blood-red hair shaved on one side, and a nose ring in her left nostril. Her outfit was controversially sexy, subverting the more androgynous look favored by punks in the early 1980s. When a lot of girls were rocking thrift-store sweaters a size too large, she wore a mid-length denim jacket with the sleeves cut off, showing off a colorful full-sleeve tattoo that, from a distance, appeared to be abstract designs and flowers. The jacket was unbuttoned over a torn Ramones T-shirt that partially revealed a black bra and a peekaboo view of modest cleavage. Just enough to turn heads without raising an eyebrow. The shirt itself had also been altered to show off contours without cutting off circulation. A black skirt stopped just a few inches above her black knee-high boots, which had more buckles than were practical. The lower bit of the ensemble looked like a black arrow pointing right at her waist. It was crystal that the girl took care of herself, and she'd fashioned an outfit that let people know it. She was laying out flowers and couldn't have given two whiskey shits that I was there, staring at her like a fucking creep.

"We're starting the memorial in about an hour," one of the bouncers said to me. Like most bouncers, he was a tattooed thirty-something. His hair was long and curly. "You'll have to wait outside."

"It's okay, Nick," said a deep, raspy voice that I immediately recognized as my friend Rad. "He's cool. Would you mind covering the door?" Nick nodded and headed outside.

"Rad …," I said, turning around.

"Alex …" Rad gave me a somber nod. "So, you heard about Jerry Rash?"

"No," I said, "I, uh, didn't. I …"

"Came for your jacket?"

"Yeah," I muttered, distracted. "Jacket."

Rad and I went way back to when he had just been Brad. It was "B. Rad" for a short time before being shortened to just "Rad." He had been a big guy even then, and I don't think he's taken shit from anyone since he was twelve. Especially once he hit six-four and 220. His size and no-bullshit attitude made people think he was much harder than he really was. Don't get me wrong, the guy was a coffin nail. A glance from him could defuse just about any situation. But he was also one of the kindest, most loyal people I knew. He was wearing his sleeveless studded denim with the *A* for anarchy spray-painted on the back. I think he'd washed it since he'd bought it from the thrift store. I think. He had thick black hair, short on the sides and longish on top. Instead of spiking it up, he usually tied it back. His arms were covered in minimalist stick-and-poke tattoos of animals and triangles inspired by the baskets in his mom's house. Because of his perpetually tanned skin, people would occasionally try to speak Spanish to him, of which he did not speak a word.

Rad went over behind the bar and grabbed my black leather biker jacket. It looked like wild dogs had been at it. The right sleeve was torn along the seam at the shoulder and held together with comically sized safety pins. An armband with a crossed-out swastika adorned the right bicep, and a Dead Kennedys logo was sloppily sewn onto the back. Rad tossed it to me, and as I slipped into it, he walked over to the bottles.

"Surprised you didn't hear about Jerry before. I tried to call you this morning," Rad said. "Even left a message with your service. You didn't get it?"

"I, uh, didn't make it home." I half-chuckled. "Woke up on a bench in Plummer Park. How'd it happen?"

"OD'd," he said, swallowing. "Heroin, they're saying."

"Intentional?" I asked.

"Fuck if I know," Rad said. "It could be. Jerry Rash had a lot of issues."

I thought about the song they closed with, "Fighting the Hydra," a warp-speed introspective meditation that drew parallels between stress and depression and Herculean tasks.

> So much shit on my plate
> Man, it's filling me up with hate
> When that stress builds up inside ya
> Feels like yer fightin' the hydra
> Can I get a minute?
> Just a fucking minute?

"Sad to say it wouldn't surprise me," I said. Taking a drag from my cigarette, I noticed a loud clomp as the girl jumped off the stage and made a bit of a show about storming into the back room. I felt flushed at the realization that she had overheard us. Rad picked the cig out of my mouth and took a drag. Holding my smoke in his mouth, he touched the shaved sides of my head.

"Got some stubble there, buddy." Rad was trying to change the subject, and I let him.

"Yeah," I said. "Been getting lazy."

With his thumbs, he stroked my three-inch-high mohawk. "Going with blue?"

"Yeah," I said. "Blue." Then he held my head tighter and headbutted me in the forehead, which in our little world is the equivalent of a kiss on the cheek.

"Goddamn it, Rad!" I blurted. "The fuck?!"

"I just wanted to feel something else, y'know?" Rad was a big fan of Bad Chemicals. And so was I, for that matter. It was dawning on me we'd seen their last show. At least, with Jerry Rash. Hard to imagine the band without him. Jerry Rash *was* Bad Chemicals. He had bad chemicals and he took bad chemicals.

"He didn't kill himself," said a feminine yet husky voice. I turned around and saw the girl there. "Jerry wouldn't do that." I hooked my sunglasses into the neck of my T-shirt and opened my mouth to apologize for running my big, stupid mouth, but she walked away and headed outside. Before the door shut behind her, I saw her fall into the arms of her friends.

"I was a fan too," said Rad, "but I wouldn't put it past him at all."

"Yeah." I was still looking at the door. "I know what you mean."

2

I stuck around for the vigil. I didn't see how I couldn't. I was at that show. The last show. Bad Chemicals was one of the hardest, most political bands on the scene. No one did it with more passion, intensity, and love than Jerry fucking Rash. He wasn't just a front man; he was a tribal leader. The San Andreas Fault could only ever dream to shake our little world more than his passing. Our foundation had cracked and was on the verge of collapse. I watched the girl throughout, and she caught me looking at her a few times. I was struck by her poise as she headed the vigil. And was amazed when she read her poem dedicated to Jerry.

> *Some want fame and some want dollars*
> *Some just to be free of their cuffs and their collars*
> *Spiky hair and a torn T-shirt*
> *Is enough for some to call you dirt*
>
> *Some say that a dog off its leash*
> *Is much more likely to die in the street*
> *But you and I could always see*
> *They were the ones who truly ran free*

Punks can cry. Sometimes. Being in the Starwood that afternoon was proof of that. Rad and I sat at the bar and waited for people to empty out. Rad poured whiskey and we both did shots. Before each one, we chanted the greeting Rash would do as he took the stage. "Fuck, fuck, fuckity, fuck, fucking, fuck, fuck you!" Then we each gave each other the finger with one hand as we did a shot with the other. When I turned around in my stool to leave, she was standing there.

"Hey," she said.

"Hi?" I responded.

"Look, I wanted to apologize for earlier," she offered. "I kinda got pissy at you."

"Oh," I said. "Don't worry about it. It was kind of a dick move to say that stuff with you right there."

"It was," she said. "Big time."

"You don't apologize much, do you?" I asked.

"No. I don't." The awkwardness made the pause in conversation seem infinitely longer than I'm sure it really was. Eventually, she added, "Hey, you're that one guy, right?"

"You're going to have to be more specific than that."

"The one who is, like, the punk private eye?"

"Alex Damage," I said, offering my hand. "*That* one guy. Yeah." She didn't take my hand, or even seem to notice it.

"Suzie Haught," she said. "ZZ Hot. Zii." Gesturing to the door, she asked, "Can we talk?"

"Sure," I said. "No problem. Just let me pay up here." But Rad made a face and gesture that told me I didn't have to worry about it. "Well, then. Shall we?"

We headed toward my office on Curson, which was also my home and not all that far from the Starwood. "Okay ...," I said after a few minutes of quiet walking.

"Not here," Zii said.

"Okay."

We arrived at my building, a white, blocky three-story walk-up a little south of the Strip. The units out front had porches, but the view was obscured by trees and power lines. The gated, partially underground parking lot was a convenient feature. Or would have been if I could have afforded it. So, when it came to parking, as with everything else, I was left fending for myself on the street. The building sat alongside an alley, on the other side of which was a tiny bungalow with a truck out front and which was always playing the theme song to *The Green Berets*.

To say my studio apartment was not much to look at would be like saying Hitler had some anger issues. The guy claiming to be the landlord hadn't exactly been on the up-and-up. Nothing had been signed, and we both liked the idea of not leaving paper in our trail.

The door opened into the sleeping area, which doubled as an office. The hardwood floor was warped and creaky. The walls bulged and were covered in stains that whispered of some sinister past. When I asked the landlord about it, he mumbled something about a murder, trying to hide it and not realizing that to my warped mind it was a selling point. He never gave me the whole story, but the more questions I asked, the more he took off the rent. Until he caught wind of what I do. Apparently, the money a few photos of his wife and brother saved him in the divorce was enough to cover rent for the foreseeable future. Favors for favors. The corners where the wall met the floor had layers of grime so thick a moderately competent archaeologist could have determined the building's age. Under the window across from the door was my bed, if you can even call it that. It was really just the springy mattress from the inside of a pullout couch. Rad's couch had fallen apart, and I figured, "Waste not want not," so I kept the mattress in exchange for helping him pitch the sofa. Honestly, it works better on a floor than in a foldout; there's no bar to dig into your back.

An archway separated the office and sleeping area from the kitchen, which also served as a dining room. The floor changed to laminate posing as tile. They say it's easier to mop, but I wouldn't know. I had one plate, one pan, and one set of silverware. All of which I had stolen from a restaurant I used to work at after they'd fired me. And all of which sat unwashed in the sink. My only appliances were a toaster and a coffee maker, if you don't count the broken blender, which I don't. The garbage can in the corner was filled with takeout bags from Oki-Dog and In-N-Out Burger. Pizza and cereal boxes were piled up in a cardboard box serving as my recycling bin. I'm a slob, not an animal. The table sunk toward the middle and was covered in books, fliers, and fanzines. There were issues of *Slash* and *We Got Power* that went back years.

I tossed my keys on it and walked over to the desk I'd found by the dumpsters behind a school. It was one of those big metal jobs, dented up and missing part of a leg, a problem rectified by folded cardboard. Getting that thing up the stairs had been a labor that would have made Hercules throw in the towel. All the lifting and turning and tilting and twisting had been like weight training while trying to solve a Rubik's Cube. The wall got banged up, and I had to remove a couple of doors temporarily to get it in the room. I'd be worried about my security deposit if I weren't basically squatting.

I pulled up a folding chair for her. The kind with armrests and padding. Duct tape had been deployed in vain to hold the cotton inside the ripped plastic casing, which the designer, in all their wisdom, had seen fit to give a wood-grain print. A rat darted across the room and crawled into a hole in the wall. Zii gasped sharply and froze.

"That's just Templeton. Don't worry about him."

"Is he, like, your pet or something?"

"Eh, more like a roommate."

She turned her attention to the Black Flag logo spray-painted on the wall, four black bars representing a waving flag. "Nice," she said.

"My own contribution. Added the day I moved in." From the bottom drawer, I took out a bottle of cheap bourbon and two tumbler glasses, pouring both.

From next door, there was yelling and pounding. A voice shouted, "You whore bitch!" followed by a slap. Someone screamed and moaned. Zii looked concerned.

"Oh. Don't worry about that. The girl next door is a hooker. Caters to a crowd that likes it rough."

"How do you know?"

"She gives good head and is not unreasonable about the price."

"You're disgusting," she said.

"I'm also fucking with you," I said. "Unless you count dinner and emotional turmoil, I've never paid for sex."

She glared a whole slasher film worth of daggers at me. I grinned.

"Drink?"

"No," she said.

I took one in a single belt and started sipping the other.

"I know Jerry's death wasn't a suicide," she said.

"So, you think it was accidental? Why'd you need to say that in private?" I sat down and put my feet up on the desk.

"I don't think it was an accident either," said Zii.

"So … what? Murder?" I asked.

She nodded.

I put my feet down, leaned forward, and set my drink aside. She had my attention for more reasons than that body now. "I'm listening."

"Jerry had been clean for over a month or so. Ever since he left that junkie, cradle-robbing wife of his. He was really focused on his music and his message. Y'know? Really getting it out there. He had a purpose. He was going straight edge. Except for the sex." She added that last part quickly. "Like me."

"Straight edge people have sex?" I asked with palpable doubt. Straight edge types weren't into drinking, drugs, or sex. It was a philosophy that was spelled out as it was belted out in Minor Threat's song "Out of Step":

Don't smoke. Don't drink. Don't fuck.
At least I can fucking think.

The way they saw it, those things were bait put on hooks by those who wanted to control and manipulate. The real hardcore types didn't even eat meat. Some punks felt the world was ending and we had to grasp pleasure in the moment, however fleeting or destructive. The straight edge types felt that self-control was the path to revolution. Or maybe it was all just cognitive dissonance because they weren't old enough to do those things anyway and they wanted to convince themselves and others they had a cool reason for it. Either way, it explained how her body was so well taken care of.

"*I* do," she said. "When *I* want to. Just not *casual*. If I feel a connection with someone, I just want to … connect. Sex is life-affirming. Drugs and alcohol are life-destroying. And getting all that junk out of his life was letting him focus on what he was meant to do."

I nodded. "Go on."

"But the last couple of days, he seemed anxious. Cagey even."

"Had he been using again?"

"I don't think so. I mean, I didn't watch him every minute. But we were together a lot. I would have noticed something."

"Junkies can be sneaky," I suggested.

"Hey!" she spouted. "Watch your goddamn mouth!"

"I'm just saying. Junk can make people sneaky once it gets a hold of 'em. You see that a lot in this life."

"It was all Nancy," Zii said.

"Nancy?"

"His wife. She's, like, thirty-five. She's the one who got him hooked on drugs in the first place. That's how she kept him with her."

"You think she did it?" I was really just thinking out loud more than I was asking.

"I can't say for sure," she said, "but she had something to do with it."

I slipped a cig into my mouth. "What makes you say that?"

"Do you mind?" she said sternly as I lit up, regarding me as one might a leper.

"Not at all," I said, breathing out smoke. She looked away with a huff.

"She came to see him last night," she said.

"What? She was at the show?"

"Yeah. She came backstage beforehand."

"Really? Huh. What was she on about?"

"She was begging him to come back. She thought she had a chance to patch things up, I guess. She didn't, of course."

"What did she say?"

"She was saying that he couldn't just walk away. That they'd taken an oath. Vows. And that those still meant something. She kept going on about 'in *sickness* and in health.' That kinda shit. She screamed he'd regret it."

"What happened after that?" I stubbed out my cigarette. Now things were getting interesting.

"The bouncers were ready to chuck her out. But he stopped them. Told everyone to leave, he had to talk with her privately." She stopped suddenly. As if just realizing something. "That was the last time he spoke to me." She began to cry.

I opened my drawer. I only kept three things in there. One was a .38 special Smith and Wesson short-nose revolver. I fucking hate guns, but when you're in the business of professionally pissing off the wrong people, you keep one around and you keep it loaded. The others were a bottle of bourbon and a box of tissues. The latter two for coping with the function of the first. I offered her the box of tissues, and she pulled out a handful of them. I set the tissues down on her end of the desk and poured myself more bourbon. When she settled down a little, I continued.

"Did she bring him any drugs?"

"I dunno." Zii sniffed. "But she was strung the fuck out for sure. I didn't want to leave him alone with her. I'd worked hard to help him get cleaned up."

"So, it's possible she brought the drugs that killed him?"

"Yes." She nodded and wiped her nose. "Definitely."

"You think she did that on purpose?"

"I think Nancy was capable of just about anything. That bitch killed him. I have no doubt. I just need some-one to prove it." She must've been pretty damn sure of her theory. Her conviction straightened her up quick. The valves controlling her righteous anger had been loosened, and when the water in her eyes turned to fire, it was hard to say no. And I'm not just saying that because it got me a little hard. Her intensity was contagious and intoxicating enough that it should have been a controlled substance. Strip away the arrogance of youth and I would have even admitted to being a bit scared.

"Listen," I said. "This sounds like a little more than I'm used to taking on—"

"I can pay," she cut me off. "I have money. Well, my parents have money. And if it means finding Jerry some justice, I'm willing to reconnect with them."

"Oh?"

"Yeah," she said. "I choose this life. I mean, they aren't *bad* people or anything like that. I just couldn't stand the whole bullshit consumerism anymore."

"Ah," I said, "you're a rich girl?"

"You can't tell anybody."

"All right," I said, smiling, throwing my hands up in playful surrender. There were plenty of people in the scene who were from comfortable middle-class backgrounds. Comfortable in the financially stable sense, at least. Even those from the upper crust had perfectly legitimate reasons to run. Still, I always had to raise an eyebrow at the rich kids trying to be poor. But the yellow, dying grass on the other side looks green when you're seeing blue.

"I'm serious. You fucking tell anybody and I'll stomp your balls flat, rip 'em off, and carry 'em in my Docs for good luck.

Got it?" She said this in a way that made me believe her. To think she'd just spent the last several minutes talking about how Nancy was unstable. I took a moment to gauge the wild glint in her eye. Somewhere behind it, a woman was doing a tightrope walk between passion and insanity. It took me the span of a Dee Dee Ramone count-off to decide she was my kind of crazy.

"Fifty a day, plus expenses?" I said. "That's my rich-kid price for murder investigations. For that price, I don't take any other cases."

"Find out the truth about Jerry and you'll get more than that."

"When you put it that way, I'm definitely in. But I'm not going into this to prove it was his wife. I'm going into this to find the truth. I'm keeping all avenues and possibilities open."

"Fine," she said, getting up. "It might take me a while to get all of the money I promised."

"I'm going against my better judgment, but I'll trust you." Pretty faces and hourglass figures'll do that to a man. I handed her a card advertising who I am, what I do, and how to reach me. She fumbled through her purse, which was so full I half-expected she was walking around with the cure to all known diseases. It seemed to have everything else. She handed me fifty bucks of what I assumed was her father's money.

"This is what I have for now."

"I'll consider it a retainer," I said.

"Here," she said, scratching her name and number onto a piece of paper. "You can usually find me at this number. If not, call this number and leave a message with my messaging service." She wrote a second number down. "And this is the address where Jerry was staying with her. I'm pretty sure she'd still be there."

"Okay," I said, pocketing the number, address, and money. I tried to make eye contact, but she avoided it.

"Well, stay in touch," she said. I watched every single step she took walking out. "If you're looking at my ass, I'll rip your face off," she said before closing the door; she was gone quicker than I would have liked, and I had to remind myself that punks don't fall in love. Cold showers and right hands, Alex. Cold showers and right hands ...

3

So, I already had a lead. The same lead there always is. The spouse. Nancy. I wasn't going to see her, though. Not yet. I needed more information. I wasn't going to show up hurling accusations all half-cocked. No. That would require a full cock. I was headed back to the Starwood. I was going to learn what other people saw, hear what other people knew, and see if anyone had heard anything that might help me connect a few more dots before I guessed the picture.

There were still mourners about, and I passed by them and found Rad toward the back of the club, keeping people from going backstage.

"Where'd you go, Damage?" Rad wanted to know.

"I'm on a case now," I said.

"Zii hire you?" he asked. "For what?"

"You know I can't reveal any of that," I said.

"Whoever heard of a nihilist with a code?" Rad chuckled. "You are a rare breed. Well, I figure only one thing would bring you back here," he said. "Any way I can help?"

"You could let me backstage," I said. He let me past.

"Hey, man!" shouted some guy with close-cropped hair. "The fuck?! Why does he get in?"

All Rad had to do was shoot him a look and the guy backed the fuck down. Because that was Rad. Real badasses don't have to say a goddamn thing.

I walked through to the green room, and the rest of Bad Chemicals were still there. The walls were plastered in old concert fliers and the occasional commemorative poster. The skunky smell of weed hung in the air. The ground was covered with more dead soldiers than a tracking shot in *Gone with the Wind*. I rolled a Jameson bottle around with my foot and looked at the band. The pot didn't seem to be taking the edge off. I'd never seen them more sober. Waking up next to an OD'd friend gives you a better jolt than coffee. They were hardcore kids. Normal but ratty clothes. The collared shirts looked like they'd done a few tours of Hell. Their hair was shaved almost military style. Even the boots looked ready to storm the beaches. I was still rocking the leather and safety pins. Perhaps it was time to update my look. But that thought made a quick exit once I realized I didn't give a fuck. The drummer, Luke Warning, was the first to speak.

"You Damage?" he asked. I wasn't sure if he was being confrontational or was just in shock.

"Yup."

"Zii talked to you then?" he asked.

"Yup."

Double Dare, the portly bass player, walked over and stuck out his hand; I shook it according to the custom. "We appreciate you coming by."

"Yup."

"She tell you anything?"

"She said Jerry's wife, Nancy, was here last night looking for him."

"Oh, she was here all right," Double said. "Just fucking out of her mind high."

"And when was this?"

"About ten, fifteen minutes before showtime," Luke offered. "The other band was breaking down. We were just getting ready to set up. So, I guess that'd have been around … ten … forty-five?" Which from my own recollection sounded about right. Reggie Reckless was still quietly sitting in the corner, looking uncomfortable. He must have sensed me staring at him, because he looked up at me but quickly looked away again.

"Where'd you find him?" I asked, calling out the

eight-hundred-pound gorilla trying to hide in the corner. Luke answered my question. Not with a word or even a gesture—he simply glanced at the couch sitting against the wall to my left. The couch was straight out of the 1960s. Fuzzy and plaid and looking like Holy Hell. Which, when it comes to couches, means it's as comfortable as true love's embrace. It looked like the type of couch that could turn you into Rip Van Winkle if you could stop thinking about which of Iggy Pop's fluids it had absorbed. I pulled the cushions off and searched inside for anything incriminating, knowing full well that the cops had probably already gone through this when they came for the body. The death of a punk was not something the pigs gave enough of a shit about to put forth a real effort. But if there had been clues, they were gone. It had been cleaned out. I didn't even find loose change.

"Who noticed he was dead?" I put the cushions back into place.

"That'd be Reggie," Double Dare said. "Tried to ask if he wanted to get breakfast."

"Reggie," I said, getting no response. Reggie was still just sitting in the corner. But nothing in his look suggested that Reggie Reckless was in that corner at all. Reggie was not in the room or even the Starwood. Reggie was not on Santa Monica Boulevard, or in Los Angeles, or California. The United States. Earth. Reggie was gone. If he was still within the Milky Way, he showed no signs of it. "Reggie!" I said again, crouching, leaning my arms on my knees. I placed myself in his line of sight, which went right through me. He'd only have seen me if I were a thousand yards out. I balled up a fist. "Reg!" Nothing. I belted him across the jaw, knocking him off the stool he'd fused himself to and sending him sprawling to the ground.

"Ahhhhh!" He stood up. "What?!" He was still coming out of it.

"I'm here to help!" I said loudly.

"Fooled me," Reggie said, checking his mouth for loose teeth. "The fuck was that for?"

"Reentry. I've got some questions about last night." Reggie looked at me. I had his full attention now. "About Jerry." He nodded. "Okay," I said. "I'm told you found the body this morning." He just nodded. "About what time was that?"

"I dunno," he said. "I guess it was about eight in the morning." I gestured for him to continue. "I was pretty fucking hungover. We all were. But Jerry said to wake him when I got up and we'd go get some breakfast at someplace on Santa Monica. His treat, he said. I walked over to the couch to wake him. I touched him and he was cold." Reggie kept his arms crossed. "I got real scared. I tried again, and this time I rolled him over and I saw he was dead. I figured he musta OD'd."

"Was he using last night?" I asked, not just Reggie, but the whole room.

Reggie was the one who answered. "I dunno for sure. I didn't see him. But I think so."

"Why'd you think it was an OD?"

"He still had the needle in his arm." Reggie's voice cracked.

I nodded. "Cops take that too?"

"Yeah." It was Luke Warning this time. "Evidence."

"And the cops have for sure written it off as an OD?"

"Yeah," said Luke. Or Dare. It didn't matter.

Reggie had slumped onto Jerry's death bed, or couch, rather. And buried his face in his hands. "It seemed like one to me."

"So, he had been using again?"

"The needle was in his arm!" Reggie said. He seemed defensive. Almost standoffish. As if the question was some kind of personal insult. Or an accusation.

"I wouldn't blame him if he'd taken a shot, personally," Double Dare said.

"What makes you say that?" I asked.

"Fucking Nancy, man," Dare said. "She was …" He made a crazy face while framing his head with his hands and shaking them. "Y'know? That kind of tension spreads. She was getting him all crazy. He was worked up pretty hard. And I mean in ways that'd send a guy back into old habits real easy."

"So, she was upset?"

"Oh hell yeah, she was upset," Double Dare said.

"What did she say?" I asked.

"She was saying how he couldn't leave her. How she wouldn't let him. She was just throwing a vicious fit, man."

"Could she have killed him?" I just threw it out there.

"You really have been talkin' to Zii, huh?" Luke chimed in.

"She ran that by you too?" I asked.

"Oh yeah," Luke said.

"And what do you think?"

Luke thought a moment. "I would not put it past her. Nancy, I mean. She's fuckin' crazy. And a junkie. I never liked having her around, really. I never knew what was going to set her off. That woman is disturbed."

"Yeah," Double Dare added. "I mean, what's a thirty-five-year-old doing running around with a nineteen-year-old kid? It's sick."

"How much of the conversation did you hear?"

"Not much. Jerry told us to go check the equipment. He knew the equipment was fine. But we could all take a hint."

"Did any of you know his dealer?"

"No," Luke said. "I mean, Nancy always got his smack, far as I knew. Before he claimed to have quit." Double Dare just nodded in agreement.

"We used to get speed off of Joe Public," Double Dare added, "until he and Jerry had a falling out."

Like Jerry, Joe Public was a scene lynchpin. He was always setting up gigs, helping people get time in studios, and selling speed. He was in three bands and had songs played on the radio by more than just Rodney Bingenheimer.

When he wasn't touring, he was always at shows. He was everywhere. Hell, I figured he had a secret twin brother, he got so much shit done. Even after his band Crumbs had started gaining some relative mainstream success with their fusion of rockabilly and punk, he would convince organizers to get lesser-known bands on the bill. He was whatever the male equivalent of a mother hen is and just an all-around good dude. Mix all that with the fact Joe had been on tour the last few months and it didn't make him a suspect.

"What happened with Joe?" I asked. Relevant or not, some gossip just sets off the saliva.

"Nothing, on Joe's end at least," said Double. "The problem was all Jerry. He was jealous, got all huffy about it. We could have played with Crumbs for their homecoming show at the Whisky in a couple nights, but fucking Jerry turned him down."

"That's a benefit gig, ain't it?" I asked. "For the people of El Salvador?"

The US involvement in El Salvador's civil war was massively controversial and a huge political talking point for a lot of bands, including the Minutemen, Joe Public, and Bad Chemicals. Reagan had started giving millions in aid each day to the El Salvadoran government, whose National Guard was carrying out torture and extrajudicial killings. Not to mention rape, murder, and other human atrocities.

"Yeah," said Double.

"I've never known Jerry to turn down a benefit gig," Luke said.

"Can you think of anything else Jerry did last night? Anyone else he might've talked to in the last couple of days?"

Luke started to shake his head and then stopped himself. "Wait. Yeah. Now that you mention it, he was talking to some HBers yesterday afternoon. It got pretty heated, actually."

"You know these guys?"

"Oh yeah. We used to share a practice space with them when we were out in Huntington Beach. Young guys. Fifteenish. Thuggish little punks. Their little hardcore band is really more of an excuse for a gang, really. The types of fuckers who walked around in leather with chains and switchblades. It's all bloodlust and faux Marine Corps bravado with these guys. Being honest, I was scared of 'em sometimes. We left to get away from those little shits. Especially after what happened."

"What happened?"

"This kid, Tom Numb, fronted their band, right? Well, he and Jerry got into it before we cut out of HB. Both of 'em damn near wound up in the hospital. Ever notice how Jerry's right eye was never really open all the way? Numb was why."

"Jesus," I said.

"No kidding," Luke said. "Jerry fucked him up pretty bad too. Numb's nose'll never point straight again. Not to mention the scar on his lip."

"What was the fight over?"

"Tom accused Jerry of stealing a song of his."

"Which is bullshit," Dare chimed in.

"'Cop-a-Feel,'" Luke said. "Cop-a-Feel" was a minute-and-forty-second thrasher about getting frisked by the police and the cop getting off on touching teenage boys. A great fucking song. But another motive floating around made my job more difficult. I was pretty sure that faking an overdose would not be part of the HBers' MO. They were less into pharmacy and more into amateur dentistry. They'd be more likely to make him bite a curb and stomp on the back of his head. Still, you pursue all leads. Fuck, I hated HBers. Obnoxious, drunk-ass thugs. They had the testosterone of a bull shark, the bloodlust of a vampire bat, and the brains of a goldfish. The offspring from an orgy of vicious, awful, stupid creatures.

"Fucking HBers," I muttered.

"Tell me about it," Luke said.

I took out business cards and handed one to each band member. "Here. Let me know if you think of anything else. Anywhere I can reach you?"

"Yeah," said Luke. He scratched a number onto the back of a concert flier that was sitting on the coffee table. "You can usually find us at our practice space."

"Can I also get the address of that old practice space in Huntington?" He wrote that down too and handed it to me. I folded up the flier and stuck it in my back pocket. "Thanks. I'll be in touch."

I stepped out past Rad. "You ever leave?" I asked.

"Not today. But I'm not working tonight. I should be out of here by dinner if you wanna hit up Oki-Dog."

"Maybe. Hey, listen, you want to head down to Huntington Beach tonight?"

"Fuck no. Maybe. Why?"

"I got a lead on some HBers. Might need some backup of the large, intimidating man-beast variety."

"Aw, I bet you say that to all the girls." He patted my shoulder. "When you put it that way, you got it, buddy. Stop by 'round five?"

"Five," I said. "Sounds good. I've got a few things I need to take care of first."

One of those things was food. It was getting on lunchtime and I hadn't eaten the day before. I found my car, a red, beat-to-hell 1971 Chevy Vega Coupe, and drove toward the address where Zii said Nancy would be. I detoured through residential areas looking for open garage doors. I finally found one after about twenty minutes and parked on the curb. I moved quickly and quietly up the driveway, making sure the coast was clear, and saw they had a fridge in the garage. I walked in and opened it. It was pretty bare except for some string cheese, packaged precooked hot dogs, and beer. I grabbed a beer, two hotdogs, and a couple sticks of string cheese. I'd practically finished it all before I reached my car.

4

The sun broke through the smog and I switched on the radio. Damned to know what I was looking to find. The only thing on the radio worth squat was *Rodney on the ROQ*, but it was far from his time slot. I flipped through stations and found nothing but the death rattles of disco. And something they were calling "new wave." Fuck that. I flipped over to the news, because it's crucial for a budding young anarchist to keep abreast of current events. I came in midway through the traffic and weather. Smoggy. Hot. Light traffic.

> *And now your news at the top of the hour. Police responded to an alleged riot last night at the Starwood Club in West Hollywood. The crowd became violent during a performance by punk rock band the Bad Chemicals.*

"Bad Chemicals," I corrected him. "There's no 'the,' asshole." So much for journalistic integrity. "Riot" was also a bit sensationalist. Cops just don't get mosh pits. When they showed up for a noise complaint or something, they came out swinging.

> *Although considered minor, this makes for the third such incident this month. Senator David Cromwell had this to say:*
>
> *"With growing violence connected to this music, it is imperative that we be vigilant as parents and citizens. As the father of a teenage girl myself, I can say that I won't allow our youth to be corrupted by music that promotes a lifestyle of violence and destruction. If*

it's a war they want, it's a war they'll get. And I know
a thing or two about war."
     Senator Cromwell was a twice-decorated war hero
in Vietnam and has played a major role in providing
assistance to the government of El Salvador in their
attempts to defeat the communist—

I turned the radio off and drove the rest of the way in
silence. Senator David Cromwell was leading the charge
against "the punk syndrome." Which, alone, is obnoxious
enough. But the whole militant right-wing idiom really
poured lemon juice on the paper cut. For now, though, a
murder investigation was stressful enough.

Rash had married young. He was nineteen, but his wife,
Nancy, was good bit older. She was easily thirty-five. They
were estranged and hadn't been living together for over
a month. Her place was in the ground unit of a building
just off Sepulveda near the 405. The neighboring house was
covered with about ten rolls worth of caution tape. Tito's
Tacos was across the street, so it made for an easy stakeout.
I ordered some food and took in the lay of the land. There
were a few palm trees out front in the walled-off courtyard,
and the building had red brick chimneys. Not super practical, but the clash of red against the white of the building
had a certain appeal if you dig on the whole "blood on the
sheets" aesthetic. After an hour of counting the leaves
pouring over the front gate, I didn't see any movement to
speak of.
     Maybe it was the bean and cheese burrito, but I started
getting antsy. I crossed the street and found the door to the
unit around back, under some metal stairs. I knocked, and
just before the third knock, the door swung open. Inside was
a woman standing there in a bathrobe. She'd been pretty, at
one point. Lingering bits of beauty were desperately gasping

for air in the last moments before drowning. Years of smack, coke, and speed had sucked so much life from her once-stunning features that she looked like a supermodel that had survived the Holocaust, and the only rings she was wearing were the ones below her eyes.

"Fuck you want?" she slurred.

"To ask about Jerry Rash," I said.

"Jerry ain't here." She spat on the ground by my steel-toed Doc Martens. "He's dead. And he wouldn't be here if he was alive. He had better things to do. Better things than his fucking *wife*. You a cop or something?"

"Lady, I look like a cop?"

"No, but they can be slippery fucks. They got undercover guys at Jerry's shows all the time. So, who the fuck are you?"

"Alex Damage. I'm—"

"That's a retarded-ass name." She tried to spit again but was dried out. I was already losing my patience.

"Yeah, well, that's the thing about nicknames. They ain't always up to you."

She pushed the door open. "Would you like to come in? Alex. Damage." She pursed her lips and stroked the collar of her robe. It was obvious she was giving me the eyes; even though they had enough luggage for a monthlong voyage under them, she wasn't subtle. But it's hard for someone to be sexy when they're struggling to stand.

"Sure," I said. "Thank you." As I went in, she didn't get out of my way, forcing me to brush against her as I passed. I felt like I was going to break her just doing that. She tried to make eye contact with me, but I avoided it. She pushed the door shut behind us and moved ahead of me to the middle of the room. There was a ratty old mattress and no other furniture. Presumably, it had all been sold to feed her habit. The floor was shittier than mine. Drop a marble in the middle of the room, it would roll toward the wall. Flyers for past Bad Chemicals shows that once adorned the walls had been ripped off in a blind tantrum of junkie rage with no hope of being salvaged, but enough remained that they could still be recognized. The kitchen was all dirty dishes and half-eaten Oki-Dogs. A smell hit my nose that almost made me believe in the Devil. I didn't know where that smell was coming from, and I thought it best to maintain my ignorance. Something had died here and died ugly.

"So, why you askin' 'bout Jerry?"

"He's dead."

"I know that."

"I'm being paid to find out why."

"I know why." She walked over to me. "He killed himself because he couldn't bear the thought that he gave up all this ..." She started to let her robe slip. I caught it and pulled it back on her shoulders.

"My client doesn't seem to think so," I said. She breathed in sharply through her nose and awkwardly tilted her head away. She tried to play it cool, but my rejection had clearly hurt her feelings.

"Who is your client?" She sat down at the end of the mattress.

"I wouldn't be very good at what I do if I just gave that information away."

"What do you want with me, then?"

"Well, guy winds up dead and there's whispers of foul play, you talk to the spouse. That's murder investigation 101."

"Why not leave it for the cops?"

"They've already written it off as a simple overdose. And they're keeping it that way. They don't give a shit. I'm sure they're happy about it. Besides, you know that's not how we do things. How long were you married to Jerry?"

"Year and a half. We were married on his eighteenth birthday." She began reaching for her drug gear by the mattress, and I pushed it away with my foot.

"Not until we're done here," I said.

"Fuck you! You ain't a cop! You've got nothing to threaten me with!"

"Lady, I work *outside* the law. I have *everything* to threaten you with. But that's not really my style. I'm all about positive reinforcement."

"You don't got nothing I want!"

"Are you sure about that?" I said, kneeling in front of her. I moved in to undo her robe. She breathed in, anticipating the previously denied pleasure. My hand quickly changed direction and pulled a baggie out of her robe pocket. "Because I think I do."

I stood up quickly, holding it out of her reach. She tried to stand, but I put my free hand on her shoulder and held her down. It was too easy, and I didn't feel good about it.

"Easy now," I said. "I can't have you any more strung out than you already are if I'm going to get you to answer my very simple questions."

"Fine!" she said, knocking my hand away and running her fingers through her dirty hair. "Fine, fine, fine, fine, *fine!*" She gave me the finger on the last one.

"Feel better?"

"Fuck you!"

"I think I've made it pretty clear that's not an option for you. Now, fan though I am of foreplay, I'm short on time, so let's get to it. I've got questions, you've got answers. I've got your stash, you've got a disgusting habit. So, let's quid-pro-quo this shit and I'll get out of your greasy, unwashed hair.

"Here's how this is going to work. I tell you what I already know. You can confirm, deny, and fill in the gaps. Then I'll give you this back and you can go back to slowly killing yourself and join your beloved husband. Got it?"

"Got it."

"What was that?!" I said, channeling my best drill-sergeant impression.

"Got it! I got it!"

"Goooood!" I said. "As I'm sure you know, Jerry died last night of an apparent overdose of heroin. A nasty habit he'd picked up during his relationship with *you*. He was trying to clean up. But he couldn't do that with you around, so he was going to break things off with you. How'm I doin' so far?"

"That cunt," she muttered.

"I'm sorry. How is that an answer?"

"That groupie of his. He was leaving me for her. She was turning my Jerry against me!" She was starting to cry a little.

"How's that?"

She sniffled. "She told him that I was to blame for his habit. She told him that the drugs were going to ruin his life." Her voice cracked. "But *I* was his life!"

This was so pathetic. I could see why Jerry wanted to bail. The drugs were what tied him to her; they were what kept them together. With him cleaned up, she'd have nobody.

"When was the last time you saw Jerry?"

"About a week ago. We'd been split up a month and he came by to talk."

"Tell me," I said, holding up the baggie, "should I just flush this down the toilet with the rest of the shit you're giving me?" I moved toward the bathroom.

"No!" she shrieked, like a mother losing her child.

"If the last time you saw Jerry was a week ago, why does everyone backstage say they saw you at the show last night?"

"I begged him to reconsider. I just thought if I could remind him how I used to make him feel …"

"Nancy. Did you bring him drugs?"

She got quiet and turned her head away, bit her nails. She was shutting down, so I backed up a bit and switched to "good cop" mode. If there is such a thing.

"What did Jerry talk to you about last week?" I asked in as sympathetic a tone as I could muster.

"He came to get some of his stuff. I asked him if he'd take me back if I got clean." Her voice cracked, and she hiccupped a few times. She stopped a moment to pull herself together and managed to choke out, "He said no!" before sobbing. I had no tissues to offer. The sleeves of her robe fell down to her elbows when she brought her hands to her face. Her arms looked like Julius Caesar's back.

"That's too bad," I offered with as much sympathy as I could. I wouldn't be able to look you in the eye to tell you I didn't mean it.

"He said that he still cared about me, but that if we were going to get clean, we needed a fresh start. That if we were together, we risked falling back into old habits. He was so full of shit."

Actually, it sounded totally reasonable to me, but I played along. "Yeah. Definitely."

"He said he didn't want to leave me to die. I told him he already had. And then I showed him the door and he left. I would have done anything to get him back." Except quitting, apparently.

"Is that why you showed up with the drugs last night?"

Her silence gave me the answer I needed.

"Where did you get them?" I asked.

"Same place I always do."

"And where is that? Who did you buy them from?"

"I'm not telling you that. Or anything else. I ain't tellin' you shit. I've said what I'm going to say. Now give me back my shit and get the fuck out of my house!"

"So, it is your house," I cracked.

"Fuck off!" she shrieked.

I looked at the baggie in my hand.

"Give it ta me!" she screamed, like a spoiled child denied candy in the checkout line. "Givita me! Givita me! Givita me!"

I ripped open the baggie, making a blizzard of heroin. With the noises she made, the neighbors, if there were any, would think she was being stabbed to death. I made a swift exit.

Brutal, right?

5

Now, I'm not that heartless. I may be a punk, I may even be an asshole, but I'm not a bully. That whole stunt with the heroin baggie? I had a reason for that. After my dramatic escape, I hid out across the street. The way she reacted told me that was probably the last of her stash. With it gone, she'd need more. I grabbed the trench coat and fedora I kept in the trunk of my car. I popped the collar on the coat and pushed the brim of the hat down. I lit a cigarette and waited. After a few minutes, she rushed out of the apartment, not even stopping to look around. Dumbass junkie. When she got a block ahead of me, I followed. I stopped abruptly when she hit a pay phone right around the first corner. Once she hung up, she continued along Sepulveda. She walked into an alley. I passed the alley and glanced in. It ended at a fence. Nancy was in there talking to a guy. They made a quick exchange and she quickly left and made fast tracks for home. The man hung back for a few and I cut across the street. I'd left my .38 in the office, so I'd have to play it carefully. I made like I was window-shopping until I saw the guy leave the alley. He passed by, giving me as much thought as the air he was breathing. I followed from a safe distance and saw him duck into a bar. I gave it a few minutes before I went in and sat down next to him.

"Bourbon," I said.

"What kind?" the bartender asked.

"Whatever's in the well," I said. He set a glass on the counter and poured me a shot. The dealer seemed uncomfortable. "Five o'clock somewhere, right?" I said.

He turned to me, looked at my outfit, and shook his head. "What the fuck are you supposed to be?"

"Oh, y'know. Just some guy."

"You Columbo or something?"

I took my shot. "Actually, I always preferred Philip Marlowe."

"Who?" he said with a look combining confusion and irritation.

"Never mind," I said. "You been by the Starwood today?"

"No," he said, not looking at me and taking a swig of his drink. I tried to look him over for signs of lying. Darting eyes, hesitation, a tensing of the muscles.

"Yeah. Big memorial service there. The singer of this punk band died last night." No response. Nothing. "What was the name of the band? Bad ... Bad something ..."

He turned to me and glared at me in a way that said he was going to kick my ass if I didn't stop gawking at him.

"Chemicals!" I snapped in the air and shook my pointer finger. "That's it. Bad Chemicals. Jerry Rash. You hear anything about that?"

"What makes you think I'd give a fuck about something like that?" he said through his teeth. Oh, I thought he gave a fuck all right.

"Just, seems to have hit the community pretty hard is all. Thought maybe ..."

He moved right up in my face; we were practically touching noses. It can be dangerous to make eye contact with a wild animal. They see it as a threat. But look away and they'll take it as weakness. I wasn't about to give him the satisfaction. And I wanted to keep his attention on my face. "Look, asshole, you don't shut your goddamn mouth and fuck off, I'm gonna kick your faggot ass."

"Oh, I won't be fucking off. Not yet, anyway." I tossed my hat down on the bar, revealing my short blue mohawk. "What are you selling?"

"Fuck you talkin' about?"

"Drugs. Coke. Speed. H. That kinda shit."

"I ain't got shit on me."

"No. I didn't think you did. You don't just hang out on street corners with a backpack. You're the house-call type. Well, dark-alley call, at any rate. You do deliveries."

"Bullshit." He started to leave.

"Say hi to Nancy for me," I said. He stopped a moment, and then he was gone.

But I had his wallet.

6

Bobby DeVaughn. 8763 Wonderland Avenue. He lived at a house up in Laurel Canyon. I'd heard of the Wonderland House. It was a known drug den. I had some time before I had to meet up with Rad at Oki-Dog, so I drove out to the canyon and found the house. It was a narrow street lined with relatively nice homes, and 8763 stuck out like a stubbed, gangrenous toe. The modernist concrete block appeared to be three stories, but the first floor was a small open-air garage that a car couldn't even pull all the way inside. Each of the other two floors had its own balcony. While swapping back into my leather jacket, I glanced up to try to gauge any movement inside, but from this angle I couldn't catch so much as a shadow cast on the ratty curtains. Some concrete steps ran up along the right of the house to the door on the side. Halfway up those steps, there was a steel gate. I jiggled the handle on the off chance it was unlocked. When I couldn't get in, I looked around and found a buzzer. I held it down. Dogs barked inside.

"Yeah?" said a gruff voice.

"I'm here to see Bobby," I said. "I found his wallet." The gate buzzed in response, I pushed my way through, and I climbed the rest of the stairs along the side of the house. The door was open, so I tapped the frame to announce my entry. "Yello?" I said.

"In here," called the gruff voice. I walked in to find a middle-aged man sitting on the couch. He had a bandanna, long hair, and a beard and wore a sleeveless shirt under a biker vest. Several patches proudly displayed his member-ship in the Aryan Brotherhood. The dogs, apparently, had been moved to a back room. They continued to bark and thudded against a door at the end of the hall. Bobby was sitting in a chair next to the couch.

"You?!" said Bobby. "The fuck are you doing here?"

"You dropped this." I tossed the wallet to him, striking him in the forehead. "Better be more careful. Word is this town's going to shit."

"You stole my fucking wallet."

"Actually, I'm returning your wallet. It was a little out of my way, too. You should show some appreciation. Say 'Thank you,' Bobby."

"Fuck you," said Bobby.

"Close enough. Know how you can thank me? 'How about some information?'" I said, mimicking his voice. "Gee. That'd be great, Bobby!" Bobby just stared. "You sold some smack to a woman named Nancy earlier today."

"What's it to you?" he asked.

"I need something to take the edge off. Jerry Rash's death has hit me pretty hard."

"Jerry's dead?" said a third man standing in the kitchen.

"Yeah," I said. "Last night. Overdose."

"Who did you say you were?" he asked.

"I didn't. Alex Damage. I'm a private dick of sorts."

"You're a dick, all right," Bobby quipped.

"Watch it, Bobby." I pointed at him. And then turned back to the new arrival. "You are?"

"John Holmes," he said.

"John Holmes?! No shit!" I said. "And here I am talking about dicks!" John Holmes was once a legend in the porn industry. Dick as big as my arm. Most famous for his private-eye character Johnny Wadd, he'd starred in over a thousand porn films. He hadn't done much in the last few years. The word was that because of his drug habit, he couldn't get it up anymore and was all washed out.

"That's right. What's this about Jerry?" Holmes asked.

"Right. Where was I? Jerry. He died. OD. I've been hired to look into the possibility of foul play." John sat down and snorted a few lines of coke.

"Yeah, that sounds like it could be possible. He used to party here. All the time."

"He stop coming when he cleaned up?" I asked.

Bobby chuckled. "Jerry? Clean? Yeah, sure."

"He ever get into it with anyone here?" I asked. Looking around the shady-ass room gave me the creeps. Guns on tables, stacks of cash, bedsheets as curtains. I'd never been into needle drugs, but if I had been, you could bet I would have at least put my used needles away. These losers couldn't even be bothered with that much. It was the kind of place where a guy could make some dangerous friends. Or enemies. Especially a guy as volatile as Jerry Rash.

"Are you kidding?" Bobby said. "That fucking guy was lucky *I* didn't kill him."

"What do you mean?" I said. I was ready to stomp him, and my tone did not hide that fact.

"I had some really primo shit awhile back. Nothing I was looking to sell. This was some stuff I'd come across from some chink broad I was nailing. So, he's trying to get some from me, and I told him, 'No fucking way!' Well, John calls my name from the kitchen and so I turn my head, but then I catch Rash trying to swap out whatever middle-of-the-line shit he had with my quality stash. I just about caved his head in."

"Anyone else you can think of might have had it out for him?"

"Asshole fucked my girl," said the gruff-voiced Aryan biker. "Primo piece of ass too. Hot young thing. I get her into the room, right? Hook her up with some to-the-moon shit. She's lying there, seeing God in the ceiling or whatever. I step out for thirty seconds to piss, I come back an' Jerry's on top of her. I threw a fit. He ran out the door. I got my turn in, though." He grinned. I tucked the rage down. I wasn't here for bullshit lies.

"All I want to know," I said, "is did you sell Nancy anything in the last few days?"

"Yeah," Bobby said. "Now that's all you get."

"I wanna buy some," I said. "The same shit you sold Nancy a few days ago."

Bobby looked over to the guy on the couch. He nodded.

"Yeah," Bobby said, "fine. But if I see you again, you're dead." He got the smack and handed it to me. I wanted to respond, "One of us will be," but I smartened up quick. Being outnumbered and unarmed in a drug den is a fucking master's course in etiquette. I just handed him the money.

"How much will this get me?" I asked. He counted it, took the baggie back, and removed half, maybe more.

"Now," he said, "fuck off."

"John," the Aryan biker said, "see him out." John walked me to the street.

"Where did Jerry die?" John asked.

"Starwood," I said.

"That's one of Eddie's places, ain't it?" he asked.

"What? Yeah. I dunno. Probably." I didn't know "Eddie" or the Starwood's owner. I was too focused on the images those fuckers had put in my head to listen to a washed-up porn star.

"I know him. I'm actually headed over to his place tonight to pick up some stuff. I'll ask." Nothing so far suggested that would be of use, but it helps to flip over all the pieces of a puzzle. I handed him my card.

"Thanks," I said. I got back into my car and drove off in a huff. I'd always been proud of my ability to keep my cool. It's what separated me from the little dipshits ruining the scene. Those angry suburban white kids with the shaved heads picking fights and blowing their stacks over everything. I shook it off and headed to Oki-Dog to meet up with Rad.

7

Oki-Dog was a dive hot dog stand in West Hollywood and a popular hangout for punks due to the casual atmosphere, proximity to the clubs, and cheap, greasy eats. Most famously the eponymous Oki-Dog, two hot dogs with chili and pastrami rolled up in a flour tortilla. If you knock it and haven't tried it, well then, fuck you.

It was a little before five when I parked in the lot off Santa Monica and walked toward Pico, where Oki-Dog sat on the corner. The place shared its signpost with a neighboring car stereo shop, but the single-story shack stood out the way that apple-red buildings do. There were picnic tables along Santa Monica and Pico. Under a blue awning was a window where you could order food. The menu itself was painted on a white wooden board on the side of the building.

Indoors, if you could call it that, was more like a screened-in porch. In there was another ordering window, and this time the menu was displayed on a Coca-Cola sign above the grill. The wood-topped tables, once again of the picnic variety, were scuffed and sticky. At night, these tables were heavily tied to status. For all the posturing, even us punks never fully exorcised the high school cafeteria. An American flag was nailed to the ceiling, along with about four trees' worth of Christmas lights. The smell and feeling of grease hung in the air, reminding you that you weren't just eating a hot dog, you were eating every hot dog that had ever been cooked on that grill.

Between the kitchen, the radio, and the Pac-Man machine in the corner, it was hard to have a conversation, so I was glad to find Rad sitting at one of the picnic tables outside. It was covered in graffiti, but a blue circle stood out from the curse words and the *wuz here*s. It was the Germs' logo, supposedly drawn there by Darby Crash himself, so people left it alone.

It was once suggested that Jerry Rash had named himself that because it sounded similar to "Darby Crash." That rumor didn't get very far. Jerry didn't take kindly to the implication that he was being unoriginal, so he supposedly beat the shit out of anyone who said it. I can't speak to that. Fact and myth blur a lot, especially in the scene. Going off hearsay and rumor isn't just amateur in my line of work, it's downright dangerous. Although they can make decent starting points, and it's not like I'm being regulated by anybody. But just because I'm unlicensed does not mean I'm unprofessional.

"Where you been?" Rad asked.

"The goddamn Wonderland House."

"The fuck were you doing at Wonderland?!" he asked, voice thick with parental concern. "Those people are dangerous. Like, *dangerous* dangerous."

"Following up on a lead. That chem major from UCLA still tending bar at Starwood?"

"Saul? Yeah. But only Fridays and Saturdays."

"Can you get in touch with him?"

"Yeah," he said with an implied *duh*.

"Have him run some tests on this," I said, slipping Rad the heroin under the table.

"What do you think this is gonna tell you?"

"Probably nothing. Maybe everything if it's the same stuff Nancy bought the night Jerry died. I want to see if there's anything off about the batch."

"Yeah, I'll talk to Saul. Can we please order some fucking food now?" he said, not really asking for my permission, because why the fuck would he need it? He stood before I could respond or offer money. "I got this."

I could hear the radio from the kitchen. Top-of-the-hour news.

> *Human-rights groups continue to demand an outside investigation into the rape and murder of four American nuns in El Salvador last December and accuse the Salvadoran government of "white-washing" the investigation. UN Ambassador Jean Kirkpatrick continues to deny the involvement of the Salvadoran military in the murders, insisting the nuns were political activists sympathetic to communist forces.*
>
> *Highs in the mid-70s. Rain expected tonight.*

Rad came back with two Oki-Dogs for each of us and a mountain of fries. Chili on the side.

"So," Rad said after he had feasted and could focus, "what the hell do we need to deal with these HBers for? Street gangs posing as punks is all those little bastards are."

"Agreed," I said, nodding, "but these HBers claim that Rash stole a song of theirs."

"Bullshit!" He pounded his fist on the table.

"That's what I said."

"Which song?"

"'Cop-a-Feel.'"

"Great fucking song." He tilted his head back, smiled, and imitated the drum roll between the verses while I recited the words. And together we shouted the song's defiant ending line: "Next time buy me dinner, you fuckin' pig!"

This, obviously, was met with stares showcasing a variety of reactions ranging from raised eyebrows to hoots and hollers. Rad and I had actually been in a band together a few years before. Not coincidentally, he was the drummer and I was the vocalist. We called ourselves Eraserheads and we played one show at a house party in 1978. We were fucking terrible. It was amazing.

"Why even follow this up?" Rad wondered aloud while munching on a fry.

"Because it doesn't matter if it's true. These guys either think it's true or have a reason to want others to think it's true. And that's motive."

"Fair enough," he said. "Let's go bust some heads."

"Okay." I stood up and took out my keys. "But not before I get the information I need."

"Oh, you're no fun."

8

After a quick stop at my office to pick up my .38, I emptied the bullets into my pocket. We were cruising along in my car at a good clip. *Rodney on the ROQ* wasn't on, so I didn't see the point in trying the radio. I grabbed the Minor Threat EP I had on tape and popped it in. It had only been out for a couple weeks.

"A guy I know in DC taped this for me," I said.

"What guy do you know in DC?" Rad mocked.

"Just, y'know, a fuckin' guy," I said.

"A 'fuckin' guy' as in 'a guy you're fucking'?" He grinned and I jabbed him in the arm, which was more like punching a redwood. I would know. I've done that. While drinking. Heavily.

"What? You jealous?" I cooed.

"Please, you're not my type," he said. "Little guy like you? Your ass would tear apart like tissue paper."

I laughed so hard I had to pull over. "Jesus fucking Christ, dude! That ... oh. You took it too far! Why do you always take it too far?!"

"That's why you love me, and you know it." Rad leaned his head back on the seat and stared at the cigarette burns on the roof as Ian MacKaye rapidly ranted about being straight edge. It was true, though. Partially. I did love the guy. But that wasn't why.

We found the address of the old practice space, a rundown storefront in a partially abandoned strip mall surrounded by an ever-encroaching subdivision of newly built homes. The yards of some of these houses were coming right up against the lot. Given another year or two, the remaining businesses would become somebody's pool.

The "band" was hanging around the parking lot harassing people walking to their cars from the stores left in the plaza, which included a check-cashing place, a long-standing family-run pizzeria, and a clothing shop advertising a going-out-of-business sale. They started following a girl to her car as she left with some shopping bags from the clothing shop. She did her best to ignore them. She was short and curvy, with straight brown hair and full lips. In short, a damn good-looking young woman. I had money on her being a college student. The sorority sweater was a clear giveaway. They were catcalling her and whistling and saying things like, "You get some new clothes? Hey, can I see you try 'em on? C'mon! Give us a fashion show, baby!"

Her boyfriend, who had been waiting in the car, got out and put himself between them and the girl. "Hey, assholes. Why don't you leave her alone?"

"Whooa ho ho ho!" one of them laughed. "The boyfriend's mad!"

"C'mon, Sandy. Get in the car."

"We wasn't done talkin' ta her!" one of them said in a cartoony voice. If his goal was to aggravate someone into taking a swing at him, his shrill, nasally tone was a great asset.

"Yeah. You were," said Sandy's boyfriend. As he turned back to the car, one of the HBers grabbed him by the shoulder, spun him around, grabbed him by the throat, and pinned him up against the car door.

"Last guy who told me what to do ain't doing so good himself," said the HBer through a clenched jaw and bugging eyes.

"Which one'a you fags is Tom Numb?" I shouted. I'm not a huge fan of that word. Sure, I crack the occasional gay joke. Certain company in my world will eat you alive if you don't play along, and I ain't proud to say that I have. But I've got friends from the early days of the scene that are gay or bi or throw on the occasional dress, several of whom could kick these guys' asses, and I've been called "fag" by plenty of rednecks and surfers. Hell, being honest, there are transient thoughts I can never fully dismiss. Still, I've found that the best way to goad macho homophobes is with their own shitty language.

"What was that?" said the one holding the boyfriend. His attention now on me, he pushed away from the scared young man, who took the opportunity to get in the car and drive off. His nose was crooked and he had a scar on his lip. I figured he must be our boy.

"We're looking for Tom Numb. We were told that he had a dick the size of a grain of rice, and, well, we just had to see it for ourselves." Tom came across the lot at me. The others followed behind.

"Fuck you! My dick is huge!"

"Is that what your boyfriend told you?" I said, pointing my thumb at the closest one to him. "That was sweet of him." As Numb went to take a swing at me, Rad grabbed him by the wrist and twisted it back, just shy of breaking it. Numb looked at Rad with a mix of absolute terror and pure hate. The hate coming from the fear, the type of hate reserved for those made to feel powerless. Whether it's a kid cornered by a bully, a Marxist rebel interrogated by the Salvadoran government, or a poseur street punk realizing he isn't as tough as he thought, there is no anger like desperate anger. There is no fear like the fear of the fucked.

The "boyfriend" pulled a switchblade, but a little peer mediation from my .38 made him realize that wasn't going to cut it. I didn't even have to point it.

"Easy, kemosabe," I said. "Why don't you put that away and we'll all step inside and have a nice little chat." I could almost see the floor falling out from under them when they saw that gun. I looked across at their faces. One was even trying not to cry. I hate these fucking things. I really do. I feel like shit no matter what end of the barrel I'm standing on. Guns turn pussies into tough guys and make people who shouldn't have power powerful. Guns mean war. Guns represent everything I am against. And yet, I'm in a line of work that necessitates being flexible with my principles. I'd clean my mirror more often if I could stand the sight of myself. Instead, I mask my self-loathing by expressing a willingness to blow someone's fucking head off. In that way, it's really no different than most jobs.

Gun still at my side, I pulled back the hammer, and the whole of Tom's crew scattered. I turned to Tom.

"Oof," I said. "That's gonna come up at the next band meeting."

The walls inside the practice space were covered in graffiti with varying degrees of skill. A drum kit sat on an old rug in the corner, surrounded by guitars on stands and a few amps and monitors. All looked to be secondhand or, more than likely, stolen. A couple amps still had price tags on them.

"Take what you want," Tom said. "Just put that fucking thing away."

"Let the kid go," I said to Rad. Rad tossed him to the ground. Tom got up and rubbed his wrist.

"Weapons on the ground," I said. Tom tossed a switchblade and some brass knuckles at our feet. As Rad leaned down to pick them up, Tom tried to spit on him.

"Faggot ass," Tom said, but quickly shrank when Rad towered over him.

"Easy, Tommy," I said. I released the hammer and tucked the gun back into my jacket pocket. "We're here to talk. This doesn't have to get violent. But, so help me, if you fuck me around, I will fuck you up accordingly. We understand each other? Good." I wasn't waiting for him to answer. "I don't have time for this, and I really don't want to fucking be here, so I'll just come out with it. Jerry Rash is dead."

"Good," Numb said. "Serves him right." Rad moved to hit him, but I stuck my arm out and stopped him.

"Word on the street is you guys had some bad blood. So, naturally, you're a person of interest."

"You're not a cop," he said.

"No," I said. "No, I'm not."

"Well, I didn't kill him. I wasn't even at the Starwood last night."

"Who said anything about the Starwood?" I asked.

"Fliers, retard," he said.

I nodded. "That's fair, but it doesn't mean you aren't lying. What was the deal between you and Rash?"

"The hell you care, asshole?

"I may be an asshole. Won't deny that. Hell, I'll be the first to admit it. But I'm a fair and reasonable asshole. An asshole who wants your side of the story. Don't think of this as an interrogation. Think of it as an opportunity."

"An opportunity for what?" He seemed more at ease now that the gun was gone, but still unnerved by its presence. I doubt he'd have felt that way if he knew it wasn't loaded.

"A lot of people know you had it out for Jerry, and a lot of eyes are looking at you. Your name is coming up in all manner of whispers about this whole thing. I've been hired to set the record straight. I'm in a position of influence, buddy boy. I could unleash the mobs or be your personal savior, so if you want the stories to stop or to ever play a show without glass bottles chucked at your melon *fucking* head, you best be real convincing."

"Yeah. I hated the guy," Tom said. "I've stomped the piss outta him a few times, and he's beaten the shit outta me. Literally, once, if you wanna know."

"I did not," I said. "Go on."

"Fucker stole my song."

"Bullshit!"

"Why the fuck are you here then?" he asked. "I mean, if that's my supposed motivation 'n' shit, and you don't believe it, why the fuck did you come looking for me?"

I'll admit he had me there. He may have been a dumb jock, thug, douche, but an intelligent point is an intelligent point. He even seemed to notice that my silence acknowledged this. He smirked, snorted, and continued.

"He *did* steal my song. I was working on 'Cop-a-Feel' when we were both using this space. He was crashing here then, so he heard us working on it, like, all the fucking time. Enough to learn it. I went to one of his shows and I saw him playing it. But *I* didn't kill him. I was at a party in San Pedro. On Cabrillo Beach."

"You got someone who can back your story up?"

"About twenty people. Especially the chick slobbin' on my knob during the Minutemen. Was with her all night."

"Got her number, did you?"

He dug around in his jacket pocket and handed me a number on a slip of paper from one of those mini notebooks that a writer or poet might carry around in their pocket to quickly write down ideas. "Paula?"

"Yeah, somethin' like that."

"She wrote 'Paula.'"

"Well, I guess it's Paula then," he said in a mock idiot voice.

"Careful," I said. "Keep talking like a retard and you'll give yourself away. There a phone in here?" He pointed to a rotary on the floor in the corner. I dialed the number.

"Hello?" said the voice of a young girl.

"Is this Paula? From San Pedro?" I said in a voice other than my own.

"Yes." She sounded confused. "Who the fuck is this?"

"Yeah. Hey, Tom Numb gave me this number. He said he met you at Cabrillo Beach last night. Told me to call it if I wanted really good head." Tom looked mortified.

"The fu—?!" He moved toward me and I pointed at him. Rad, quick as a snap, grabbed him and held him in a full nelson.

"He said *what?!* That fucking asshole! You tell that worthless little shit that I ain't no whore! You tell him last night was a huge mistake! And *you* can blow *yourself!*" She hung up so hard I almost felt it on the other end of the line.

"The hell, man?! I wanted to hit that again! You just fucking ruined that shit for me!" Tom tried to break free to hit me, but Rad just held him tighter.

"You should smile, buddy." I slipped the number back into his jacket's breast pocket and patted him on the cheek a few times. "Your story just checked out."

"We done here?" Rad asked.

"Yeah," I said. "We're done here."

Rad chucked Tom across the room and we made a hasty exit to my car. As we got back out into the lot, a bottle sailed by my head. Some of Tom's ballsier crew members had returned. We piled into my car and I threw it in reverse right at them, bottles smashing against the trunk. They stopped long enough to dive out of the way, I threw the car back into drive, and the tires squealed, drowning out the curses and insults. Just like that, we were off into the night, laughing our asses off until we realized we'd just lost another lead.

9

Much of the ride after that point was in silence. We got back into West Hollywood late.

"Drop me back at Oki," Rad said.

"Yeah," I said, "sure." When we pulled up, it seemed like everyone from the scene was there. I decided to stick around and see what I could find out. I got out of my car and Rad and I observed the crowd. A few years before and I would have known everybody there, but I was having trouble picking out faces. Rad saw some people he knew, girls I might add, and trotted off to try to get laid, leaving me to my business.

"Good luck," he said, barely looking at me as he waved. I began polling the crowd and dropping a few eaves. Normally the conversations here would range from topics like asses kicked to Reagan, US involvement in Central America, music, or gigs both recent and upcoming. In a just world, people would have been talking about the Crumbs homecoming show. But tonight, Jerry was the only topic of conversation.

There was a fair share of people who were totally full of shit. But it was generally easy to tell who had good information and who was lying. Like the poseurs wanting to make a name by having the tragedy sound closer to them than it was. No, telling him "Great show" that one time after a gig does not make you close, personal friends. Some people really seem to get off on it. Having someone they know die. As if the drama and pity validated them somehow. I don't get it. They think death is something cool and romantic when, really, they just listen to too much Christian Death.

One guy was even selling bootleg tapes of the last Bad Chemicals show. He claimed to be "preserving history," but really it was a shameless cash grab capitalizing on a tragedy. Of course, I still bought one.

Eventually something someone said caught my attention. I turned around and saw a stoned-out looking kid with the calm, charming smile of a psychopath. He was dressed pretty average, like so many hardcore types. An old, worn collared shirt under a black jacket. He had short, dark hair with an *X* shaved across the top. Definitely the type you have to keep your eye on. He had the vibe of someone who got off on violence. HBers were one thing. Guys like this could be totally stoic, right up until the moment he beats your face to pulp with a chain just because he's drunk. He was saying something about "Jerry's crazy-ass father." I walked up to X-Head, whose name was Michael, assuming the name on his jacket was to be believed, or that it was even his jacket and not bought from a thrift store or taken off some other kid.

"What were you saying just now. About Jerry's father?" I asked.

"The fuck are you?" he asked in his haze.

"Alex Damage," I said.

He squinted as a toothy smile crept across his face. "You're that dude," he said.

"Yeah. That dude. So. Jerry's father?"

"He's fucking crazy, man. My stepdad knows that guy. Fucking drunk and crazy. He hated Jerry. Jerry hated him. They fought all the time. Used to hear 'em screaming down the street."

"Yeah? You got an address? A name?"

He told me the address but didn't know the name. I jotted it down on a napkin and got the hell away from the kid. I wasn't a hundred percent sure I believed him, so I asked around more. I got confirmations that, yes, Jerry Rash had a father in LA that he fought with. Not one of them could tell me his damn name, however. But I had an address. Unverified, but an address. I decided to give it a try once the sun came up.

I walked along the streets as day broke. The paperboys were already on their routes, chucking the morning edition at front stoops and lawns as they sped by on their bikes. I walked up a random driveway, picked up the paper, and flipped through it until I found the blurb about Jerry. It was buried in the music section and penned by my friend Aaron Craig. He'd started a zine a few years back, which was good enough to land him a regular gig at the *Times*.

> *Singer Found Dead*
>   *Gerald Rhodes Jr., 19, better known by his stage name, Jerry Rash, was found dead yesterday morn- ing from an apparent drug overdose. Rhodes was the front man for the local punk rock band Bad Chemicals. Authorities have notified the family, who could not be reached for comment.*

If the article hadn't been written by Aaron, who had origins in the scene, I would have doubted that they even tried. But one major revelation was that Jerry's real name was Gerald Rhodes Jr. I thumbed through a phone book and found the address for Rhodes, Gerald. It matched with Michael X-Head's napkin. I decided to pay a visit to the father.

10

I tapped cautiously on the frame of the rusty screen door. That amount of contact alone had me considering a tetanus shot. Doors in El Salvador have seen better days.

"Come in," said a shaky voice still containing the death throes of long-lost authority. The hinges shrieked like a battered wife. "In the kitchen," he said, more demanding than inviting. He was angry, yet there was an aloofness to his voice. The house was filled with open trash bags collectively containing hundreds of pounds of burnt toast. A scraggy, unkempt man stood in the corner of the kitchen. Every surface in the kitchen was covered with loaves of sliced bread. A power strip was attached to every outlet, and each one was full of toasters. Dozens upon dozens of toasters. The man was frantically waiting for his toast with a junkie's anticipation. "C'mon, c'mon ..." His voice was as heartbreaking and disturbing as if he were pleading for his very life. When the toast finally popped, there was a kind of desperation in his moan that cut into me. I didn't know whether to help him, pity him, or beat the shit out of him.

"Lord?" he coughed, looking at each side of every piece. "Lord?!" Begging again. "Fuck!" he screamed with all the anger and sadness of a man being stabbed in a dark alley. He ripped the toaster from the wall and heaved it across the room toward me. I stepped aside just in time to avoid it, and it crashed against the wall behind me.

"The fuck, old man?!" I yelled. "Chuck another one at me and they'll be able to make paper out of your face!" It was then I noticed the white collar around his black, untucked shirt. He had the patchy gray beard of a bum and the stench of cheap, gut-rotting gin. All the earmarks of a disgraced man of God. Jerry Rash's father was a fucking preacher? Or had been at one point. Impossible to tell how long ago. More toast popped. He grabbed it, looked at it, and brought it over to me.

"This!" he babbled. "This this this! Does *this* look like Christ our Lord?" He showed it to me. It looked like burnt toast. I just slowly and quietly shook my head. His eyes welled up, got even glassier somehow. "Mhmn," he whined and got back to his toasters. "It'll happen," he muttered. "Eventually. It has to!" I shook my head, praying, in my own atheistic way, that I would never end up this way. Drunk, stinking, twelve steps past crazy, burning toast and looking for Jesus. One thing was for goddamn sure, I wasn't going to find any answers here, so I left the old man to look for his.

11

Every corner was another brick wall smeared with the shit of vagrants. I went back home to take stock, have a drink, and get some fucking sleep. I hoped all that crap about tomorrow being a new day and a new start would prove true and things would begin to look a little clearer, because things were looking damn blurry, and my bearings were shot to all kinds of hell, especially since yesterday had blurred into today. I didn't feel any closer to solving this than I had at the start. I had to be missing something. Sleep was not forthcoming, so I rang Zii. Maybe she would remember something she'd forgotten to tell me.

"Hello?" Zii said. It was enough to make me forget what I was going to say. "Who is it?"

Oh, right. I was going to say my name. "Hey, Zii. It's Alex."

"Alex! What have you found out?"

"Not much, I'm afraid. I'm exploring a few angles but keep hitting dead ends. Which might be good. At least it means possibilities are narrowing down."

"Did you talk to Nancy?"

"Yeah. She tried to fuck me."

"Gross!"

"Tell me about it. Led me to her dealer, though. I'm waiting to get some stuff tested, maybe see if it was a bad batch or something. Can we meet?"

"I'm actually at my parents'. But … yeah. Okay." She gave me an address on National Ave in Toluca Lake, near Burbank Studios. And I told her I'd be there in fifteen minutes. Sleep could wait. And even if it couldn't, it would have to.

Twenty-five minutes later (traffic) I pulled up in the

driveway. It looked like the *Leave It to Beaver* neighborhood. This was prime real estate. She was sitting outside doing whatever it is nonsmokers do when they sit outside. She walked over as I was getting out of the car.

"Sorry I'm late," I said. "Cahuenga was backed up. Car accident. Brutal. Real *Red Asphalt* kind of shit."

"S'okay. What have you got so far?" She crossed her arms across her chest, and I glanced over at someone watching us from the window. "My dad," she explained.

"Did Jerry ever talk about his dad?" I asked.

"Not much. Why?"

"I went to see him."

"You … met Jerry's dad?" She seemed agitated for some reason.

"Yeah …"

"And how did that go?" Her hands moved to her hips.

"Not well. He's nuts. Did you know he used to be a preacher?"

"Jerry did mention that once, yeah. All Jerry ever told me about his dad was, 'He doesn't approve of my lifestyle and I don't approve of his.' Jerry didn't like to talk about it." As she talked, I tried to pay attention. Honestly, I did. But the man in the window, Mr. Haught, was still staring at me with a look of disapproval I'd normally get a kick out of. This was more like the figure in the window of the house behind the Bates Motel. Zii noticed how uncomfortable this was making me. Then she looked at her father and a sly smile crept across her face. "Do you want something to eat? We were about to have some brunch."

"Are you … ?"

"Trust me," she said as she took my hand and led me inside. I don't scare easy. I'd stood up to a lot in my life, and there wasn't much left I was afraid of, but something in me was terrified. I wasn't even admitting it to myself. The curtain shut, and her father was standing at the door when we walked in.

"And just who said you could invite your thug friends over?" he said to her. He was an intimidating man. It was clear he hadn't made his money by being cuddly. His presence alone demanded attention, answers, and whatever the fuck else he wanted, on the grounds that if he wanted it, he felt he had the right to have it. And they say people on welfare think *they're* entitled.

Zii's demeanor was not shaken in the least and, just as if he had asked nicely, she said, "This is my friend Alex. He's been helping me through Jerry's death."

"So, Alex. Are you trying to scam my baby for drug money too? Or just looking to fuck her?"

I stuck out my hand. "Pleasure to meet you too, Mr. H." He took my hand and shook it. He squeezed tight. I squeezed tighter, so he squeezed tighter. I squeezed to match him, and eventually it broke off with neither of us rubbing our hands but both wanting to.

"Are you going to answer my question?" he demanded.

"I would prefer not to," I said, summoning Melville.

"Because you don't want me to know I'm onto you," he shot back.

"No. Because it's presumptuous and I didn't feel like dignifying it with a response. It's the same way you'd feel if I were to ask you how many families you put out in the cold with that company takeover you negotiated. But I don't know you, I don't know what you do, and so why would I ask you a question like that? That would be rude. I've lived in the gutter, but I wasn't raised there. I still have manners." To be honest, I would totally ask him that kind of question, but he'd have seen a direct attack like that coming. Whatever was happening was putting a grin on Zii's face.

"Oh, don't give me that. You think you are the first of my daughter's punk friends to come in here and give me shit for how much money I make? What I do is legal."

"What *I* do is honest." Mostly.

"Dad ...," Zii said.

"Come in, come in," he grumbled. "But don't steal anything!" Now, under other circumstances, I totally would have stolen something, but only because he told me not to. Zii led me through the house, which, from the front, had appeared to be a modest ranch house. But it went back far and was much bigger than it looked from the outside. She took me into the backyard.

"Your dad seems kinda ..."

"Oh, he's all right. He just doesn't get the whole punk thing. If you'd walked in with a button-up shirt and a sweater draped over your shoulders, he'd warm right up to you. Course, if you were dressed like *that*, you wouldn't be walking in with *me*. You handled that well, though. No one talks to him that way."

"I can't imagine why," I said.

"He's not that bad. He just talks to everyone like an employee." She bit her lower lip.

"What does he do?"

"He has an investment firm. Commercial real estate mostly. So, you had some more questions?"

"Jerry really never talked about his dad?"

"Well, he did say he'd gone to see him recently. But he was real tight-lipped when he got back. Kind of shaken."

"He say why?"

"Just that his dad had 'finally lost it.'"

"Do you think they argued?" I asked. Her mom came out and handed us eggs and toast without saying a word and quickly moved back inside. Zii waited for her to close the sliding glass door and then shook her head. I wasn't sure if it was at her mother's behavior or the question.

"Honestly, I wouldn't know."

We sat and ate in silence for a few beats. I couldn't think of other questions to ask.

"So, did you really need to come here?" she asked. I looked up from my eggs to find her looking at me. "Do you really think I know about Jerry's father? Or did you just want to see me?"

Busted.

"Hey," I said. "Which one of us is the investigator?" We both smiled. I stood up and said, "Which I need to get back to, speaking of." She stood up and we both turned to look at the window, where her whole family (mother, father, and a brother who seemed close to her age) was watching us.

"Take the side gate," she said. I nodded and started to go.

"Damage," she said. I turned and she grabbed me by the collar and pulled me to her and kissed me deeply. A tongue stud clicked against my teeth. It could have melted ice caps. When I peeked, I saw her momentarily glancing back at the window before closing her eyes again. When she broke away, she bit my lower lip. Her family had left. "Call me when you know something," she said. All I could do was nod. If I had tried to talk, my voice would only have embarrassed me, so I walked out the back gate feeling like I'd just spent a month at sea.

I collapsed onto my mattress and felt the faux tile floor right through the horrid little springs. I rolled over onto my back and closed my eyes. A midday nap would set me right. But my mind raced with everything I'd found out and failed to find out. Jerry Rash was dead. His wife was crazy and distraught that he was leaving her. He had tried to rip off a drug dealer. He'd allegedly stolen a song from a gang of HBers, who seemed to have an alibi. His estranged fallen-preacher father was so far gone it would take an Apollo mission to reach him. It took another two hours to fall asleep.

My phone rang late that afternoon, waking me. When ignoring it didn't work, I blindly fumbled it off the hook and mumbled something that hopefully sounded like a greeting but was probably closer to "Mmemmo?"

"Alex." It was Rad. "I talked with Saul last night. Gave him the stuff. He's running the tests on it soon. Says he should be ready in a few hours."

"Then give me a call in a few hours, asshole." I hung up, rolled over, and fell back asleep. When the phone rang again, I couldn't have said if it was a few minutes later or several hours. When it wouldn't stop, I relented and answered. "Whoever this is, I'm warning you, irrelevance is punishable by death."

"Get down to the UCLA lab, Alex. You're going to want to see this!" The voice was familiar but could not be immediately placed.

"Whooizzit?" I grumbled.

"It's Saul, man," he said. "I got your stuff tested."

I rubbed some crust out of my eyes and said I'd be there soon. I headed west down Santa Monica and parked just off campus. It didn't take me long to get stopped by security.

"Can I help you?" he said, but he was really asking what the hell I was doing there.

"Can anybody really ever *help* anyone?" I smiled.

"Okay, wise ass. What's your business?"

"Meeting my friend Saul in the lab about test results."

"Test results for what?"

"A gentleman never asks and a lady never tells."

"Just a minute," he said, less amused than Queen Victoria. He walked into his little booth and talked on the phone a second, then checked his clipboard and nodded. "Oh yeah. Here it is." He hung up and looked back at me. "Name?"

"Alex Damage?" I said. He just stared. I sighed. "Alexander DiMaggio." I showed my driver's license.

"Yeah, okay," he said, handing me a guest pass. "You can go on ahead then." There is a special air that people in minor positions of authority have. It's almost higher and mightier than those in positions of *actual* power. A security guard, a tollbooth operator, the woman at the DMV, they lord their

ability to inconvenience you over your head with the arrogance and pettiness of a Greek god.

I walked into the lab and found Saul standing by a chem-
istry set in the back corner. He was an excitable, wiry little
man with unkempt hair. To help fund his extracurricular
activities, he worked at the Starwood part-time. I'm not the
cocktail type, but word was he made a helluva martini. Nice
guy, good for a laugh. But most important for my purposes,
he was a third-year chem major on a full academic scholar-
ship. He turned when he saw me come in and came over to
shake my hand. He handed me a pair of safety goggles.

"Alex," he said. "Good to see you again. I don't have much
time and I gotta get cleaned up before a class comes in here,
so I'll make this quick."

I hardly had a chance to say, "Okay," before he continued on.

"See, it wasn't easy, because it's kind of limited how I
can test this stuff. Basically, I try to boil out impurities and
what have you to see how pure the stuff really is. I hope you
didn't take any of this stuff. What am I saying? Of course you
didn't take this stuff. If you'd taken it, you'd be dead. Or, or,
comatose at the very least. Especially when you consider the
other stuff that was in there. See, when—"

"Whoa," I said. "Stop right there. Back that up. Other
stuff?"

"This here is lethal. There's cyanide in here."

"Cyanide?" I said.

"Poison," Saul said.

"I know what cyanide is. That's not what … never mind.
You're sure it was cyanide?"

"Oh yeah. Definitely. This stuff isn't a drug. It's a weapon.
They call 'em 'hot shots.' Drug dealers use them to kill people
and make it look like an accident."

"Shit. This is the stuff that was sold to Nancy when she
brought drugs to Jerry the other night," I said.

"Well, if he took it, it's no wonder he wound up dead."

"So," I said, "let me get this straight. This stuff is the murder weapon?"

"Absolutely."

"Shit!" I must have said. Or something very much like it.

"What's wrong?" Saul asked.

"Nancy!" I was out the door before I'd finished the word. I darted past security as he shouted something about needing to sign out, but I was in my car and on the road before he could do a damn thing about it. I didn't have time for that. Hell, I was probably too late already. I had to get to Nancy. Several possibilities were floating in my head and not one put time on my side. She'd killed him. Now she might be on her way out. Either out of the country or the world of the living, and I had to get there before she bailed in whatever way she was planning on bailing. I pulled up to the apartment and began banging on the door. No one came. The door was locked, but the wood was so rotten that it didn't take more than throwing my shoulder into it to make it give way.

Right there, in the middle of the room, Nancy was sprawled out on the floor. I ran over to her and the smell hit me. She was lying in her own shit with her robe and eyes wide open. I gagged and covered my mouth and nose with a handkerchief I keep in my back pocket. The needle was still in her arm. I pulled the needle out. She was still warm. As I took her wrist in my hand to check her pulse, her other hand reached over and grabbed mine.

"Shit!" I shouted. "Hang tight. I'm calling an ambulance." But she hung tighter on my hand and let out a little moan. Then a rattle. Her faint pulse faded to nothing. I found the phone and called an ambulance. I was far from a doctor. Maybe something could have been done.

While I waited, I took inventory. Other than her gear and drugs, there was nothing else near her body. I picked up the baggie of heroin just as I heard the sirens. My heart stopped.

When you live in West Hollywood, you learn the difference between an ambulance siren and the sound of the police. I turned around from the body to make my way out the back only to see two pigs standing in the front door, guns drawn. Not a paramedic in sight.

"Hands in the air!"

Well, shit, I thought. *This does not look good.*

12

There is a long list of things you do not want to be doing when the pigs walk in on you. A *long* list. When you're a punk, that list includes, well, pretty much everything, really. But no matter who or what you are, near the top of that list is standing over a dead body with a bag full of heroin. I've always credited myself with having at least half of a brain, so I complied. My hands went up very slowly. Thank fuck my gun was at home.

One carried the weight of perpetually being in charge. He hovered around six feet, round but clearly carved from oak. His black hair was going white at the temples. He had a thin black mustache and brown skin. LAPD's diversity hire, it would seem. The other a was younger, pale, white, fresh-out-of-the-academy type.

"Drop it!" They were moving in now. They were getting further agitated. I was being totally calm; they hated that. They loved making the punk kids piss themselves. I was denying them this satisfaction. It's not like this was the first time I'd ever had a gun pointed at me. I tossed the drugs lightly to the floor. They patted me down.

"Who are you? What are you doing here?" they shouted at me.

"Alexander DiMaggio," I said. "I was checking up on my friend because her husband died the other day, and I found her this way."

One cop pulled my business cards out of my pocket. "Alex Damage," he read out loud, "Private Investigator. You got a license for that, punk?"

"Not with me," I said. It wasn't exactly a lie.

"Why the hell not?"

"I'm not on a case." Okay, *that* was a lie.

"Know what I think?" he said through his teeth.

Nothing of substance, I thought.

"I'm talking to you, faggot!" he said. I hate when they try to get you to swing at them first. "You better answer me!"

"What?" I said. "What do you think?" He shot me a long glare. "Officer," I added, looking at his nametag, "Hernandez."

"I think you're here dealing. You had the stuff when we walked in. She OD'd and you're trying to cover it up. That's what I think. Now, what do you think about that, pussy-ass punk faggot?"

"I *think* all of your evidence is circumstantial. I *think* you can take me in for questioning but you've got nothing to hold me on. I *think* I've got rights."

"I also think you're resisting arrest." He took out his baton.

"I'm not resisting!" I shouted, hoping that someone would hear. "I'm not resist—" After that, things got kind of fuzzy. I've taken worse beatings before. In pits, from cops, in fights, and from doing martial arts in high school. None of them are coming to mind, though. I'm not sure how many concussions I've had, but I'm pretty sure it's more than doctors would recommend. I'm probably well past my fair share of cracked ribs too. Up to this point I'd managed to get by with nothing more than the occasional light sensitivity and soreness. Nothing completely debilitating, but I dreaded turning thirty, I can tell you that.

I was still conscious and breathing okay when they dragged me out to the car. Nothing felt broken.

I'm getting too old for this shit, I thought, and I was only a month past my twenty-second birthday. The handcuffs cut into my wrists, and my head hit the door frame of the squad car when they stuffed me in. My endorphins were working overtime to numb the pain, so it didn't even register.

"Jesus, Mike," said Hernandez's partner.

Sometime later I found myself cuffed to a bench in a police station. This was also not a first for me. I never slipped fully into unconsciousness after the beating. But it left me feeling sore and put the world into a blur. A man is measured more by the beatings he can take than the beatings he can give, and by that measure, I had just proven to be a beacon of masculinity. The cuffs were on so tight it was like I had another heart beating in my hand. While I have no problems with the color purple itself, it's not the color I would choose for my extremities.

"Hey!" I shook my hand, trying to get the blood to flow. "These cuffs are too tight!"

"Shut the fuck up!" A pig at his desk looked up at me and glared. I glared right back, then smiled and shot him a wink. He just shook his head and went back to work.

"Ugh!" I groaned. "Uggggh!"

He pounded his fist on his desk and looked back up at me. "What did I *just* tell you?" he said.

"I dunno, I wasn't listening." I smiled almost flirtatiously. That got him out of his chair and right into my face. I love fucking with pigs' heads. "Does this mean I get my phone call now?"

All the nine circles of Hell were burning in his eyes. "If you don't shut the fuck up right now, I will …"

" … give me something nice to tell my lawyer?" That shut him right the hell up. The big fat dump I'd just taken on his sad little fantasy changed his tone real quick, and since I was looking him right in the eyes, I could watch as they lost something. It's the same face a kid makes when they find out there is no Santa Claus and the Tooth Fairy has been Daddy the whole time. He muttered under his breath as he loosened the cuff on my wrist, unhooked me from the bench, and walked me to a phone.

"A little privacy?" I told him, disguising it as a request. He just stared at me. "Seriously, where am I gonna go?" He walked away. I called Zii.

"Hello?" Just hearing her voice stirred something in me. I wanted to pretend it was only in my cock, but ...

"Zii. It's Alex."

"Alex! Where the fuck have you been? Why the fuck haven't you called? What the fuck is going on?!"

"If you promise to calm down, I will answer all of those questions."

"Have you found anything out?"

"Yeah. You're going to want to sit down for some of this," I told her.

There was a pause. "Well?" she said.

"Are you sitting?" I said.

"Ugh. Fine. Yes, I'm sitting." The sound of a chair scooching came over the phone line.

"Okay." I took a breath. "You were right to be suspicious. I tracked down some of the heroin that was given to Jerry, and it was a hot shot. Cyanide laced. The batch was made to kill. And Nancy's dead. Same batch, it would seem."

"So, she killed him, and then herself?" Zii asked.

"That's what it looks like, yeah."

"Alex! You're amazing!"

"Yeah, I know. It's always nice to hear, though. Listen," I said, "I need a favor ..."

Zii sent her family's lawyer. Legal shit is boring as fuck, though. Trust me. I had no idea who this guy was, but the pigs sure as hell did. If they'd shit themselves any more, they'd need to change buildings, not to mention pants. They had nothing they could charge me with. I had walked in on a dead body and was only picking up the heroin to see what it was. The truth *had* set me free. Also, threatening to sue for brutality picks a few locks.

I went back to my place in the closest thing I could be to a good mood, and when I opened the door, I saw something that took me the rest of the way. Zii was sitting on the corner of my desk. Totally naked. I pinched myself and was thankful when it hurt.

There were star tattoos on her left breast, right by the nipple. Her shoulder-length red hair hung over one eye, and she was wearing black lipstick. Her sleeve-tatted arm rested on her pale legs, which had been hidden from the sun by knee-high boots. A birthmark was on her inner thigh. At least it looked like a birthmark at first, but it was, in fact, a small tattoo of a cat. It was a sexy joke I was glad she was making now but knew she would one day outgrow. A patch of dark hair sat between her legs. It was getting harder and harder to play it cool. I swallowed my heart back down to its proper place in my chest.

"You didn't have to get all dressed up for me," I said.

"Shut the fuck up, Damage." She came across the room and kissed me. Her sharp tongue slid across my teeth before inviting itself in. I hadn't thought she was the type, and it seemed awfully soon. But was I going to question this? Fuck no. I expected any minute to come to in a hospital bed, all this being a fantasy brought on by painkillers.

But I continued on. Lifting her off the ground and sitting her back on the desk as all her limbs wrapped around me and she undid my belt. She guided my hand to the patch of hair and started me on the rhythm to help ready herself. She pulled her mouth away from mine and flicked my chin with her tongue. I moved in to kiss her, but she moved her open mouth away, teasing me with hot breath. She licked along my jawline and nibbled my ear. I moved in and kissed where her neck met her shoulders. My pants were at my ankles, and she gripped with the tender firmness of the schoolteacher that makes a boy realize he's hit puberty. Her mouth was on mine again. As we broke for breath, I heard myself talking.

"Damn, baby. I thought you were straight edge." She slapped me across the face and glared at me. We were locked in that stare for a few beats before our mouths were on each other again. "Left drawer," I said. "Left drawer." She leaned back to reach behind her and pulled out a condom. She placed her foot on my chest and kicked me back onto my mattress. Then she was on me, rolling on the Trojan expertly, and then I was in her. She was grinding and bouncing, and I did my best to keep up. She gave a sharp gasp as I sat up, held her by the shoulder blades, and continued from a seated position. She moaned and screamed but was silent when she finally came the first time. I flipped her under me and lifted her legs to help support me. I leaned in and our flicking tongues met. Then she gasped loudly and her eyes went wide with climax. A few beats later I felt the slow bursts of my own. We collapsed into each other, panting, twitching, and satisfied.

13

I woke up in a better mood than I usually do. I had solved the biggest case I'd ever had, stuck it to the pigs, and the beautiful naked girl lying next to me had a lot to do with it too. How long had it been since I had awakened with a smile on my face? Zii half-moaned and rolled over on the mattress. I sat up, threw on some pants, and stepped outside to swipe a paper from the guy in the bungalow. I could count how many times I'd seen the guy on a partially dismembered hand. He was an obsessive recluse who had seen *Rear Window* about ten too many times. The glances I'd gotten suggested he was in his late thirties and well-built with military hair. He looked like the type of guy who wanted to be a cop more than anything but had been rejected from the force once they found out he'd made a necklace of ears while fighting in 'Nam voluntarily.

When I noticed papers piling up on his doorstep, I started taking them. I'd been doing this for months, and since I always did it when he was blaring Marine Corps Marching Band records, he'd never caught me. A sign on his lawn advertised that he was the head of the neighborhood watch. Which is kind of disturbing when I stop long enough to think about it. Not that I do it all that often. I love it, though. It's a fun little reminder that the people watching over us can't even look out for themselves. Hang the "we call the police" signs in your windows all you want. You'll be robbed and gutted long before your neighbor reaches their phone. And the amount of time they'll have left to do things to your body before the cops finally show? Please. It's all a joke. Good for a fucking laugh and little else.

I bought some coffee and doughnuts from the nearby gas station and headed home. Zii was up and wearing just a T-shirt. I handed her a doughnut and coffee. I thought, *Nothing can ruin the mood I'm in today! Nothing at all.* Except for the newspaper, apparently. "Fuck."

"What is it?" Zii asked.

I tossed the paper down on the desk sharply. "Fuck!"

The goddamn newspaper. And I had been in such a good mood, too. They had printed a story about Nancy's death.

Nancy Rhodes, 35, was found dead in her home yesterday afternoon of an intentional heroin overdose. Police found a suicide note clutched in her hands that confessed to the murder of the late local musician Gerald Rhodes Jr., 19, better known by his stage name, Jerry Rash, whose own death earlier this week had been ruled a suicide.

The note stated: "I cannot live without my Jerry. If I could not have him, I did not want anyone else to. I killed Jerry to keep Jerry. I cannot live with the guilt. I am sorry, but we must be together again in the next life."

"So?" said Zii after reading the story. "What's wrong with all that?"

"There wasn't a suicide note," I said, folding my arms and leaning back in my chair and bumping my head against the wall. "Ow."

"What?" she said.

"I was there before the police showed up. She died holding my hands. Not clutching a suicide note."

"Maybe you just didn't notice it?"

"If there was a fucking note I would have fucking seen it!" I fell forward in my chair and slammed my fists on the table. "Goddamn it!"

"Alex," Zii asked. "What are you thinking?"

"Something ain't right," I said. "I would not have missed a note. Someone planted that note."

"What? Who? Why?"

Without answering her I tossed on my Clash shirt, grabbed my jacket, and shot out the door. I needed to think. This wasn't right. Why would the pigs plant a suicide note at the scene? What the fuck was going on here? I thought I'd had this one in the bag, but something far more sinister was at play. Nancy was just a pawn. A sacrificial lamb. Misdirection. I had some theories kicking around. Someone else wanted Jerry dead. Someone with enough clout to get the pigs to cover things up by planting a note on Nancy's body. If they'd just left that shit alone, I would have bought the lie, but they oversold it. I needed a smoke and I needed a drink. One of which I had in my pocket. I pulled out my pack of cigs and noticed a squad car driving slowly down the street; it seemed to be following me. This happens all the time when you dress like I do. Every punk has been in this spot. I stopped walking and put my cigarettes away, waiting for them to get out of the car and hassle me with the usual routine. But the car just stopped. And it just sat there. I stared at them; they stared right back at me. I recognized one as Officer Hernandez. His partner was saying something into the radio, but I couldn't hear what. I waved at them and they peeled out and drove off. Now, *that.* That was not common.

I was sitting on the curb. It had only been about ten minutes since the staring contest with the squad car, and I was already finishing my third cigarette. I suck 'em down like pixie sticks when stressed, and this had me on the edge. I like the edge. But the edge was really giving me a good fuck-around. I thought I'd been on the edge before. I didn't have a fucking clue. Something was up. I knew it. They knew I knew it. And now they knew I knew they knew it. Fuck. I flicked the butt down a sewer grate. My adrenaline was pumping so hard, my heightened senses heard the *pssst* of the cigarette going out when it hit water. I was still covered in bruises from my beating the night before, and I could feel my heart thumping in every one of them. I ran back to the office and found money and a note from Zii on my desk.

> *Alex,*
> *What the fuck?*
> *Call me.*
> —Zii

I opened my drawer, checked to make sure my gun was loaded, then took a long pull on the bottle to make sure *I* was loaded. With a gun in my pocket and booze in my blood, I was out the door and into my car and headed toward the only lead I had left. The drugs. I would follow the drugs. Someone at the Wonderland House was in on this shit. I'd been pulled into whatever had gotten Jerry killed. I had sniffed the wrong dog's ass. I wasn't just going through the looking glass, I was going to shatter that fucker with the goddamn hammer of Thor! I wasn't tumbling down the rabbit hole, I was fucking swan-diving! No, you eat *me,* motherfuckers! You. Eat. *Me!* Alex in Wonderland, cocksuckers!

14

Pulling up, my tires were banshees. John Holmes was sitting on the lower balcony of the house and saw me getting out of the car.

"What the fuck, man? The hell you doing back here? Wait!" he said. "Wait right there!"

This fucking guy. A washed-up, coked-out porn star is about the last person I wanted to be dealing with, but if he had the information I needed, I was willing to put up with his bullshit. He came out through the gate, looking more wired than a power plant. I had caught him in a rare moment of sobriety before. His mustachioed face was beet red, his eyes bounced around like pinballs, and his curly hair was frizzing into a full-blown afro. He looked like a before picture for a skin cream ad in Hell.

"You shouldn't be here, man. What are you doing? These guys, man—"

"I got questions, Holmes. Shit is going down and I demand information!"

"I said I'd let you know if I found out things, and there's nothing to find out. Now get the fuck out of here before—"

I grabbed him by his greasy, frizzy hair and slammed his head against my car's hood so hard he'd have to explain the mark on his temple to his friends later.

"Here's how it is, you pathetic, washed-up man-whore, and I'll be sure to use small words so your drug-addled, coked-out, VD-riddled brain can understand. You so much as move and I will see to it that you collect on the insurance money for that legendary cock of yours. Jerry Rash was killed with a hot shot that his wife, Nancy, bought off your people.

That same batch was used to kill Nancy, ya following me so far?"

"Maybe she killed herself because she killed him? You ever think of that?" His voice was cracking.

"I did think of that, Johnny, I did. But someone fucked up. See, I was at her place before the cops showed. I don't really like to talk about it, it was kind of traumatic, but the papers said a suicide note was found at the scene, a suicide note that *wasn't* there before. So, even you can probably understand why that's had me scratching my head a bit. Now I got people following me around. Maybe you see now why I want to know what the *fuck* is going on!"

"We just sold it! We didn't cut it, I swear! These guys, they rip off drug dealers. Steal their money, their weapons, and their drugs, and then I fence the stuff. Sometimes we get paid with money, sometimes with drugs. I swear I don't know anything about it!"

"Bullshit!"

"It's true! I swear it! The heroin they sold, the stuff you're talking about, was given to us as payment for a job. I don't know anything else!"

I leaned right in his ear and sang, "I dooooon't belieeeeeeve yooooou!"

"These guys don't fuckin' respect me, man. They treat me like I'm some kinda fuckin' pet. Like a fuckin' freak! They make me whip my dick out, like a goddamn sideshow act. They don't let me in on nothing."

"I'm not buying that. Who have you been dealing with?"

"I don't know! The gang, they steal the stuff. I just fence it."

"Fine. Who should I be talking to, Holmes?"

"I'm not telling you a goddamn thing!" he shouted.

"Fine," I said, drawing a switchblade from my coat and flicking it open. "At least no one can say your dick went to waste."

"Eddie Nash! Eddie fucking Nash!" he screamed. I backed

the fuck away. That was the "Eddie" he knew? Goddamn. Not
Eddie Nash. Fuck. This was bad. A huge part of me wanted
to get away from this case, pack what little I owned, and
get the hell out of Los Angeles. Eddie Nash was LA's real-life
Godfather. Word was, after arriving from Palestine in 1960, he
had a hot dog cart. By the end of the 1970s, he owned dozens
of bars and clubs. He was also into drugs, prostitution, stolen
goods, and weapons. There was hardly a pie baked in this
town without him sticking his dirty, freebasing fingers into
it. He carried a lot of political power too. This was the type
of guy who dined with the fire commissioner once a week.
While under investigation for arson.

"Why in the fuck would I want to talk with Eddie Nash?
How is Eddie Nash mixed up in this?"

"You were asking about the guy ..."

"Jerry Rash."

"Rash. Yeah. Punk guy, yeah?"

"Yeah." I was losing my patience more and more. Holmes
was cracked out of his mind.

"Eddie owns the Starwood and he's my friend. So, you
should talk to him, right? I can get a meeting with him."

"Okay," I said. "In return for what?"

He teared up a bit. The guy was beyond a mess. He was
a disaster area. Like if Hiroshima were a person. My bullshit
detector was in full-on code red. "I could really use some
money right now," John said, scratching his neck. I shelled
out some of the money Zii had given me. "Come on, man,"
he said. "A little more than that?" I chucked a few coins into
his chest, and he scrambled around the street picking them
up. "Man ..."

"If you think you're getting any more, you've lost your
cracked-out little mind."

"Show some respect, asshole! I'm Johnny fucking Wadd!"

"And when was the last movie you did? Huh? How'd that
go?" That shut him up. "Now take me to Eddie Nash."

We decided to take his car because it would be recognized as friendly when pulling up to Nash's mansion. I got in the passenger side and Holmes went back to the trunk and took out a briefcase full of gear. He took a few hits of freebased cocaine. Fucking baseheads. The only thing you can trust about a basehead is that you can't trust them. In that area they are consistently reliable, spewing out disappointment and treachery like Old Faithful. He got in the car and we drove up to Studio City. The houses were incredible. Some were tucked back behind huge yards; others came right up to the property line, covering every inch of space. People think punks are shady, dangerous, and evil people. But I bet if you looked into how these people were able to afford these places, it wouldn't be the guy with the spiky hair in the leather jacket and Doc Martens you'd cross the street to avoid. It would be the fucker in the Armani suit and Berluti loafers.

Nash's house was in a cul-de-sac. We pulled up and there were quite a few other cars there. People were coming out as we were going in, and it seemed to be the norm for the place. When we walked in the door, there was a huge dark-skinned man, easily three hundred pounds.

"Hey again, Greg!" Holmes waved.

"That's three times today, Holmes. Who the fuck is this?" Greg wanted to know.

"Oh. Don't worry about him. He's with me."

"It's cuz he's with you that I'm worried 'bout 'im."

"Hey, Greg. Be cool, man! It's okay!"

"Johnny Wadd! Hello again, my friend!" shouted a very cracked-out-looking Arab in nothing more than a colorful banana hammock. Holmes smiled and walked over to him. They hugged and the Arab held a pipe up to Holmes's lips and he took a hit. "Good stuff?"

"Yeah, Eddie," Holmes agreed.

"Who is this guy you bring into my home?" the Arab, who was apparently Nash, asked. I'd heard the name and I knew who he was, but I had never seen him before. Except maybe in grainy newspaper photos. Which didn't quite do him justice but did him plenty of favors.

The place was packed with people. Some naked, a few passed out. Some were fucking on the couch next to me. Everything was elaborately decorated. There were velvet curtains, Persian rugs, and marble statues. I thought it was tacky as hell, but it definitely seemed like the type of thing that would creep into a twisted mind when it imagined the American wet dream.

"Oh. This is Alex. He's—"

"What do you want?" Nash asked me, losing his party-time voice so quickly it scared me. In this deck, all the cards were wild. "Tell me, please. Or why don't I just have Greg here beat you?" I had to choose my words carefully. A savage beating by a three-hundred-pound musclehead was not exactly on my to-do list.

"I ..."

Nash turned his attention to Holmes. "Why do you bring people here?"

"Eddie, calm down. He's ... y'know, like ... ," Holmes stuttered.

"I'm looking for some of the good shit," I said. "I booked some gigs for an out-of-town band that likes to party. They got a madman singer, crazy stage antics. Gets hurt a lot. And he needs a little horse before he goes onstage to dull the pain. Holmes tells me you got the hookup."

"So?" said Nash. "Why you come to me?"

"Why do—? Why do I—?" I laughed. "This fuckin' guy. Because you're Eddie *fucking* Nash! Everyone knows your shit is the best shit! What? Am I gonna waste my time with some middleman? Some guy who cuts his shit with diced-up Tylenol? No fucking way, man. I got a reputation to uphold. I need to get my boys the best of the best. And for that, there's only one guy to see ..."

"Eddie fucking Nash!" he said with a level of enthusiasm that is universal among those in love with the sound of their own name. He reached out and put his arm around me, pulling me in close and embracing me in a manner that ran closer to a headlock than a hug. "I like you. But what are you hanging around with this guy for?"

"I'm right here," said Holmes, to zero acknowledgment. I was dangerously close to feeling sorry for the guy. As much as one can feel sorry for a washed-up, drug-addicted porn star. He was a piece of shit, no doubt. But good, sweet fuck, was he pathetic. I had scraped things off my shoe that were more worthy of admiration. He got no respect because he didn't deserve any. And he knew it. And that made him dangerous.

"That you associate with him gives me great trouble. It hurts my trust, you know?" Nash said to me. "I think what we need here is trust. You want to go into business with me, you want a regular supply for your rock and roll friends, I need to know you are not a cop or something."

"I'm not a cop. Look at my hair," I said, gesturing to the short blue mohawk.

"I'm not a fool," Nash said. "So many people, they watch too many movies. They think cops must tell you they are cops when asked. I'm not a fucking idiot. I know this is not true. The only way is to test."

"What kind of test?" I ask.

"You see Johnny over there?"

"Yes."

"Shoot his fucking dick off," he said.

"What?" John and I both said at once.

"Shoot," Nash said, picking up a semiautomatic pistol from an end table and forcing it into my hand, "his fucking dick off."

"Okay," I said, feeling the gun in my hand. Without hesitation, I aimed for John Holmes's monster cock and pulled the trigger. John screamed a high-pitched wail and winced. The gun just went *click*. Nash and everyone else went into hysterics. Every last person in the room was howling with laughter, except for John, who was having a panic attack and looking around the room trying to figure out why he wasn't dead and why there hadn't been a gunshot. Then he looked down and, realizing he had pissed himself, a look of absolute dejection crossed his face. Without looking, I handed Nash his gun back.

"You must have ice for blood," Nash said. "I thought for sure you would be crying too. Fuck, man. Remind me not to fuck with you. Ha ha ha!" As a result of his little prank, Nash now thought I was a cold-blooded killer. Which is a drop of good fortune I intended to milk dry. Odd how it never occurred to him that I knew the difference between the weight of a gun that was loaded and one that wasn't. "Come on, eh? It was funny! A joke. Joooohn, I love you," Nash said, embracing John but leaning forward to avoid his piss-stained crotch. John looked at Nash with pure hatred. "It was funny, yeah?"

"Hysterical," John said. But everything about his face said, *I will get you for this*.

"Come on!" Nash said. "Somebody clean this up, yeah? John, you can borrow some clothes. Actually, keep them. My gift. Pick out anything."

"Yeah. Thanks," John said before walking into the back room. As he walked down the hallway, he shook his head to rid himself of all the thoughts that were too dangerous to say. When a guy like Eddie Nash makes a joke at your expense, all you can do is pretend to be in on it. Smile. Laugh if you can. Your life depends on it.

Nash put me in yet another borderline headlock. "Come to my office. Let's talk business, then we can have fun, yeah?"

His office was lavish in the way that a poor man thinks a rich man lives. Silk curtains with gold trim, expensive rugs from the Orient, a marble statue, antique furniture, and shelves with more books than most people can reasonably be expected to have read. I scanned the bookshelf and had a lot of trouble picturing a drug lord digging into Ayn Rand. But, hey, you never know. I've known punks to absorb everything from Pynchon to Nietzsche. He pulled a robe off a coat rack and slipped it on but did not bother to close it.

"Do you like my statue?" he said, pointed to the marble sculpture of a woman in the corner. It was pretty standard. Smooth, white, naked, sans arms.

"It's beautiful," I said.

"I like her big titties," he said. As I looked at it, he took a book off the shelf and brought it over to the desk. Classic misdirection. And it might have worked if I hadn't given the bookshelf a scan earlier. It was a copy of *Atlas Shrugged.* Or so it appeared to be from the outside. It was, in fact, a ledger. And a thick one at that. "When do you need? Now?"

"No," I said. "Gig's not until a bit later this summer, and I don't want to hold on to it that long."

"Ah," he said. "Smart guy. When is good?"

"July first?" I said, pulling the date completely out of my ass.

"Good, good," he said. He jotted something down in the book and slammed it shut. Then he looked me up and down in a way that made my skin scrabble. The guy oozed sleaze in the way only drug kingpins with connections to the porn industry can, and I could see way too much of the whites of his eyes. I opted to keep putting on tough-guy airs.

"The fuck you lookin' at?" I said, lowering my voice to hide the squeak in my throat and the shiver in my spine. His nostrils flared, and he slammed the book down. His eyes widened, and he moved toward me and pulled a gun out of the pocket of his wide-open robe. He got right up next to me and locked eyes. They looked ready to leap from their sockets to take refuge in mine. I held his gaze. To back down would be dangerous. Plus, I was desperately trying to take my attention away from the blood-red, tiger-stripe banana hammock barely holding back his cock.

He put his hand on my shoulder, and I fought off every instinct telling me to wince. Then he tossed his head back and sent himself into hysterics with a joke only he understood.

"I have an idea," he said. I waited a few beats for him to continue before it occurred to me that he wanted me to ask.

"What's that?"

"You do me this one little favor, and we're even."

"Even?"

"Yeah, even. Square. For the drugs you asked. What do you say?"

"I say that all depends on the favor," I said.

Again, he laughed. "Smart. So smart. This is why I want you to work for me. You are smart, so I think maybe you are smart enough to know that I am not asking you." He smiled and patted my cheek.

"So, what do you need me to do?" I asked.

"That is better. That is the attitude that I like," he said as he walked over to the bar to pour two tumblers of bourbon. He walked back and handed me one. "I think you like it neat, yeah?" I had to admit, he was a perceptive man.

"Yeah," I said. "Neat."

"There is a guy. He owes me money. I think you know him. He is punker. Like you."

"We don't all know each other. Not anymore at least."

Nash's eyes turned to ice picks.

"Who's the guy?"

"Joe Public," he says. I was quiet. "You know?"

"Yeah," I said.

"See? I know." He tapped his head, then pointed at me. "He gets speed from me. Not directly. From my people. But he owes me thirteen hundred."

"Jesus," I said, suddenly realizing where Joe had gotten

the money for that top-of-the-line equipment he had. I knew he sold speed. I used to buy it off him. But it seems he racked up quite the tab with his supplier. "Is it possible he doesn't know that he owes *you?*"

"It's possible," Nash said before finishing his drink. "But it doesn't matter. Go now."

I stepped out of the office, but there was no sign of Holmes. I checked out the window and saw his car was gone.

Touché, Johnny Wadd. Touché.

15

I wasn't about to ask one of the most dangerous crime bosses in Los Angeles County for a ride. It was tense enough being in the home of evil of this caliber. A lot of punks get off on being in situations like this. Of being in danger. Transgression is kind of our bag. Still, I wasn't about to be in a small speeding box with him. Even if it was only a six-minute ride. Every sense I had was screaming to get the fuck out of there. While I spun the possibilities in my head, my eyes wandered the living room. It gave the sense of perpetually being in a state of the morning after. What brought my eyes to a screaming halt was a framed picture hanging on the wall of Nash and Senator David Cromwell. Why would a right-wing senator be doing photo ops with criminals? Of course, on the record, Nash was a "community leader and businessman." There was a banner in the background saying something about a fundraiser. For what was cropped out. Part of the date was obscured by Cromwell's fat fucking head, but it appeared to be October of 1976.

"Staying for the party?" Nash's voice snapped me out of my trance.

"No," I said. "I got shit to do."

"It seems your friend has left you," he said, looking out the window. "You need a ride?"

"I—"

"Brandy!" Nash shouted. A jaw-dropping beauty walked out of the powder room. Her blonde hair was done up with curls, and her makeup was freshly applied. She wore shiny silver short shorts that barely classified as underwear and a strapless rainbow crop top. If she was over eighteen, it was by a few weeks. Tops.

"What?" she said.

"Take care of my friend here," Nash said.

"Ewww," she said. "I don't want to fuck a punker."

"Give him a ride home!" Nash said. "And hurry back. I need to take a shit, and I want you to wipe me." He licked his lips at her, and she rolled her eyes and grabbed keys from a hook. She blew past me without so much as cursory glance, much less a "Come on." I followed anyway. We got into the car and sat there in silence.

"Where?" she said. I turned to look at her, but she held up her hand and said, "Don't fucking look at me. Just tell me."

"8763 Wonderland Ave. It's—"

"I know where it is." She pulled sunglasses from her purse and started the car.

"What finishing school did you go to?"

"Kiss my ass," she said. I had about a dozen comebacks kicking around in my twisted head. But it seemed below the belt, even for me. I'm not in the habit of kicking people when they're down. Ass-licking jokes were off the table. I opted for raising my hands in mock surrender.

"I think we got off on the wrong foot," I said. "I'm Alex." But she was playing the cold shoulder. Every woman's trump card.

I didn't know much about Brandy. I spent the next five minutes trying to piece together her story in my head. It's a professional hazard. She had a hint of a Southern accent that she was making great efforts to hide. She was pretty success-ful at it. Nothing about her suggested she was strung out. I figured she had done drama in high school, was told she was good at it. Which I couldn't speak to. She damn sure had the looks for it. So, stars in her eyes, she trotted off to Hollywood. Figured she'd take a year off school or ditch college alto-gether. Or just see how things went over the summer. But she got here and found it was just shithole neighborhoods and street gangs. A few weeks was enough to burn out her modest savings, so she got a job slinging drinks at a club until one night the owner asked her to join him at his table. Said he'll make her a star but neglected to mention what kind. I had basically just piled a bunch of clichés on the girl. But this was Hollywood. Clichés are safe bets.

She pulled up next to my car and stopped suddenly enough to give me a bit of a jerk. She didn't even say, "Get out." She didn't have to. I'm a big boy and I figured it all out on my own. She drove off before I could finish closing the door. The momentum took care of that.

I didn't see John's car. Which was just as well, since I had no desire to see John. I decided to get the hell out of there before someone saw me. I drove back down to West Hollywood. I got myself a shitty slice of pizza and a large soda.

I was trying to gain Nash's trust before asking him anything. You don't get as far as he had by just trusting anyone who walks into your home. Blue mohawks sure as shit didn't help. I had just been talking with the remaining Bad Chemicals about the Crumbs homecoming show at the Whisky tonight, so I knew right where to find Joe Public. Hell, I needed a show to clear my head anyway.

It was time to go shake down a personal hero.

With the show starting at seven, I figured I could find him there around five for sound check. The Whisky-a-Go-Go sat on the corner of Sunset and Clark. Clark Street ran at a slight incline, so the intersecting sidewalks gave the building a disorienting, almost non-Euclidian look. The building itself was a violent shade of red with black awnings and trim. The iconic cursive logo sat above a marquee advertising the Crumbs show later that evening. When I got there, the doors were locked, so the front door was out, which I had expected. But no harm was ever done by jiggling handles. I heard the sound check from outside. It didn't sound like Crumbs, so I figured it was the opener. Openers tend to sound-check last;

that way their levels are all ready to go. Which meant Crumbs were already done. I headed around back to the small lot off North Clark. Joe was back there smoking cigarettes with a small group. The eagerness of their body language gave them away as fans. Friends don't fawn. Besides, compliments from friends made Joe uncomfortable. With fans he was humble enough to take in the accolades with genuine appreciation. Adulation often means more coming from strangers.

His back was to me as I approached, and he only turned around when the fans looked past him to see if I was anybody worth seeing. There were more looks of recognition than blank stares, for the record. Joe just put his cigarette in his mouth and gave me a hug.

"Holy shit," he said before backing away to get a good look at me. "If'n it ain't Alex Damage himself."

"Joe Public," I said. He spread his arms wide and leaned back, his cigarette held in the corner of his mouth.

"In the flesh!" He was in his typical outfit. Leather vest, no shirt, blue jeans held up by a snake belt, and black cowboy boots.

"How was the tour?" I asked.

"Great, man. Great." He ran his hands through his perpetually disheveled hair before finally taking the cigarette out of his mouth.

"How'd you come out?" I asked.

"What do you mean?"

"The tour. You actually turn a profit? Or did you lose out like everybody else?"

"Ah. Made a bit of scratch. Sold a shit ton of T-shirts, actually. They ate up the new album too, man. It was great. Why you ask? You need some money or something?" He laughed but stopped when he saw I wasn't.

"Can we talk?" I said.

"Uh-oh. That's the serious face." He looked back at the fans, then back to me. "Yeah. Sure, yeah. Let me just …" He gestured to the fans. I nodded. He turned to them, thanked them for coming out, and told them to enjoy the show. I followed him inside and he waved off bouncers as we headed backstage.

"What gives?" he asked. I filled a whole tumbler glass with the bourbon they had on their rider, because his band was actually at the point where they had a rider. I drank the whole thing and then refilled a respectable two fingers. I turned to Joe, still holding the bottle.

"I saw Eddie Nash today," I said. Joe immediately grabbed the bourbon from me, stared at me in an attempt to get a read, and didn't take his eyes off me as he took a long pull from the bottle.

"What are you doing hanging around Eddie Nash?"

"He said you owed him some money. Asked me to get it from you."

"So, what? This whole punk rock Matt Scudder thing you got goin' ain't workin' anymore? You runnin' errands for Eddie Nash now?"

"No. Kinda. Not exactly."

"Then what's this about?" His bandmates came in. "Fuck off, guys." They backed out slowly. "You happy? I just told my friends and *my wife* to fuck off."

"No, Joe. I'm not happy."

"Not until you get your money, right?"

"Joe, I don't need money. I just need you to listen."

"Well, I'm listening."

"Are you, though?"

"Yeah."

"You sure?"

"Yes! Cut the shit!"

"You heard about Jerry, right?"

"I did. I mean, we just got in this morning. We were in Portland, but Luke called me at the hotel when it happened."

"Well, I'm looking into his death. His girlfriend thinks it wasn't an accident …"

"Suicide?"

" ... or a suicide."

"Murder?"

"She thinks."

"And you?"

"Have evidence to suggest."

"Fuuuuck. And you think Eddie Nash is connected?"

"That's what I'm trying to find out," I said.

He rubbed the back of his neck and took it all in. There was a very clear moment when the light clicked on and all the pieces started falling into place. Then he nodded and pointed at me.

"And you're trying to get closer to get information, so you went to him and he wants you to get money from me?" What did I tell you about this guy? No dummy.

I tapped my nose twice.

"Okay. I can get the money. I just have to let the band know what's up. How much?"

"Thirteen hundred."

"Jesus!" he said.

"Is it a problem?"

"No," he said. "It won't be easy. I mean, there goes all the T-shirt sales. Just, damn, didn't realize I was in that deep."

"There's one more thing," I said.

"What?"

"I gotta ... break your legs."

"What?!"

"Nah. Just fucking with ya. But a black eye might help with the credibility." I was serious. If I was going to curry favor with Nash, I was going to have to further the whole cold-blooded rep I had cultivated with him. A willingness to rough up a friend over money would certainly cement that.

"No. No fucking way. You can have the money. I owe it anyway, but you can't fuck up my face."

"Do we want to sell this thing or not?"

"Sell this thing?! I'm *willingly* giving you the money. I hadn't paid yet because I was on tour. What's to sell?"

"Fine," I said. "No face-punching."

He walked over to his guitar case and took out the thirteen hundred. "Here." He smacked the wad, mostly tens and twenties, into my hand. "Sorry, man. Merch sales, y'know?"

"Yeah."

"You stickin' around for the show?" he asked.

"I think so," I said. "I could stand to cut loose a bit. I'm going to go put this in my safe and head back in a bit."

"Sure thing."

Just then his wife, Leah, who was also the bass player and vocalist, walked in and saw me with the money.

"The fuck is this shit?" She made a move toward me, but Joe jumped in.

"Honey, honey, take it easy!" He explained the situation to her with more detail than I would have liked him to, but you know how married couples are. No secrets and all that. At least the good marriages. Then she hauled off and punched him. Right in the eye.

"You're still dealing with Eddie Nash?! What the fuck did I tell you about dealing with that psycho?" She kept whacking him in the arm and shoulder but stopped long enough to smile at me and say, "Hey, Alex. Enjoy the show tonight. If I don't see you after, good luck with the case."

16

I stuck the money in my safe and then dialed up Nash.

"How'd you get this number?" was how he answered his phone.

"You gave it to me," I said.

"Alex!" he said. "How'd everything go with our friend?"

"Fine. Perfect. I got the money. I'll bring it by tomorrow."

"He give you any trouble? How bad did you hurt him?"

"He'll be walking around with a shiner for a bit."

"What? This is all? A black eye? I wanted you to fuck him up!"

"Didn't need to," I said. "He handed it over right away. Sends his apologies. The tour, y'know?"

"I can't have people get away with these things."

"He got away with nothing. He has a shiner. I have the money. That's what you fuckin' wanted, ain't it?" Templeton crawled up on the desk and squeaked. I mouthed, "*Dude, I'm on the phone.*"

"You got a lot of balls talking that way to me," he said. "Lucky for you, I like balls."

"That why yours are hanging out all the time?" It was a knee-jerk response. It's easy to forget who you're talking to over the phone. There was silence on the other end. I winced and thought about what I wanted on my tombstone. I was looking for a pen to write "All of my things go to Rad" on a sheet of paper when I heard he was laughing.

"You're funny. Come to a party tomorrow night. Bring the money then." He hung up. It was not an invitation. I reached into my drawer, pulled out a bottle and a glass, and poured myself a double. It went down even quicker than

I had planned, so I poured another. Templeton squeaked again. I looked around for something to feed him and found a potato chip on the ground. I set it down on the desk in front of him, and he scurried off to the corner with it and ate it in quick little bites.

I rubbed my temples. I was in desperate need of some live music. It lifts you up, soothes the soul. Which, when it comes to punk, a lot of people might find hard to believe. To an outsider, a pit must look like a scene from Hell. But for us, it's a slice of Heaven, a way to cut loose. It has more in common with some Pentecostal parishioner falling to the ground and speaking in tongues. It's just getting caught up in the moment. All in good fun. Or at least it used to be. Now, more and more, there are people who show up with every intent of hurting somebody. Some of these shitheads were the very macho surfers that had been beating the crap out of punks just last year. Still, there was something thrilling about it. A lot of the people had left the scene as things had started getting more and more violent. I wasn't about to get scared off by a bunch of violent assholes.

I headed back up toward the Whisky. I parked a couple blocks away. Walking along Sunset, a car blew past and someone shouted "Faggot!" at me. If I'd been holding a bottle, I'd have thrown it. If I weren't lost in my own head, I would have had time to shout something back, not that they'd have heard it, but it still feels good to push back. As it was, I did nothing, and it would eat at me for days.

I passed by the line outside the Whisky and walked past the bouncer with my fist out. He gave me a nod and stamped my hand. There was outrage of varying degrees from the ones who didn't know me. Probably some of the new kids coming up from OC to see what this punk rock thing was all about.

"How come he gets to just walk in?" someone protested.

"He's on the list," the bouncer said. Damn right I was on the list. I'm always on the list. One of the benefits of my lifestyle is that I've done a lot of people a lot of favors. That kind of reputation, everyone is willing to pick up your tab, put you on the list. This is usually how I get paid.

I beelined for the bar and ordered a beer. I'd been hitting the liquor pretty hard all day, and I needed to change things up to calm it down a bit. "Liquor before beer …," they say. Jury's still out on that theory. The kids like to throw that one around, but any respectable alcoholic knows it's about pacing. Never really drunk, never fully sober. Slam the first two, then one every hour and a half. That's the way to do it. I'd been spacing out my full tumblers of bourbon, but they were catching up to me. A beer's just easier to nurse. I got myself a good spot by the stage as the rest of the crowd began to pour in. Those who knew me waved. I gave them the finger. They gave it back. Others who had seen me walk in ahead gave me dirty looks, and to them I smiled and raised my bottle.

The opening band took the stage. They were all right. I wouldn't knock their talent, and they had energy but it felt a bit forced. Given a few more shows, they'd find some confidence, and with that, stage presence. Assuming they lasted more than a few gigs or weren't just a one-off.

I got a tap on the shoulder between sets. It was Zil. We both moved in for a hug, had a moment of awkward hesitation, then went for it, trying not to make it too sexually charged, for appearances' sake.

"What's this I hear about you shaking down Joe for Eddie Nash?"

"I'm working a lead," I said. "I need info from Nash. That was my in."

"The black eye your handiwork?"

"Leah's," I said. "But don't go telling Eddie Nash that."

"Well, be careful. Nash is dangerous. He's also a fucking pig. Just thinking about him makes me want to take a shower."

"You know him?"

"Not something I really want to talk about," she said.

"Listen, Zii. I'm thinking there's a connection between Nash and Jerry's death. I traced the dose of heroin that killed Jerry to Nash."

"Why would Nash kill Jerry?"

"I don't know. All I know is the heroin came from him. Whether or not it was poisoned before or after that, I can't say. But it's the best lead I've got so far. Someone in that distribution chain is connected."

"Before Jerry started trying to get himself cleaned up, I had to go pick him up from there," she said. "He called me from the party and was in a real bad way. Nancy had ditched him and he needed a ride. At least that's what I pieced together from his rambling, incoherent call. When I went to get him, Nash answered the door mostly naked. He tried to get me to tongue his asshole."

"Gross."

"After he'd just taken a shit."

"Yeah, he was trying to get a girl to do that to him earlier. Fuck. That's ... fuck."

"That's the only time I met him. But he's definitely unhinged."

"Unhinged enough to be buddy-buddy with Senator Cromwell," I said, remembering the picture on the wall.

"Really? How?"

"I dunno. Some fundraiser from a few years back. That's another thing on my to-do list. Wanna hit up the library tomorrow and scan the microfiche for every news story from October 1976?"

"That sounds ... terrible."

"Oh, it's mind-numbing as fuck. In the meantime, I was hoping to just enjoy myself."

"Oh. Okay. Have a good evening then," she said.

I grabbed her hand as she walked away. "I was thinking you'd be part of that."

"Were you now?"

"Yeah. I mean, why not?"

"Okay. Buy me a drink?"

"Of course."

"Proper buy. Like with money. None of this 'your money's no good here' stuff that you keep riding on."

"Sure. Of course," I said. I walked over to the bar and wound up next to Reggie Reckless.

"You move in fast, don't you?" he slurred.

"What's that supposed to mean?"

"Jerry's not even cold yet, and you're going after his girl like that?" He looked right at me. I had to give it to Reggie, he was not one to shirk confrontation. It was easy to see why he and Jerry were constantly at each other's throats. I hadn't even thought about that part of it.

Maybe I am being a selfish fucker, I thought. She was still grieving. Had all the flirting been manipulative? No. A lot of people grieve that way. Sex is life-affirming, right? It's only natural to want to feel something positive when your mind is awash in grief. I don't know. Was it disrespectful to Jerry? She had been his girlfriend. Even if it was on the side. Not that he was in any position to object or be hurt by it, nor did he have much moral high ground. But still, he'd been a personal hero. Maybe it was shitty to do him like that. Or shitty to take advantage of her. Maybe Reggie had a point. Hell, I knew he did.

"I don't know what you're talking about, man," I said.

He snorted. "Bullshit." He turned away and stared at the back of the bar.

"What can I get ya?" the bartender said.

"Sprite," I said, going for my wallet.

"Don't worry about it," he said.

"I insist," I said.

"Dude. It's a Sprite."

"I. Insist." I dropped a dollar on the bar. He rolled his eyes and gave me the change. I took the drink back to Zii.

"What's this?" she asked.

"Sprite," I said.

"Aw, you remembered," she said, stroking behind my ear, then pulling me in for a kiss. Which definitely got us some inquisitive looks. I glanced back at the bar and saw Reggie. He raised his glass to me. "You didn't get anything for yourself?"

"I'm, uh, still working on this one," I said, lifting up my half-empty beer.

"Well, come on then." She took my hand and led me out to the floor. We pogoed and moshed. I ordered more drinks, paying for Sprites and not paying for beers.

Midway through Joe's set, a fight broke out. One that I had nothing to do with, thankfully. Just some rival crews butting heads. But it was enough to stop the music and bring the lights up. The cops were on their way. We all spilled out into the night, and Zii followed me to where I'd parked.

"This is my car," I said, tipsier than I'd realized.

"Maybe I should drive," she said. One of the benefits of your date being straight edge is you've always got a designated driver.

"'Kay." I got into the passenger seat and handed her the keys. It's a weird feeling being a passenger in your own car. I don't know about anybody else, but it's similar to the feeling I would get as a kid when I stayed home sick from school. It's familiar territory seen from a new angle, or in different lighting. Something about it seems off. Like you're not supposed to be there. I kind of half-dozed. But then I realized we'd been in the car awhile. Much longer than we should have been.

It dawned on me we were going to her house. She shushed me before we went in, and quietly led me upstairs. I sat down on the bed and then fell backward. She slid off my boots and then my pants. She got naked, climbed on top of me, and slid me in. No protection, which gave me a moment's hesitation before she started to slide up and down. I'm not going to call it rape. I was a participant, even if I was too drunk and tired to be an active one. But I have to say, situations reversed, I wouldn't have even considered it. She did all the work and pulled off me a few moments before I came. She wiped me off with a towel as I passed out.

The next morning I woke up staring at a Johnny Thunders poster on the ceiling. It was black and white and featured Johnny giving a coy, sideways glance and come-hither eyes. His trademark mussed hair blended in with the black border. Pink stenciled lettering down the sides read "Dead or Alive." I rubbed my eyes and rolled over. There was a note on the side table.

> *Taking a shower. Breakfast is downstairs. Great cock.*
> *xxxooo*

I got dressed and walked downstairs. Her father was sitting at the breakfast table. I froze.

"Have a seat," he said. I didn't comply right away, nor did I say much of anything. I wanted to be anywhere else. "I said, 'Have a seat.'" He put down a plate of eggs, bacon, and toast. I sat.

"Eat."

I ate.

"Listen to me," he started. "I don't like you. I don't get this whole thing." He gestured on his own body to indicate my manner of style and dress. "My daughter is a smart girl. A smart girl, you hear me?"

"She is," I said. He was caught off guard by my sincerity. I took a sip of what I assumed was my coffee.

"Except when it comes to men," he said. I stopped eating. "Look, I have no doubt that you've ... *fucked* ... my daughter. She's not trying to hide it."

"I'd say she's rubbing your face in it," I said.

"Yes," he said. "If you wind up being anything like that last little shit she brought home, I will end you."

"An odd thing to say," I said. "Suspicious, considering."

"Considering his death? I had nothing to do with that. But it didn't surprise me."

"What makes you say that?"

"He was slimy. He was turning my daughter against me. Poisoning her mind."

"I think you did that yourself."

He winced when I said that. He tucked in his lips and breathed deeply. Apparently, I was salting wounds.

"Am I a perfect father? No. Maybe I'm a bit distant. I haven't been there for her like I should. I was busy putting food on the table and keeping a roof over her head."

"Well, congratulations on doing the bare fucking minimum," I said.

"What was that?"

"You don't get a trophy for providing for your kid. If you think that's all being a parent is, then you really don't deserve to be one. You want a pat on the back for not tossing her out in the cold and letting her starve, is that it?"

"No," he said. "I'm a cold man. But it doesn't mean I don't care."

"Then put forth some effort," I shot back.

He leaned in close. "That's exactly what I'm doing right now, you little prick. I will not let you put her through the same shit Jerry put her through. I won't let you get into her head like that. I saw the bruises on her. I heard her crying when she came home. And still she defended him. He would—" He stopped when we heard her coming down the stairs.

"Morning, Daddy," she said.

"It's been a while since you called me Daddy," he said.

"I wasn't talking to you," she said with a smile before kissing me. I *really* did not want to be there anymore.

"Well," I said, "I should get to the library. Where are my keys?"

"Table by the door," she said, pointing. "Good luck. Call me later."

"Okay," I said. Moving quickly.

"Remember what we talked about," said Mr. Haught. I don't know how I could forget. And I wished I had heard the rest of it. But the main thing on my mind was escape. Swift. Fucking. Escape. Zii walked me to the door and kissed me one more time. Long and deep. In view of her dad. My eyes were open and I saw him standing at the end of the hall, arms crossed, leaning against the wall, as a man does when he's losing a battle but has his eyes on the war.

17

I drove downtown to the Central Los Angeles Public Library. This white love child of Mediterranean and Egyptian architecture was covered in mosaics of sphinxes and snakes. On top of its central tower was a pyramid featuring a mosaic of its own, a hand holding a torch as an over-the-top metaphor for the power of learning or some such shit. Unlike authors, architects aren't generally celebrated for their subtlety.

The indoors also walked a line between beautiful and ostentatious. Whichever side of the line one fell on, everyone could agree it was colorful. The lobby had an elaborate chandelier and even more bright, primary-colored mosaics. The only thing I could think to compare it to was the time I dropped acid and read a bunch of golden age comic books. The stacks themselves were ornate. Rows of books, with all their book smells, were lined up along dark wooden shelves. Windows ran from the floor up to the high, raftered ceilings, and the walls had painted murals of scenes from what I assumed was the Bible or some other book I had not read. Of course, the microfiche was in the basement. Which featured off-white walls, an old mashed-down carpet, and enough fluorescent light to classify as a form of torture.

I requested all of the newspapers I could get from October 1976 and I began my grind. Normally in the movies they montage over this shit. Whole days can be spent slogging through microfiche. What I wouldn't give to be able to do this in the span of a couple fade-outs. I occasionally sipped from my flask. There were hundreds of articles to dig through. Many of them about the last election. Some things about the swine flu outbreak and mass immunization. Plane crashes. West German elections. Assassinations in Spain. A massacre at a school in Thailand. Not so long ago that I had forgotten, but long enough that I had to be reminded.

Then I found it. October 23rd. *LA Times*. Page 3. Nash shaking hands with Senator Cromwell. It was the same photograph that had been hanging on the wall in Nash's living room. Apparently, Nash had hosted a fundraiser for Cromwell at one of his more upscale nightclubs.

> *With dining and entertainment provided by prominent local businessman Eddie Nash, Senate hopeful David Cromwell was able to raise an estimated three and a half million dollars for his campaign.*

Jesus, that's a lot of money for one event. What were they charging per plate on that? It would certainly explain how a crime boss on the level of Eddie Nash could fly under the radar. He must have a ton of people in his pocket. Keep your friends close, et cetera. I requested a copy of the story and tried to find what I could with it. I figured I could go to Nash's party and try to sneak into his office. If I could get a hold of his books, I could try to find any large numbers. I was working purely on a hunch. I just had to prove it.

The next election was just a little over a year away, and Jerry had started getting very political. One of his more recent songs had been getting some mainstream radio play. "San Andreas Fault" was a criticism of the class divide in California.

> *In California there's a growing divide*
> *And it's already pretty damn wide*
> *But I ain't talkin' 'bout dirt and silt*
> *I am talkin' 'bout greed and guilt*
>
> *No it's not San Andrea's fault*
> *Some get stepped on so others stand tall*

No it's not San Andrea's fault
You get buried if you don't play ball

Given that he blamed Republican policy for said class divide, he was very openly and very publicly anti-Cromwell. I knew he'd been making it a goal to be a thorn in Cromwell's side. I found it extremely unlikely. But every possibility, no matter how unlikely, needs to be pursued. Nash himself wasn't off the hook either. The cover-up attempt was damning. The only people I had linked to this whole thing with the connections to pull off something like that were Eddie Nash and David Cromwell. Or the cops themselves.

If I had a sense of self-preservation, I would've called it then. Just walked away. When it comes to good ideas versus bad ideas, digging around in the interactions of the most powerful man in the state with the most dangerous ranks somewhere between jumping into a shark tank while bleeding and starting a fistfight with a wild grizzly. I never expected to live long, but I figured I'd have liked to make it to twenty-seven. I tried to think of ways it could have been anybody else.

Mr. Haught? He'd pretty much threatened me. And he didn't care for Jerry. He seemed to think that Jerry was physically and emotionally abusive to Zii. He was well connected. But in a very different world. Did those connections extend into organized crime? It was certainly possible. Or to the senator? Did he know about Nancy?

Maybe it was one of the guys at the Wonderland House. They were the middlemen between Jerry, Nancy, and their drug supplier, after all. None of them seemed to be fans. Bobby had mentioned Jerry's behavior at parties, and whether he was lying about that or not, it seems Jerry had done something to piss him off. And it's never a good idea to piss off one's dealer. It's that connection to the pigs, though. Maybe they had an in with some dirty cops.

Tom Numb? I'd written him off too easily. Hell, his

bandmates. Still, I didn't have any of them pegged for it. But more questions might point me more toward who else would want him dead. Or at least start clicking in some pieces to connect the senator to it. All that would have to wait. I had a party to get to.

I stopped by my place on my way up to Laurel Canyon. I showered, got changed, and got the money out of the safe. When I pulled up to Nash's house, there was a line of cars around the cul-de-sac up and down the block. This time I walked right in. A sign on the door displayed a warning about no cameras. My senses could have pressed assault and battery charges on that house. Music and chatter and moaning came at the ears with switchblades; smoke and unwashed sex bashed the nose in with a bat. This wasn't just a party. This was an orgy. John was there, reclining on a chaise longue and being straddled by a girl who looked barely out of high school, if she'd even started it.

"Where's Nash?" I asked. John just pointed to the back office. I stepped over a few writhing bodies and headed down the hallway, pushing my way past the couples making out or fucking up against the wall. I bet if I'd scanned the room more carefully, I'd have found more than a few public figures. No wonder they didn't want cameras. This was a potential blackmail farm. I rapped on the door and got no answer, so I rapped a bit harder and heard a muffled "Come in."

I stepped inside to find Nash standing there with his bathrobe wide open and his dick wrapped firmly in the mouth of a famous porn starlet. "Alex!" he said. "You have my money!" This was not a question. I reached into my jacket pocket and handed him the envelope of cash, averting my eyes the whole time. There are moments to make eye contact with a man, and there are moments to not. I heard him count it.

"Perfect!" he said. "And for my end of the deal!" He handed

me the drugs I had negotiated earlier. Which, considering I'd told him I didn't want it until July, was both confusing and annoying. It must have shown in my face.

"Something wrong?" he said.

"No," I said. "This is perfect."

"Great! Now go! Party!" Again, this was not an invitation. I pocketed the drugs, slinked out of the office, pushed my way to the kitchen, helped myself to an unopened bottle of top-shelf bourbon, and snuck out the back. A sign on the door made it very clear there was to be no fucking in the pool. I lit a cigarette and then noticed a girl sitting on the edge of the pool, staring at her feet in the pool light. It's a scene no LA party is complete without. When she turned around to see who had come outside, she gave me a very recognizable look of disdain. I took off my jacket and tossed it over the back of a pool chair.

"Brandy, right?" I said.

"Fuck off, punk," she said.

"Hey, whoa, I come in peace," I said. I held my hands up, then patted my pockets. "Afraid I'm fresh out of white flags, though." I plopped down next to her with my legs crossed. I offered her a cigarette, which she begrudgingly accepted. I busted out my Zippo and lit it. I snapped the lighter shut and stuck it back in my pocket. I stretched my arms behind me and exhaled a few smoke rings straight into the air. She watched them a moment before rolling her eyes and looking away. As if she wasn't impressed.

"Are you even old enough to smoke?" I asked.

"Yes, I'm old enough to smoke," she said, enunciating each word to give it that snobby tone only teenagers are capable of.

I broke the seal on the fresh bottle of bourbon and christened it with a long sip. "Are you—?"

"Do you care?" she interrupted me, and snatched the bottle and took a big sip before immediately spitting it all out.

"Such a waste," I said as she handed the bottle back to me.

"Ugh! That's disgusting!"

"It ain't a California Cooler, that's for sure."

"How do you drink that stuff?"

"How do you—? Never mind."

"How do I what?"

"Nothing. Forget it. Never mind."

"How do I *what?*" she said.

"How do you ... find yourself in a place like this?" I said, putting things as euphemistically as possible.

"Good save," she said. "I came to LA to be an actress. And, well, y'know, it's not what you know, it's who you know. I'm just doing this for now. It makes more than waiting tables, and you meet the right people."

Nailed it.

"You gotta sip it," I said. "Don't just gulp it down." She took a smaller sip, actually swallowed it this time, but winced at the burn, shook her head, and handed the bottle back.

"You don't care for punks, do you?"

"Does anybody besides other punks?"

"I guess not."

"Just a bunch of violent, obnoxious drug addicts."

"You're watching too much *Eyewitness News.*"

"I'm speaking from experience."

"How's that?" I offered her another cigarette by quietly holding out the pack. She took one, and I lit hers before getting a fresh one of my own.

"A few of them used to party up here a lot," she said. "With Eddie."

"Really?"

"Yeah. Eddie owns all those clubs, y'know? And he likes to invite a lot of the rock stars to party here. Even those shitty little punk bands. 'Hey, come to my place. We'll do drugs and fuck porn stars.' What nineteen-year-old is going to say no to that?" She looked at me as if looking for an answer.

"I was also gonna say, 'What nineteen-year-old is going to say no to that?'"

"Y'know, fucking rock stars is pretty cool. But one of those punk guys, he went way off the menu."

"How's that?"

"He got rough," she said. "Like really rough. Violent, even."

"What did he do?" I asked. "Sorry. Can I ask that?" There was a long silence. She stared at her feet as she swished them around in the water. She sighed and looked up at the night sky.

"Promise you won't laugh?"

"Why would I—?"

"Promise you won't laugh."

"Okay."

"Say it." Her voice cracked.

"I promise I won't laugh."

"I can't believe I'm going to tell you of all people this." She took a drag on the cigarette. She was either processing a lot of information or milking the suspense. I couldn't tell.

"He slapped me around a lot. He was into spanking and he overdid it. Which, y'know, happens sometimes. But then he pinned me down and he started choking me. He'd bring me right to the point of passing out, then loosen his grip and let me breathe, then he'd do it again."

"Jesus," I said.

"Then he said he wanted to 'put it in my tight little Dixie ass.' And I told him I don't do the ass. So, he hit me. With a closed fist right here." She pointed to her forehead. "And here." Right eye. "Then he choked me until I passed out. When I came to, he was ..." She took a long drag on the cigarette and regained her composure. "He was fucking my ass. He pulled out, came on my back, and tossed me a towel. Told me to mop myself up." She went really quiet. My own breathing slowed as I processed what she had shared with me. She'd decided to trust me with this, and I wanted to say the right thing.

"Fuck. That's awful," I said. "Why would you think I'd laugh?"

"He did."

A rush of blood warmed my body as rage coursed through me. To do that to someone. To laugh about it. This subhuman bastard deserved to be set on fire in public. A savage flogging, at the very least, was in order. My fists and teeth clenched.

"Who was it?" I asked before turning to her. "I can make sure he's straightened out. Free of charge."

"I wouldn't worry about it," she said. "He died the other day. Overdose." My heart fell through my body like a pachinko ball.

"Jerry Rash?" I asked.

She tucked her lips in to choke back the memory but managed to nod.

"Did you tell anyone about that?"

"No."

"Not even Eddie?"

"God, no! Especially not Eddie. If it got out that I was causing trouble for his clients ... You won't tell anyone, will you? Shit, why did I tell you? Forget I said anything!" She started to get up, but I held her hand.

"Brandy," I said. She looked over to me, and for the first time since meeting, we met eyes directly. "I swear to you, your secret is safe with me. Thank you for trusting me with it."

"Thank you ..." She searched for my name.

"Alex," I reminded her.

"Right. Sorry. Alex."

"I'm hurt, Brandy. I thought I was more memorable than that."

She bicycle-kicked her feet in the water. "Actually, it feels good to talk about it. So ... thank you for that too, I guess."

"Yeah," I said, spaced out now.

"You okay?" she asked. "You look sick." I took a sip of the bourbon. I don't say this often, but thank fuck for Kentucky.

"How else did Jerry act at those parties?" I asked.

"Like a fucking asshole," she said. "Why?"

"To everybody?"

"No. No, actually up until then he was charming. Sexy too. Except..."

"What?"

"One time he was really high. And he saw that picture of Eddie and some senator. He went on some rant. He and Eddie had some fight about it. Why do you want to know?"

"I'm supposed to be finding his killer," I said.

"I thought it was his wife. Some kind of murder-suicide?"

"That's the official story. But I'm not so sure."

"He's dead. He deserves to be. Leave it at that," she said. I just stared into the night. She stood up and shoved me into the pool. I sputtered to the surface.

"What the hell?!" I was partly pissed but mostly thankful I hadn't been holding the bottle. She picked it up.

"Y'know, Alex," she said, taking one more sip of bourbon, then replacing the cap, "you're actually kind of sweet when you want to be. You should drop the tough-guy act. It doesn't suit you." She tossed the bottle into the water. I watched her sashay back inside. I swam over to the bottle, grabbed it, and got out of the pool. The water poured out from my pants. I sat on a lounge chair, dumped the water from my boots, and dried myself with an abandoned towel. I didn't want to draw attention to myself, so I slinked out the side gate, leaving it unlocked. As I stood on the street, a cop car slowly rolled past me. It looked like the same guys as before. Mike Hernandez and his partner. But they all look alike to me. Cops, that is. Their eyes singled me out from the partygoers. I gave them a nod, and the one in the passenger seat signaled his partner to drive on. I went to pull out a cigarette, but they were soaked. I crumpled the pack and tossed it on the lawn.

18

I was too drunk to drive. Not hammered, but tipsy enough to give the cops following me an excuse, so I put my keys under my car, leaned back in the driver's seat, and dozed off a bit. I awoke to the sound of everyone leaving the party just before dawn. I watched as the cars left, some paired off, others on their own. It takes a certain kind of person to go home from an orgy alone. I waited for the crowd to dwindle and watched for the lights to go out. I fumbled through the back seat and pulled out my camera. I tucked it into my jacket and went around to the side gate that I had left unlocked.

I slowly opened the sliding door and heard nothing in the way of noise. Eddie's bedroom door was open, and he was passed out between two naked women. I quietly checked the office door. Locked. There having been a wild orgy here just a few short hours ago, it didn't take long for me to scrounge up a couple of bobby pins. I bent one back and bit off the rubber end from the straight side with my teeth. I bent the other into an L to make a tension wrench, and with a minimal amount of effort, I set the pins and was in. I scanned the bookshelf, looking for *Atlas Shrugged*, but it didn't seem to be in any sort of order. Any normal person would have it alphabetized by author's last name, but I wasn't dealing with a normal person. Hell, I wasn't sure I even knew how to deal with normal people anymore. I'd started to lose any sense of what that meant. "Normal" is just a euphemism for people who aren't comfortable with themselves, so they act like everybody else.

It made sense that the book would move around. He wouldn't want to put it back in the same place each time.

Eventually I found it somewhere in the corner. I opened up the book and flipped through it. It contained names and numbers. Amounts paid and who they were paid to. These looked to be the legitimate books of his illegitimate business. A handy thing to have around, but risky. I couldn't figure out why he hadn't locked them up. But I didn't have time for dental exams on gift horses. This type of book would give him leverage over anyone listed in it. There was mail in here of the blackest pitch. But there were hundreds of pages. Thousands of entries. If Nash wanted to sell people out, this book would take a lot of people down. *Atlas Shrugged* may have been a disguise, but the book was still a bible of self-interest.

I flipped through the dates and went back a few years until I found October of 1976. I couldn't find anything. I flipped back a few weeks to September and saw David Cromwell's name a few times. These outgoing payments were listed as "contributions." I flipped ahead through the years and took pictures of any page that seemed suspicious. I paid especially close attention to anything with Cromwell's name attached. It seemed to pop up a few times a month, starting in early 1976, for more or less the same amounts. Usually around two to three grand. When I got to a few months prior, I noticed along the seam that a few pages had been cut out. If I hadn't been careful, it would have been easy to miss. They had been cut right along the inside of the spine with a knife. I took a photo of that too. I checked the last few pages and saw an *incoming* payment from Senator Cromwell. For nine grand. Three days before Jerry died. Speaking of Jerry, his name was in there. A lot. Right up until the end. There's no way he was buying that much to use without Zii noticing. I was in too much of a hurry to take time to process and interpret this information—that's what the photos were for—but it was obvious. Jerry was dealing.

I put the book back, careful to not disturb anything. I locked the door on my way out too. I went out the way I came, slinked back into my car, and wondered if the photo booths had opened yet. When I saw the clock on my dash, I realized that, no, no fucking way. I had a few hours to kill.

I drove off quickly, even though I had nowhere to go. No one to see. Everyone else was still asleep or, more than likely, had just gone to bed. I decided to get myself some coffee. Turns out a few winks of drunk sleep in the front seat of your car is not the soundest. I had too much to do before I could rest again.

I found a coffee shop easy enough, and after a few minutes I managed to find parking. I stepped in and heads turned. They didn't immediately turn away, and for a moment it felt like 1978 again. In West Hollywood, my look wasn't raising as many eyebrows as it once had. But in some of the more affluent neighborhoods, it still managed to bring in the wide-eyed stares. The place went quiet for a moment, and the manager was clearly wondering if she should call the cops. A couple came up to me and asked shyly in a Midwestern accent if they could take a picture with me. I'd heard of some punks that hung around Mann's Chinese Theatre and charged people to "have their pictures taken with a punk," and I figured I could pay for my coffee.

"Five bucks for three pictures," I said. The man reached into his wallet and handed me a crisp five-dollar bill, doing far too little to hide the wad of cash he had in there. I took the fiver and jammed the bill into my jacket pocket.

"Would you mind?" the woman asked a man from a neighboring table. He was far more agreeable than I'd be. The couple came up on either side of me, and I put my arms around their shoulders and curled up my lip into a nice sneer. In one pic I gave the finger. Just a fun little show for their friends back in Des Moines or Carbondale or wherever.

"Thank you so much!" she said.

"Sure thing," I said.

"How do you do that with your hair?" the man asked.

"Jell-O powder," I said.

"Jell-O powder," he told his wife.

"Well, Jell-O powder and hair conditioner," I said.

He turned to his wife. "What do you think, honey? New look?"

"Don't you *dare!*" She swatted him on the arm, laughing. And they sat back down. I don't know why I waited a couple seconds for a goodbye. But I did. I knew it wasn't coming, and when it didn't, I walked over to the counter and waited in line. Part of being a punk is being treated like a freak show. Some people complain about that. They complain about the staring or the harassment. Or the tourists who want a little souvenir of the crazy punk they saw. But those people are whiners. Why be a punk if you don't want to turn heads or freak people out? Why do it if not to shake things up? I get wanting to be left alone to do your own thing, but don't try to shake things up and then complain about the turbulence. I've got no patience for that shit.

I walked up to the counter and handed over the now-crumpled five-dollar bill.

"Coffee, please," I said.

"What kind of coffee would you like?" said the woman behind the counter. She was older than me by about three years. Brunette, hair cut into a bob. Her glasses did little to cover her tired eyes. She had "grad student" written all over her.

"What?"

"What kind of coffee?"

"Shit. I dunno. Coffee coffee," I said. She rolled her eyes at me and rang me up and got to work on my order. She had it up as quickly as possible and in a to-go cup. I got the feeling it had less to do with providing good, fast, efficient service than it did with just getting me out the door as quickly as possible. I looked at her, glanced behind me, and read the air.

The message was clear, I was making people uncomfortable. The couple who had taken their picture with me had left as well. I turned back to the woman, reached to my left, and grabbed a copy of the *LA Times*.

"And a paper," I said, pausing before adding, "please." She rang me up for that too. I took my paper and my coffee and picked out an open table. I sat down, propped my feet up on the opposite chair, read the paper, sipped my coffee, and reveled in my small victory.

I hit up a photo booth in the parking lot of a mall, then browsed through some shops while waiting for them to get developed. Nothing in the shops looked good, and it was all out of my price range, so I walked into the record shop and browsed some. I picked up X's *Wild Gift* on cassette. I checked my watch and headed out to the car. I picked up the photos and cranked my new tape. All I had to do now was comb through these photos for anything to prove my theories or at least point me in a new direction. Truth be told, I was desperately hoping for the latter. I got back to my office to find a note pinned to my door.

> *Alex. What the fucking hell am I paying you for?*
> *I need a fucking goddamn status report.*
> *Call me at this number. And tell me what you've found*
> *if you want to see your money. Or anything else ...*
> *—ZZ*

Jesus. Even her handwriting made me hard. Fuck. I'm a scumbag. I ripped the note off the door and stepped inside. She was sitting at my desk. Feet propped up on top.

"Don't put your feet on the desk. You'll scuff it up," I said, closing the door. She looked down at the surface of the desk, covered in scuffs, slashes, scratches, and other *S* words for damage.

"You're kidding, right?" she said.

"Yes," I said. I dropped the photos on the desk, making her move her feet.

"What the hell is that?"

"A fucking goddamn status report," I said. "Wait. How the hell did you get in here?"

"What's the status?"

"Eddie Nash's books."

"Fiction or nonfiction?"

"Financial ledger." I started to slip off my shirt.

"Fiction or nonfiction?" she asked again.

"Whichever kind you keep hidden," I said. She was busy flipping through the photos. I tossed my shirt aside and moved in for a kiss, but she backed away.

"Whoa, what the fuck?" She pushed me back. But not in the sexy, knock-me-to-the-bed-and-fuck-my-brains-out way.

"Oh, I mean ... I thought ..."

"That I'd reward you for playing fetch by sucking your dick or something?"

"Jesus ... when you put it that way, it sounds ..."

"Accurate?"

I was at a rare loss for words. She slapped me in my dick with the back of her hand. "Oof!"

"Not this time. Shirt on." She snapped and pointed. I complied. She turned back to flipping through the photos.

"I mean, just because before ..."

"Before I wanted to. Right now, I don't," she said without looking away.

"Is it because ... ?"

"You were fine. If that's what you were going to ask." She turned to look at me. "Good, even. But it's not about that. It's got fuck-all to do with you. This is about me. And what I need right now. I sleep when I'm tired, eat when I'm hungry, and I fuck when I'm horny. I'm not here to satisfy your needs, and I don't need anyone else, man or otherwise, to satisfy mine. When I need help, I ask for it. When I can give it, I offer it.

Right now, I don't want food, I don't want sleep, and I don't want to lay or get laid. I want justice for my friend."

I opened my mouth to say something but got cut off.

"The fact I was sleeping with him has nothing to do with it. I hate injustice. That's why I'm a punk. Because the system is built on injustice, and I'm sick and fucking tired of it. And now that that shit has hit me personally, I'm going to stuff it right back up the system's ass. And you can either continue to help me or take the money I owe you and fuck off."

I waited a few beats so I could be sure she was done. "You realize that only turned me on more, right?" And, honestly, I didn't just mean sexually. I smiled.

She smiled back.

Then swatted me in the dick.

19

I had gotten a nap in while Zii searched Nash's books for anyone she knew who had it out for Jerry who I hadn't considered. I rinsed out my coffeemaker for the first time since the Carter administration midterms and made us a couple of cups.

"Cream or sugar?" I asked.

"Black," she said.

"Good. I don't have any of that other stuff." I set the cup down next to her on the desk.

"Thanks," she said. She reached for the cup and took a sip while never looking away from the log entries. "Your coffee tastes like shit, by the way."

"Oh, you give me way too much credit," I said, looking into my mug. "Shit tastes way better."

She started with a low chuckle, which quickly burst into laughter. "I needed that," she said. She stood up and planted a kiss on my cheek that made me never want to wash my face again. "I'll go get us some real coffee."

She took my cup and emptied it in the sink. "See if you notice anything else in the books. When I get back, we'll make a plan." This time she let me watch her leave. I looked at the pile in front of me and sighed.

Slogging through evidence required bourbon. I opened my desk drawer.

Empty.

God. Damn it.

Zii returned with the coffee and some doughnuts. "I wasn't sure if you wanted cake or glazed, so I got both." She broke off a piece a gave it to Templeton, whose presence she had become accustomed to.

It was my turn to give looks now. "Zii," I said, my voice wearing a calm mask, "where is my bourbon?"

"I did you a favor and dumped it out."

My eye twitched. "You ... did *what*, now?"

"I got rid of that crap you keep poisoning yourself with. I'm straight edge, remember?"

"*I'm* not." I did not do a good job of hiding my inner child's temper tantrum.

"Fine. But as your client, I can't have you putting my case on the line because of your little habit."

"Do you realize what you've *done?!*" I said. My body was not happy with me. I was a diesel engine chugging and out of fuel. I ran to the bathroom and puked. Fucking hell.

"That's just the poison leaving your body," she said.

"No," I said, "this is my body denied drink." I spit into the bowl.

"Pathetic," she said and walked back to look over the photos of the books.

"I ain't arguing that," I said, spitting one more time before flushing. "But you can't—"

"Did you find anything?" she said.

"Well, as I'm sure you noticed, Jerry's name comes up an awful lot in there," I said. She went quiet. "Like, *a lot* a lot."

She turned to look at me. She started to say something but stopped.

"Oh my God," I said. "You knew, didn't you?"

"That Jerry was dealing? I ... kind of."

"Kind of? What does that mean? Kind of?"

"I suspected it was possible, but I didn't really know for sure."

"How could you not have known your boyfriend was—"

"Look, Jerry was ... he was secretive. He was a good liar

He made you *want* to believe him. So, people believed him. They always believed him."

"I thought you were straight edge. Why didn't you confront him for the drug dealing?"

"Jerry was … he was charming and passionate, and he had a lot of problems. There were whole parts of his life he didn't share with me. I was trying to get him to let me in. I was making progress, but—"

"Did he ever get rough with you?" I asked. I didn't mean to interrupt, but it wasn't the kind of thought I wanted taking up residence in my brain any longer than it already had. It was making too much noise and needed to be evicted. She stopped talking, but only for a moment. Then, as if I had said nothing, she continued with her previous thought.

"But he kept saying it was all for a reason. There were things he kept from me because he said it was for my protection, and that it was all for a reason."

"And you believed him?"

"What choice did I have?" she said. I had to think about that. Not believing Jerry would force a lot of uncomfortable questions and situations. And, I was beginning to think, a few dangerous ones as well.

"Okay. But we can say now, certainly, that Jerry was selling drugs," I said.

She nodded.

"Senator Cromwell comes up in here a lot too," I said. "I'd noticed it earlier, but—" Again, she shifted her weight away from me. "Oh, Jesus Christ …"

"Jerry researched the hell out of the guy and told me less than three days before his death that he had something that could humiliate Cromwell, maybe have him impeached," she said. She was a dam of calm holding back torrents of annoyance and rage. It took me a moment to process this information as my brain gasped for air after a blow to the gut.

"Why didn't you fucking say that sooner?!" I said.

"You didn't let me finish."

"Earlier!" I drew out the word. "When you *hired* me!"

"Because I wanted it to be Nancy, okay?!" She was crying now. I'd made her cry. *Bravissimo*, Alex. Way to fucking go. You ass.

"Why did you wa—"

"Because I was scared! Okay?! If it was Nancy, that would have been so simple. A jealous, junkie ex wife—"

"Estranged wife."

"*Shut the fuck up!*" she howled. I took her advice. I could have lit cigarettes with those eyes.

"Jesus Christ," she moaned. "But if it *is* him ... I just don't know ... I just ..." I let her cry a moment before I walked over to her and put my arm around her. She buried her face into my shoulder. "You must be loving this. I am a hysterical woman, after all." I gave her a minute to let it out before I said a damn word.

"I don't love it," I said. "Don't even like it. Loathe it, actually. You are so not a hysterical woman. I am pretty damn sure you've got more balls than I do. I don't want it to be him either. Cuz I'm scared too."

She just nodded. "Brush your fucking teeth," she said.

"Right." I got up and brushed every inch of my mouth and rinsed with mouthwash. I snuck a drink from a nearly empty bottle under the sink I had forgotten about, and the burning in my throat restarted my brain and my balls. Oh, sweet bourbon. Let's never fight again.

"What did Jerry find out?" I asked, screwing the cap on quietly and slipping it back under the sink.

"I dunno. He didn't tell me. He just said it would change everything. Get the piece of shit out of office."

We sat there and let that sink in. What was the information that Jerry had on the senator, if anything? Was there something in Jerry's drug dealing that could have gotten him killed? It left me with a few avenues to pursue. But it kept bringing me back into Nash's orbit. Which was not a place I particularly wanted to be. But I had some ideas.

"I think ... I have a plan?" I said.

"Are you sure?" she shot back. "The upward inflection doesn't exactly inspire confidence."

"I'll go to Nash. I'll tell him I want Jerry's client list. That I want to take his old job. I'll see if anything comes up there. Any other possible leads. It will at least give us more of a sense of who else he was seeing. Who else he might have pissed off." I leaned against the wall. "For now, I think we should contact our state representative."

Multiple calls to the office got us nothing. Just answering machines. It was as if they were deliberately trying to avoid talking to their constituency. In other news, grass is green and water is wet. I left a message pretending to be from a conservative magazine at one of the area colleges. I figured that had a better shot at getting through a call screening than a concerned citizen.

"We are big admirers of yours and want to do an article on your plans for your new term. The left-wing *rag*-azine is putting something out about you too, and we want to beat them to the punch. So, please call me back as soon as you can, and we'll send out a reporter to meet you." I left my number and hung up. "That should pass through their screening process like a microwave burrito," I said. "You want to help?"

"Fuck yes, I do. What do you need me to do?"

"I want you to pose as the college journalist. Get a blonde wig, wear something conservative. Try to get an interview with him. In a public place. Ask him a few questions, nothing too pointed, but enough to rattle his cage. See if his reaction tells us anything."

"I *know* what rattling someone's cage means."

"Of course, sorry. Just make sure it's in—"

"A public place. That way, if I rattle him too much, there'll be witnesses, so he can't do anything about it."

"Right."

"Do you think I'm stupid or something?"

"No."

"Then shut the fuck up." She grabbed my face and gave it a little staccato shake along with the last four words. Then she kissed me softly on the mouth. "You do your job. And I'll do mine."

"Right." I headed to the door. "I gotta go see a man about a horse."

"What?"

"I am hitting up people for information."

"See now, *that* idiom is new to me."

"Stay here. Wait for them to call back. Until then, lay low."

"On it." She saluted. Sarcastically. Which made it hotter.

"Oh!" I had almost forgotten. "Money."

She shelled out what she owed me.

"Got a little extra?" I asked. "I may need to grease some palms."

"That sounds really—"

"*Bribe* people," I said.

She handed over another twenty. "I know. Teasing. Off you go then." She slapped my ass on the way out the door. Jesus.

20

I went to see Nash. Hopefully for the last time. I got the usual pat-down from the burly bodyguard and was shown into the living room. Brandy was sitting in the lounge chair. I gave her a nod of recognition and she failed to hide a smile.

"Alex Damage!" Nash proclaimed as he came in from the kitchen. He kissed Brandy, then took a line of coke off the glass coffee table, which was covered in enough residue to have a sizable street value. "What brings you to my home?"

"You had Jerry Rash working for you, yeah?"

"Who told you that?"

"Oh, you know. Little birds on the wind and all that."

"He didn't work for me. I supplied him. He did whatever he wanted."

"I want to replace him. How does that work?"

"How does any business work. I supply you. You sell for more than you bought it for. You pay me." He went back for another bump. "You want some of this?"

"No," I said. He grabbed Brandy by the knee and gave her legs a little shake.

"How about some of this, yeah?"

"No." I turned to Brandy. "No offense."

"None taken." She gave a sneer, but it was not for me.

"Ah, right," Nash said. "Brandy does not like punk rockers, eh?"

"Right," she said, then got up.

"Where are you going, baby?"

"For a swim," she said.

"She is hot stuff, yeah?"

"Yeah, she's cool. You have Jerry's old client list?"

"Why would I have a thing like that?"

"Well, Eddie—can I call you Eddie?—I figure the way you see it, anyone who owes him money owes you money. If they don't pay him, he can't pay you, and you catch me as the kinda guy who wants the shit to roll down the whole fucking hill, yeah?"

He gave me an approving finger wag. "You. This is why I like you. See? You. You get me," he said. It was the most insulting compliment I'd ever received. See, I'm more prone to taking insults as compliments. A jock or yuppie on the street calls me a "freak" or a "faggot," it bumps my chin up. But this, this just made my skin crawl.

"So, you have it?" I asked.

"Yes. I have," he said. He took one more bump and gave his nose a little flick. "Come." I followed him to his office. He flipped through a Rolodex, pulled out a card, and handed it to me. It was a list of names. Two columns, one of names, one of addresses, front and back.

"Jerry gave you this?" I asked.

"Yes. It is like you say. People don't always pay. Just in case he needed help. He never really needed help. Ha ha. You call if you need."

"What kind of help?"

"You're funny."

"Thanks. I'm told I should try stand-up," I said, and I moved toward the door quickly enough to get out of there fast but just slow enough to not make it obvious I was in a hurry. At least that was the idea. My awkward pacing just made it look like I had a limp. Or a mental defect.

"Something wrong?" Eddie asked. It may have been genuine concern—even the vilest of men are capable of some level of social awareness—but, like with everything he said, it sounded like an accusation. Whether that's due to his paranoia or my own I couldn't possibly tell you.

"No," I said. "I just ... my leg's asleep."

"Too long on the shitter, eh?"

"Yeah. Yeah, that must be it. Whiskey shits, you know how it is," I said. What I really needed to do was shut up and get the fuck out of there. I had what I'd come for and was really hoping it was the last thing I'd need from there. Jesus fuck, did I hope it was the last thing I'd need from there.

I got in my car and took a look at the list. I figured I'd start off with the people I knew and then work with the strangers. The number of strangers was not really as shocking as the number I knew. How many people knew Jerry was dealing? It was starting to look like my finger wasn't as on the pulse as I had previously thought. I had once again overestimated myself. One name on the list that I recognized was simply written down as "Rapunzel."

A few things to know:
1. Rapunzel is a dude.
2. Rapunzel is a British transplant.
3. "Rapunzel" is ironic because ...
4. Rapunzel is a skinhead.

I tapped on the door to Rapunzel's house. It was not a tower. It was a garage. The garage door slid up and Rapunzel was standing there, holding the door from going all the way up. The garage had a bed in the corner with a mini fridge next to it pulling double duty as a side table. There was an old workbench that had a hot plate on it. There were soiled rugs on the floor, and a giant swastika flag took up the whole back wall. The other walls were covered in fliers for Rock Against Communism and Punk Front shows and posters for bands like the Dentists and the Ventz. He had on a home-made Tragic Minds T-shirt. Oh yeah:
5. Rapunzel is a neo-Nazi.

A lot of people think that all skinheads are Nazis. Well, that pile of bullshit could not be more steaming. Not all skinheads are Nazis, and not all Nazis are skinheads. There are white skinheads, Mexican skinheads, Black skinheads. I met an Asian skin once. She was cool. Skinheads run the whole political spectrum from ultra-liberal to apolitical to uber-right cunts like Rapunzel. Most of the skins I know and love are simply just working-class kids. That's the true commonality of skinheads. Working class. Guys like Rapunzel are what happened when neo-Nazis started convincing these poor white kids from broken homes, hungering for a sense of belonging, that it was "the Blacks and the Jews" keeping them down. Because they are fucking Nazis and that's what fucking Nazis fucking do.

"The hell you want, Damage?" He spat on the ground by my feet.

Right. Enough history lessons.

I shrugged. "An old friend can't stop by to visit?"

"That was a long time ago. You made your choice." He started to close the door, but I caught it and tossed the garage door all the way up.

"Sounds like you don't think I made the right one," I said, walking inside.

"Sure, you did. For you. But—stay the *fuck* outside!" He turned and pointed.

"Okie dokie then," I said, doing a little backward walking dance out onto the driveway.

"You don't think I've forgiven you, do you?" he said.

"Hmmm," I said, checking my pockets, "I seem to have misplaced the fucks that I give. Where could they have gone?"

"You think you're pretty clever, don't you?"

"I do. But I was told chicks dig confidence."

He just glared at me. Well, he didn't *just* glare. When a man who lives to hate is directing all of it at you in one Antarctic gaze, you can't call it *just* a glare. To cover my fear, I rolled my eyes.

"We were mates," he said.

"Yeah. *Were*, as in past tense."

"You're supposed to have your brother's back, Damage. You *used* to know that."

"You're not my brother. And you *used* to be a halfway decent human being. But then you let that slimy 'British Movement' fucker manipulate you. You changed. And you had it coming."

"You stood there and did nothing while that fucking *golliwog* put me in hospital," he said.

"Because *you had it coming.* You pulled a knife on his thirteen-year-old brother just for playing basketball in the park. What did you *think* was going to happen?"

"I didn't even see him there. You did. You said nothing."

"Because I was about to beat the shit out of you myself. He just saved me the trouble."

"That's a load of shite. You turned your back on me. After everything I did for you."

Right after I had burned out of school, Rapunzel had helped get me a job degreasing engines. It was a good gig and we were both active in the union. But a trip home to Merry ol' England and a few circle jerks with his newly fascist school chums and suddenly the rest of us guys were 'commie fags' for wanting a goddamn cost-of-living adjustment.

"You're giving me shit about turning my back?" I scoffed. "Yeah. I turned my back on you. Maybe I just wanted to show you the fucking knife you stuck in it."

"Why did you even come here?"

"Jerry's dead."

"I already knew, and I don't give a toss."

"Really? You don't care?"

"Not at all," he said, spitting again as punctuation.

"I figured you would. It's a pain in the ass to find a new drug dealer."

"Who the fuck told you that?" His confident stance melted. I had him on the defensive, if only for a second. I used it.

"People far scarier than you," I said.

"Oi, mate. I hadn't bought shite off him all year. I've been clean for months."

"Cool, good for you," I said. He seemed thrown by my apparent lack of sarcasm.

"New job involves a lot of drug testing," he said matter-of-factly.

"What are you—"

"Security," he said, far too quickly for it to be the whole truth. Most people think hesitating is a sign that someone is lying, but I typically find that the opposite is true. Prepared responses are said with zero hesitation. But there're ways of prodding for what you need.

"Really? Wow. Never figured you for a rent-a-cop."

"Fuck you, mate! I'm not mall security!" Once I had him nice and riled up, I could make him slip up. That's the thing about pride, it's easily manipulated. You appeal to someone's pride, or belittle it in any way, and they become malleable. Hell, I'm surprised "pride" isn't an ingredient in putty. It's the same way the Nazis work. Appealing to pride. Pride in your country. Pride in the white race. Which is stupid shit to be proud of. Who the fuck takes pride in that? What's there to be proud of in being white or being British or being American? I'm not proud to be an American. I'm proud of *my* accomplishments. Solving cases, helping people, playing in bands. Being American or British? Being white? These are *not* accomplishments. They're accidents. But I digress.

"So, what? Like construction sites then?" I asked.

"It's *personal* security," he said with a smile. "VIP type shit."

"Nobody that important could be desperate enough to hire *you*." I chuckled.

"Loyalty goes a long way. Some people respect honor. Not that you'd know anything about that." He folded his arms and looked smugger than ever.

"Yeah. You got me. I lack the honor needed to pull knives

on children. What a coward I am. Your rap sheet wasn't a deal breaker?"

"More like a selling point." His smugness had reached a boiling point. His self-satisfaction brewing just behind the eyes. It clicked with me.

"So," I said, "you're a hired goon." I leaned over to peek around him and get a view of the garage, and he leaned over to block my view. "Rapunzel, Rapunzel, what have you gotten yourself into?"

"You were here to talk about Jerry? I assume you're 'on the case' or some shite?"

"Yeah," I said. "I have a few questions."

"Why? I didn't fucking kill him," he said.

"Wasn't saying you did. *Necessarily.* But you were tied to illegal activities with him. He was your dealer, after all. He knew things about you you didn't want others to know. Some might call that motive."

"Jerry was an arsehole. And a lefty scumbag cunt. But I always paid up. He never had a reason to hassle me, and I had no problems with him."

"Never thought he'd use that information to benefit himself?"

"The fuck do I have that he wants?"

"I dunno. Maybe your client does, though. Or—"

"Fuck right off!" he said loud enough to catch me off guard. Up until this point, his hostility had just been percolating. This was a sudden burst, like a jump scare in a bad horror film. He was telling me a lot by trying to shut it down.

"Whose goon squad are you part of?"

"Part of? I'm *in charge*, you moist little twat." He was in my face now. "I give the fucking orders."

"After having them handed to you from …"

"You want to stop with this line of questioning, mate. I'm far too good at my job to slip up on this. So you best stay on topic, innit?"

"In it?" I asked. "In what?"

"Isn't it?" he said.

"Isn't it what?"

"For fuck's sake. Isn't it *true* that you should stay on topic?"

"Let's keep the slang on *this* side of the pond, yeah?"

"Jesus, I fucking hate you," he said.

"See. *That's* better. *That* I understand. Now we're communicating!" I patted him on the shoulder.

"Touch me again and I'll bust your fucking head open." His jaw clenched and he made a fist. I tried my damnedest not to flinch, and I'd like to think I was successful.

"So, your experiences with Jerry as a dealer? How was that?"

"Fine. He brought drugs. I paid him."

"He never burned you or anything?"

"No. Only got high-quality shit from him. He never burned me."

"He seem like the kind of guy who might?"

"I can't say. I just know he always hooked *me* up with the good stuff. He knew what would happen if he tried to pull that shite on me."

"What kind of stuff?"

"Coke. Speed, 'ludes, GHB. A little pot every now and then."

"Jerry was selling GHB? The narcolepsy drug? For what?"

"Like you don't know." He gave a knowing smile that made me want to start practicing amateur dentistry. Not just because he was drugging women, but because Jerry had been selling the means and Jerry's ass wasn't there to kick. My desire to make Rapunzel choke on his own teeth must have shown all over my face. "What? You want to hit me?"

"Can't say I'm surprised you need that shit."

"The fuck is that supposed to mean?" He was right in my face now. Close enough to feel the breath from his nose. Close enough to tell he'd had boiled eggs for breakfast. If I'd puckered my lips, I could have kissed him.

"Like you don't know."

"Always the clever little cunt, *innit?*"

"Always."

He raised a fist just as that cop car rolled by. I guess I should have been relieved I was still being tailed.

"Besides, that's all in the past," he said. He leaned back against the edge of the door, finally giving me a decent view of the room. I took a quick stock of the place. I scanned over the obvious things until I noticed an old steamer trunk under the workbench. It had a big padlock on it and looked like something from a pirate ship. It became apparent to me why Nash hid sensitive information in an Ayn Rand book. Crooks and cops and everyone on the thin line in between go straight for the safe. But who the fuck would look at *Atlas Shrugged*?

"I suppose the women you and your crew dosed feel the same way?"

"Those who remembered never complained. Some of them shagged me sober later anyway." It often surprises me what people do to justify themselves and their actions. They do these mental gymnastics. A whole floor routine of aerials and tucks, layouts and pikes. *She likes to fuck. I don't remember. She was hammered. Real men take what they want.*

"Besides," he repeated, "that's all in the past." And with that, he stuck the landing and vindicated himself in his own mind. Ladies and gentlemen, we have a winner. He gets to sleep at night!

"Go die in a fire, rice dick," I said.

"Oh, just take a swing already, mate. You know you want to." He opened up his stance as he was talking. "Come on then. A free shot. I'm sporting like that." I balled up a fist, but quickly loosened it. I knew better. I wanted to break his face, and I probably could, but not without getting badly fucked up myself. I knew better than to fuck with a skinhead. They're not a solo breed. They're pack animals. Just like the HBers,

Bloods, Crips, or La Mirada Punks. They run with crews. It's never just one man you're in a fight with. It's everybody he hangs out with. Even if I won this fight, it would bring down a world of shit on me.

"I don't have time for this crap," I said. I started walking away, walking backward the first few steps with my hands up. I wasn't turning my back to him. Not a chance.

"Oh, a nancy all of a sudden, innit? What happened to the big, clever tough man?" He followed a little, but then laughed and went back. As he closed the garage, I gave him the backward peace sign, a little taste of home.

I went to the next name on the list. Misty. Misty was not a punk. Misty wasn't a new waver. She wasn't into the neo-rockabilly scene or any of the subcultures the first wave of punk girls had moved on to once things started getting too macho. Misty, in fact, had never been punk at all. Misty was a student at USC. Her address was some sorority house. It was a white two-story colonial with red shutters and a second-floor deck held up by wooden columns. There were three giant letters bolted to the banister that were all, well, Greek to me. Needless to say, I did not receive the warmest of welcomes when I arrived.

"Who are you and what do you want?" said the girl at the door. She had the air of being very experienced in dealing with assholes. Her dark hair reached the middle of her back and came over the right shoulder. She was wearing a red sundress with the straps tied behind the neck and lipstick to match. She was very clearly getting ready to go out.

"I'm Alex and I'm looking for Misty," I said. She gave me the once-over twice and repeated her question.

"Who are *you* and *what* do you *want?*"

"You don't, uh, get a lot of my kind around here?" I asked. She pushed her tongue to the back of her lower lip and started to close the door, but I blocked it with my foot.

If I had been wearing my Vans instead of my Docs, she might have broken it.

"I'll scream so loud," she said.

"Look, I just want to talk to Misty," I said.

"Misty's not here," she said.

"Do you know when she'll be back?"

"If she were ever coming back, I wouldn't tell you when. Now get out of here before I call the cops." She started to close the door again.

"If she were ever … ?" I stopped the door again.

"Who is it, Kelly?" said a voice from some unseen corner of the house.

"Nobody," said Kelly.

"Look, my name is Alex Damage, er, DiMaggio. I'm a private investigator, of sorts, and I'm looking into—"

"Listen, Alex," she said, barging out on the porch and sticking her finger in my chest. "Misty is gone. Misty is not coming back, because the last time someone who looked like you showed his face around her, shit went sideways real fast. Now you need to fuck off out of here before my sisters and I tear you the fuck apart."

"What happened to screaming and calling the cops?" I said, in an attempt to lighten the mood. Her look suggested it had failed, so I just launched into it. "Did Misty ever mention a guy named Jerry? Jerry Rash?"

"That would be the name of the reason Misty isn't here anymore."

"Was he her dealer?"

"He was … something like that, yeah."

"He's dead," I said.

"Good," she said without a single beat skipped. "I hope it was painful." I decided to leave my own opinions as per Jerry out of it. Trying to defend him wasn't going to give me the answers I needed, and it was becoming apparent he wasn't worth defending.

"No love lost, huh?" I said.

"I never liked that she brought that skeezy bastard around here. He was hot. But dirty. And he was crazy. She said he had the best weed and the best speed, and he did. For sure. But he was dangerous, and I tried to tell her, but—"

"But you would still take the weed and speed he was dealing?"

"Look, maybe if you'd been to college—"

"I went to college," I said. The ice in my veins came out in my voice. This whole ordeal had turned my vessels into the arctic fucking tundra. But the more I tried to dig, the harder and colder the ground got.

"Speed helps with studying," she began.

"Weed helps you come back down. Yeah, yeah. Spare me. You're not the one on trial here. Not yet, anyway. Jerry is dead, and there seems to be a bigger how and why than 'he partied too hard.' I'm trying to figure out what that is."

"Well, I can tell you whatever happened, he deserved it."

"I'm not interested in if he deserved it or not. It's not my job to figure out if he had it coming or not. My job is to find out who, if anyone, had him killed."

"Working your way down his client list?" She folded her arms.

"Something like that, yeah." I put venom into it. She was trying my nerves. She was living a life I had no connection to or interest in and she was lording it over me. I don't much mind being stared at, but I hate being looked down on. To her I was nothing but a dirty drug dealer's friend. We were good enough to buy drugs from but not worthy of anything more than a condescending comment and a laugh. I had known her kind too well when I went to school.

"Jerry and Misty had … an arrangement."

"What kind of arrangement?"

"The kind where you don't pay for the drugs," she said, raising her eyebrows and her voice to punctuate the key words. She gave one more nod to see if I got her meaning. I did.

"Oh," I said. "Did she meet him through the punk scene?"

"God, no," Kelly said. "She wasn't involved in any of that."

I gave a mock look as though my feelings had been hurt. If she noticed, she didn't care or had made the choice to ignore it. "Any idea how she would have met him then?" I asked.

She pursed her lips, wrinkled her nose, and looked skyward with a squint, as if consulting with the LA smog for answers. "I really can't think of where she would have met somebody like that," she finally said.

Again, it was a barbed comment, with or without intention. But it stung with a sense of truth. Girls like Kelly and Misty didn't stop to give someone like Jerry the time of day, much less fuck them in exchange for drugs. But Jerry, as usual, was an outlier. For every rule there is the exception, and that exception always seemed to be Jerry Rash. Jerry was unmistakably a punk rocker, but he was good looking enough that if he cleaned up, he could walk right into a yacht club and be swooned over by debutantes as easily as he could punkettes. He had all the charisma of a fascist dictator, sans the nationalistic ideology.

"Where is Misty now? Have you been in touch with her recently?" I asked.

Somehow, she looked even more pissed off than before. "Are you trying to be funny?" she said, her voice nearly cracking. So much so, in fact, that I was taken aback.

To my own surprise, I lost the hard-assed tone I was trying to maintain. "Surprisingly, no," I said.

"Misty killed herself," she said. She hiccupped and put her hand to her mouth, taking a moment to pull herself together. "Sorry," she said. "Sorry. You couldn't have known that. Of course you didn't, you showed up asking for her."

"And you think she killed herself because of something that happened with Jerry."

"I *know* that's why she killed herself," she said before I had even finished my own sentence.

"What happened?" I asked. She sighed and stared off into space.

"He stole something from her. A bracelet or something. He just took it one night after he had sex with her. She went to confront him about it, but he said he needed to borrow it. He'd give it back later. But he never did, so when she went to get it back from him, he slapped her around. Beat her, tied her up, burned her with a cigarette, and raped her."

I was in shock. I thought back to a story that Jerry had told me once. Or rather had told a group of us at Oki-Dog after a show one time about a time he was with a sorority girl and tied her up. He said she was really into it. He said she was dripping wet, that she moaned with pleasure. To hear him tell it, he had a sexual conquest with a girl who was full-on into sadomasochism. We thought it was so cool that a sorority girl lusted after a punk, that he had dominated the type of girl who'd only look at us just to sneer. When we heard that story, we laughed and cheered. I high-fived him. Now, I was damn near ready to throw up. I felt the acid at the back of my throat.

"She said 'rape'?" I asked.

Kelly nodded. "She was scarred. She refused to go to the police or to counseling, because then it might come out about the drugs. She did nothing about it. It just ate at her, so she …" She couldn't finish, and I wasn't going to make her. I'd gotten the important parts anyway. The why is what mattered. The gritty details of the how were not a scab that needed picking.

I thanked her for her time and handed her my card. I headed back to my car and started breathing heavily. It's a gut punch to hear this kind of shit about friends and heroes. I wanted to believe that she was full of shit. She was a liar. She was just some sorority slut talking down about punks.

She wasn't part of our world. She didn't know. But the more I thought about it, the more I punched the dashboard of my car, the more I realized she didn't have a reason to lie. That, on top of Brandy's story, wasn't something that I could just write off as "he said, she said." Not when so many were saying the same thing. It was a pattern of behavior. Then I thought about what Zii's father had said. I caught myself in the rearview mirror and—you can't tell this to anybody—saw that I'd been crying. Kelly had gone back inside. It was then that I also caught sight of an all-too-familiar-looking squad car. I got out of the car and looked back at them. The car started and drove toward me. As they passed, they slowed down and gave me a knowing nod.

Fuck, I thought. *Who needs a drink?*

I walked into a campus bar and showed the bouncer my ID. I was drinking age, but he looked wary about letting someone of my ilk into the establishment. I took my ID back and blew past him and he said something to me, but I wasn't listening, and if it was something about me not being welcome, he didn't have the balls to actually confront me about it.

I sat down and the bar and said, "Whiskey." The frat boy working it gave me a dirty look, so I said, "Whiskey," once again, louder and angrier, and he poured me a neat glass of whatever was in the well. I took it in one shot and signaled for another, which he poured. I was getting stares from the other patrons. It was still pretty early, but the place was already filling up with summer school kids. Frankly, I was surprised at how lively a campus bar was in the summer. This place must have been elbow to elbow during the school year.

The news was on. They were interviewing Senator Cromwell about his efforts in El Salvador. I couldn't make out much of what was being said, but standing behind him in a black suit and tie, sunglasses, and that curly fucking wire sticking out one of his car-door ears was Rapunzel, "working

VIP security," just like he'd said. That rat-fucking bastard. I had to wonder why a bodyguard for one of the most powerful men in the state was living in a garage, but I figured Rapunzel just liked it that way, or the majority of his funds were going elsewhere and so he skimped on rent.

He had to know something. There was no way he didn't. No doubt he was bound to some kind of nondisclosure agreement. Fortunately, those of us technically working outside the confines of the law aren't tethered by such concerns. I hadn't a surplus of rat's asses. He wouldn't be giving it up willingly. But I knew a thing or two about Rapunzel. He was an ambitious bastard. The type of guy who is always thinking, *How can I use this?* and, *How can I get one over on them?* It had everything to do with his standing in the neo-Nazi community, not to mention all the red on the path he had taken to get there. If he heard shit, he kept a record of it. Probably in, oh, say, a padlocked steamer trunk.

I was so caught up checking out Rapunzel on the TV that I didn't notice the group of frat boys crowding around me. One tapped me on the shoulder, and I turned around to find three burly-looking fuckers in matching gray and purple sweaters sporting the same Greek letters. Damned if I knew which ones. Their beer guts hid how much they worked out.

"Hey, man. You can't be here. This is a Theta bar."

"Bullshit," I said. "It's cuz I'm Black, ain't it?" They looked confused, what with me being white and all.

"Look, just fuck off, all right?" said the one on the right. He was ginger and had a good six inches on me in either direction.

"Pledge shouldn'a let you in. Don't worry. He'll be dealt with," said the one the middle. "This bar is for Thetas and their guests only. Now, I didn't invite you. Chet didn't invite you. Barry didn't invite you. You ain't the type Thetas are supposed to be around, so I'm damn sure nobody else invited you either."

"Okay," I said, finishing my drink. "I'm gone." As I slipped my jacket on, I looked around the room. "And here I had heard gay bars were supposed to be inclusive."

"The fuck did you just say?" said the ginger. He took a swing at me, which I managed to dodge. I socked him in the gut and brought my knee up into his nose as he doubled over. But the others were on me before he hit the floor. They gave me a good kicking, but nothing like the ones I'd taken from the cops or skins. These were tough guys, but they were law-abiding citizens. They held back, because unlike cops or skins, they feared consequences. I was chucked out onto the sidewalk. I got up, dusted myself off, and smiled at them as they slammed the door on me. I heard the lock latch shut. I gave myself a look-over. Neither my pride nor my body bruised. Nothing more than a good mosh pit would have given me.

As I walked back to my car, I heard the "whoop whoop" all too familiar to punks walking by themselves in half-way-decent neighborhoods. I stopped and put my hands up. I knew the drill. A couple officers got out of the car, and one walked over to me.

"Stop right there, DiMaggio. Turn around," one said. I complied. Sure enough, it was my friends from Nancy's. Mike Hernandez and—I had to look at the young pal one's nametag—Burke.

"Afternoon, Officer Mike," I said. "What's the trouble?"

"There was an altercation at a bar just now," he said. "A man fitting your description was involved."

"Yes. But don't worry," I said. "I don't plan on pressing any charges."

"Hands on the vehicle," he said.

"It was self-defense, officer. I—"

"Hands," he said, removing his nightstick, "on the vehicle." Again, I complied. He put his nightstick away and started to frisk me. Thoroughly. *Very* thoroughly. He took my flask out of my coat pocket.

"What's this?" he said.

"A flask," I said.

"No shit. What's in it?"

"Whiskey, usually. It's not illegal."

"I'll decide that," he said. He opened the flask and went to take a sip, only to find it empty. Hell, maybe I *do* have a problem. I was just glad I'd left my switchblade in my glove box. My hands were still on the car, and he slipped the flask back into my coat pocket. As he did, he got so close to my ear I could feel the scratchiness of his mustache.

"Walk away from this, Alex *Damage*. You don't want to dig into this any further. Or I will personally make your life hell. You get me?"

I said nothing.

"You hear me?" he repeated.

"Yeah. I heard you," I said. He pulled me off the car and pushed me down the road.

"We're watching you," he said. "And that little girlie, too."

I stopped in my tracks a moment, and about a thousand scenarios turned over in my head.

In one, I turn around and say, "Fuck you, Officer Mike. I'm never backing down. You want to stop me, you're gonna have to kill me!" At which point he pulls out his gun and shoots me dead in broad daylight, then places a knife on me.

In another, I simply turn around, point at my eyes, point at him, and then walk on down the street.

Or I grab him, slam him against his own car, and he tells me whose payroll he's on, who killed Jerry, and why. I pressure him to make the arrest, justice is served, Zii falls madly in love with me, we get a small cabin in the woods, and we never leave our bed.

Or, and this is my favorite, I turn around, walk right up to him, and bust him across the jaw. He's out before hitting the ground, which he hits like a sack of overpriced potting soil. I kick him in the ribs and face, undo my fly, and piss on him while his partner watches, stunned and slack-jawed.

Or I just walk away. Forget the whole thing. Move on with my life.

But I wasn't about to do any of that. I'm too damn stubborn. I know that. But I never take comfort in finding out that I'm not paranoid.

I knew Rapunzel wasn't home. He had just been on live television. I drove back to his garage. I gave the area a quick look around to make sure no cops or neighbors were about. I pulled my switchblade out of the glove box and tucked it into my pocket. I went around to a side door and managed to pick the lock with the bobby pins I'd used earlier. I was glad I'd hung on to them. You'd think a guy paranoid enough to believe in approaching race wars would spring for better locks, but you should never underestimate laziness, stupidity, or thrift.

The place was quite the dichotomy. Free weights were out in the middle of the room, and the floor was covered in discarded beer and whiskey bottles. But the bed, or cot rather, had been made with military-level precision. I looked around for anything that might have been informative. Of course, right there on the mini fridge serving as his nightstand was a little black book. I flipped through it, looking for names I recognized. I saw mine, crossed out with the word *FAG* written in all caps next to it. Either he was calling me a cigarette or he'd picked up some stateside slang after all.

There were also some of the guys from our old job, a few girls, his gang, and Tom Numb, which I found odd. I could think of zero reasons those two would have to speak to each other. I pocketed the book. I looked at the safe. It had a combination lock, and I thought for a moment. I took the address book out and looked under *S*. Sure enough, listed under "Safe" was the combination. Sometimes it really is just that simple. Although what was there wasn't of much interest to me. Or, at least, my case. Just some drugs, cash, and what looked to be an authentic SS officer's hat. I helped myself to the cash, slashed up the Nazi hat with my switch-blade, and left the drugs. "Clean for months," my ass.

Tom Numb was back in the picture again. He had an alibi for the night in question. But that didn't mean he wasn't involved somehow. I had started out on this thinking it was a normal, everyday, run-of-the-mill murder with an obvious suspect with a clear motive. To be fair, that's because most of the time, that's exactly what it is. But now it apparently involved junkies, thieves, drug dealers, HB thugs, neo-Nazis, one of the most influential gangsters in Los Angeles, and a goddamn senator. Was I in over my head? Absolutely. But honestly, that's the only time I can really breathe.

21

I slapped Rapunzel's little black book in the palm of my hand as I rocked in my chair. It was helping me think. Zii had left. There was a note explaining that when the senator's office had called, they had just offered to send along a boilerplate press kit. She had given them a fake address but had then had to leave to follow up on something. Whatever she was doing was probably dangerous. But she was tough as fuck. Hell, I'll admit that I was a little scared of her. When it came to something she believed in, that girl had eyes that flared up to say, "Stay the fuck out of my way!" That level of passion for shit that actually matters was dying in the 1980s, and I realized where all the fucks people used to give had gone. They'd gone straight into Zii. She was carrying it for the rest of us. I just hoped it wouldn't fuck her up too much. Before I was a nihilist, the world almost tore me apart. Meeting Zii started to make me think that becoming a nihilist meant it already had. A crack was forming in my walls, and the masons were helpless. I half-expected a tiny red-clad version of myself would pop up on my shoulder and convince me to hate her for that. But it didn't happen. It wouldn't. I couldn't.

I had called Rad and told him to meet me at my place. He'd been waiting outside when I got there. Now he paced back and forth, drinking cheap beer. He was itching to know what our next move was going to be. I got up and he followed me out the door.

"What we doing?" he asked. "What's the game here?"

"I need fresh air, a stroll, and a proper fucking drink," I said. We walked the short distance to a liquor store, and I bought a half-pint of bourbon. I took a long pull from it and

handed it to Rad, who took a sip, winced, and then handed
it back to me.

"Good stuff," he said. It wasn't.

I killed the rest of the bottle, then bought one more.
We stepped out into the unseasonable cold snap posing as
a summer night. I lifted the collar on my jacket to block the
breeze and lit a cigarette. I hadn't had one since Zii came
by. It had been too long and I was starting to get crabby.
Then I noticed Rad staring at something. I turned to see
what it was, but all I saw was a lamppost covered in fliers.
Rad pointed. I took a closer look and Lady Luck shot me a
flirtatious smirk. There was a show tonight at the Whisky-a-
Go-Go. Tom Numb and the Goons were playing in the middle
of the lineup. It was almost enough to make me believe in
God. Almost. My car was parked close by. If we hurried, we
could make it.

We got to the Whisky and paid the three-dollar entry fee. The
bouncer was new and we didn't argue. I appreciate it when
I get an open door, but I never take it for granted. That level
of entitlement is for the ones who live in the Hills. The first
band was finishing up as we walked in. Tom Numb and the
Goons started setting up. We hung toward the back so they
wouldn't see us. Tom walked up to the mic with his guitar
hanging too low.

"We're da Goons!" he said, pouring on his tough-guy
voice way too thick. Then they launched into "Cop-a-Feel,"
and it was … Really. Fucking. Good. Jerry had put a lot of
feeling into this song. But the emotion coming from Tom
Numb was different. Out of Jerry it sounded like satirical
commentary. Out of Numb it sounded honest. It was not
gallows humor for him. It was not a political statement; it
was a personal one. I turned to Rad and could tell by his face
he was having the same thought I was: Jerry *had* stolen this
song from Tom.

I bet that you like touching me there
Why the fuck are you smellin' my hair?
So much time with yer hand on my sack
I just hope that's a gun in my back!
You just wanna cop-a-FEEL!
Cop-a-FEEL!
Cop-a-FEEL!
Cop-a-FEEEEEEEEEEEELLLL!

The audience was going ballistic. Guys were jumping up onstage, thrashing around, diving back into the crowd, and surfing a sea of hands and shoulders. People were running in circles and plowing into each other. Sweat was dripping as they took their raw angst out on each other. One guy stood alone in the middle and flailed around like a cracked-out marionette. Until a 250-pound skinhead mowed into him, sending him sprawling. The two ran at each other, threw their arms over each other's shoulders, and spun around, plowing into the people on the edge of the pit whether they wanted to be part of it or not. I exploded into the crowd and Rad followed. I pointed up and Rad lifted me. I crawled on top of the crowd and surfed all the way to the stage. Tom's eyes were wide when he saw me. I landed on the stage next to him. He stared at me and stopped singing. I shouted the lyrics into the mic. When it got to the bass hook, I said in his ear, "Rapunzel says hi." He looked at me. "We need to talk after the show." He nodded and I jumped into the crowd.

"Think he's gonna run?" Rad yelled into my ear. I grabbed his shoulder and pulled him down to my face level.

"Oh yeah. Can you cover the back exit?" I asked.

"Sure." He patted my back. The Whisky was another place Rad had worked, and he still knew people.

After the Goons set, I walked into the alley behind the Whisky, pulling a long drag on a cigarette. Rad was holding Tom. His bandmates were not around. I wasn't sure if it was a reason to be relieved or worried. I considered flicking the cigarette into his face but then decided to try a new course of action. I flicked the butt off to the side and then nodded at Rad, who let Tom go.

"Dude," I said, "that was fucking amazing in there tonight." As I expected, it caught him way off guard. "I'm serious, Tom. That was easily the best version of 'Cop-a-Feel' I've ever heard." It's incredibly easy to be convincing when you are telling the truth. I lit another cigarette and offered it to him, and to my surprise, he actually took it. We both leaned up against the hood of a car. "Listen," I said.

"Don't," he said. "Just don't ask."

I just nodded. "Yeah . . ." I drifted momentarily. "Yeah. Okay, I won't. But I believe you now. The way you played tonight? You could only have done that if you wrote it." I chose my words carefully. He finished his cigarette and I let him. I offered another but he shook it off.

"So," he finally said, "what's this about Rapunzel?"

"I found your name in his little black book," I said. "Why might that be? He doesn't hang in your neck of the woods."

"He's a fascist asshole," Tom said.

"I said the *exact* same thing!"

"But I ain't no snitch." He folded his arms and looked at his feet as he scraped his right boot on the ground.

"So, there *is* something you *could* snitch on him for?" I noticed a car coming down the alley. Tom saw it too and turned as pale as a death rocker. The car pulled up. I recognized the man inside as none other than Officer Mike Hernandez. Tom, for some reason, recognized him too.

"Hello, Thomas," Officer Mike said with a grin as he leaned to the open passenger-side window.

"Officer," Tom said with a nod, but looked away.

"I'm off duty, Thomas. You can call me Mike." He still had that grin. Like the grin the kid who made you eat dirt in grade school would get.

Tom said nothing.

"I saw you were playing here tonight. Did I miss it?"

Tom just nodded.

"Hey, look," Officer Mike continued, "you want me to give you a ride home?"

Tom was frozen, and I could barely tell he was shaking his head.

"C'mon, buddy. Why not?"

"We've got him covered," I said, stepping forward, getting between Tom and the car window. Mike gave me the face you give year-old takeout you find in the back of the fridge.

"You watch your ass, DiMaggio."

"I'm not too worried. I'm sure you're looking at it plenty." I smiled. Officer Mike didn't. He just drove off. I looked at Tom, who had turned away from us.

"Hey," I said, reaching out to touch his shoulder. He just swatted my hand away. I could hear sniffling. He cleared his throat and made a failed attempt to compose himself. Finally, he got it together enough to look at me with his red, wet eyes.

You should be honored, Officer Mike.

Not everyone has a song written about them.

22

I convinced Tom to come back to my office to talk. The old proverb "The enemy of my enemy is my friend" held up even in 1981—maybe *especially* in 1981. It definitely explained Los Angeles. Officer Mike had done me a huge favor, in a warped sort of way, by showing up. I laid out everything I knew to Tom. I was taking a huge fucking risk by letting him in on any of it. With that in mind, I omitted what I needed to and sprinkled in some misdirection, but the gist he got was, "I think Officer Mike is involved in Jerry's murder. And I can take him down. But I need your help."

Tom nodded and mulled over his options. "You really think you can get this guy?" he asked.

"I'm trying my ass off over here," I said. "I know you weren't Jerry's biggest fan. But I also know you want Officer Mike off the streets." Tom started to look uncomfortable, so I backed down a little, a new concept for me.

"Rapunzel found me," Tom began. "It was when I was up here for a show. He came and pulled me aside. He said he knew I shared a practice space with Bad Chemicals. He asked if I would do him a favor."

"What was it?" I leaned forward.

"Can I finish?" he said.

"Sorry." I gestured for him to go on.

"I told him I didn't do favors for nobody didn't do a favor for me. He said it wasn't anything big. He just wanted me to keep tabs on Jerry Rash."

"Keep tabs?"

"Yeah. Watch him. See where he went, what he did, who he did it with. Everything. It was like he wanted me to find stuff out. Like, bad shit. Or even just, like, where their shows were and stuff."

"Did he say why?"

"No. I just told him to fuck off. If he wanted to know things about Jerry, he should talk to Jerry. I ain't no spy and I ain't no rat. I started to walk away and ..." He started to get that look again.

"What?" I asked.

He could barely get it out.

"Tom! Stay with me. What did Rapunzel say to you?"

"He'd tell Mike where to find me."

"So, did you do it?" I asked.

"Fucking *of course!*" he blurted. "What would you do?!" You look at these thugs. These HB punks, all macho anger and testosterone, and it's easy for you to forget they're just kids. We're all just kids. Zii was a kid. Jerry was a kid. Rad, Rapunzel, me. Tom couldn't tell anyone about it. Who would've listened?

"Did you take notes?"

He nodded.

"Do you still have them?"

He shook his head.

"Rapunzel?"

A nod. I hadn't seen anything at Rapunzel's place like a notebook filled with Jerry's movements. I'd have seen it too. It definitely wasn't there. I had a few theories about where it was but had access to none of them by any stretch of the imagi- nation. I didn't know where "police evidence locker" ranks on the list of places that are hard to break into. But I'm sure it sits pretty close to "a senator's home or office." It was looking like it was time to pay my favorite neo-Nazi a visit again. This time I could not go in alone. I needed help. And I needed my gun.

"Get some rest," I told Tom. "Use my bed if you want. I've got some stuff to take care of."

I put on some leather gloves and wiped my prints off my gun, loaded it, and stuck it in my pocket. I called up Rad and I called up the Bad Chemicals guys, laying out the plan to each of them. Tom was quiet and just walked over to my bed to lie down. Just a day ago I wanted to bust the kid's face in. Now I felt a sudden instinct to protect him. What the fuck was that about?

We all met outside my office and made our way to Rapunzel's garage. The rest of his cronies were hanging around, drinking, smoking, and licking their wounds from some brawl with whatever minorities they had been assaulting that evening.

"That fag almost kicked your arse!" one of them said, razzing his "mate."

"Shut up!"

"Who'd have thought that dress-wearing queer would have had it in him, eh? Tough as coffin nails, he was." Their talking silenced real quick when I strolled up. I just stood there and said nothing. Rad, Double Dare, and Luke Warning stood behind me. Reggie was off doing his part.

"What do you want?" Rapunzel said.

"Just returning this." I tossed him his address book.

"You talked to Tom, didn't you?" he said. Oh, Rapunzel, were all your brains in your hair? Is this like a Samson sort of thing? Except with intelligence? "I knew that little poofter would talk. Well, I ain't got what you want. And good luck getting it, because I ain't telling you where it is. Especially not after cutting up my hat." I smiled for the first time in the whole conversation. "You couldn't if I did!" He got up into my face. "You gonna say something?"

Silence got more of a rise out of him than insults ever could. I should have tried it years ago. My watch said eleven p.m. That's when I reached for my revolver.

"The notebook," I said, pointing it at him. Rapunzel just looked at me and the gun and laughed. We looked at each other. He grabbed the gun and pointed it at me. He smirked with the smug confidence someone can only have when they have no fucking clue what's going on. I removed my gloves and chucked them into a neighbor's yard.

"Still doing those little metaphoric gestures?" Rapunzel asked.

"Until the day I die," I said.

"You're such a twat."

He fired.

I had told Reggie to call in "suspicious persons" at Rapunzel's address a few minutes prior. By the time Rapunzel had fired the blank, police were already close enough to hear the gunshot. We were surrounded. My ears were ringing and I had spots in my eyes. The police drew their guns and everyone's hands found sky.

"Drop the weapon!" shouted a loudspeaker. Rapunzel did as he was told. "Get down on the ground!" it ordered. We all did as we were told. On our way down, Rapunzel gave me a look of pure hatred. I winked. The police came over, guns drawn, and cuffed Rapunzel. As I had hoped, one of them was Officer Mike.

All of us were taken in for questioning. By the standards of the LAPD, not one of us looked innocent. But the ones with the guns looked comparatively worse. Rapunzel's claims that the gun wasn't his weren't getting him anywhere. It wasn't registered, only his prints were on it, and they'd found more in his garage. None of them were registered either, and filed-off serial numbers tend to raise all manner of red flags.

When my turn came around, I saw Officer Mike talking to one of the detectives. I could make out some of what he was saying: "This kid is from my neighborhood. I know his family. Let me talk with him a bit first or he's not going to talk."

Or something to that effect. This little exchange was incredibly informative to the right kind of ears. It told me:

1. Officer Mike *was* a fucking liar.
2. Officer Mike wanted to talk to me.

3. This detective was not in on whatever Officer Mike was a part of.

All of this was very useful. I was taken into a room by Officer Mike, a scary concept. The kind that makes your shit back up. Hell, I thought I may never shit again. The way I saw it, Mike was going to play it a number of ways. He was going to try to make me look bad. Play up the conflict between me and Rapunzel so that I looked like the instigator. Which I was. He would play it this way if people were listening and watching.

Or he was going to try to intimidate me into backing off the Jerry Rash case. He would do this only if nobody else was listening or watching. This would be ideal, because it would confirm my suspicions and give me the possibility of finding further leads and connections. It was possible he'd take this approach if whoever was listening was also in on it. But the fact he'd lied to the detective in order to talk to me ruled this out.

There was a third, and final, possibility that he was going to feel me up like we were slow dancing at the junior prom. But I ruled that out, because I hadn't been a minor in over four years.

I took my seat and he took his.

"Now, Alex," he said, "do you want to tell me your side of the story? What happened tonight?" He was going with option one. People were listening. I had to think of a way to gauge his intentions and change them to the ones I needed.

I started to hum "Cop-a-Feel."

His face was the final scene of *The Wizard of Oz*. Color one moment, monochromatic the next. I swear I felt the temperature drop. He reached over to the microphone on the table and turned it off.

He whispered through clenched teeth, "Okay, you little shit. You listen to me. I dunno what that kid told you—"

"He didn't say anything. Your reaction says *everything*." I grinned, feeling pretty damn proud of myself.

"Hassling the skinhead, hanging around Tom, poking around the junkie's … don't think for a *second* I don't know what you're up to."

I shrugged cartoonishly in mock confusion.

"Don't play dumb with me," he warned.

"Tell it again about da rabbits, George."

Officer Mike pounded his fist on the table. "*Bicho! Hijo de puta!*" he shouted, suddenly slipping into Spanish. "I don't know what you think you know," he began. "But we never touched that kid."

We? Hel-lo.

"Which kid?" I said, tilting my head.

"Numb is a liar. He's a thug just trying to start trouble."

"Why did you say I was from your neighborhood?" I asked.

"I'll ask the questions here. And if you know what's good for you or that sexy little groupie, you'll be really careful how you answer them. You know what they say about how the truth hurts." He turned the mic back on. He'd told me a few things already, but I needed more.

"Why were you at Mr. Kaminski's residence this evening?"

"Mr. Kaminski?" I asked.

"Stuart Kaminski," he said.

"Ohhh. You mean Rapunzel. The *neo-Nazi* skinhead?" I said, looking him in the eye. "Well, Officer Mike, I heard that he and his neo-Nazi buddies were planning to go 'gay-bashing' this evening. I was concerned about a gay friend of mine, so I went by to ask him to call it off. Rapunzel and I used to be friends once, before he got into the Nazi thing, and I thought he might listen. But instead, they ganged up on me and called me 'fag' and threatened me. Thank God someone called the police, who just happened to be nearby."

"You were there earlier?"

"No," I said. He'd been tailing me. He knew damn well where I'd been. I BS'd my way through the questioning. I didn't want to overplay my hand. Officer Mike didn't call me out on anything. He needed the truth hidden just as much as I did. Maybe more.

We had all planned out our stories together. Our stories were consistent. We were there to talk them out of committing more hate crimes. Rapunzel's crew had been taken totally by surprise. They all had to lie, but they were coming up with different lies, making the lies obvious. Reports of the attacks they had committed earlier that day seemed to confirm our story, and the police couldn't connect the gun to me. They were fucked; we were free to go. I was the victim this time, after all. I just hoped they didn't post bail too soon.

With Rapunzel in jail, I had time to comb over his place. As I drove past, I saw flashing lights. But this time, it was fire trucks. Rapunzel's garage was in flames. I kept driving.

I went to Al's Bar. Al's was on the ground floor of the old American Hotel over on Traction and Hewitt. At four stories, the white brick building wasn't large as far as hotels go, but the place had become a hub of sorts for the art community. Al's was a dive bar for the countercultural types. Punks, artists, poets, and skid row bums shared the space like a boardinghouse for undesirables. The walls were decorated with pieces by the local artists who called the hotel home or were just regulars at Al's. The whole complex was basically one giant art gallery. The windows on the Hewitt-facing side had red awnings that matched the paint on the ground floor. They had live music most nights. The type that would never get radio time. The bathroom reeked of shit, and every wall of the place was covered in so much graffiti that the bar itself was less an art gallery and more like a piece of abstract art in and of itself. There was nothing resembling air conditioning.

Finally, I felt at home.

I took a seat near the TV and watched some news, which only ever makes me want to drink more. Come to think of it, it's probably why so many bars always have it on. I wasn't much feeling like sitting out in the open, so once I'd ordered my bourbon, I found an open table in an alcove. I needed to collect my thoughts. I had a mass of winding roads I could walk down and couldn't figure out how or where they intersected. I needed to take my mind off of shit. Fortunately, I had just the thing for that. Drinking alone.

At least that had been my plan before Joe Public sat down across from me, turning the chair around so he could lean forward on the backrest, because that's the kind of guy he is. He was holding an empty rocks glass and a full bottle. It was my brand of bourbon. He topped me off without a word. Because he's that kind of guy too. He poured a glass of his own and raised it. I raised mine and we drank. He poured two more. We raised our glasses again and sipped, but neither of us took it all.

"What's the occasion?" I asked.

"Jerry, I guess," he said. Although he seemed distracted by all the graffiti and Polaroid photos on the walls. The place was even noisy visually. Some people can't stand the sensory overload. Too much shit on the walls makes normal people anxious, I guess. It straightens me out, though. I'm the type of guy that needs constant distraction. Too little to see, too little to hear, and my mind wanders down roads I'd just as soon wish it wouldn't.

"Drinking to his honor?" I said, making no attempt to rein in my ambivalence.

Joe just sighed. He started to say something but stopped himself. He killed his drink and poured another.

"What's up, Joe? You look like you've got something to say."

"I do." He nodded. "I do. But I'm nowhere near drunk enough to say it."

"Well, then." I finished my drink and he refilled it. I lifted my glass. "Let us grease the wheels of honesty." We drank.

Joe went back for another bottle eventually, and after one from the new bottle, his tongue was looser than the bolts on a carnival ride.

"Fucking Jerry, man," Joe said.

"What's on your mind, Joe?"

"Did you know we didn't get along?"

"I seem to recall a band rivalry. But I thought it was of the good-natured type." Bands butted heads all the time. There was often a strong sense of competition between some of the larger-than-life personalities. Often these conflicts were only known to one party. The other remained completely unaware of the rivalry.

Joe shook his head and waved his hand. "No. Nothing good-natured about it at all. I mean, I thought that too at first, y'know? I thought that too. At *first*. But no. That guy, he hated me. I mean he *hated* me. Which, like, that hurt me. Y'know? It hurt, cuz I liked the guy. We coulda been friends. But nah, man. He had none of that."

"What was his problem with you?"

"Well, like, you know. People look to me. Up to me. Like a leader or something. And, and I try. Y'know? I try to help people out. I get them on shows. I book things. Tours. Or like hook people up if they need equipment or get people in touch with other people to make bands and stuff."

There was no denying that Joe Public was a scene leader. Jerry was as well. But there was a difference in personalities that melded as well as oil and water.

"Yeah," I said. "What was his issue with that?"

"I dunno. Jealousy? Or envy. Whichever. There's, there's a difference, y'know."

"Sure." I nodded.

"It was like he was keeping score or something. Like how many *followers* we had. He thought he deserved to have more *followers*."

"Followers?"

"His words." He gave a sloppy drunk shrug. "He tried to pick fights with me about it. Or like would talk shit about me all over."

I hadn't heard Jerry speak ill of Joe. I considered the possibility that that bit was all in Joe's head. But then I remembered what Jerry's bandmates had said a couple days before. Honestly, part of me just felt left out of the loop. I only cared about gossip in as much as it helped me out in my line of work. It was my job to have my ear to the ground. But I wasn't upset because I felt like I had failed somehow by not picking up on that; I felt excluded. I couldn't help feeling shitty about it. Then I felt shitty for feeling shitty. So, I drank again.

"He tried to kill me once," Joe said. I stopped. I must have looked like I was trying to catch flies in my mouth. "Alex, I never. I never told anybody about that. And, I, I didn't want to tell you. I mean I did, but I didn't, but I knew I should and … but. Yeah. Jerry Rash tried to … tried to kill me."

"What the fuck are you talking about, Joe?"

"Man. See? I fucking knew you wouldn't believe me."

"I don't know what I believe yet. I believe that you believe it. I definitely believe that Jerry was capable of some pretty horrid shit. But I'm gonna need to see some more cards before throwing any chips into the pot."

"Well, that's fair enough 'n' all. But he fucking bloody well did," he said. Joe Public was drunkenly slipping into a fake British accent. Did I tell you this guy was a trendsetter or what?

"What makes you think—I mean, how did he try to kill you? What happened exactly?"

"It was at an afterparty for the homecoming show for the tour. Not this one, obviously, the tour we did for our second record, *Blood Moon Eclipse*. The single we'd put out to promote it was actually getting a lot of airtime. And not just on Rodney. Everyone was just, like … gushing over us. They were asking all sorts of questions. Talking about, like, the lyrics and stuff. We started getting a bit high and, like, I was waxing philosophical. Everyone was just li—listening, y'know? Really eating it up. Someone turned the music down, turned it down so, like, people could, could listen. And, and, and … it was like giving a speech or something. Or like a sermon or something. Jerry, Jerry was not happy about that."

"He did always like being the center of attention."

"He was fucking pathological, man!" Joe pounded his fist on the table, which only drew the attention of the pool players for about half a second. Joe took a drink he did not need, rubbed his face, and continued with his story. "So, Jerry offered to cook me up a shot …"

"Was this before or after he went straight edge?"

"Hey, man, Zii may have bought that line, but it was just that. A line."

"He never … ?"

"Fuck no, he never stopped. Can I finish my fuckin' story?"

"Yeah. Please."

"So, I was like, 'Hell yeah, man.' So, he got his shit. Fresh needle, cooked up a shot and handed it to me, then just walked off. But I was talking to this girl and she asked if she could get a hit, so was I like, 'Sure.' I wasn't really feeling like a hit much anyway, so she tied off and shot up. Her eyes rolled up into her head and she started to convulse and shake. Jerry comes back in when he hears people start to panic. It was like, *bam!* All of a sudden, he was back. And he has this look of anger. And he was looking right at me."

"What did you do about the girl?"

"What did I—? I bit the fucking bullet and took her to a hospital! I'm not gonna let her fucking die!" The booze had loosened his tongue but also boiled his blood. He reached for the bottle, but I gently pulled it away from him. He smiled big, and his face crinkled in a way that showed he was just past thirty, but his eyes had the glaze of a man twice that. He wagged his finger approvingly at me for cutting him off.

"So, you think … ?"

"Jerry tried to cook up a hot shot for me? Yeah. You know, when … when you drop a girl off for OD'ing, they don't tend to let you … let you see her. But, uh, my wife managed to talk … talk to her sisters. They managed to, y'know, save her, but it was a potentially fatal shot."

"When was this?"

"About a year ago." He squinted and scratched the stubble on his neck.

"Why didn't you ever mention this to anybody?"

"I couldn't prove it. That's not the type of shit you just toss out into our little world. The schism that would cause? Are you kidding me?" He was getting worked up again, and I signaled the bartender for water and coffee.

"He ever try it again?" I asked.

"No. No, I don't think so," he said as the bartender brought over the coffee and water.

"Don't think so? You mean, you're not sure?" I asked.

He just gave a sad chuckle and shrugged. "Who can be sure of anything anymore?"

I figured I'd head home and get some food and rest. I could also check on Tom and make sure he didn't set fire to the place.

I stopped by an In-N-Out to pick up some food for Tom and me. The drive-through was packed, and it took me forever to find parking when I got back to my place. I walked into my apartment and found the door unlocked. "Yo, Tom! I thought I told you to keep the door locked!" There was no response. "Tom?" I glanced around. I wasn't sure where I thought he'd be. It was not a big place. Tom was gone. A note sat on my desk.

Back off or you're next.

A draft came in through the open window, chilling me to the bone. As I went over to close it, I saw a black car driving slowly by, loudly playing "Light My Fire" by the Doors.

23

I was shaking like the San Andreas. My heart pounded in my ears like John Henry while my brain swam the English Channel. Someone had been in my home. Someone who meant me harm. There is no way to explain the level of violation. But damn it, I'm going to try. To come into someone's home is to crawl under their skin, burrow to their most sacred parts, and take up residence there. Los Angeles in 1981 was intimidating on the best of days. Hell, the whole world was terrifying. The general consensus, especially among my peers, was that the world was going to end at any second. Nothing mattered and nowhere was safe. But there should always be one place where that's not on your mind. One place you can let your guard down. And that was your fucking, goddamn home. Suddenly, the very place I lay my head was as scary as the darkest West Hollywood alley. And every single one of my meager possessions was now caked in filth.

I had no idea what had happened to Tom. His walls may have had some scary-looking graffiti and razor wire on the ramparts, but they had turned out to be made of Styrofoam bricks. Trauma and partially developed frontal lobes are a volatile mix. He was either dead or would have that possibility hung over his head as a means to some horrible, dog-fucking end. I closed the door behind me and turned around. Templeton had been pinned to the door with a hunting knife.

They'd taken my witness, threatened my client, destroyed evidence, and murdered my roommate. If they were trying to scare me, they'd done it. But fear is quite the motivator. And they kept showing their hand. Making the kind of power plays that only served to narrow down my leads. Half this city had wanted Jerry dead. Seems even more had a reason. But not all of them had cops in their pocket and black sedans in their motorcade.

I went outside and knocked on my neighbor's door. He wore a gun on his hip. From the looks of it, the list of states it was legal in was short and did not include California. Fuck me with razors. I'd been stealing papers from *this* guy? I was lucky to be alive.

"Hey. I'm Alex. I live in the building next door. I was wondering if you saw anything suspicious earlier this evening."

He sized me up and decided he didn't like the look of me. "You're kiddin', right?" he snorted.

"Earlier," I said. "Did you see anyone come or go from that building?"

"I saw the cops arrest some punk kid. Nothing odd about that. Now get outta here." He closed the door, but I blocked it with my foot. He did not like that. At all.

"Do you know what they arrested him for?"

"No. He was probably drunk 'r high 'r somethin'. He was yelling. I heard 'em and looked out the window. They dragged 'im out of the building. He was resisting. Took a swing at one cop, so they cracked him one. Stuffed him into the car and drove off. Now, if you don't get the fuck off my property, they'll be back here again real quick. Capeesh?" He started to close the door and found my foot again.

"Just a few more questions."

"No! Get the fuck outta here, you fuckin' punk! I'll bet you're the one's been stealin' my paper!" He pulled his gun but didn't point it at me. "Get the fuck out of here right the fuck now, or they'll be sendin' an ambulance too!"

I backed away from the door slowly. He watched to make sure I left. "What time was it?" I asked quickly. He just slammed the door. I turned around and ran to my car. I figured he would be calling the pigs, and I did not want to be around when they showed up. Officer Mike would probably put a bullet in me and claim I was attacking him. I had been warned, and now they would know I was asking questions again. I should have backed down when I saw this guy was a wannabe cop. Stupid, Alex. Really stupid.

Whoever killed Jerry had pull. I had a few pieces to the puzzle, but most were upside-down and spread all over the table. The only certainties were hunches and my own personal grudges. I had to retrace some steps. Which meant flying some white flags. I tracked down the remaining members of Bad Chemicals at their home and practice space. They rented out the garage-slash-guest-house unit behind Luke's parents' place in Fairfax on a tree-lined side street just south off of Melrose. Being that it was late evening, everyone was home and parking in front of their Spanish-style houses, so I had to find metered parking a block or two up on Melrose. Melrose was lined with all sorts of shops and restaurants, but even without that, the sidewalks were so narrow that the foot traffic was a battle.

I had never known where the band crashed or practiced. Guess that can be added to the long list of things I learned today. Apparently, they had decided to continue on under an as-of-yet undecided new name. Reggie Reckless was pulling double duty as vocals and guitar. They were ripping into a new one as I walked up to the garage.

> *Jerry!*
> *Why'd you go?*
> *Jerry!*
> *You fucking asshole*
> *Jerry!*
> *You said you were through*
> *Jerry!*
> *But that wasn't true*

Jerry!

You fucked your life on drugs
Ruined shit for the rest of us
You were supposed to be a leader
You were nothing more than a monkey feeder!

Jerry!
You deceived us
Jerry!
So where does that leave us?
Jerry!
You had to scratch that itch
Jerry!
You took the apple from the witch
Jerry!

So now that you are dead
You've left behind fear and dread
You gave us all hope
But threw it all away to cop some dope!

Jerry!
Why'd you go?
Jerry!
You fucking asshole
Jerry!
You said you were through
Jerry!
But that wasn't true

Jerry! Jerry! Jerry! Jerry! Jerry! Jerry!
Jerry! Jerry! Jerry! Jerry! Jerry! Jerry!
Jerry!

Clearly, they were working through some issues.

"I was wondering when you would show up again," Reggie said to me. "What have you found out so far?"

"Privileged information," I said.

"Priv—privileged information?" Reggie was incredulous. "How the—we're his band! His friends!"

"Ain't *my* client, though," I said.

"Don't we have a right to know who killed our friend? Our leader?"

"I haven't found out enough to say for sure who did it," I said. "I wouldn't want to show my hand."

"Are you saying we're suspects?" asked Double Dare.

"Until I find out—"

"I found the fucking body!" Reggie took his guitar off and came at me with an intimidating sense of purpose.

"You say that like it absolves you," I said. I might as well have punched him in the gut. Sometimes, when you can tell someone is hiding something, you throw some fear into them. If you can make them think that they're a suspect, and in Reggie's case I had almost considered it, they might be more forthcoming with information if it absolves them. Cops had tried this one on me before. "I mean, it ain't exactly a secret that in the early days of the band you and Jerry fought for creative control. You butted heads over that shit right up to the end. Publicly."

"I didn't kill Jerry."

"Well, his death seems to have worked out pretty well for—" I didn't finish my sentence before taking a very well-deserved punch to the face. He stormed out of the room. Luke and Double just looked at me and waited for the door to slam. "If there's something I need to know that you guys aren't telling me, you should tell me. And let's just assume that I need to know everything."

"Jerry was dealing drugs for Eddie Nash," Luke blurted out.

"Knew that," I said. "Had to piece it together myself, though, didn't I?"

"Well, we couldn't exactly let it get out," Luke said. "Jerry was supposed to be straight edge, remember?"

"Which leads us to …"

"Jerry never went straight edge," Double chimed in.

"Yeah. I didn't think so. Come on, guys. Break my heart."

"He wasn't just fucking Zii," Luke said.

"Right …"

"He, uh, got out of line a lot. Really took advantage of girls who wanted in on his inner circle," Luke continued.

"What was this inner circle?"

"He wanted us to be more than a band. He kept telling us how we were going to spearhead a revolution," Double said. "That's where he and Reggie butted heads."

"They both wanted to lead the revolution?" I asked.

Both of them laughed, only for a moment, before catching themselves.

"No," Double said. "Not at all. Reggie couldn't give a fuck about revolution. He was just in it for the music."

"Did Reggie disagree with Jerry's politics?"

"Not really," Luke said. "I mean, I think he largely agreed with the points Jerry wanted to make. He just, like, couldn't be bothered. Reggie figured the world was fucked either way. He didn't figure anything would change. He thought it was a waste of time."

"Jerry ever say much about his plans for revolution?"

"He played those close to the vest," Luke said. "He kept telling us he had a need-to-know basis. He kept saying we were only in phase two. Although …"

"Go on."

"Okay, so phase one was the band. Get a following. That kind of thing. Phase two was getting media attention. I dunno anything much about three. Dare, didn't he say something about phase three pretty recently?" Luke asked.

"He just came into practice one day and told us he was just about ready for it. For phase three, I mean. He said he had something that was going to fast-track us to phase three."

"Were there any indications about what that was?" I asked.

"No," they both said.

"When was this?"

"A few days before he died," Luke said.

"So, right around the same time he told Zii that he had something on Senator Cromwell."

"Yeah, he did not like Cromwell. None of us do," Luke said.

"What else did he say about this revolution?"

"Same stuff he said onstage a lot. 'The revolution is coming!' 'California will be ours!' That's what the song 'Burn It Down' was all about."

I thought about the lyrics to that tune.

We're gonna burn it down
Burn it all, straight to the ground
We're gonna burn it down
Play in the ashes and roll around

"Y'know," Dare said, "behind closed doors he referred to our fans as an army."

"Really?"

"Yeah," said Luke, shuffling his sticks nervously. "He did do that."

"This thing he said would fast-track phase three, was it about the senator?"

"Yeah," said Reggie from the door. "It was dirt on the senator." He walked back into the room; he didn't apologize for hitting me. I wouldn't have either.

"He say what it was?"

"He showed it to me," Reggie said.

"What?" Luke said. "He let you in? What the fuck, man? Why would he show it to *you*?"

"I was trying to talk him out of this whole revolution thing. That it was a waste of time. You know, our usual bullshit. When he told me he had dirt on the senator that could bring him down, I told him to fuck off. He must have been high or proud—knowing him he was probably both—because he slapped the papers down in front of me on the table."

"What was it?" I asked. He was crouched in front of his guitar, checking it for damage.

"Now what kind of storyteller would I be if didn't hold you blokes in suspense?" Reggie grinned.

"A shitty one. But a damn fine witness," I said.

"Records. Financial records and photos. Of Senator Cromwell's dealings with Eddie Nash."

"What kind of dealings?" I asked. Knowing some but not all of it.

"Drug deals, hookers, bribes, kickbacks," Reggie said. "Perfect blackmail material. Probably why Nash had it."

Questions popped up in my head: Did Nash know Jerry had taken them? Did the senator know they were missing? Did he even know they existed? And, most importantly, where the fuck were they now?

"Any idea what he did with it all?"

"No," Reggie said. "No clue."

"Well …," Luke began.

"Well, what?" I asked.

"I don't know if this is related, but about a day after Jerry died, someone broke into our van."

"What did they take?"

"That's just it. Nothing. Some of our equipment was tossed around, cases were opened, but it was all accounted for. Except, the spare tire compartment had been pried open."

"They left the instruments and amps but took the spare tire?"

"We, uh, didn't keep a spare tire in the spare tire compartment," Reggie explained.

"You think Jerry could have been hiding his blackmail material in there?"

"Could have," Luke said. "He kept all kinds of contraband in there."

"Well, shit," I said.

I may have said this before, but the more answers you find, the more questions you'll have.

There was a lot to process. Jerry *had* taken blackmail material on the senator from Eddie Nash. Which strengthened my working theory that it was one or both of them. It was widely known, among the band at least, that Zii was being played by Jerry. Her father had even seemed to get it too. As much as I didn't want to admit it, she was a blip on my radar that was becoming increasingly hard to ignore. She didn't have the connections to pull on the thin blue line herself. But could she have sold him out to those who did?

Dinnertime had made Melrose sidewalk traffic even worse. I was pushing my way through the crowd on the way to my car when I caught the smell of weed emanating from a parked car. I turned and saw an idling Camaro with fogged windows blasting Foghat's "Slow Ride." Weed had never really been my thing. I'd tried some I stole off my parents when I was twelve, and I just felt tired and hungry. Given smell's connection to memory, I felt both now and became suddenly distracted by the display case of an erotic cakes shop. The baker had done a helluva job drawing a detailed vagina with various shades of frosting. You had to admire the talent and dedication. Although it made me think how when I eat pussy for real, I don't want to taste birthday cake.

A moment later, I heard huffing coming up the street. I turned to see Double Dare approaching in a light trot. If I hadn't stopped to contemplate a cherry clitoris, he'd never have caught up with me.

"I'm so glad," he panted, "I caught you." I urged him to catch his breath before he continued. He nodded with gratitude. We had to press up against the window of the cake shop to let people by. Between that and the traffic and car horns and the idling Camaro's Foghat tape, I gestured for us to move to my car.

By the time we sat down in my car, he'd caught his breath enough that he could speak. "There's something I think you should know, but I didn't want to say it in front of the other guys."

"Do tell."

"The riot. At the Starwood, the night Jerry died?"

"Vaguely. My skull remembers better than I do. What about it?"

"Jerry was the one that called the cops."

"What?"

"Jerry called the cops."

"What the fuck are you talking about? Why would he do that?"

"I dunno. But I heard him on the pay phone. He didn't know I was in the bathroom. But I heard him. He told them a riot was ready to break out."

"The riot didn't start until after the cops showed up," I said, peeking through the haze of my memory. "Right?"

"Yeah. Definitely after the cops tried to bust up the show."

I rubbed the bridge of my nose. It was all I could think to do.

24

I found a bar, ordered a whiskey, and asked for the phone. The bartender gave me my drink and a cocktail napkin before pointing me to a booth in the back. There was a stool and a little shelf bolted to the wall for setting down drinks. I dropped a coin into the phone and dialed Zii.

"Hello?"

".Jerry was fucking other people," I said. If you asked me why I would start a phone call to Zii that way, I'd tell you I didn't know. But deep down, that's horseshit. I knew exactly why. You're smart, you can piece it together. The response, unsurprisingly, was a deep breath through the nose.

"You really suck at phone calls," she said, her voice breaking slightly.

"Yeah," I said.

"And delivering bad news."

"Yeah."

"Jesus. You don't really *get* women, do you?"

"No argument there," I said. There was a long, awkward silence that hung in the air the way they only can during phone conversations. The phone has a way of turning three-second pauses into minutes. However long it actually was, it gave me time to contemplate the condensation on the side of my rocks glass. I watched as one drop rolled down the glass, gaining size as it collected the smaller, weaker drops before hitting the bottom and soaking into the napkin. The smaller, less-greedy drops managed to hang on.

"Who told you that?"

"His bandmates."

"Why wouldn't they tell me?"

"You don't really get *guys*, do you?" I said.

"Fuck. Well, thanks for confirming what I already knew," she said.

"I'm told that's what I do best." I ran my fingers along the glass, then licked the water off the tips, because, apparently, I am still a child. Another pause, long enough to ponder mankind's existential dilemma, passed. "He was also lying about being straight edge."

"You do realize you have yet to say, 'Hello, Zii. How's it going?' Right?"

"Hello, Zii. How's it going?"

"Hey, Alex. It's shitty. Thanks for asking. What's new with the case?"

"Jerry was lying about being straight edge."

"You're doing it again," she said.

"Telling you things you already know?"

"Yeah. Well, confirming suspicions at the very least."

"That's pretty much what being a PI is, though, right? If no one had suspicions, it would not be a very lucrative profession."

"Is it anyway?"

"It is not."

"So much for marriage prospects," she said, I would presume, with a grin.

"Ouch," I said. "Good thing for me everyone dies alone anyway."

"Hmm, good thing for you I'm not the marriage type," she said, putting just enough sultry husk behind it to get the blood rushing where it needed to go. I swallowed.

"Ha ha, yeah." I laughed nervously. "Who needs it? The … traditional institutions …"

"*Don'thurtmelikehedid.*" She said it so quickly, I almost didn't catch it.

"What?"

"Nothing," she said, almost as fast. "Don't worry about it."

"If there's something you're not telling me about Jerry …"

"Look, Alex, you just confirmed all of my worst fears. It's a lot to process. I'll call you later, okay?"

"Wait," I said. She didn't say anything, but there was no click. "I won't," I said. "I promise." There was another minutes-long three-second pause before the receiver clicked.

I had to find Tom. Which meant connecting the growing number of dots I had accumulated. I figured Officer Mike was involved somehow, which had to mean he was connected to everybody's favorite gangster. If I could find something on him back at Nash's, I might find Tom. I drove over and parked down the street just before Nash's cul-de-sac. I walked up to the door and knocked. There was no answer. I glanced inside and saw no movement. I jiggled the doorknob, but it didn't budge. I walked around back, hopped the fence surrounding the pool, and snuck toward the door. A familiar voice half-whispered, "Hold it right there." I damn near jumped out of my skin. I turned around and saw Brandy sunbathing naked. She certainly had the body to be a movie star. Curved hips, a taut belly, and perky symmetrical breasts that were far from being comically large, the way far too many women in this city shoot for. Proper proportions are rare in this town. And there she was, in all her glory, and there I was, with half the blood in my body rushing to my face and the other half to my dick.

"I, uh …," I sputtered.

"What are you doing here?" She placed her hands on her hips, making no attempt to cover herself.

"I was looking for, um, Eddie. Is he here?"

"Did anyone answer when you knocked?" she asked.

"No," I said.

"Well, I guess that answers that, then. But you try to get in anyway? Why are you really here?"

I knew she wouldn't be keen on helping me if I told her the truth. That I was here trying to find information on a corrupt cop to track down a kidnapped witness that would lead me to Jerry Rash's killers. Her *rapist's* killers. I spun a wheel of options in my head, and the arrow landed on "half-truth."

"I'm trying to dig up some dirt on a corrupt cop who's been harassing some friends of mine. I want him to back off, and I have reason to believe that Eddie has him in his pocket."

She looked me up and down as if scanning me for any tells. "Okay," she said, standing up. "I buy it. Follow me."

"I might need a moment," I said.

"Too late," she said. "I already see your hard-on. Pig."

I followed her into the house. And, given my tendency to shake every package gifted to me, I had to ask her.

"Why are you helping me?"

"Does it matter?"

"I have no idea. That's what scares me."

"Well," she said, "for one thing, I hate the cops that Eddie brings over here. They tend to get real handsy, and they're not good about tipping. They act like the girls are gifts from Eddie, and he lets them believe it. But where does that leave us, right?"

"Right?"

"I'm sick of Eddie and his bullshit altogether. He's nothing but a wad of sick fetishes and broken promises."

"Yeah …"

"Plus, you listened to me the other night."

"Well, I aim to please," I said.

She turned around, walked up to me, kissed her finger, and touched my nose. "Mmm. So do I."

She smiled. I swallowed. We walked into Eddie's room, and she lifted the mattress of his bed to reveal a hidden safe and put in the combination. She looked over her shoulder and smiled when she saw me trying and failing not to look at her ass. We opened the safe to reveal massive amounts of cash. Brandy took the cash out and set it aside. Under the cash was another hidden compartment containing a box of files.

"How did—?"

"When it comes to a girl they want to fuck, guys tend to talk a bit too much. Especially when they're constantly coked up." Brandy removed the lid from the file box. "What's the name of the cop?"

"Hernandez. Michael Hernandez."

"Officer Mike? Ugh. You don't want to know what *that* guy's into. Or, I guess, maybe you do."

"I already have ideas."

"He likes the boys," she said. "And he likes them young. Too young. Ah. Here we are. Hernandez, Michael." She took the file, returned the lid, and closed the hidden compartment. "You gonna take that fucker down?" She lifted the file above her head.

"Something like that." I reached for it, but she pulled it away.

"Come here," she said. I did as I was told. I tried to reach behind her, and she used this chance to grab hold of me. She wrapped her arms around me as she planted a wet kiss on my mouth. She handed me the file. I opened the lining of my jacket and slipped the file into my hidden pocket.

"Clever," she said. She started to rub my cock through my jeans and kissed me again. I thought about Zii for a moment, but I was frozen. She undid my belt and took out my dick. "Oh," she said. "It's cute."

And it was then, while my cock was in Brandy's hand and a pile of cash sat next to the open safe, that Eddie Nash walked in. He looked at me, he looked at Brandy, then at the cash, and then back at me. And I wouldn't have believed it if I hadn't looked back at him, but I swear to you that the look on his face was one of utter betrayal.

25

I never liked flying. Airplane seats have an embarrassing lack of legroom. But I will say this: they've got it all over the trunk of a car. Which is typically where one can expect to find themselves after they're caught stealing from the city's most dangerous drug dealer and pimp while getting a hand job from said pimp's best girl. The bag over my head didn't make having limited air any easier. It could be argued that I put *myself* in these positions. However, I am not a drug-dealing pimp who conspires with senators and dirty cops to murder abusive, rapist, rock-star drug addicts. So maybe, just maybe, I was not *entirely* to blame for the unfortunate situation in which I had found myself. Just putting that out there. Luckily the cash had provided some unintentional misdirection. He never checked for missing files.

Of course, under other circumstances I might have very well enjoyed being tied up with a bag over my head. Zii might be into it. I figured if I got out of this, there would be no harm in asking.

The beating I had undergone at the hands of Nash's hulking personal bodyguard had left me a bit woozy. Course, part of that could have been the sodium pentothal. The injection point on my neck was the sorest part of me.

I wasn't sure how long I had been out, so I had no clue how far I was from Studio City. I tried to listen for other traffic and came to the pants-shitting realization that there wasn't any. We were outside of the city. Maybe somewhere in the woods or mountains. Why the fuck they didn't just kill me and be done with it was both baffling and a relief. I figured on them having a few questions for me that were not related to my dick being in the hand of a nineteen-year-old aspiring actress. I spent the rest of the car trip trying to anticipate those questions and coming up with answers to them, like they always tell you to do before a job interview. I guess being sent to the guidance counselor wasn't a total waste after all. *Who do you work for? What do you know? Who sent you?*

As I was pulled out of the trunk of the car, I could hear crickets. My nose was hit by the scent of pine and tree sap, and I could feel that the driveway was dirt and gravel. Given how long we'd been driving and the strong smell of trees, I figured we were up north. Probably Sequoia or the Sierra National Forest. I was pushed along with a gun in my back and stumbled up the steps to a cabin. Boards creaked as heavy footsteps clomped on wood floors. I was shoved into a back room and heard a door slam behind me. They tied me to a chair. Arms, legs, torso. All of them tight enough to retard the flow of blood. There were at least two other people in the room pacing aggressively, and then they left. The door slammed and the door locked. I moved my head as much as I could, trying to get a sense of where I was. A short time later, I heard them unlocking the door. I started anticipating their questions again. *Who do you work for? What do you know? Who sent you?* Someone grabbed the bag on my head and ripped it off, taking a bit of my hair with it. And I found myself face to face with Senator David Cromwell.

"Where is she?" he asked.

Okay, *that* one I had not anticipated.

He was beefier than he looked on television. He was always wearing some big, double-breasted suit that betrayed his soldier's physique. But here, in suspenders, with a blue striped shirt with a white collar and cuffs with the sleeves rolled up, it was clear that what was about to come was going to hurt a great deal. He hit me in the gut. Apparently, while in shock, I had failed to answer his question in a time frame he felt adequate.

"Oof!" I coughed and sputtered.

"Where is she?" he repeated, as if that was going to help.

"Where is who?" I asked. He punched me again. In the face this time. "Sorry. Should I have said *whom*?" His eyes went wild and he hit me again. "No. No. It's *who*. It's definitely *who*." Another gut shot.

"I suppose you think you're funny, huh?" he said.

"Now that you mention it, I *have* been working on a tight five for the Comedy Store. Try this one. 'Did you catch Senator Cromwell's speech about the "gay agenda"? The man clearly spends a lot of time thinking about it. Makes you wonder …'" That one earned me a straight shot to the nose. Everything went white. "Fuck!" I cried despite my best efforts to hold my cool. My eyes stung and watered. The fucker could throw a punch.

"Everyone's a critic," I said.

His next hit practically caved in my chest. "Where. Is. She?!"

"I'm not telling you where she is! Hit me all you want!" As ballsy as that sounds, it was a very poor choice of words. Because he did. And it turned out he wanted to hit me a lot. Silver lining: the tooth he knocked out was crooked anyway.

"I'm not going to ask you again!" His face was redder than mine, and mine was covered in my own blood.

"Good. Because I'm not going to reveal my client's whereabouts."

"Please," he scoffed, "Susan Haught means nothing to me. If I wanted that groupie dealt with, she *would* be."

"Wait. I'm confused," I said. "Who are you looking for?"

"Lisa, you punk! My daughter!" Suddenly it felt like someone had busted open the airlock. Every ounce of oxygen was sucked out of the room, and the pressure dropped. The floor fell out from under me, and something in my head momentarily shut down, then came whirring back to life. Truly, this night was full of surprises.

"You have a daughter?" I said.

"*Had* would be more accurate," he said, shaking off his hand.

"Had? Is she dead?" I asked.

"She may as well be," he said. "All the debauchery she started to engage in. At first, she was happy to oblige me to stay out of the public eye. But active defiance? Helping others tear down everything I build? I will not abide sedition." It's a funny thing. When you're tied to a chair, people really open up to you. "And all this started when she started listening to punk rock."

"Of course it did," I said, rolling my eyes with my voice.

"One Bad Chemicals record!" he said defensively. "One! She started cutting up her T-shirts! Slathering on dark eye makeup! She got defiant! Of *course* that's what started it!"

"Or maybe, just *maybe*, she felt constrained by her overbearing, power-hungry, *fascist* father, who cared more about money and power than her, and finally found an outlet." I knew well enough to brace for the punch this time. I shook off the pain of it and turned to face him.

"Sorry to put you through all this trouble, what with the stuffing me in a trunk and the long drive and the beatings and all, but I don't know a goddamn thing about your daughter." I spat out the blood that had pooled up in my mouth. "Actually, I don't even know *any* Lisas, come to think of it."

"Bullshit!" he said, backhanding me. "You've been digging around in the life of Jerry Rash! She wanted to join his cause! You know *something* and I will find out what it is!"

I have, in the past, been boastful about my ability to take a beating. This beating, I am not ashamed to say, forced me to reassess a crucial point of pride. His training showed. It showed. It showed in his jabs. It showed in his hooks. And it especially showed in his uppercut. Even if I hadn't been tied to a chair, I can't imagine myself faring much better. Sweet, merciful fuck, did it hurt. The scariest bit was, I knew he was holding back. He wanted to drag out the pain and keep me lucid. There was that military training again. Cards on the table: I pissed myself. After that, I just kinda zoned out.

A bucket of ice water shocked me into consciousness. It was a sharp, painful cold. The best thing I can say about it is that it took my mind off the pain from elsewhere. I had passed out, but nothing felt broken. The nose, lip, and forehead bleed a lot with very little effort if you hit 'em right. It's scary as fuck but keeps people you want to talk cognizant.

"I apologize for being overzealous," said the senator. Both clearly lies.

"Don't beat yourself up over it," I said, lolling my head.

"I assure you, I won't." He pulled up another chair and slid it inches from me. He sat with menacing purpose. But maybe it just seemed that way to me. When someone has spent several hours beating the shit out of you, everything they do would seem to be done with menacing purpose. He'd cleaned himself off. The stench of blood, sweat, and top-shelf gin had been replaced by the smell of designer cologne, pomade, and top-shelf gin. "And I won't let anyone use my daughter to ruin me." I always find it disconcerting when people threatening my life are this revealing. I didn't have a lot of time left. *Fuck it*.

"Is that why you had Jerry killed?" I said.

"That doesn't trace to me," he said. It was his *lack* of a reaction that most struck me. Of course, it didn't mean he was guilty, just that he had anticipated the accusation. Which, alone, still fills in gaps.

"No. Just to the drug dealers you're in bed with," I said.

"Eddie Nash and I have a certain understanding," he said. "He is, at the end of the day, an important man in an important town."

"All money is green if you ignore the blood," I said.

"*All* money has blood," he said. "Don't be a child." And for the first and only time in my life, I found myself agreeing with Senator David Cromwell. "Last chance."

"I don't know where Lindsey is," I said.

"*Lisa.*"

"Her either." I looked him in the eye; he didn't break away. In fact, he tilted his head to get a better look. He looked deeper into my eyes than anyone I love ever has, and then he nodded.

"I believe you," he said. "But it's not going to save you."

"Never expected it would," I said.

"You're a smart kid. You get it." He stood and knocked a certain pattern on the door. Two men entered. "Walk him up the trail. Chuck him off a cliff. Make it look like a hiking accident. Keep working on the other kid. If he doesn't talk, give him the same. Wait for a few hours and do it during my press conference."

He was sticking with his MO at least.

26

Escape or die. Since I wouldn't be able to fight my way out of the house, I waited and planned. Two armed men entered the room. They were big and bulky and, of course, adorned in the types of suits and sunglasses that suggested the existence of some kind of Goons "R" Us. Both of their heads were shaven, giving them the air of skinheads playing Secret Service dress-up. I figured them for some of Rapunzel's boys. One held a gun to me while the other loosened my restraints from the chair. I was bagged and shoved back into the car. The back seat this time. It was more comfortable, but a gun was pressed into my side the whole time. The stench of the henchman's cheap cologne made me long for the trunk again.

We stopped and marched through the woods for a while. It would have been too far to carry me. I started tripping over anything and everything, until one got annoyed and removed the bag from my head so I could see where I was walking. Phase one, complete. I managed to read a trail sign saying that we were somewhere near King's Canyon.

We got to an overlook that provided a view of a tree-filled valley. Pillars of green stood in defiant contrast to the rock-faced mountains. The setting sun had turned the sky the color of a fruity cocktail and had stained the clouds that still dared to hang on a sensual shade of pink. As spectacular as the view was, it was hard to feel on top of the world when I was moments away from being thrown to the bottom. But I had to say, as far as last things to see go, I could have done a helluva lot worse. Valleys beat gutters for places to die.

Still, I was hoping some other hikers would come along

and see the scene unfolding. But it became more and more apparent that I was on my own.

They couldn't chuck me over the cliff with bonds on and have it look accidental. So, one of them began to cut my hands free while the other kept a gun trained on me. As soon as the bonds were cut, I moved. I was dead either way and I'm too damn proud for surrender. I lunged forward and grabbed the gun-wielding goon's wrist with one hand and the gun with the other. I twisted the gun outward and pried it out of his hands and ducked to the side so that I had them both in the line of fire. The other goon, who had cut my bonds, was reaching for his own gun. Plus, I knew he had a knife.

"Drop your weapons!" I said to him. He scoffed.

"You don't have the—"

Blam! Blam! I put two in his chest. His friend backed off and put his hands up. Just a reminder, I hate these things. But given my current situation, principles were not a privilege I had.

"Keys," I said, moving closer. He moved his hands to his left jacket pocket. "Stop!" I shouted. He froze. "They're in your other pocket."

"No," he said. "Let me—"

Blam! In his head. I walked over to the body and checked his pockets. Sure enough, his left jacket pocket contained a concealed handgun. I wiped my prints off the gun I had used, disassembled it, and chucked it off the edge of the cliff. I grabbed the keys, pocketed the smaller gun, and ran down the hill toward the car.

The two-lane road cut through thick forest. Occasional breaks in the evergreens allowed for views of the mountains, and I thought about how I had never learned the names of trees. As I wound farther along the road, I found a cliff face on one side and, on the other, the canyon that had very nearly been my grave. The rubble along the cliff face gave credence to the signs warning of falling rocks. Along the side of the road, tourists who had pulled over to take photos at sunset were getting back in their cars. Having almost been thrown into that valley and having shot more than scenery, I was considerably less content. Being in flight mode, my thoughts were more on escaping than what I was escaping from. Or what I had done.

Every now and then I'd catch some headlights and would get an awful glare. I was able to shake it off with a few rapid blinks, but I had to accept that, given recent events, I probably had a concussion.

I drove around until I recognized road signs. I was in the Sierras. I whooped in victory upon seeing signs for LA. Then it hit me.

Tom.

Cromwell had said something about another kid. He had to mean Tom. If there was a chance he was back there, I had to take it. I just had to hope they'd kept him alive. Of course, having been bagged and trunked before, I had no clue where the cabin was. I pulled off into a parking lot of one of the observation decks and searched the car for clues. The glove compartment only had the user manual for the car and, well, gloves. But clipped behind the passenger-side sun visor was a marked-up road map. One of those marks appeared to show a road that was not on the map. I turned around and headed back toward the cabin. I found the private road, and the bumps seemed familiar. I pulled up to a cabin.

It was a two-story log cabin stained a light brown. The ground floor, more of an exposed basement, was flat-face rubble stone, and there was a chimney to match. The second floor walked out onto a large deck. Floor-to-ceiling windows went all the way up to the steeply sloping triangular roof. It was one helluva weekend home. Meanwhile, a family of five somewhere was crammed into a two-bedroom.

There was a car out front, a black sedan, that matched

the one I was driving. Black sedans. It's always black sedans. Nothing looks more conspicuous than looking inconspicuous.

Of course, there still were other men inside. Which meant that there was something or someone inside that still needed guarding. Hopefully. I was waging a lot on it being a particular obnoxious, hyperviolent surfer thug turned punker from HB. I drew the gun, parked the car, and walked up to the door. It was locked. I had keys but decided on a different approach. I stood to the side of the door and knocked. When one of the senator's men opened the door, I recognized him as one who had been in the room with me earlier. I put the gun to his head. It was quickly dawning on me that I had killed two men only a short time ago. It wasn't a feeling that I much cared for, despite the arguable necessity. Either way, I preferred to get out of this without sending another man into soulless oblivion. When you don't believe in an afterlife, you believe in the value of this one. Which is a helluva lot easier to say when someone isn't pointing a gun at you.

"Don't move. Don't make a sound. So much as clear your throat and I swear to your boss's god I will blow your head all over this charmingly rustic porch." I pulled back the hammer. "Now be a good little sycophant and walk toward the car." He did as he was told. "You got keys for that one?"

I gestured to the one I hadn't been driving. He nodded.

"Good," I said. "Open the trunk."

He opened it and put his hands up. This was a man who didn't want to die. Most don't. Some just don't realize it until they're toeing the line.

"One last request," I said. "Is Tom inside?"

He nodded.

"Excellent." I cracked him over the head and he fell forward into the trunk. I lifted his legs up and shoved the rest of him in. "Now you know how it feels." I shut the trunk, tossed the keys into the woods, and ducked into the bushes.

I whipped a rock at the window of the car. It bounced off. I fired the gun once and ran toward the side of the house. I heard two more men run out the front door shouting.

"Phil! Phil! Where are you?" Apparently, the name of the guy in the trunk was Phil. "Phil! Are you okay?" They were seized with panic. "Fuck! What the fuck is going on?"

I slid open a side window and slipped into the cabin. I was in a small bedroom with bunk beds on two of the four walls and a twin just under the window. Two dead. One in the trunk. Two outside. I peeked out the bedroom door and got a straight shot down the hall to the still-open front door. Just a screen door between me and presumably armed guards. I could see them passing through the porch light occasionally. I lined up my shot down the hallway. I had a clear shot at the door. The hallway had become my own rustic Thermopylae. I ducked back into the room until I heard one come through the door. He cocked a shotgun, causing the stock value of his life to plummet. As I spun out of the room, I fired two shots down the hall, hitting a shoulder and chest. He fell to his knees but was able to aim the shotgun at me. I dove back into the room just as the molding exploded in a hail of splinters.

"What the fuck?" said the remaining henchman. "Jim?! Jim!"

I fired down the hall and hit him in the shoulder while he was checking on Jim. After that, the gun went click. He picked up Jim's shotgun and did more damage to the molding. Luckily, the tree-trunk walls could stop shotgun blasts. If it'd been drywall, I'd be a dead man. Buckshot scraped my cheek. More blood on my face at this point was straw in a haystack. I was starting to hope Zii would let me include medical expenses in my fee. I was not looking forward to the adrenaline wearing off.

He was coming down the hall. He approached slowly and cautiously. He didn't know I was out, but if I went too much longer without firing back, he'd soon piece that one together. I had spent the last several hours being beaten and tenderized. Even looking at a lamp had started to feel like staring at the sun. The edges of my vision blurred. On top of the beatings, the closest thing I'd gotten to sleep in the last twenty-four hours was a sodium-pentothal-induced nap in the trunk of a car. Which is not super restful, by the way. In short, I was a snowball going against a blowtorch.

I took a quick inventory of the room I'd scrambled into. Which appeared to be some kind of walk-in utility closet. *Fucking hell*, I thought, *I've lived in smaller places than the closet where this guy keeps his fucking wasp spray.* Resourceful little fucker that I am, I grabbed a can of Raid off the shelf and crawled behind the door.

Just as he started to come into the room, I kicked the door shut, hitting him right in the wrist. I managed to grab the gun from him. Or at least I got a hold of the barrel and pointed it away as it blasted a hole in the ceiling. I sprayed insecticide right in his eyes. He screamed as he fell forward, and I managed to pry the gun away and cracked him over the head with the barrel. There was a sickening crunch as part of his skull cracked open.

I found the room I had been kept in. My jacket was in the corner and, by some miracle small or massive, the file was still hidden in the lining. I tried the room next door. Locked. I thought a moment and took out the keys for the car I had stolen. I tried a few of the keys on the ring, and one worked. Sure enough, there was Tom. He was barely hanging on to life. His face was swollen, and he had more loose teeth than a bad dream. He'd been worked over far worse than I had. If he hadn't been tied to a chair, he'd have collapsed on the floor.

"Tom? Tom! It's Alex." He gave a groan that I assume was expressing familiarity. "I'm gonna get you out of here. Okay? Can you hear me?" I ran to the kitchen and got a knife. I ran back and cut his bonds. I caught him as he fell out of a chair, the weight of him made all the heavier by our injuries. My muscles were beaten to dough, and he was dead weight.

I managed to carry him out to the car I'd stolen earlier and fix him up in the passenger seat. Phil was still in the trunk of the other car and I'd chucked his keys. I hoped there was enough fuel to get us back to LA. I'd been too distracted to pay any mind to the gauge earlier. If someone hadn't contacted the authorities yet, someone at a gas station certainly would. I checked the other car's glove box and found a loaded .38, which I pocketed. We had half a tank of gas. I was probably going to have to stop. I considered siphoning some gas from the other car but figured others could return any minute. I was, in fact, lucky enough that they hadn't already. One look at my face in the rearview mirror was all the indication I needed that I didn't have any luck left to push. I put the car in drive. Maybe we'd arouse suspicion at a gas station, maybe we wouldn't. I'd jump off that bridge when I came to it.

27

Tom was still dozing as I drove us out of the mountains, which left me alone with my thoughts. In this line of work, I'd doled out some savage beatings. Mostly to stalkers, bullies, and rapists. Roughing up scumbags wasn't anything I'd lost sleep over. But killing three, possibly four, men? This was a whole new beast. And it was rabid. The short breaths and rushing blood of a panic attack set in. Unable to drive safely, I pulled off to a scenic outlook to pull myself together. I fought back tears and took slow, deep breaths. It had become brutally clear that if I was going to make it out of this ordeal alive, I was likely going to have to be the reason other people didn't.

"It was them or me," I whispered over and over to myself. "It was them or me." I couldn't fully numb myself. Honestly, I hoped I wouldn't. There are some things people should never be numb to. I couldn't flip a switch, but I could dim the lights enough to function. Can't say I had a choice in the matter. I could worry about affording therapy later. I took one last breath and pulled back out onto the road.

We were somewhere just outside of Bakersfield when thoughts of Brandy's fate started to overtake me. The girl had wiles. I hoped she had been able to talk herself out of some horrid fate. I already knew from personal experience the cost of betraying Eddie Nash. If she was as devious as I hoped she was, she could have told him that I had forced her into it. But it didn't exactly look like I was forcing her hand into my lap. If anything, it had clearly been the other way around. I had to stay focused and just hope for the best. I couldn't go back to Nash's house. Hell, I couldn't go back to mine.

Tom started coming to.

"Hey," I said. He just looked at me, wide-eyed. "Look. We gotta ditch this car pretty soon. Maybe we can catch a bus out of Bakersfield." What we really needed to do was get to a hospital. But we found a bus station and I parked the car a few blocks away. Tom still hadn't said anything. His jaw was at the very least severely bruised.

"Jesus!" said the guy at the ticket booth.

"You should see the other guy," I said. "Two for LA."

"Should we be going back to LA?" Tom croaked out. I'll admit he had a point. Maybe it was better to lie low. But if they'd been following me as closely as I feared they had, I had to figure they knew where to find Rad and Zii. I wasn't about to bail on the two people in this world that I loved. Or at least tolerated. Which, relatively speaking, is a lot for me.

"I am," I said. "You can do whatever you want. But considering that I just saved your life, I'd take it as a kindness if you were to tell me everything on the bus ride."

In response, he looked away from me. I held up the file.

"This contains dirt on Officer Mike. Proof that he was taking kickbacks from Nash, and photographic evidence of his proclivities. Emphasis on *graphic*." Tom stared at me, confused. "It's pictures of him fucking underage boys, Tom. Evidence. He'll be off the streets. And with a bit of luck, being force-fed his own medicine for the better part of the next decade."

Tom nodded.

On the bus ride, Tom communicated as best he could that they had taken him to the cabin after they'd busted into my place. They'd asked him what he'd told me, but he hadn't said anything. They'd beaten him, obviously. He said he never saw the senator but that Officer Mike had been by a couple of times and had said Tom was "too beaten up to be cute anymore." Tom said they'd asked him about Jerry's cult, but he didn't know what they were talking about. He'd told them he hated Jerry and wouldn't have been part of any inner circle. They'd remained unconvinced. Tom said that he'd started feeding them some lies, as a means of staying alive. They'd mostly wanted to know what I knew, he told me. But I hadn't told him much. He also said they'd asked him about Rapunzel.

"I thought he worked *for* them," I said.

"He did. Does. I dunno," Tom said. "Officer Mike said something about Rapunzel getting arrested. And that he had done what he could do but mentioned that he'd been held. Then someone said something about posting his bail."

Fuck, I thought. Rapunzel and his crew would probably be looking for me too. Seattle was starting to look pretty good. Hell, maybe Chicago or DC. Just get the fuck out of California. But I knew I couldn't. It was too late for that.

Tom dozed off, understandably exhausted. I decided to do some reading. The kind where you have to check around you first to make sure no one is looking. I opened up Officer Mike's file, keeping the photos out of sight. I slogged through some of his background information. Nash had had a lot more dirt on him than pederasty. It turned out Officer Mike's actual resume included the Guardia Nacional. As in *of El Salvador*. Mike's name wasn't even Hernandez. It was Gonzalez. Miguel Gonzalez. He got his job in the LAPD with a letter of recommendation from Senator David Cromwell. Cromwell, who had supported the US involvement in El Salvador. And, it would seem, may have been involved in training the Guardia.

We got to LA and I called Rad from a pay phone. He came by in my car, which he had managed to find where I had left it. The cost of the ride back was a lecture.

"This is why you *don't cut me out*," he said. "You need backup. You need a partner on this. Look what happens to you when you don't ask me for help." He turned the rearview mirror toward me. "You *see?* You see what happens?"

"If you'd been there, this would have happened to you too," I said. Rad just started laughing. "Just what the hell is so damn funny?"

"When are you going to learn that I'd take a fucking bullet for you?" he said.

That shut me up. We sat in silence for a few moments.

"You guys make a cute couple," Tom said.

Rad pulled up to a hospital, prompting me to sit up quickly and ask him what the fuck he thought he was doing.

"Look at yourself!" he said. "You're hurt!"

"How many brawls have you seen me get in? I've had worse!"

"No! You *haven't!*" he said. "I don't know how you're still standing right now!"

I had to admit that with the adrenaline wearing off, I was in a bad way. Despite my best efforts, I winced at the pain.

"I knew it," Rad said. "You're going to the ER. Tom too."

"We can't afford that!" I protested.

"I can," Tom said. "I'm on my parents' insurance."

"Of course you are," I said. "Fine then. *I* can't."

"We'll figure it out," Rad said. There was no use fighting him on it. We went into the ER, and I checked in under an assumed name. We told them that I had been mugged. I was given something for the pain and told to wait. It looked like it was going to be awhile. I decided to try to call Zii from the lobby pay phone. Her father answered and was disgusted to find me on the other end of the line.

"She's not here," he said.

"Is she not-there not there, or is she there's-no-way-in-hell-I'm-letting-*you*-talk-to-her not there?"

"She's not here. There'd be no point in lying to you."

"Well, I appreciate your honesty then?" I toyed with the phone cord and read the lewd things that had been scratched into the pay phone console. And I thought this was supposed to be a family hospital.

"There'd be no point in lying, because I don't know where she is either. I figured she was with you."

"How's that now?" My mind began to run laps around an obstacle course full of worst-case scenarios. "Mr. Haught, I need you to think carefully. Have you seen any black sedans around your neighborhood lately? Have you been in touch with anyone from Senator Cromwell's office?"

"What the hell are you talking about? What does that have to do with—have you gotten my daughter into some kind of danger?"

"Meyers, Richard. Meyers, Richard," the PA announced. It was the alias I had used when checking into the ER.

"I gotta go," I said. I hung up, cutting off his "What the fuck is going on?!" by about half.

I had contusions to the ribs and cheekbone, that much was obvious, possibly a mild fracture to the former. The jury was still out on a concussion. They wanted to keep me for a day or two to make sure there was no internal bleeding. They didn't think there was, but they said it was best to err on the side of caution in these cases. Which really means, err on the side of a larger hospital bill.

"Am I stable?" I asked.

"Well, it's too early to tell," said the doctor, a dark-skinned man in his early forties, his hair and beard prematurely white from the stresses his profession brings. "We haven't done enough tests to say for sure. You seem cognizant enough. I'm not noticing any slurring in your speech. Your pupils seem fine. But not all symptoms show right away, and you mentioned fogginess and light sensitivity. I'd really like to do a CT scan. X-ray those ribs and—"

"And I'd like to get the fuck out of here before I go into debt for the rest of my life. So, give me something for the pain, an ice pack for my face, and let me get the hell out of here."

"Irritability and paranoia are also symptoms of a concussion."

"Motherfucker, this is my baseline."

"I really recommend—"

"Do I look like I can afford several nights in a hospital? Huh? I don't have the money, and I *really* don't have the time. So, send me on my way and go back to healing the rich in a system that leaves the poor to die."

I could tell by looking at him that my armor-piercing mini rant had struck a chord. For all I know, this guy had gone into the medical field with the best of intentions. Helping the sick should be a noble profession, and not everyone participates willingly in the cold, uncaring capitalistic cycle. His face turned from one of genuine hurt into one of a defiant purpose. He left but reappeared a short time later and tossed me a pill bottle.

"Two every four hours for the pain," he said, then tossed a second bottle. "One every six hours for the swelling."

"Thanks," I said with a clear air of confusion in my voice. He walked over to a freezer and tossed me a cold blue square.

"Here's your fucking ice pack. I assume you used a fake name?"

"Umm …"

"That's what I thought. Door at the end of the hall goes to the alley. I may have left it propped open after my cigarette break."

"May have?" I asked.

He shrugged nonchalantly; his face showed nothing. "One way to find out. Now, if you'll excuse me, I have to go and perpetuate a broken system that falls more and more apart with each passing day." And with that, he left, which meant it was time for me to follow suit.

As promised, or at least as highly suggested, the door

was open. I slipped around the front and found Rad in the parking lot.

"Everything good?"

"Yeah," I said. "Let's go. We gotta find Zii." We got to the car and I took my first bits of medication and stuck the ice pack on my face.

"Where is she?"

"I don't know. We'll start looking at some of her haunts this evening and ask if anyone has seen anything."

"It's already late afternoon," Rad said.

"What? Jesus. Well, no rest for the wicked, I guess."

We strolled around West Hollywood. We poked our heads into cafes, pizza places, and bars. Most of the venues weren't open. But I ran into Sally Fitz, one of Zii's close friends and Luke's girlfriend.

"I haven't seen her in a few days," Sally said. "But last week we made plans to see Bad Religion at Club 88 tonight. So, I'm hoping to see her there."

"Thanks, Sal," I said.

"Don't call me Sal," she said.

"—ly," I added quickly. She gave me a playful punch to the arm. I smiled and nodded to hide the fact that against my bruised and battered body, her swat felt like some twisted medieval torture. My eyes welled with tears I prayed she did not see.

Rad and I decided to split up and meet at the show. I decided to risk heading back to my apartment to look for clues—and possible signs that Zii had been there. If I'd told Rad my plan, he would have tried to talk me out of it, and he probably would have succeeded. When I got there, I approached the door cautiously. I still had the .38 that I had swiped from one of Cromwell's cars. I burst in the door.

It was the smell that hit me first.

Sitting at my desk was the headless body of a young

woman. Her head sat on the desktop, facing her. Her hands
had been nailed to the top of her head. This was a tactic
used by Salvadoran death squads to send a message to the
rebels. I was no longer dealing with men. That much was
clear. I shook and I cried as every ounce of guilt forced its
way out of me. I walked over to the body. I could barely tell
it was naked, it was covered in so much blood. The cut along
the neck had been clean, as if with a razor-sharp machete.

"No." I sputtered out the words. "No. No, no, no." I turned
to look at the head. I'd always thought it was lame when
people brought their hands up to their face or chest when
shocked, but it turns out it's absolutely a reflex. My throat
closed up and the room dropped away. I was spinning in
the dark and the temperature dropped. My ears started to
ring like I'd spent all night standing next to triple-stacked
Marshall amps. The room became an impressionist painting.
I floated in nothingness. A void. For a second, I remembered
when I was six. I'd almost drowned in my cousin's pool. Up
and down had become mere myths as my lungs filled with
something they were not meant to breathe. So it was now,
standing in my room. This was how people imagined death
in the absence of an afterlife, and it filled them with a fear
so great that they had to invent religion. But there are no
gods here. Not if this can happen.

Brandy's eyes were still open. They didn't even spare
the poor girl that dignity. Conflicting emotions of relief and
guilt brought me to my knees. Relief that it was not Zii, and
guilt not only at the relief but in the knowledge that this
was *my* fault. Blood was still dripping from the table and
onto my jacket.

Some people only think they're tough because they have
never encountered something that sends them instinctively
into a fetal position. I've never felt worse, but I felt a strange
sense of relief that I felt as horrid as I did. Vomiting at least
meant I still had something inside me.

I managed to pull myself together enough to look out the window in a panic. Right across the street was Officer Mike in his squad car, calling it in. Fucker had been waiting for me. I looked back at the body. It had to have been Mike, bringing in old tricks from his old job.

"I'm sorry," I whispered. I went out the back way and waited for him to go in the front. I made a break for my car and drove off.

I cleaned the blood off my leather jacket in a gas station bathroom, called Rad from a pay phone, and drove up to Club 88 to look for Zii at the Bad Religion show. I parked my car somewhere along Pico Boulevard, stashed the .38 in the glove box, and walked toward the club. I stuffed my hands into the pockets of my jacket to hide how much they were shaking. My eyes were bloodshot to fuck. The guy working the door grinned at me. I must have looked high as a fucking kite. But really, I was just exhausted and wired at the same time. My face still looked like all nine circles of Hell. I took some meds.

I walked inside and Rad was waiting for me. He looked right at me, came straight over, and hugged me. Not a headbutt, not a loogie to the face, no backslap. Just an honest-to-God *hug.* "What the—?" I started to say. But he squeezed a little harder and I realized just how much I fucking needed it. I bought my arms up and hugged him back. Some dickless piece of shit shouted, "Get a room!" but we finally broke off the hug without shame.

"You seen Zii?" I asked him.

"Are you okay?" he asked, even though I had explained everything to him over the phone.

"Sunshine, lollipops, and rainbows. Where's Zii?"

"You don't seem—"

"Peachy. Fucking. Keen. Where is Zii?"

"Ain't here yet. If she is, I haven't seen her." He handed me a straight double whiskey in a rocks glass. I took the whole thing down in one gulp and went to look for her. There was no sign of Zii. During the breaks between sets, I asked around about her. Everyone knew her, or knew *of* her, but no one had seen her. Terrible possibilities swarmed in my head as I pushed through the crowd. I saw her standing toward the front and touched her shoulder. A girl who was definitely not Zii turned around.

"Sorry," I said. She turned back just as Bad Religion took the stage. They launched into it, and the crowd became bedlam. In the chaos, I spied a guy on the edge of the pit who was staring at me. I didn't recognize him. He had on a plaid shirt, torn jeans, Doc Martens, and close-cropped hair. He was dressed like a lot of other people there. But much older looking. He pushed his way into the pit and hit me, but not in a mosh-pit kind of way. The fucker was out to hurt me. And with a possible concussion, bruised ribs, and blood full of painkillers, it wouldn't have taken a whole helluva lot.

People hardly noticed and the band played on. He kept trying to get me to go down; he wanted to trample me and make it look like an accident. But one thing my time in the pit had taught me was how to keep my center of gravity firm. I managed to dodge a punch and throw one or two ineffectual ones myself, but it was taking everything I had to stand up. And even that ability was dwindling.

It had been enough to get Rad's attention. And just in time. The guy finally got my feet out from under me, but Rad plowed into him just before a bootheel crushed my forehead and then scooped me up from the floor.

My assailant bolted for the door and burst into the alley. I pushed my way through the crowd and ran outside. The guy was a ghost. My mind was in such a fog, I didn't see the battered skinhead coming. Rapunzel grabbed me and pinned me against the wall in the alley. He looked like hell. He was covered in blood that had been hastily wiped away by hand. I couldn't believe nobody had noticed him, but absolutely believed no one who had would have said anything. His eyes were as red as his hands.

"What did you do?" he whispered. If his teeth were any more clenched, they'd start cracking.

"What the hell happened?" I said. He slammed me against the wall again.

"What did you do?!" He didn't whisper that time. His voice shook, and his lip quivered. He'd been crying and was about to start again.

"Stuart," I said, using his real name. "Stuart. Listen to me. Tell me what happened." He took me off the wall and put his hands to his face. I went to put a reassuring hand on his shoulder, and he swatted it away.

"My boys," he said. "They're dead."

"How?"

"What the fuck have you gotten me into?!" He swung at me. I ducked aside, grabbing his arm. I couldn't have given less of a damn about his band of hate-filled jizz bags. But the shithead had information that could chart a course to salvation.

"*Talk* to me!" I shouted. "I will fill you in if you fill me in." I had my ideas. Everyone else connected to this had disappeared or been killed. If Brandy was on the hit list, of course Rapunzel was. I started to think about Rad. I started to think about the remaining Bad Chemicals.

I pulled a flask out of my jacket, took a pull, and handed it to Rapunzel. He took one twice as long, wiped his mouth, and handed it back. I took a second pull before pocketing it again.

"What the fuck is going on, Alex?" he asked. I sighed, put a cigarette in my mouth, offered him one. He took two. I lit mine with shaking hands and handed him the Zippo. I started to fill him in on everything so far. About halfway through, Rad found us. By the time I brought them both up to speed, the three of us had killed most of the pack.

"Your turn," I said. Rapunzel had told me that earlier that day he'd gotten a call from Senator Cromwell's office. He and his gang had been hired as security for them before. It was his day job, after all. The call was about a job doing security detail at a private event. A fundraising dinner. Rapunzel gathered his crew and showed up at the address, but when they got there … no event. No dinner. Just an empty building. And an ambush.

"I thought it was weird that the fundraiser was down on the docks, at first. But they'd told me on the phone it was a fundraiser for rebuilding the old industrial buildings. We figured we were early. But when we walked in, it didn't even look like anyone was planning on being there. These guys, they came out of nowhere. I didn't even hear 'em. This wasn't some gang. They were pros. We didn't … we couldn't …" He took a panicked drag from a cigarette. His eyes darted about.

"Did you get a look at any of 'em?"

"Naw. Ski masks. In the dark. They killed everybody."

Rad grabbed him by the collar and lifted him up.

"The fuck, man?!" Rapunzel shouted.

"If everyone's dead, why the hell are you still alive?" Rad said. It was a fair question. And I was too stressed, tired, and stupid to have thought of it. I'll blame the possible concussion.

"I ran."

"And they just let you go, huh? Is that it? Why would …" I looked at Rad, and he got quiet as the realization struck. This did not bode well. Rad put Rapunzel down. The three of us began looking over our shoulders.

"Okay," I whispered. We ducked into the nearby Mexican restaurant. The place was full of punks from the show, so we blended in just fine. My eyes pinballed around the room, looking for my assailant. Looking for Zii. I hoped she'd caught wind of all this and blown town. We each ordered an all-meat burrito and got our bearings. I got about three bites into mine when the nausea hit. I kept it down but stopped eating. It was Rapunzel who finally broke the silence.

"So. You going after Cromwell?" he said.

"Keep it down," I said.

"Yeah, well. I want in."

"Sorry," I said. "Wasn't that long ago you were working security for the guy."

"That was before. This is now."

"So much of our relationship can be summarized with those six words …"

"Shut it, DiMaggio."

"Whatever you say, *Kaminski*."

Rad stepped in. "Guys. Guys, look. Obviously, whatever is going on, we're all in this together."

"Only because Sam fucking Spade over here's gotta go stepping on all the wrong toes."

"Hey. What the fuck was I supposed to do? Jerry was murdered. Justice—"

"Ohhh. Justice?! Is *that* what this is all about?! And I suppose that sweet little piece of ass had nothing to do with it?"

I started to stand, but Rad put his arm across me. "Hey. Easy. Emotions are running high here. Let's not let our judgment get clouded. We lose our cool, we could wind up in a grave. Okay? They've come after all of us."

"Wait," I said. "When did they come after you?"

"After we got released from the station. I got home, someone was there. He got away from me but left with a limp."

"Why didn't you tell me?"

"I didn't want you to worry and lose focus."

"Give me a break," Rapunzel hissed.

"Will your nose do?" I asked. "Oh, that's right. I've done that already!" Silverware jumped when I slammed my hand on the table.

"Fine. I guess I'll just take all my damning evidence and go home." Rapunzel started to get up.

"You walk out that door, and you're dead," I said.

He paused. "That a threat?"

"No. It's a reminder," I said. He mulled it over for a couple ticks of the watch and sat back down. Fate had tied all of our ankles to cinder blocks and chucked them off the same pier. I placed a cigarette in my mouth and fumbled for my Zippo. Rapunzel lit it for me, but I didn't thank him. We weren't there yet.

"Well," said Rad. "What's our move?"

"We need to get somewhere we aren't being watched," I said. "Once we're more secure, Rapunzel here is gonna fill us in on what he knows. But first I need to find Zii. I can't get in touch with her, and I'm worried. We got to find her before she tries to go back to my place. She doesn't know it's compromised."

"Okay," Rapunzel said. "Let's just get to your car. Keep a lookout for tails. Three sets of eyes, blah blah blah."

"Let's move," said Rad. We paid up and headed out the door. Our heads were Disneyland teacups. Everywhere it was teenagers and punks. It was not an easy crowd for our enemies to blend in to. Thank fuck. Rapunzel grabbed the first guy over drinking age he saw and slammed him against a wall.

"You come to finish the job, asshole?" He got in the guy's face. The look of sheer terror and confusion in the man's face suggested he was either no assassin or *was* an assassin and had passed on a promising career as an Oscar-worthy actor.

"I, I dunno what yer talkin' about, m-man. I, I just wanted a t-taco."

"Down, boy," I said, pulling Rapunzel away. I'd seen that look in his eyes before, directed at me. He let go, but his eyes were locked and his nostrils flaring. "Piss off," I said to the stranger, who didn't waste a second following my suggestion. I guess he wasn't that desperate for a taco after all. When we got to my car, Rapunzel stopped me a moment.

"Wait here," he said. He got under the car, clearly looking for something. After a minute or two, he got up, dusted himself off, and said, "Clear." The most disturbing thing was that I wasn't surprised that he knew what to look for and where to look for it.

The drive back to my place had less dialogue than a Buster Keaton film. But we had a stop to make on the way.

Officer Mike was still sitting in a car outside my apartment. On his own. Something told me he was off the clock. Which is to say, *everything* so far had told me he was off the clock. I pulled up across the street from him. I immediately had his attention. The morning had come. I strolled up to his car, the newspaper we'd bought on the way there tucked under my arm. He saw me coming but made no attempt to get out of his car. I tapped on his window and he rolled it down.

"You got some huge balls," he started.

"Tell me about it. I can barely get my jeans on in the morning."

"You just keep fucking around where you shouldn't," he said.

"We got that much in common," I said. "Shame we couldn't be friends."

"What's that supposed to mean?" he said.

"Staking my place out all night, huh? Must be boring. I just figured I'd bring you something to read." I dropped the paper into his lap.

"What the hell is this?"

"It's a newspaper, Mikey."

"That's *Officer* to you."

"Is it, though?" I winked. Realization swept over his face as its color drained.

"What … ? What did you do?" He frantically opened the paper. He was all over the front page.

Corrupt Police Officer Caught on Camera with Underage Boys, by Aaron Craig

His breathing became erratic and he started dry-heaving. His face started becoming a deep red and he reached for his gun. A call came in over the squawk box but he ignored it. He pointed his gun at me and I ducked away as he fired. People were out walking their dogs, jogging, and sitting on porches. A woman screamed. Officer Mike tried to get out of the car and stumbled into the street, still huffing and heaving and red. He could barely stand and used the car to support himself.

"I'll ki—" He heaved again. "I'll kill—" Again a heave. A little bile dribbled out this time. Other cops started to arrive. First one squad car, then two, until five surrounded us. Not a moment too soon. Rapunzel had timed his phone call well.

"Drop the gun, Mike!" came over a speaker. "It's over. We know everything! Put it down." Cops were behind their open doors, their guns on him, but my hands were the ones up. This wasn't my first mosh pit. Mike just looked at me. Pale again. Tears streaming. Looking too pitiful to inspire pity.

He looked me in the eyes when he did it. Right in the eyes.

It all happened so fast it was hard to say what happened first. From where I was standing, it was almost as if one of the cops sensed it before it happened. Maybe it happened all at once. But the cop shouted, "Miiiiike!"

Mike brought the gun to his own head and pulled the trigger. The left side of his head burst. Time slowed. I saw the bullet leaving his head. I saw the vapor trail. I swear I did. He collapsed to the ground. The whole time he never took his eyes off me.

As the bullet went through his head, one thought went through mine.

One less thing to worry about.

So, what does that say about me?

28

As I walked down the steps of the police station, I stopped a moment to light a cigarette. My first in what seemed like days. Fucking pigs didn't offer me any when I was in interrogation. I hadn't been arrested, so it really wasn't "interrogation," it was questioning. I was a witness, or more accurately, I was the victim, but because of who I was, they treated me like a fucking suspect. Of course they did. They made me wait in that room for hours, hoping that I'd sit there stewing. What they'd really given me was a chance to get some sleep. The fog had cleared, somewhat. My head still ached, but I wrote it off as a lack of coffee. Cops hadn't offered me any of that, either. The cops in the bullpen scowled at me as I walked out, and I gave them a wave that was really a middle finger.

I had done their job for them, basically. Naturally, they wouldn't have seen it that way. I exposed, at best, their incompetence. The more accurate way of putting it would be to say that I had exposed the fact that they'd turned the other way or even aided and abetted corruption and pedophilia among their ranks. Internal Affairs was all over the station when I was brought in. They were questioning everybody, and I had to hope that the right paths were followed. Nash had been compromised by the piece as well. He, however, was still at large, and he was likely to come through this unscathed. In the meantime, it gave him something else to worry about other than me. Architect of his discomfort though I was. I sure as shit couldn't go back to his place. I had no reason to see him anyway, and I just had to hope he wouldn't come looking for me. They didn't ask me about Brandy, and I didn't expect to see anything in the paper. The poor girl was being swept under the rug. I hoped, though, that by driving her killer to suicide, I had provided something resembling justice. Even if it was only revenge.

With the news about Officer Mike out there—the pederasty, the corruption, the Guardia connections—all hell had broken loose. Riot control was holding people back from the police station. People were shouting and lifting picket signs. Police were rounding up everyone who looked vaguely punk or a few shades left of center. Cops were being assaulted, and not just by punks. They had known about Mike's behavior and helped cover it up. Well, some did. Others were found guilty by association in the court of public opinion. To see it on the news, you'd think the city was at war. It sure as hell seemed that way out here too.

Seeing the chaos playing out in the station and on the streets, it dawned on me that this was exactly what Jerry had wanted. It was the revolution he'd always ranted about while pacing manically onstage like a caged lion. Even in death his chess game with Cromwell continued. I had triggered this by outing Officer Mike. Pawn takes pawn.

I pushed my way through the crowd to the street, where Rad was waiting for me in my car. Rad climbed out of the driver's side door and leaned on the roof of the car.

"You want to drive?" he asked.

"Fuck no."

"Okay." He climbed back in and started the car. I got in the passenger side and pulled my cheap Wayfarers out of the glove box and slipped them on. Light sensitivity, it seemed, was still going to be a whole thing. "Get some food?" he asked. I hadn't been able to eat my burrito the day before and was feeling lightheaded. The cig wasn't doing its job curbing my appetite.

"Sure," I said. "I could murder a burger right now."

"So, is that it, then?" Rad asked between handfuls of fries.

"What's what, then?" I asked, mouth full of beef. Not the

best of manners on either of us, but we weren't exactly the finishing-school type. But nor did we have the desire to dine at any Ritz-Carltons, so I didn't see any problems. I was just glad I was keeping food down.

"We took Officer Mike down. IA should follow up the chain, right?"

"This isn't over," I said. "Not yet. We still got to find the girl."

"Zii?"

"Her too, I guess. I meant the senator's daughter. Lisa. Apparently, she had been hanging around Jerry."

"Lisa?" Rad mulled that name over. "Lisa. Lisa … I don't know any Lisas. Least not from the scene."

"Think about it," I said.

"I … just did?" he said. He was confused enough to stop eating for a moment. But he started eating again as I started talking.

"If you were a senator's teenage daughter and you were hanging around a bunch of punk rockers who hated your dad's guts and were very open and public about that hatred, would you be using your *real* name?" I asked.

He finished chewing and swallowed. "I *don't* use my real name," he said before washing down his food with some Sprite.

"And you got a helluva lot less to hide," I said.

He pointed at me with the hand holding his drink. "You've got a point there. Any theories about who she could be?"

"She was an underage teenage girl who hung around Jerry."

"That doesn't narrow it down. Especially if we're talking pre-Zii."

"Maybe. Maybe not," I said.

"What do you mean?" he asked.

I sighed. "He wasn't exactly loyal," I said. "He wasn't

exactly ... good." I expected Rad to get belligerent. Rad was a
huge Bad Chemicals fan. In his world, in our world, I had just
spoken blasphemy. He was just calm. He didn't yell or curse;
he didn't even look angry or hurt. He just nodded quietly.

"You boys want any dessert?" our waitress asked.

"Coffee's fine," I said. She looked to Rad, who just turned
his coffee mug up. She came back and filled us both up. He
added some sugar and cream to his. I just stared at mine.
The music on the jukebox faded to nothing, drowned out by
Rad shaking sugar packets. Or so it seemed.

"I just ..." I stopped a moment to sip black coffee and get
my words together. "I just been learning a lot lately. About
the man behind the scenes, y'know?"

"I think," Rad said.

"Jerry sucked," I said. I just came out with it. "He was
fucking terrible, and the more I investigate his death, the
more I've dug into his life ... I ... I can't believe I looked up
to that guy. I can't believe I could have someone like *that* as
a friend. How did I miss all of that?"

"What did you learn?" Rad said, still calm. Calm in a way
that was hard to read. I looked up from my coffee and our
eyes met. It was only then that I realized I was on the verge
of tears. Something about looking another person in the eyes
makes you so much more conscious of your own.

"Do you want to ...," I started.

"Yes," he said flatly. I took a deep breath, sipped my
coffee, and looked up at Rad. I told him about the sexual
assault, the drug dealing, the blackmail, the cheating, the
song stealing, the attempted murder of Joe Public, the abuse,
and the theft. When I was done, he pounded his fist on the
table. I will admit, in that moment, I was scared of my friend.
I had torn down statues in his mind. He hit the table three
more times.

"Hey!" the waitress shouted.

Rad quickly moved toward the door. I threw money on

the table and went after him. He was pacing on the street, balling and unballing fists.

"Rad …," I started.

"Stop! Just … *stop!*"

I stopped. For a few beats at least. I had to kill that silence. "I just thought you should know."

"Yeah, well, I know now. Thanks for that." His words hit me like a snakebite. He sat on the curb. He buried his face in his hands. When I thought it was safe, and I couldn't tell you how long that was, I sat next to him. I lit two cigarettes. He reached for one.

"What are you doing?" I said. "These are both for me." That got a chuckle out of him. Progress. I handed him the pack and lighter. He copied my two-at-once idea, then handed the pack and lighter back.

"The worst part …," he started. "The worst part is that … shit, I dunno what the worst part even is. I mean, obviously the abuse and sexual assault toward fans and women and stuff. Those are the worst bits. But, like, I worked for that guy. I *admired* him. So …" His voice broke. "So, what does that say about me?"

I didn't know what to say to that. I'd been struggling with that question myself, so I sure as shit didn't know what to say to someone else.

He took off his denim vest and stared at the Bad Chemicals patch on the back for a long time. I took a safety pin out of my jacket and handed it to him. He took it, undid the stitches, and ripped the patch off. He chucked it into a sewer drain.

"Guess I got some space to fill now," he said.

We got into my car, this time with me in the driver's seat.

"So, what now? Does Jerry even deserve justice at this point?" he asked. Sixty-four thousand big ones to whoever had the answer to that question.

"Doesn't fucking matter. This isn't about Jerry anymore. I'm finishing this either way," I said. "Because it's the only way we're getting clear of it."

"And how the hell are we gonna do that?"

"We find the girl," I said.

A shit-eating grin suddenly filled Rad's face.

"The fuck you smilin' about?"

"You said, 'we,'" he said, still grinning like some simple-minded, canary-devouring cat.

"Shut the fuck up."

"I'm just so happy," he said, as if I'd just proposed to him or something. Fucker even pantomimed wiping away a single tear. Who does shit like that? My best friend, apparently. He bugged the shit out of me sometimes. But what ate at me more was that I knew I needed him. I've never been too keen on needing anybody. That's why I'd bailed on home at seventeen. I'd finally admitted to Rad and to myself that this was not something I could do alone. And Rad, being Rad, was going to milk that until we were old, gray, and leeching off the system to play bingo. Truth was, that annoying son of a bitch is the only man I would ever really love. I started to think maybe it was time I told him that.

"Fuck you," I said.

"*We* make such a good team, don't *we?*"

"Rad ..." My tone was a warning.

"Fuck you. You love it."

I snorted and shook my head. It was all I could do not to cry.

29

I wasn't really sure what to do next. Most of what I knew about detective work I'd picked up from books, movies, and television. In those, they have all these dots they just can't seem to connect, then some seemingly random thing triggers this eureka moment and, like Archimedes in the bathtub, they suddenly have the whole thing figured out. Which is all a steaming pile of horseshit. Truth is, it's mostly dumb luck. And considering that in the last several days I'd been arrested, beaten, kidnapped, beaten again, and shot at, been the cause of a senseless brutal murder, and fallen into the crosshairs of some of the most dangerous and powerful men in the state of California, I wasn't going to be placing any bets anytime soon. Yeah, I could definitely rule out luck.

I tried to think of the younger girls I knew from the scene. But the truth was, I didn't spend much time hanging around the *really* young people on the scene. There were kids as young as twelve at shows or milling around the scene in general, but I was in my early twenties. I had no interest in or business hanging around twelve- and fourteen-year-olds. I wish to hell I could say that about every guy on the scene, but let's face it, countercultures can draw in some scummy fuckers. Not to mention, recent years had seen a shift in the scene. It was far more macho than two or three years ago. It used to be a more woman- and gay-friendly scene, but a lot of the women I'd come up with had moved on to new wave and rockabilly revival. They'd traded in their Bags for Stray Cats. Couldn't say I blamed them. In 1981 more and more of the new punks, surfers mostly, were the same people who'd been kicking the shit out of us in 1977. The violence had turned it into a boys' club. Jerry, even with his endless list of faults, had at least tried to maintain some of the old ways. Or, at least, he'd tried to maintain that appearance.

But I should have known. This is fucking Hollywood, after all. The city's whole legacy is facades. Even when a city is built around the industry of creating overpriced illusions, we act surprised at the realization that the wool has been pulled over our eyes. It's not confined to the movie sets. It permeates everything. The people, the culture, the politics, and the economy. Eventually the smoke clears, the mirrors get nudged, the truth reveals itself, and we gasp and clutch our pearls and padlock pendants, having completely forgotten the lesson we learned the last time, and the time before that, and the time before that. Our whole lives are spent pretending to be surprised. It's a habit we carry from womb to tomb.

"Where'd you go just now?" Rad asked. We were back at my place, which had been scrubbed spotless. Frankly, it had never been cleaner. The conspirators had done good work. Conspicuously inconspicuous. He was lounging on my mattress. I was sitting at my desk next to the phone. I guess I was hoping Zii would call. I wasn't sure if my place was safe. Actually, I was pretty sure it wasn't. But with riots breaking out and me being a poster child for it, getting around the city wasn't much of an option. So, I sat at home. I was tired of trying to hunt people down, and I figured I'd sit where they could find me.

"Huh?" I said, coming back from my internal monologue. "I just feel like an idiot."

"Don't worry," Rad said. "You are." I could practically hear the canned laughter.

"I don't know what's going on with me," I said. "I'm just looking back and realizing how ignorant I've been. Thinking about my own behavior. I don't know what's different." We both sat in thought for a moment.

"How long since your last drink?" Rad asked. Surprisingly, I actually had to think about it.

"Uh, shit," I said. "I dunno, actually. A day or two?" We both looked at each other.

"Dude," Rad said. "You're *sober*." I tilted my head and folded my arms, tucking my tongue between teeth and lower lip.

"Mmm," I grunted.

"Should probably give it a rest then," he said, "at least until you recover from the concussion."

"*Possible* concussion," I said.

"Sure, right. *Possible* concussion. Either way, probably not a great idea to drink while on those pain meds. Or, like, when people are trying to kill you. In fact, can we make that a new rule? No drinking when people are trying to kill us?"

"Fine," I said. I took out some of the pain meds from the doctor and took them with the glass of lukewarm tap water on my desk. I sighed. Rad took the whiskey bottle on the desk away. I dunno what he did with it and I wasn't going to ask. "What happened to Rapunzel?" I asked.

"I dunno," Rad said. "After the whole thing with Officer Mike, he just kinda vanished. I gotta imagine he's in hiding somewhere. Could have hopped a plane out of the country, for all I know."

"Can't say I blame him," I said.

"Want to go to the airport?" Rad asked.

"To look for Rapunzel? Or to bail?"

"Either or." He shrugged.

"I want to take a shower," I said. I realized I'd been wearing the same clothes for a number of days now. I was starting to get a bit crusty. I went to the bathroom, stripped down, and sat under the hot water for a few minutes without doing anything. I twisted it to cold and sat under that, then brought it back to steaming, then back to cold. It's a trick for hangovers. Shock the body. Hit reset. *Get it together*, I thought. My mind drifted to encounters with Jerry. As things became clear to me, I tried to think more toward the past. I'd been looking at all the stuff he'd hidden that I'd failed to think about, and how I'd never reflected on the stuff that had always been right there in front of me. What I said about learning about detective work from TV and movies? Well, I guess I'd ignored the trope where the hero detective gets chastised for being "too close to this."

Jerry had *It*. Capital *I*. His charisma was intoxicating. His passion was infectious, and when he gave you a compliment, you wouldn't even realize that was exactly what you had needed to hear. He could make men in their twenties and thirties feel like fourteen-year-old girls. I thought back to the first time I'd met Jerry. It was back in 1978 at the Masque, when that was still a thing. I was adding some graffiti to the wall. At first, it was his exploding liberty spikes that caught my attention. Rings pierced the brows above steel-blue eyes, one on each side. He was pale, and it was hard to tell if he was lean or just malnourished. He flashed what was, if not for one offset tooth, a perfect smile.

"Nice," he said. And, God help me, I actually blushed. I felt myself blush. This was before the Bad Chemicals era, but he had It, even then. Most scumbags do, I suppose. At least the particularly scummy ones. How else could they get away with it for so long?

He and I became casual friends after that. We'd talk politics and drink together. One time we took some speed and pushed a flaming dumpster down a hill. It got pinned on the Germs. I realized now that was his intention all along. To make Darby Crash look like an asshole. Or, you know, more of an asshole.

I thought of every time a young girl hung on his arm. I said nothing. I thought it was none of my business. Wasn't that just being a rock star? Weren't they old enough to make their own choices? If his actions spoke to his character, I started to feel like my silence spoke volumes about mine.

I never considered us *close* friends. But I guess I thought we were closer than we were. I wasn't part of his inner circle, although it seemed even his own bandmates were on a need-to-know basis and didn't need to know. It was becoming apparent that all that talk of revolution was bullshit anyway. At that point, I was glad I didn't know him better. But I still felt complicit. And, perhaps, even guilty of lesser crimes myself.

30

I got out of the shower and felt refreshed, clearheaded. Rad was sitting at my desk sipping day-old coffee when I emerged from the bathroom.

"What's the plan?" he asked.

"We find the girl. Lisa."

"So you keep saying. I'm just not sure why that's our problem."

"When the senator was doing this to my face, he said something about Jerry turning his daughter against him. So, I gotta figure she must know something. We don't know what name she went by when she was hanging around the scene. We'll have to find a picture of her. Or find someone who can ID her. Rapunzel used to work security for Cromwell. Maybe he can. You find Rapunzel and I'll head to the library and skim old newspapers for any pictures of the senator and his whole family."

"Okay. There's that Alex Damage confidence we've been missing!" Rad said. "Let's do it then." He got up and stuck out his hand, palm down.

"No," I said.

"Come on," he said.

"This isn't intramural soccer, Rad."

"Do it."

"Ugh. Fine." I put my hand on top of his.

"Three, two, one, break!" he chanted.

I once again found myself sitting in the fluorescent light of the Central Library's basement. I'd been down there for the better part of the day. I had shown up when they'd opened, and the fact that my stomach sounded like a dogfight suggested that it was getting on dinnertime.

Very few of the senator's stories featured anything about his family. Maybe two had a photo of him with his family, and neither featured an adolescent girl. Each article mentioned that Lisa Cromwell was not pictured, as she was attending boarding school. He'd mentioned keeping her out of the public eye. I had to figure he would have been ashamed to be pictured with a daughter dressed in black with dyed hair and wild makeup. Me? I would have been proud. But maybe that's why I'm not a senator.

I took a break and went to the lobby to call Zii from a pay phone. Nobody answered. I called the other number she gave me, the one I hadn't tried yet. It was a messenger service. I told the stoned-sounding girl on the other end to have her call Alex.

"Any idea when she'll check in?" I asked.

"I don't know, sir," she said in a spaced monotone.

"When did she check in last?"

"I'm afraid I can't give out that information about our clients. It's policy."

I have to admit I have a certain level of respect for people who can be loaded and manage to remain professional. Which reminded me that I was flying dry. I reached for the flask in my jacket pocket. Rad would have been disappointed in me, but Rad wasn't there. Not that it would have mattered. The flask was as empty as I was.

By the time they kicked me out of the library, I wasn't any closer than I had been when I'd started. Senator Cromwell had gone to great lengths to keep his daughter out of the limelight. He'd tried to sweep her under the rug, and now he wanted to find her. And he was putting people in the ground in the attempt.

As I reached the bottom of the library steps, I lit a

cigarette. I'd barely closed my Zippo before a Town Car pulled up and a Black man in a suit, sunglasses, and a gold earring emerged from the back seat. He stood well over six feet and was as wide as I was tall. He looked the wrong kind of familiar.

"Alex Damage," he said, "put that out and get in the car."

"Heeeey, you," I said. "If it isn't ... um, y'know, I've forgotten your name. I wanna say ... Gary?"

"Greg."

"Right. Greg."

"Eddie Nash would like to speak with you."

"You tell Eddie Nash that he can—"

The car window rolled down.

"—expect me to comply fully!" I finished. "Eddie! Hiya! Been a while."

"Get in the fucking car," he said.

"Yeah, sure. Of course." I took one last long draw and flicked away the cigarette.

"You are going to litter in my city?" Eddie said.

"I mean ..."

"Pick up the *fucking* cigarette butt!" he screamed.

"Yeah. Sorry. I'll ..." I went over and picked up the butt, killed the cherry on my boot, and tossed it into a nearby trash can. I did this because when the most dangerous man in the state of California tells you to pick up the fucking cigarette butt, you pick up the fucking cigarette butt.

I got in the car and Eddie immediately slapped me with his ring hand. Several times.

"Fuck! Eddie! You turnin' that ring in, man?"

Eddie turned his ring back out. "My father told me to never hit someone with a closed fist." Eddie then hit me in the face with a closed fist. I suppose I should have seen it coming.

"I was about to come see you," I lied.

"Alex, Alex, Alex ...," he started. "The thing that hurts the most is that I liked you. You were such a fun guy, so I do not understand why you would betray me in this way."

"I can explain," I said.

"You have no idea how many times I have heard this only to be disappointed."

"What? Like fifty?" I said. He stared at me hard. "*More* than fifty? Seventy-five! One hundred?"

"That humor of yours. I found it charming. Before you lied. Before you stole from me."

"I may have lied. But I gave you the money you sent me to collect."

"What you have taken was much more valuable than money. You took certain … information."

"Look, if this is about what happened with Officer Mike, I didn't—"

"I do not care about Officer Mike. He was a liability. With his exposure and death, I have been done a favor."

"Even if the photos were from your house?" I asked.

He shrugged. "My house looks like many houses. Besides, they did not blame Jack Nicholson for Polanski. I will be fine. No, I mean the other information."

"What other information?" I asked.

"I am in business with certain people. Some of these people, well, to stay in business with them requires persuasion. Information is power, you see. People want to know things. And people don't want *other* people to know things."

"You don't have copies?"

"Of *course* I have copies. A man does not turn a falafel cart into an empire by being a fool."

"So …"

"So. This kind of power, it does not divide. It only works if only *I* have this information. Some other man, if he uses it, if he gives this information away, my power is less."

"Okay," I started, "I get it. You have blackmail material and you want the exclusive publishing rights. But I didn't take your blackmail material. Honest. Like I said. I can explain."

"Yes. So you have said. Do not disappoint."

"It was Jerry," I said.

"If what you say is true, Jerry took several pages from a ledger in my office. This contained sensitive information about certain parties ..."

"Senator Cromwell?" I asked.

"Certain. Parties."

"Eddie," I said, "it's going to be hard for me to be helpful if you're not honest with me."

"Honesty!" His eyes bugged out and he foamed at the mouth. "You, of all people, speak to me of honesty?!"

"It's true. I have not been honest with you. I was trying to find out who killed Jerry Rash. Certain information came my way, and I didn't think it was an accident or a suicide. And yes, I used you. I followed the drugs to some of your dealers. Then, when I came to talk to you, I realized he worked for you, and I used that as a chance to dig around in his life. What I found out is that a lot of people had good reasons to kill him. Senator Cromwell was one of those people. See, I think Jerry stole the blackmail material you had so that he could take Cromwell down. At first, I thought he knew Jerry had it, but he's just looking for his daughter. So, I didn't take it. Jerry took it."

Eddie stroked his ring while he considered everything I had laid out. I sat there and wondered if I had said too much. Actually, I was damn certain that I had said *entirely* too much, and I was just anticipating what the consequences of that might be.

"I do not trust you," he said. "However, I trusted Jerry less. He also took some ... home movies. You find these things. You bring them to me. You hope I believe you when you tell me there are no copies. Then I will decide if I should kill you."

I sighed. "I'm gonna have to think about that."

"What?"

"Here's the thing, Eddie," I said, scratching my bruised face. "I have to work under the impression that you're going to kill me anyway. That's not really a great motivator for me. You've got me in your vehicle, and your boy Friday here has what I hope is a gun digging into my side. I'm at your mercy. And I'm really fucking tired, Eddie. I am so. Goddamn. Tired. I haven't had a decent night's sleep all week. A week in which I've been beaten, arrested, kidnapped, beaten some more, shot at, had many very unkind words spoken about my character, found out that the guy I looked up to is a horrendous piece of shit, slogged through countless old newspapers, and bottled up the suicidal levels of guilt *you* should be feeling for Brandy's death. Oh, right, and two of the most powerful men in the state want me dead. Yourself included. So, you know what, Eddie? Fuck you. Kill me."

"And mess up this interior?" Eddie said. "No. I won't kill you here. Driver. Take us to the studio."

The rest of the drive was long and awkward. Silences are much more loaded on the way to your inevitable murder. Eddie just stared at me. He was even scarier sober. Sure, he was unpredictable high, but at least then, letting me live was a possibility. His bodyguard looked to him for a signal. I tried to glance wistfully out the window. I would have liked to think that on the way to my death my mind would have been more reflective. Maybe a somber and damn beautiful song would play in my head as I heard the voices of people saying things that had stuck with me. But none of that happened. The only things I could think about were Eddie Nash's eyes burrowing into the back of my head and how sticky the Naugahyde felt.

31

"The studio" was, well, just that. A studio. This one appeared to be set up in an old warehouse or factory. A security guard was watching the door, and I thought I recognized him as one of the bouncers at the Starwood. A burly thirty-something white guy with old-school sailor tattoos and long, curly hair. I'd couldn't recall his name, but he'd caught me crowd-surfing a few times. Never threw me out, though. He'd attended Jerry's memorial service too.

"Anyone filming today, Nick?" Greg asked.

"Nah," Nick said, "last of 'em just went home. I was locking up."

"Let us in, then fuck off," Greg said. Nick saw Eddie, now the one holding the gun to me, swallowed, and did what he was told.

Inside was a wide-open space, and what few windows there were were high off the ground and covered in so much unwashed filth as to render the need for curtains irrelevant. The smells of industry had been replaced with the smell of sweat and cum. There were well-lit corners, sectioned off with beds and mattresses. There was a faux fireplace with a bearskin rug. Again, I should have been thinking about the gun pressed up against my medulla oblongata, but I was thinking about how one goes about cleaning protein stains out of bear fur. Your life, as it turns out, does not actually flash before your eyes in the moments before death. Really random thoughts do. I guess it doesn't kick in until the split second the trigger is pulled.

They walked me through the main room and down a back hallway. Some doors to the rooms had been left open.

Each had its own theme going. One looked like the Middle Ages, all faux stone walls and wooden furniture with straw mattresses. One had a Moroccan vibe, with hookahs and pillows. There was a stereotypical teepee, with a fire in the middle, animal skins, and various sexual positions painted on the walls. Another seemed to pull inspiration from Egypt. But it was the PI's office set that caught my eye. None of the rooms or spaces were being used. I guess even the adult film industry keeps regular hours and takes days off. Probably not Sundays, though. I didn't even know what day it was. Without a typical nine-to-five, my only real reason to keep track of the days was to know when shows were.

We walked down into the basement, which, in a place like this, raised extra alarms. The walls were covered with leather paddles and rubber toys of varying imaginative shapes. The farther down the hall we walked, the more twisted the fetishes, the more menacing looking the toys. Naturally, we walked all the way down to the last door. I was shoved into the room and chained to a bed that was clearly stained with more than cum. There aren't many times I've said to myself, "I hope that's menstrual blood."

"It is not," said Eddie Nash, before squinting. "Not all of it."

After they finished locking me into place, one of his men turned a crank so that the bed would stand upright. As I was being raised up, I had to wonder how many times a grown man can be kidnapped in a week before it constituted a pattern of behavior. Sweet fucking Christ, what a week it had been. I had to wonder why they didn't just fucking kill me. Why chain me to the bed in a fetish room in the basement of a porn studio? *What could possibly be the point of this?* I wondered. It occurred to me, pretty quickly, that I was asking myself questions I didn't actually want the answers to. Professional hazard, I guess.

"You probably are wondering why have I not killed you yet?" Eddie said, as if reading my mind.

THIS RANCID MILL   223

"The thought had occurred to me. But I always figured I would die while chained to a bed in a porn studio," I said. "Maybe that was just wishful thinking."

"Funny guy." He pointed at me, wagging his finger as he spoke. "That is why this will be so fucking hard to kill you. You made me laugh. But you betrayed me, so I have to not only kill you but make an example, you know this?"

I looked him dead in the eyes. "Yeah. Brandy mentioned something about that."

"Hmm. That was shameful. Lovely girl. Officer Hernandez would get carried away. But this was not why he was a problem."

His men started to bring in cameras and lighting equipment. *Well, fuck*, I thought. I already knew where this was going, but I was afraid to interrupt him further.

"We will make a film, yes? And I will mail it to everybody who I am in business with. This way they will *know* what it means to betray me. Maybe, if they are thinking about it, they will think twice."

I nodded. "Makes sense. Glad to be of assistance."

The cameras and lights shone on me. The lights were hot, and I could barely see the surgical cart roll in. There were standard surgical tools. Scalpels and clamps and the like. But they were joined by corkscrews, claw hammers, pliers, and a pair of wire cutters.

"Admiring the props?" Eddie asked.

"What?" I said. "No dentist drill?"

"Mr. Alex Damage," Eddie said, "it was a pleasure. I leave you in the care of my friends now." After Eddie left, there was a brief exchange of dialogue in the hallway. Three men entered the room. One wore a black beret, a black turtleneck, and black, thick-framed glasses. His black boots came halfway up his shins. And where one might have expected black pants, he just wore a baby blue Speedo with a dark blue male symbol on the crotch. He carried an acoustic megaphone and a folded director's chair, which he snapped open with one hand. He sat, set down his megaphone, crossed his right leg over his left, formed a steeple with his hands, and brought them to his mouth. His desperate attempts at cliché told me he was the director.

His coworker was a large man in surgical scrubs and a gimp mask. It didn't take a genius to guess his role. The third guy looked pretty normal. Plaid shirt, jeans, backward baseball cap. He moved over to the camera.

The director formed a rectangle with his hands and held them out to me, framing the shot. He snapped his fingers and made a quick gesture to the cameraman, who brought the camera in a bit closer to me. Finally, the director rose. He paced around me and stroked his chin. He did several laps. I'm not sure how many. I wasn't counting. Who would? No one spoke. Not even me. Which was kind of hard to believe. Eventually, he reached over and grabbed my chin and twisted my face hard toward the camera.

"Now," he finally said, his breath reeking of clove cigarettes and gin, "you will look at the camera and you will say, tears in eyes, 'My name is …'"—he paused a moment while he checked a note written on his hand—"'Alex Damage. I am a dirty, rotten traitor. I betrayed the trust of my business partner. This is what happens to those who betray.'"

I started, "My name is—"

He slapped me hard across the face. "Not yet!" he shrieked. "You speak when I say, '*Action!*' Amateur!" His accent was some kind of central European. But he couldn't seem to decide if he wanted to go with French, Italian, or German. So it drifted between the three.

"I'm sorry," I said. "I've never been in a snuff film before."

He slapped me again. Then twice more. Open-palmed. Then he strutted back to the chair. He picked up his megaphone, which was highly unnecessary considering the size of the set, and shouted, "Ac-*tion!*"

I turned toward the camera. "My name is Alex Damage. I am a dirty, rotten traitor. I—"

"*Cut!*" he shrieked into the megaphone. He walked over and slapped me twice more. "I said *tearful!* Tearful. Have some regret in your voice, for *God's* sake." He walked back to the chair, lifted the megaphone. "Ac-*tion!*"

"My name is Alex—"

"Cut! Cry! You must cry! Ac-*tion!*"

I put as much tremble in my voice as I possibly could. "My name—"

"*Cut!*" he shrieked again. He walked over to me and grabbed my face with both hands, squeezing with a surprising amount of force for someone so scrawny. "*Faaaaake!*" he screamed, long and drawn out, spitting into my face. "I don't believe you. *No one* will believe you! If no one believes you, what could possibly be the point of this endeavor?"

"I guess I'm just not all that invested in this project," I said.

"*Again!* And this time do it *right!*" He sat back down. Megaphone. "Ac-*tion!*"

"My name Alex Damage. I am a dirty, rotten traitor. I betrayed the trust of my business partner. This is what happens to those who betray."

He sat there quietly for a moment, fingers framing his mouth. "Cut," he said quietly. He walked over to me, megaphone in hand. He held it up so close, my head was practically in the cone.

"*Wrong!*" he shouted. He hit me with the megaphone, drawing blood. He tossed the megaphone across the room, and it landed on the floor by his chair. "Allow me to motivate you," he began. "That man over there is going to do terrible things to you soon. Awful, awful things. He will start with the wire cutters." He snapped. The gimp surgeon lifted the wire cutters. The director ripped open my shirt. "He will clip you!" He pinched me. Hard. "Over and over and over again."

He pinched me again and again with each *over*. "He will do this as a warmup. After that, I do not know. He likes to, how you say, 'play jazz'? Maybe he slices you. Maybe he uses this." He picked up the corkscrew and tapped my crotch with it. "I can't say. I love to work with him because he always surprises me." Tears began to well up in my eyes. "I see you understand now?"

"Yes." My voice cracked. Even I barely heard it.

"Good," he said, dropping the corkscrew on the table. "Use it." He walked over to his chair, picked up his megaphone, sat down, crossed his legs, leaned one arm on the armrest.

"Ac-*tion!*"

I somehow managed to blubber my way through "My name is Alex Damage. I am a dirty, rotten traitor. I betrayed the trust of my business partner. This is what happens to those who betray." After I got through it, I wept. Finally, he stood up and applauded.

"Yes!" he shouted. "Yes! Cut! Yes!" He walked over to me, grabbed my face, and kissed me on the mouth. "Excellent! Perfection!" He walked back to his chair. "Let's get some clipping in, then we will break for lunch, yes?" He turned to his cameraman and the surgeon. "I think we should already have him standing over there when we start rolling. This way he just seems to appear. Much creepier that way, don't you think? I want an *otherworldly* feel to this film."

Gimp Surgeon walked over to me.

"Good, yes," said the director. "Pick up the wire cutters. Stand shoulders back. Let us see how tall you are. How big. Alex, please look to the camera, same place as before." He came over and turned my head. "Yes, here." He went back. "Okay, when I say, 'Action,' I want you to slowly reach over to Alex and clip him just below his left nipple." He turned to the cameraman and said, "Slowly zoom in on the spot where he clips. Left nipple. Everyone ready? Ac-*tion!*"

Pain is a funny thing. Not ha-ha funny. Funny like, strange and difficult to understand. The brain can only take so much. Then it shuts down. Like an overheated engine. Same goes for fear. You hear a lot of talk about the fight-or-flight response. But there's also freeze. This is just a somewhat long-winded way of saying that somewhere around the third clip, I blacked out. Some might say that makes me a pussy. Those people have never had anyone clip their nipples with wire cutters. A loud crashing sound from the hallway brought me back to reality.

"*Cut!*" the director screamed. "Robert! Go see what that was! Find who to blame for wasting my precious film!"

The cameraman stepped out in the hall. "A camera fell down the stairs," he said.

"What? How could that happen?" the director shouted. "Go see! Go see!"

Robert the cameraman did as he was told, just like a good cameraman should. Suddenly there was a great racket and a scream. Robert stumbled back into the room, bleeding profusely, a broken piece of a movie camera sticking out of his shoulder. He collapsed on the floor. The director gave a scream.

"What the fuck?!" he shouted, no trace of an accent. Least of all European.

Gimp Surgeon picked up a knife from the table and charged toward the door. Just then, Rad stepped in holding a boom-mic pole, broken and pointed at the end. He ducked down and drove the pole right into Gimp Surgeon's gut. The gimp fell to the ground and writhed on the floor with muffled shrieks. The director came at Rad with surprising speed.

"You motherfucker!" He struck Rad in the face. Rad managed to block the next one. But when he took his own swing, the director moved in, got his arm over Rad's, and locked his arm into place and headbutted him. Rad managed to move his head down in time to avoid a shot to the nose, and they cracked foreheads. This was more dazing for the director, and Rad managed to break free. He tried to grapple the director to the ground, but the spry little bastard was as slippery as he was quick. Rad couldn't quite get a hold on him. Finally, after taking a few strikes, Rad managed to grab the director and toss him to the ground. The director tried to crawl for the door, but Rad got on top of him from behind, got his arms around the director's head, and snapped his neck.

I was trying to say, "Thank you," but the words wouldn't come out. Rad searched the body of the director and found the keys. He unlocked my arms, and before he could get to my legs, I threw my arms around him and sobbed. He held me a moment. The way he sniffed, I could tell he knew I had shit myself, but he didn't say anything.

"I'm sorry," I said through sniffles, my voice shaking. "I, I pooped …"

"It's okay," he said, holding me. "It's okay. You're okay."

I just nodded.

"Let's get the fuck out of here and we'll get you cleaned up. Sound good?"

I just nodded again. It sounded great. But we didn't move for a few minutes. First, I just needed to be held. And to sleep.

32

I came to in a hospital bed. Which was odd. I didn't remember blacking out again. But I guess that's kind of how blacking out works. In a three-day span, I had probably used more legitimate medical care than I had in the previous three years. Jesus. Rad was sitting next to my bed.

"How did I get here?" I asked.

"Well, good morning to you too," he said. "I brought you here."

"You brought me to a hospital?" I asked.

"Uh, yeah. You should have seen yourself. Actually, on second thought, it's probably better that you didn't." He lifted the lid off the food tray and spun the tray table toward me.

"How long has this been here?"

"Not long," he said.

"That's vague," I said. "How long is 'not long'? Not long to one person might be—"

"Two days," he said. "Well, you have. Food's from last night."

"I've been here two days?!"

He took a bite of what looked like peach cobbler. "Yeah, it's still fine." He sat back down and turned to the TV on the little platform by the ceiling.

"Fine?" I asked, poking at the steamed chicken entree. There was a thin layer of skin on the cold gravy. Which, as a kid, I had loved. I probably still did for all I knew. Not a lot of gravy in my diet in those days. While that may sound like a good thing, you have to keep in mind that my diet was mostly hot dogs and chili. Even though it hurt like a motherfucker to swallow, and even though I winced with practically every bite,

I cleaned that cafeteria tray. That pain, however, inspired me to look at what had happened to my body.

I was a mess of cuts, bruises, and sutures.

"You lost a lot of blood," Rad said. He pulled himself up using the armrests. He fluffed my pillow, then leaned in close and whispered, "Part of me is inside of you."

"What the fuck?" I pulled away. Something about people whispering in my ear gives me a spasm. Some people get off on that. Which, hey, no judgment, but I am absolutely *not* one of those people. Rad just grinned and showed me the bit of gauze taped to his inner elbow.

"Universal donor, motherfucker!" he said. "We're blood brothers now!"

"That's cool," I said with all the energy of a strung-out sloth.

"You don't sound like you mean it," he said.

"No … no," I said. "I do … I'm just … sleepy." I really did mean it. Or I meant to mean it. But modern medicine was working its magic, and I wasn't about to heckle the magician. Just as I was about to curl up in the lap of drug-induced unconsciousness, I snapped awake.

"We're not safe here!" I said. I reached for the tubes in my arm, the first step on my immensely foggy and still-forming escape plan. But Rad, with the advantage of sobriety, was quicker.

"Hey, easy," he said. "It's taken care of. I took care of it."

"The cops, they own the—"

"Hey," he said. "Easy. It's fine. Shhh." He actually stroked my head. I raised an eyebrow and he stopped. He was about to jab me in the arm as an antidote for all the tenderness he'd been showing but, thankfully, remembered the state I was in before striking. He gave me a light tap, which still hurt like a nightmare. I tried not to show it in my face, but the single tear no doubt ratted me out.

"What do you mean, it's fine?"

"We're covered. I got people on lookout," Rad said.

"What? How?"

"You're not the only person who has favors to cash in," he said. Finally, I fell back into sleep.

Rad had thought of everything. Rad had a friend, Dr. Thompson, that owed him big, although he was forever mum on the specifics of their arrangement. All I could piece together was that she was a friend of his mother's. They talked a bit about how his mom was doing as I was dozing in and out. I could never tell for sure, but I got the impression that there was an "abusive piece of shit" that was no longer in the picture and Rad was to thank for it.

I was checked in under an assumed name and we wouldn't be paying for anything. Rad had also called in some of his bouncer buddies. Quite a few of whom had moved on to being professional bodyguards. Turned out I had my own security detail. When I saw one of them was Nick, from the Starwood and the studio, the question I'd yet to ask aloud was answered. I wasn't sure how many favors Rad had called in, but I figured I was going to have to get him more than an LP for Christmas that year. Nick, it seemed, was at least owed a card.

When I came to fully sometime later, I had a vision. Zii was asleep next to me. Well, she was sitting in the chair next to my hospital bed, leaned in with her head and arms resting next to my hip. My waking caused her to stir. She looked up at me and smiled. It wasn't until she kissed my lips that I realized, *Holy shit, this is not a hallucination.* I was ecstatic. All of the concern and anxiety I'd been bottling up drained away. She was okay. She was *okay. She was okay.* I was so relieved I wanted to break down and sob right there. So, of course, the first thing I said was, "Where the fuck have you been?"

"Well," she said, "nice to see you too. I'm glad you're okay."

"I was kidnapped and tortured by the minions of a psychotic gangster. I don't know how much fucking further I could be from okay."

"I know. Rad filled me in. I'm sorry."

"I didn't know what to think," I said. "I thought maybe they got to you. Maybe you were dead, or … or worse."

"Worse? What's worse than death?"

"Did I mention the part about being tortured by the minions of a psychotic gangster? I feel like I mentioned the part about being *tortured by the minions of a psychotic gangster*." I started to hyperventilate. Zii started to reach for the nurse call button, but I held up my hand and pulled myself together on my own. Ultimately, it was Zii who had the courage to say what we were both thinking, because I didn't have the balls for it.

"I don't want to think about what would have happened if Rad hadn't found you." When she said this, I visibly shivered. She sat on the edge of the bed and put both arms around me.

"What I don't want to think about is that if it were you, I wouldn't have been there to save you," I said.

"Okay, then don't think about it," she said.

"How can I not think about it? I was assuming the worst."

"First off, do I *really* catch you as the damsel-in-distress type?" I must have been visibly caught off guard by this, because she eventually threw in a "Well?"

"No," I said. "I guess not."

"Damn fucking right I'm not. Now, let's make *one* thing absolutely clear as we move forward in our relationship. I. Do not. Need you. To *save* me. Are we *absolutely* clear on that?"

"So, I'm not allowed to worry about you?" I asked. "Is that it?"

"You can worry however much you want. I was worried about you too, you know?"

"Oh, but not enough to reach out to me or return a fucking phone call?"

She sighed and poured herself a small cup of water from the pitcher on my side table. She poured another cup, dipped a sponge in it, and touched it to my lips to help me hydrate.

"Oh, Alex. Honey. We have a lot to talk about."

"Wait," I said. "Did you say we were in a relationship?"

"Shhh. You're getting off topic." She stuck the sponge in my mouth and left it there. "That's not important right now."

I spit the sponge out. "Really? Because it feels like—"

"I found Lisa," she said.

33

My mouth was still hanging open when Rad walked into the room.

"Oh good, he's up." He didn't seem at all surprised to see Zii there. Apparently, she'd been there for hours. He was also holding two coffees, and neither one was for me. Doctor's orders. He handed one to Zii. Zii smiled in thanks, sipped her coffee, cleared her throat, and brought us up to speed on her end.

"While you were off doing your whole Mike Hammer thing, I thought I'd work my own angles and leads. Talk to some people who might not want to talk to you."

"Like who?" I asked.

"Women," she said.

"What is that supposed to mean? I talked to women!"

Rad did a terrible job trying not to laugh. She smiled and patted my cheek when she saw I was legitimately hurt. "Can I continue now? Uninterrupted? Thanks."

I decided to shut the fuck up for once. Something about being kidnapped, tortured, and soiling yourself in front of your best friend before passing out and waking up in a hospital bed under an assumed name can really shatter a man's confidence. I figured I could stand to learn something. When she was satisfied she had our attention, she started her story.

After you left, when we made the connection to the senator, I started thinking about the one thing politicians all seem to have in common other than lies and bullshit. Prostitution. Either they're sleeping with them, looking the other way as their staff does, taking kickbacks from it, or they're whores themselves. I know some girls who work the streets. Some are pretty hot and young and have had some higher-end johns. I figured there was a good chance one had been with someone in the senator's circle.

I tried my luck at a corner where I know some of the girls from the scene work. Not to talk about the senator or anything. They're tight-lipped while working. It was just to say, "Hey! Let's catch up tomorrow!" That kind of thing. Some of these girls are fifteen or sixteen, you know. They try to hide their age with clothes and makeup, but ... Anyway, I kept walking. I didn't want to stick around longer than I needed to. Just seeing who is still working West Hollywood these days and getting them thinking about me was enough.

I tried to avoid attracting attention from any of the pimps. But after about fifteen minutes, this greasy-haired creep walked up to me and said, "Hey, baby." He didn't look like a movie pimp. He wasn't tall or Black with a wide-brimmed hat and matching velvet suit or anything like that. He looked like a crackhead. Just a skinny white dude with a faded AC/DC shirt. Not a feather on him. The scuzzy little fucker had come out of nowhere. He had a camera with him.

"You wanna make some money?" he asked me. Said I looked like I could "pull real good."

"I'm sure I could pull really well," I told him.

He said, "I can get you work, baby. C'mon with me."

I asked him what he had in mind. He said he just wanted to take some pictures. Claimed he was "real good with a camera." I wanted that camera. Or what was on it, more like. If I read this sad little man right, he'd have snapped off shots of people picking up the girls. The way I see it, there're two ways to intimidate people, physical force or information. And, trust me, nothing about this guy was physically intimidating. But he oozed confidence. I figured he had cards up his sleeve. He'd have to keep them somewhere. So, against my better judgment, I decided to play along and asked if he had a studio.

"Oh, I do, baby. You know I do," he said, showing teeth in a way that made me want to knock every single one of them out of his mouth, then shove them one by one up his dickhole.

Sorry, but this guy, just thinking about him makes me need a shower. Anyway, I followed him. There was no doubt in my mind that I could kick his scrawny little ass from here to the Bay Area. He had no idea, of course, which just gave me more of an advantage.

I followed him a few blocks away into what looked like a warehouse. We walked in and I was shocked. He actually had a pretty nice setup in there. There were boxes of "business cards" for "escort services" and "massage parlors." In the corner was a desk, a safe, filing cabinets, a line of phones, and PhoneMate answering machines. The guy had quite the operation.

He kept calling me "baby" and told me to make myself comfortable on the bed in the corner while he got the camera ready and set up the lights and everything. He handed me a glass of something and told me to "have a drink."

"I don't drink," I said.

"Aw, c'mon, baby," he said, "It'll help you relax."

I told him again, "I. Don't. Drink."

He kept pushing me. Said shit like, "You'll like this one, baby. It's nice. Don't be nervous." He smiled and I smiled back. I took the drink in my hand and tossed the glass, liquid and all, across the room. It shattered in the corner. His smile turned to a frown real quick. All he had to say to that was, "Fine, baby. Whatever. Have it your way."

Straight edge or not, I wasn't touching that drink. I wondered how many girls he'd doped up, photographed, and fucked. It was the only way a guy like that could get laid. That or money. Drugs. Anything other than looks or personality.

I watched as he carefully took the film out of the camera and put it into a tiny plastic tube. As he started loading in a new roll, I looked at the ground and saw some cables. I used the heel of my boot to get a good hold on one and dragged it over to me. A syringe sat on the desk. I pocketed that, carefully, in my jacket.

When he came over to set up the lights, he was moving around the cables. I waited for just the right moment and pulled on the cable, and he tripped and fell, bringing the fixture down with him. I moved in and wrapped the cable around his skinny neck. When he tried to get up, I dug my heel into his back.

"I'm guessing you got this place because no one can hear girls scream. What a pity it's backfired on you," I said. He just gagged and choked.

When I asked him to repeat it, he claimed, "Girls come here by choice."

"Sure. Sure they do," I said. Holding the cable with one hand, I pulled out the syringe. I brought the needle to his eye. "It's all about choices."

He was shitting himself, saying, "Wh-what is this? Y-you want drugs?"

"I'm straight edge," I said.

Little creep started blubbering. "So ... so what you here to ... get rid of the drugs? I'm not a dealer. I, I just ..."

"Yeah," I told him, "I know what you 'just.' But I'm not here about that. I'm here about your photography skills."

He swore all the girls that he "worked" with were of age. I tightened the cable.

"On your life?" I asked. He said nothing. "I'm here about your other photography project."

I had him whimpering. "Wh-what? Which girl?"

"It's not your stable I'm interested in, pimp," I told him. "It's your clientele."

"I have no idea what the fuck you are talking about!" He was practically sobbing. I lifted him up. I was surprised how easy it was. I marched him over to his desk. I kicked him to the ground, so he was facing the safe under the desk. He started eyeing a drawer. I opened it and pulled out the gun before he could and stuck it to his head.

He yelled, "Bitch, you are so dead!"

"Oh. Changing your tune now," I said. I clicked back the hammer. "Don't think I've never used one." I mean, I only ever shot clay pigeons as a kid and hated it, but he didn't need to know that. I told him to open it, and he did as he was told. He handed me a file. A big brown accordion-looking thing tied with string.

"Look, baby...," he said. I pressed the gun harder into his head. He winced, cleared his throat, and tried again. "Look, ba—ma'am. I can cut you in. Whoever paid you to get these photos, I'm telling ya, you can get more if we just blackmail 'em."

"Oh, I don't care about any of that." I fiddled in his drawer and found some pills. I poured a drink, dropped 'em in, and handed it to him. "Here," I said. "Have a drink. It'll help you relax."

34

I left as soon as he passed out. I'd put in enough of whatever it was to keep him down the rest of the night and kill his memory. Or him. Either way, I didn't care. He's a scumbag. OD'ing would be too good for him. I got back home. My parents said something. Probably asking where I'd been for the last few days. I went straight to my room and threw on the new Wipers album. I cranked it to drown out distractions. I opened the file and started looking at pictures. I had to give the pimp credit. He was able to get some great angles of the johns. License plates and faces. If I'm being totally honest, his sense of light and shadow was ... forget it.

After about thirty minutes of looking at scumbag after scumbag, and stabbing them to death in my head, I came across a photo of Senator David Cromwell talking to Kimmy Davies. You know Kimmy? Blonde curly hair. Pouty lips. Slightly upturned nose. Absolutely adorable. Well, the pimp had pictures of her getting into Cromwell's car. Which is a great back-pocket card to play against a politician who got their seat running on morality and family values. I wasn't looking to blackmail. I was looking for who I needed to talk to next. And I had it.

I found Kimmy eating at Canter's Deli on Fairfax. She saw me come in and smiled and waved me over. We used to hang out a lot before I started dating Jerry. It had been a few months. She stood up and we did the whole girly hug-and-kiss-on-the-cheek thing. But I couldn't hide myself from her. My body language was too tense, and she sensed something was wrong.

"Suze?" she asked.

"Let's sit," I said. She sat. The concern on her face was thicker than her makeup. The silence held until I said, "There's no easy way to go about this. And I'm not here to judge you or what you choose to do with your own body or judge how you make your money." I saw her face contort and worried I was losing her, so I said, "Look, Kimmy. Do you want justice for Jerry?"

Like everyone else, she thought Nancy did it. Read in the papers Nancy was dead.

I told her, "The papers are full of shit."

I hate to stereotype blondes, but she goes, "Nancy's not dead?"

"No," I explained, "Nancy's dead. But Nancy didn't do it."

So, she asked, "Who did it, then?"

I leaned in close and whispered, "I think Senator Cromwell had him killed." Kimmy just went real quiet, and all the rouge in the world couldn't cover how white she got.

"Why ... why are you telling me this?" she asked.

After a long pause, I whispered, "Damn it, Kimmy. Don't make me say it."

"Say what?" Kimmy looked at me. "Say what, Suzie?" I opened my mouth but quickly closed it. "Say it," she said.

I reached into my bag, made sure no one else was looking, and slid the pictures to her with a piece of paper on top of them. She looked under the paper, quickly put it back and slid them back to me, and demanded to know where I got them.

"Your ... manager has an interesting hobby," I told her. "He hangs out on fire escapes with a camera and gets himself some nice blackmail material."

"Can we talk about this somewhere less public?" she asked. "Please?"

I put the pictures back in my bag. "Yeah. Sure," I said.

She glanced at the bill for her Reuben. I threw cash on the table, and we walked out together quietly. I knew she'd been staying nearby, and I assumed we were headed that direction. She looked ready to run the entire time. I could tell. But I couldn't tell if she was ready to run from me or from somebody she was afraid was watching. We made it to her friend's place without her breaking into a sprint. There weren't any lights on. I followed her around the back to a pool house. She unlocked it, and the place was set up for her like a bedroom. She sat down on the bed. I sat on a beanbag chair and waited for her to speak. It took a little while.

Finally, she said, "What?"

"I'm not ..." I paused. "I'm not here to judge you." It was a lie. I was judging the hell out of her for sleeping with David Cromwell. For money or otherwise. Of course, it was possible she didn't know or care who he was. This is Kimmy, after all. "I just need you to think," I told her. "While you were with the senator, did you overhear anything about Jerry?"

She said she didn't even know who he was at first, and I believed her. He took her to this apartment and she got the feeling he didn't live there live there, y'know? Like, a "love nest" kind of thing. And there were security guards.

I asked how many times she went there, and she said, "I dunno. Um, a couple. Maybe three. He always asked me questions after. And I thought if I had information he wanted, he might keep paying me."

"What kinds of questions, Kimmy?" I asked. "Was he asking about Jerry?"

She said, "No. Not ... not exactly. I mean ... he was asking about someone else."

"Who?" I asked.

"He wanted to know if I knew Lisa."

I wasn't sure which Lisa she was talking about. When I asked, she said, "Lisa Cromwell. His daughter." We both got quiet when headlights passed. Not that it meant anything. But we were both pretty shaken. It was obvious she knew more than she was letting on. Maybe she was afraid of how

I'd react. She couldn't keep my gaze, and it wasn't because she was lying. It was guilt. Pure and simple. She had told Cromwell something she wished she hadn't, and she was worried how I'd react. Scared, even. She fucking should've been. If she had given that bastard anything that helped him kill Jerry, I would grab her by the hair, drag her out to the pool, and hold her head under until she stopped moving. She brought her clenched hand up to her face and started chewing her knuckle.

"He has a daughter?" I asked. She nodded.

Then Kimmy said, "He showed me a picture and I said I knew her. But her name was Claire and her hair was blue. Not blonde like in the picture."

I must have spoken sternly when I asked what else she'd told him, because all of a sudden she was scared. Defensive.

"I didn't know!" she said.

"What else did you talk about?" I asked. "I have to know, Kimmy."

"Look," she came back, "I needed the money. I was hungry!"

I grabbed her wrist and turned her arm, revealing needle marks. "I'll bet you were," I said.

Through tears, she said she was scared. "I didn't know what he could do to me!" she said. That I could believe. Not only that, I could empathize with it. I remembered the fear I felt when I first learned the senator might be a suspect. I couldn't imagine the fear of having him interrogate me, alone in a room together.

"It's not pleasant," I said. "He's got a helluva left hook."

"And Kimmy's an eighteen-year-old girl. You're a grown man."

"You'd be surprised how easily being tied to a chair renders that irrelevant."

"Really? Jesus, you have had a rough few days." She

stroked my hair. "You poor, poor thing. Can I get back to my fucking story now?"

"Yes. Sorry."

Kimmy said, "He asked where I knew her from. I just told him parties and concerts."

"Did you tell him where these parties were?" I asked. She confirmed it with silence. But I wanted to make her say it. I repeated the question.

"He gave me five grand!" she said. "Five fucking grand! I can change my life with that kind of money!"

I tried to ask which parties she told him about. But she claimed she didn't remember. "Just, like … some of the places," she said. When I didn't say anything, she started getting upset. "Suzie! He was looking for his daughter!" I didn't have to hear what she mumbled under her breath to know it was "My dad never did."

"His daughter ran away?" I asked. "I don't blame her. He didn't say anything about Jerry?"

So, she said, "Well … kinda."

And I said, "What do you mean, 'well … kinda'? Do you mean he asked about concerts? Shows?"

Then she told me he took out a Bad Chemicals tape and asked if she knew about it.

"And what did you say?" I asked.

She told him yeah. Then he asked Kimmy if she'd seen Lisa with the band. She thought over what to say to me next, and she decided on: "It was so much money, Suzie …"

And I couldn't hold back anymore.

"Well, Kimmy. Congratulations," I said. "You helped kill Jerry Rash." I stood up to leave. I still needed more; I was just pissed.

"What? What's that supposed to mean?!" she burst out. "I helped a man who was trying to find his daughter!"

At this point, I was screaming at her. "You helped a man

track down and kill Jerry Rash! You fucking blew it! All for
your goddamn drug habit!"

That pushed her too far, because she started shouting
back at me. "Fuck you, bitch! I was gonna use that money
to get clean!" She stood up. The rouge on her cheeks just
blended in with the rest of her face.

"Whatever!" I said. "You fucked up! You want to make
this right? Tell me everything! And I mean everything!" *Then*
she collapsed on the bed and started sobbing. Fucking junkies, *was my first thought. Then I felt bad. I sat down on the*
edge of the bed and put my hand on her back. I mean, I hesi-
tated at first. But then I put my hand on her back and gently
stroked her shoulders. "I'm sorry I yelled, honey. I was upset."
I sat in silence while she cried. I told myself I was giving her
a minute, but really, I was thinking about how we all repeat
the sins of our parents.

"Go away . . . ," she said into her pillow. I already knew
the pillow would be stained with makeup before she finally
looked up at me. "Just go!" It took me a moment, but I finally
did. I stood up and walked to the door. I paused before leav-
ing and considered apologizing for half a second before I
realized I had nothing to apologize for.

35

If Cromwell's daughter had been spending time with the band, I knew where to look for her. I was surprised I didn't know her. Maybe because she'd been using a different name. It was obvious there was a lot Kimmy hadn't told me, and I was pissed at myself for pushing her too much and making her shut down. Especially after all I went through to talk to her. I had gotten some crucial information, but I still felt like I'd blown it.

I headed to the band house on Fuller in West Hollywood. I figured either Cromwell's daughter would be there or someone who knew her would. But I didn't know how open she was being about her true identity. My guess was not very.

As usual, I walked right in. It was late, and some of the touring bands were sitting around the kitchen table, drinking. I was told to be quiet, though, as the rest were sleeping on the floor in the living room. There were sex noises coming from upstairs. The TV was playing on mute. It was the news. A few of the girls were hanging onto the guys. Sarah was there. You know, the girl with the bleached hair and all the earrings? And I'm pretty sure she was giving the touring singer a hand job under the table.

"Anybody know Claire?" I asked.

"Claire whom?" Sarah asked.

"Who," I corrected her.

"What?" she said.

"Never mind," I said. "Claire. She hangs out with Kimmy."

She was all, *"Yeah. Yeah, I think so. Blue hair? Real young? Bad Chemicals groupie?"*

I said that sounded like her and asked where I could find her. Sarah told me if Claire wasn't upstairs giving head, she'd probably be at the Girls' Squat. That's when some guy walked out of the living room naked. He had tattoos and a beer gut, but a really nice cock. Sorry, unnecessary detail. But it was.

Anyway, he overheard us and asked, "You guys talking 'bout Claire?"

"Yeah," I said. "Have you seen her?"

He said, "She left," as he walked back into the living room with a beer, without looking at any of us.

"She say where?" I asked.

"Nope," he said, turning the corner.

Sarah said she was pretty sure Claire was staying at Girls' Squat. She wiped her hand on a dish towel and asked why I was looking for Claire. I thought for a moment and decided not to say too much.

I lied and told her, "She owes me some money."

"Oh," said Sarah with a tone that caught me. "Oh. Okay."

"What?" I said.

And she went, "What? What what?"

So, I said, "What did you say that like that for?"

"Say what like what?" she said.

"Say, 'Oh. Okay,' like that?"

Then she said, "Oh. I mean … I thought maybe you were looking for her because you found out Jerry fucked her. But I guess that doesn't really matter anymore, does it?"

"No," I said, after a few seconds of feeling the silence. "No, I guess it doesn't." I turned to leave for Girls' Squat.

Sarah is a cunt.

You might know, Girls' Squat is a house in the southernmost part of West Hollywood. No one owns it currently. Apparently, no one wants to buy the place. They say there was a murder there in the late '70s. A lot of the girls who run away from home crash there. I lived there for a few weeks last spring. It's nice. For a squat, I mean. Not so nice if you're *straight edge, though. I tapped the code knock on the back door, and a few seconds later Cassie, who kind of "runs" the place, for lack of a better word, opened the door.*

"Hey, Zii!" she said. "How are you?" You know Cassie. Redhead, freckled, and just a little chunky in the middle? Kinda short, but cute as hell and tough as nails?

Oh, I knew Cassie, all right. Cassie was the type of girl who saw a guy she liked, grabbed him by the hand, and just led him away. Sometimes the guy won't look entirely sure he wants to. But what Cassie wanted, Cassie got.

I was still a bit shaken from Sarah's comments. Cassie isn't nearly as big of a bitch as Sarah. But Cassie has a big fuck-ing mouth, so I decided to be a bit more selective with my honesty. Told her I needed to get away from home and asked if I could crash there maybe for a couple of days. Okay, I decided to be a lot more selective.

"Of course!" Cassie said. "I mean, you're ZZ Hot! Of course you're always welcome. Surprised you bothered to ask. Come in! Come in!"

"Thanks," I said as I walked past Cassie into the kitchen.

"Hey, everyone! ZZ is here!" Of course, she announced everything to the room. If I had told her I was looking for the senator's runaway daughter who may or may not have fucked my dead boyfriend, she'd have busted out a mega-phone. Everyone looked up. A few said hey and others just smiled and nodded.

I scanned the room for anyone I didn't know. I finally spotted a young girl passed out on the couch. I thought I recognized her, but I had never actually spoken to her. "Who's that?" I asked.

"Claire, I think," Cassie said. The girl was young, easily under sixteen. She had short, bleached hair. Some blue from a previous dye job was still visible. Despite her young age,

she was surprisingly developed, boobwise. Her face was round and pretty. The makeup added a few years.

"Is … is she okay?" I asked.

"Yeah, she's fine," Cassie said, a bit too dismissively. "Just super wasted."

"Wasted?" I asked. "On what?"

"I dunno. Little of everything," Cassie said.

I walked over to the couch and saw some works. She'd been shooting up. "Goddamn it," I muttered. Jerry was the exact same way when we got together. If I was going to get anything from this girl, I was going to have to gain her trust. But first, I needed to get some sleep. I plopped down in the easy chair next to the couch and dozed off. If she got up, I would hear her.

But I must have been more tired than I thought, because when I woke up, "Claire" wasn't on the couch. I heard some-one moving around in the kitchen. I stepped over the girls sleeping on the floor and saw her eating a bowl of cereal at the kitchen island.

"Morning," I said. She stopped chewing a moment and looked at me. She looked a little dazed as her eyes searched for recognition. They almost seemed to find it. "Claire, was it?"

She said, "Yeah," but was real hesitant, and said some-thing like, "You are … I know I know you."

I said, "Maybe," and introduced myself. That struck a chord.

"ZZ Hot! Right! You dated Jer—" She cut herself off. "Um, sorry. I didn't mean—"

I told her, "You can say it. I dated Jerry Rash. Yeah."

Even though she said, "Cool," she was obviously super nervous. She was stuttering.

I asked her, "Why is that cool?"

She couldn't look me in the eye as she stammered out, "What? I mean … he was a cool guy. I didn't mean because, like … because, y'know. Fuck. I'm sorry."

"It's okay," I said. "Did you know him?"

"Oh yeah!" she said way too eagerly for my liking. "Totally!"

Zii continued to act out their conversation, taking on a higher, breathier voice for the young, so-called Claire.

"I see," I said. "You, like, hung out and stuff?"

"Yeah. Like … he was really nice, y'know? Took care of me after, y'know, after I ran away. He probably hated my dad more than I do. Ha ha ha!"

"Jerry knew your dad?"

"No," she said, then shut up fast.

"What do you mean he hated him then?"

"I mean, because I told him a lot about him? Told Jerry about my dad a lot. Told him a lot about my dad, I mean. So … so, Jerry didn't like him."

"What did you tell Jerry about your dad?"

"Just, y'know, stuff."

"What kind of stuff?"

"Jesus. It's personal stuff, okay?" she said, suddenly defensive. I learned my lesson from Kimmy and decided not to push too much. I was learning a lot. Teenage girls can't lie for shit.

"Okay, okay. Geez. I was just curious, is all. Take it easy." I knew just how to play her. "I just … wanted to talk about Jerry. I miss him." I brought my hand to my face.

"Oh! Oh, I'm sorry! Please don't cry! I miss him too," she said.

"It's okay. I wanted to know how he helped you."

"He just … was very protective. He never talked about me?"

"Well, I couldn't really go to a lot of afterparties. That wasn't … comfortable for me," I told her.

"See, and that's how I knew him mostly. He would really look out for me at parties and stuff."

"Did you do drugs together?" I said, looking at her arm.

She stopped herself from saying something, then started to do her dishes. "Did you?" she asked me.

"No. I'm straight edge."

"Oh. Right, yeah. He, um, talked about that sometimes," she said, then continued with her dishes without much of a word.

"Look … Claire. I don't mean to interrogate you …"

"Feels like you do," she said. Smart girl.

"I just … because of how he died. With the heroin. He … he told me he was clean."

"And you believed him?" she said.

"I wanted to," I said. "I really, really did."

"Well …," she said. "Don't be so high and mighty about it. Yes. We did drugs together."

I felt so fucking stupid. I think part of me noticed things. Part of me knew he wasn't clean, that he was lying. You were right, Alex, when we met. About how sneaky junkies are. I let myself ignore it, and I started wondering about all the other things I've let myself ignore. I thought I was so fucking smart. Clever, y'know? But I'm not. Men are horrible. It doesn't matter if it's the senator, or my dad, or even Jerry. No offense, but you all pretty much suck.

Anyway, I asked her where they did drugs together.

"Places," was all she said.

"Look, Claire, if that's your real name, and I doubt it, Jerry is dead. People around him are dying, and if you don't get your shit together, clean yourself up, and tell me what you know, it's possible you'll be next." She froze when I said that. Panic set in. Her mind was a screaming argument between fight or flight. She almost ran but thought better of it.

"Help me," she said. I walked over to her and held her. She told me everything. Well, almost everything, as far as I could tell. Yes, she was Lisa Cromwell, the senator's daughter. She was a drug addict and a runaway. Jerry had charmed his

way into her life, just as he had charmed his way into mine. Jerry was charming. Jerry had a plan. He believed he could change the world, and he let you believe you were part of it. There is no doubt in my mind Jerry knew exactly who Lisa really was. What better way to start his revolution than by recruiting the daughter of the very man he was rebelling against.

Lisa and I left the house quietly. We found a motel, and I set up for getting her clean, just as I had done with Jerry. Or so I had thought. You pretty much know the rest.

36

I sat in bed and processed everything Zii had just laid out. There were so many twists and turns going on in my head, I could have sold weekend passes. I must have been lost in thought, because Zii lost her patience.

"Well?!" she said. It still took me a few beats before I turned to look at her, and I had to wonder, for real this time, if all these blows to the head weren't doing permanent damage.

"Which motel?" I asked.

"I can't tell you that," she said.

"Zii, you can trust me."

"It's not you I don't trust," she said. It was then I remembered Rad had taken up residence on the chair in the corner.

"What? Rad? You know we can trust Rad," I said. Rad wasn't looking at either of us; he was just staring at the jar of tongue dispensers. He'd barely touched his coffee, and it had no doubt gone cold.

"I trust Rad more than I trust you," she said. I looked to Rad, expecting a pithy retort at my expense. Still nothing. I looked back at him, but he still wasn't looking at me. Just the jar. I turned back to Zii.

"But you *do* trust me, right?" A surge of pain shot through me that reminded me a bit too much of the wire cutters. This time, though, it was somewhere a lot more internal.

"Of course I do, sweetie."

She scratched behind my ear and kissed me on the corner of my mouth. "Try and get some rest. When you get out, call this number. It's a message service ... of sorts."

"What kind of sorts?"

"The kind of sorts that requires a passphrase. I will leave a message for you. You just tell them, 'We're gonna wreak havoc on this rancid mill,' and they'll give you the message."

"Got it," I said.

"Rest," she said. "Please. I'm going to need you. But first you need to heal." She kissed me once more, fully this time. Then left.

"Bye," I said as she walked out the door with more caution than I'd ever seen her display.

I looked at Rad, who had finally broken whatever spell that coffee had had over him. "You're awfully quiet for once."

He just stared at me, and I hated the way he was doing it. It was a look full of fear, pain, and confusion. I'd had plenty of that trio already. I knew that look. My mother had had it when she'd told me about my grandfather's cancer. My father had had it when he'd told me he wasn't going to be living with us anymore. My college girlfriend had had it when she'd told me she'd slept with someone else. He wouldn't know how to say this ...

"I don't know how to say this ..."

But ...

"But ..."

"But what?" I said.

"Kimmy?" Rad said.

"The girl who told Zii about Lisa?" I said.

Rad just sighed, then quietly nodded.

"What about her?"

"Dude. Kimmy died three weeks ago," he said. "OD."

If this were a comedy, that's where the record would have scratched.

37

I was out of bed. Pacing. Dragging the IV with me as I walked hurriedly around the room. It hurt like hell to move. Who the fuck knows what I was trying to accomplish.

"So, you're saying she's lying?!" I said. Apparently, I'd said this a lot.

"I don't know any more now than I did the first time you asked me," Rad said. "Or the fortieth time, for that matter!"

I paused. "I asked you that forty times?"

"That's just when I stopped counting."

"What else could it be, though?" I said, starting my pacing again.

"Alex, you have to *sit still!*" he shouted. He was right, of course, but I couldn't. Even though every step I took felt like being clipped again. Even though the sutures felt like they were going to tear open. And even though the aches felt like I was still being beaten. The physical pain was way better than what I'd feel on the inside if I denied myself the distraction.

"What does it mean, though?" I said.

"It means we need to be careful," Rad said. "Now, all I am saying is that she's not being fully truthful."

"Otherwise known as *lying*," I said.

"Sure. But why?" Rad said. "I mean, yeah, it could be she's up to something. But equally possible is that she just doesn't fully trust us. Either way, we need to be careful there. Or maybe she's protecting somebody."

"Or she doesn't want us to know how she really found out," I said.

I finally sat. The physical pain stopped. But then the thoughts set in. If you are ever presented with the option of being tortured with corkscrews and wire cutters or being betrayed by someone you love, I would recommend the former. I had already cried in front of Rad. Shit in front of him too. I wasn't about to let myself cry in front of him again, so I just sat there, breathed heavily, and clenched my jaw. He sat down next to me and put his arm around my shoulder.

"What now?" he asked after a few minutes. He took his arm off me and drummed on his knees.

"First, we get the fuck out of here. It's not safe, and we've already been lucky for too long." I looked at Zii's note. She'd dotted the *i*'s with hearts and signed with *x*'s and *o*'s. "Then, we call Zii. I'm just hoping time ain't fucked us quite yet."

"What are you thinking?" he asked, finishing his coffee.

"I don't like to say it out loud when I hope I'm wrong."

Rad got my clothes out of the closet, and I slipped them on. They were still covered in blood. But laundry isn't covered under the "admitted to the hospital under false pretenses as payback for shady favors owed to your best friend" insurance plan. You need BlueCross BlueShield for those kinds of services. Rad had also recovered my jacket. Zipped up, it managed to hide the more head-turning elements of my ensemble.

My adrenaline was upshifting, and a familiar numbness started to set in. Either that or my pain receptors were tired of the unpaid overtime and had staged a walkout. We slipped out of the room as though we were two visitors. Rad nodded to some guys who were hanging around the waiting area, and they nodded back. One was Nick. Rad shook his hand and patted him on the shoulder. A doctor was standing at the nurses' station; she saw us coming but made almost too much of a show of not showing it. Rad smiled at her, and she smiled too while watching him from the corners of her eyes. I watched her walk away as we waited for an elevator. Rad just watched the ceiling.

"Anything you want to tell me about there, killer?" I asked as the down arrow dinged.

"No," he said, shoving me onto the elevator, his usual playfulness completely truant. It's usually the habit of young men to rib their buddies for such self-seriousness. Especially in a subculture that was seemingly getting more macho every weekend. But everything about Rad's monosyllabic response told me to shut the fuck up and let that shit go. So, I shut the fuck up. And I let that shit go. Rad had just saved my life, so he'd hate to have to kill me. I harbored no delusions about his ability to do so.

We got into my car. I didn't ask how it got there; I just handed Rad the keys. I was still full of the kind of medicine that advises against operating heavy machinery. Rad drove me to a pay phone about a mile from the hospital, but he drove double that distance, snaking around side streets, to shake any tails.

I called the number Zii had given me. Given what Rad had told me about Kimmy, I had few reasons to trust it and every reason to cut and run. But running's a Band-Aid on a flesh wound. If I wanted this over, I needed the straight. And the only way to get that was to play along. I couldn't let her on to the fact that I was on to her.

"Canyon Messages. This is Kara. Can I have your name and account number, please?" The rhythm of her voice had a rehearsed cheeriness to it, but her tone suggested her grip on the waking world was on the verge of slipping.

I gave her my name and read off the account number that Zii had jotted down. Her nines looked like fours, but apparently I had guessed right.

"One moment, Mr. DiMaggio," she said. As she rustled through papers, I tried to remember the last time someone had called me Mr. DiMaggio for reasons other than to scold me. Nothing came to mind. "Yes, I have a message for you, but there's a passphrase for—"

"We're gonna wreak havoc on this rancid mill."

"Thank you," Kara said. She gave me a message. Just an address.

38

The address was in Burbank. A motel on Olive Ave. Room 205. The motel was a '50s retro job, complete with neon sign, Spanish tiles, and a stone chimney at the lobby. We pulled into the lot and parked so we had a good view of 205. There was a window with a curtain next to the door. My eyes watched for fluttering shadows with a fixation that jumped the line into obsession.

"All right, what's the plan, then?" Rad asked. "We gonna stake her out? She's expecting us, ain't she?"

"Dunno what we'd be walking into," I said.

"But, dude. It's Zii."

"Yup."

"Still worried you can't trust her?"

"Yup."

"Because she was lying about Kimmy?"

"Yup."

"Alex," he said. His tone reminded me too much of how my parents would sound whenever we "needed to talk." Just like I did with them, I said nothing.

"You gotta let me know what yer thinkin'," he continued, undeterred by my childish use of the silent treatment. But it's hard to put your cards on the table when you're unsure of the hand. Especially when you've been tossing chips in the pot, holding out on the hope that the last run of the river would be your vindication. But only amateurs play their own hand. The real pros play their opponents'. I'd been playing *my* cards. I *should* have been playing hers.

"Fuck," was all I said. But what I'd meant to say was

that it's hard to say something out loud that you desperately hope is untrue. That's the power of denial. The devout belief that something unspoken can never be true. That the truth is somehow like the Devil. It only has power if it's acknowledged. That's what I'd meant to say. But I just said, "Fuck." Again. With a cracked voice. And I hated myself for it.

"Hey. Talk to me, buddy ..."

"I think Zii is setting us up." It came out of me like a breath held too long.

"Why?" Rad asked. "I mean, she did lie about Kimmy. But ... I guess I want to know your theories."

"Let's just go in and talk to her, then," I said. "I'll lay it out to her. You just listen."

"You can't fill me in now?" he asked as I cracked open the car door. It took me a few ticks and a handful of tocks to get my words right.

"No," I said.

"Why the hell not?"

"Because I don't want to hear myself say it more than once."

Night had fallen. The neon sign splashed across the windshield. Damned if I knew how anyone on this street got any sleep with that thing. It was a miracle that planes weren't landing on Olive Ave. The curtain fluttered, and I smacked Rad on the shoulder without moving my eyes from the window. We moved through the parking lot as though it were a sea of broken glass. We made our way up the stairs and along the balcony until we reached 205.

I'd barely tapped on the door once when it flew open and I found a gun in my face. When my sight changed focus, I saw it was Zii. She was without her usual overabundance of makeup. Where there had been dark lipstick, there were only flesh-toned lips. Where there had been mascara, there were just eyes, dark and shiny. Where before the skin had been smooth and pale, there were freckles and pores and a small blemish on her left cheekbone. Fuck me running, she was beautiful.

She grabbed me by the shirt collar and pulled me in, then rushed Rad inside behind me. She held me. She kissed my lips. I thought she had some nerve doing that.

"You got my message," she said. "I'm so glad you're here."

I grabbed her shoulders and put light between us. "Yeah, I'll bet you are. Your last loose ends are here. All ready to be tied up."

"What the fuck are you talking about, Alex?" she said, swiping my hands off her shoulders.

"You lied to me," I said.

With a widening of her eyes, she shifted from confusion to panic. "Alex. I didn't lie to—"

"When did you say you talked to Kimmy? Within the last couple of days, was it?"

"Yeah," she said. Defiant, stubborn. She knew damn well what I was driving at, but she wasn't going to cop to it. She wanted *me* to say it. "Something like that. Why do you ask?"

"You into Ouija boards now, then?"

"Not since middle school. Why?" She crossed her arms, cocked her hips, and tilted her head. Full-on "fuck you" stance. Her feet were planted; her ground was held. She was gonna make me say it.

"Kimmy's dead," I said. "She OD'd three weeks ago."

Her stance fell loose and she rolled her eyes. "Yeah, okay. You're right," she said. She tossed her hands up. "I lied."

"Why?" I asked. "How could you *lie* to me?"

She folded her arms. I'm sure it squeezed her breasts together, like it did all the other times I looked. This time, though, I was frantically reading her face, searching for fuck knows what. Clues? Hints? Some kind of tell? Or maybe I thought that if I looked her in the eyes, she would tell me the truth. Or at least be unable to lie to me more. I hoped she cared about me at least that much. I really, really hoped.

"I dunno, Alex." She shrugged her shoulders, arms still crossed, guard still up. "You seem to have it all figured out. You tell me. Do your fucking Poirot thing."

"I think you killed Jerry. Or at least set up the circumstances for him to kill himself. And I think you did it because you started to realize that he was a horrendous piece of shit. You found out that not only was he using and was he dealing, he beat you and raped women. He was a fucking piece of human waste. He deserved to die, sure. And in ways far more painful than he did. He was shit. But still, he was leading the charge against Senator Cromwell. He was going to start a revolution. You were helping him make that happen. Or was *he* helping *you* make that happen? You put a lot of work into getting him cleaned up enough to lead. To be the voice of a disenfranchised generation. But his godawful behavior would have derailed all of that. Everything you worked for. He was about to fuck it all up because everyone was getting wise to his shit. Well, if he couldn't be a hero, he could at least be a martyr. You knew he fucked Lisa Cromwell. The fourteen-year-old daughter of the senator. That was too much. Maybe it was jealousy. Maybe she was just a loose end that needed tying up. But—"

Then she hit me. Not a slap. Closed fist. Knuckles of the pointer and middle finger right to the cheekbone. A proper fucking punch. Damn near spun me around. I barely managed to stay standing. I turned back toward her.

"How dare you?" she asked. "How *could* you? You can't … honestly …" She fell to her knees and cried. "Just stop." Her eyes were flooded with tears. "Just. Shut. The. Fuck. Up." I looked at her and then to Rad. His eyes were wide enough to serve dinner on.

I heard a rustling from the closet. I threw open the door

and heard a squeal. Huddled in the corner, behind the spare linens, was a fourteen-year-old girl with faded blue hair.

"Aw, shit."

And I usually know just what to say.

39

Zii and Lisa sat on the motel bed together. Lisa had her legs pulled up to her chest and rested her chin in between her knees. She stared at the matted motel carpet, with its tacky '50s pattern and thirty years' worth of stains. She rocked nervously. Zii's arm was around her, stroking her shoulder to try to calm her down. They looked pretty sympatico, considering I had just pretty much accused one of killing the other.

I was holding a plastic bag of ice to my face. Rad had got some from the machine down the hall. I checked my face in the mirror, but really it was just a flimsy pretext for avoiding Zii's gaze. Some women have a glare that could turn back whole armies. Zii sure as hell was one such woman. She was also the one with enough sand to break the silence.

"Yes," she said, "I did lie to you. Well ... not lied, really."

"You told me you talked to Kimmy. Kimmy died before any of this shit went down."

"I did talk to Kimmy. I didn't lie about that. I just ... may have withheld when that conversation actually took place."

"So, what you're saying is ..."

"I talked to Kimmy three weeks ago."

"But ..."

"Alex. This 'shit' has been 'going down' for a while. *You* only came into the picture a few days ago. This isn't *your* story. You're just a late addition. Hard as it may be to believe, the world doesn't revolve around you."

"Fine. Whatever. But I've been forthcoming and truthful, and you've got more tales to tell and fog to clear before you can start getting sanctimonious with me about much of anything."

"Your theory isn't entirely off base. Jerry was shit. He had the potential to be a charismatic leader, but he was shit. And he was full of shit. Jerry wasn't really planning any major revolution. He didn't *actually* have any plans or phases like he was on about. He just liked the attention that gave him. He was abusive. And he cheated on me. And he stole from me. But I didn't kill him. I was getting ready to leave him. I thought, really thought, there was a good guy in there. A leader. But, no."

"What about Kimmy?"

"Most of what I told you about Kimmy was true. It just happened a few weeks earlier. I was trying to find proof that the senator was fucking hookers. I found out that he had been with Kimmy a few times. And that's when she told me about the senator's runaway daughter. Except I didn't blame her for killing Jerry. He wasn't dead yet. She died of an OD shortly after. Then Jerry died in a similar way. I figured out Claire was Lisa. But she disappeared after Jerry …" She looked at Lisa and Lisa looked away. Her fixation now on the neon sign. She mouthed the words *raped her* to me. "I panicked. And I knew I had to find her before something happened to her. Or to me. But while I looked for her … I mean, I knew where to look, but I needed …"

She was having trouble saying it. But my faith in my ability to fill in gaps had just been shaken. So, I did the smart thing and kept my mouth shut.

"Alex," she started, but then stopped herself for a few more beats. "Alex, I never meant for you to … get hurt."

I couldn't bring myself to ask what she was saying. The tables were turning like a fucking Tilt-a-Whirl and I could not enjoy the ride. Just felt like tossing up. She looked at me and breathed heavily. "I figured with you scratching at the front door, I could sneak around back."

"You fucking bitch," I said softly.

"Alex, I'm sorry."

"You used me," I said, still quiet. Disbelieving.

"I did what I had to do!"

"You *used* me!" I shouted, chucking my ice across the room at the tacky landscape painting above the bed. "What the fuck?! I was just a distraction?! So, what? I go out, shake a few trees, maybe get knocked in the head, but that's fine so long as you get some fruit out of it?! I got that right? That sound *accurate?*"

"I wasn't expecting to care about you," she said.

"Oh, great. Here it comes. The fucking doe eyes. You play me for a sap and I'm supposed to let that go the second you tell me that you've fallen for me? You let me fumble in the dark, trip over all kinds of horrid shit, and I'm supposed to let that go now that you're batting some eyelashes and whispering sweet nothings? To think I actually bought it when you acted hurt when I accused you of—"

"I *was* hurt."

"You don't have the right to feel hurt!" I moved toward her, pointing intensely with each word.

"I have the *right* to feel however the *fuck* I want!" She stood up. We were face to face now.

"I don't like being *used!*"

"And *I* don't like being accused of killing fourteen-year-old girls!"

"Enough!" bellowed Rad. "Enough," he said a second time, much calmer. All four of us looked back and forth at each other. Lisa still hadn't said anything since I'd found her in the closet.

"Since it seems I have to play the voice of reason *yet again*, I feel the need to point out that you're both just being fucking terrible right now. And for *now*, at least, we need to stop focusing on what *has* happened and start focusing on what's *going* to happen. Because, need I remind you all, some of the most powerful and dangerous people in the state of California want us all dead." He looked at Lisa. "Well, three of us anyway. Now, you all can hash out whatever the fuck this whole used-accused thing is later. Because I dunno about the rest of you, but I want to at least make it to thirty before I die tragically young. Can we at least agree on that?"

"Yes," Zii and I said, not quite in unison.

"You guys are really fucked up," said Lisa.

At least *someone* was telling the truth.

40

I stepped outside for a cigarette. I didn't even want one. Not really. I just needed a reason to get the fuck out of that room for five minutes. Inhaling poison was just as good of an excuse as any. I fell into a trance watching the neon arrow blinking, beckoning people to come in and get some rest. Of course, it'd be a lot easier to rest without the goddamn blinking arrow. I made a half-hearted attempt to find a metaphor in there somewhere, but I had nothing. I couldn't get my mind off the argument. Or off the fact I'd been played from the beginning. Defining myself by having no strings had just made them that much easier to pull.

My cigarette had gone to ash before I got my nicotine fix, so I lit another. Maybe two or three after that, who's to say? When I walked back into the room, Zii turned her nose up at the smell of me. But it could have just as easily been at the sight.

"So," I finally said. "What's the plan, then? Where do we go from here?"

"The plan?" Rad interjected. "I'm not even one hundred percent clear on the situation."

"Zii. Lisa. Would you mind enlightening us? And lay it out straight. If I stay in the dark much longer, my eyes are going to adjust permanently."

Zii and Lisa looked at each other. Lisa was hesitant but nodded to Zii. Zii stroked her hair and looked back at Rad and I.

"Even though Jerry didn't actually have a planned-out revolution, he did want to try to embarrass Cromwell, and he would grab opportunities to do that. Just was sloppy as shit about it. The whole 'catching Cromwell with a hooker' thing was my idea. And when he told me he saw a picture of Cromwell with Eddie Nash at Nash's house, I convinced him to dig up dirt there."

"So, you already knew about the missing pages from Nash's ledger," I said.

She nodded. "I did. That was going to be our ace. But when Jerry found out one of his fans was actually Cromwell's runaway daughter, well, he saw that as an opportunity." Lisa squirmed a bit. Zii looked at me looking at her.

My eyes darted about as inferences eliminated themselves as options. I walked over to where she sat on the edge of the bed. I crouched down next to her to meet her on her level. Physically, at least.

"Lisa," I said. "Can you tell me what happened?" She turned away from me. "Lisa, I want to help you." She still didn't look at me. "More than that, I need your help. We *all* need your help."

Zii touched Lisa's chin and gently turned her face so she could look her in the eyes.

"It's okay, honey," Zii said. "He may not trust me anymore, but I still trust him." She gave me a look that was either tender or accusatory. I'd lost my ability to tell, and sometimes that line is not so clearly defined. Lisa got up and walked into the bathroom without saying a damn thing to anybody. She walked over to the toilet, eyes fixed forward, fell to her knees, gripped the porcelain, and spewed up what I hoped to hell was tomato soup. Zii was in there in a flash to hold her hair back.

"She's detoxing," Zii said. That's when I saw the track marks on Lisa's arm. They didn't come as a shock, but there they were. More proof of Zii's story. Even if her timeline was a bit skewed. "Do you mind?" Zii gestured to a half-empty bottle of Gatorade sitting among a collection of full and empty bottles on the table. I fetched it like the good little doggy that I was.

"Here," I said.

"Thanks," she said. We avoided each other's eyes, and Rad rolled his. "You done, honey?" Lisa nodded. "Here. Have this." She unscrewed the cap for Lisa, who took the bottle with both hands and drank two small, dainty sips.

"No rush," I said.

Zii shot me a fierce look.

"What?" I said before it dawned on me. "I wasn't being sarcastic." Zii pushed past me. "Why does everyone always assume I'm being sarcastic?"

"Fine," she said. "Whatever."

Rad just shrugged. Lisa emerged from the bathroom. All heads turned. All eyes fell. She rubbed her upper arm and gazed at her feet as if her toes were holding cue cards. It's my understanding that fourteen-year-old girls don't like a room full of eyes on them in the best of circumstances. Describing abuse you faced at the hands of a man you admired to a room full of virtual strangers sure as shit ranks a great deal lower than that. Rad, old-school gentleman that he is, pulled the chair over from the desk for her, and she sat down.

"I ran away from home about six months ago. Well, not *home*. The boarding school my father put me in. He covered it up. Like he covers up everything. He sent me there because I dyed my hair blue. He thought I would embarrass him. Part of me wanted to, I guess. Maybe I just wanted him to notice me? I don't know. Really, I just did it because I wanted blue hair. I thought it was cool. Anyway, I ran away. And I came to Hollywood, and I started going to shows and parties, and it was just great. I had to change my name. But my dad never really tried to find me. I thought if he wanted to, he would. I lived on the street for *six months* because he *let me*. He didn't want to find me."

"I've got some bruises and stitches offering a fairly compelling counterpoint," I said.

"Alex?" said Zii.

"What?"

"Shut the fuck up."

"I'm just saying he's trying to—"

"Shut. The fuck up."

"Shutting the fuck up!" I threw my hands up in surrender.

"Go ahead, sweetie," Zii said. "You won't be interrupted again. I promise." She looked at me with enough steel in her gaze to build a city.

"He didn't want to find me, until I gave him a reason to." Then she started to cry. Zii started to get up, but Lisa shook her head and pushed through it. "I started hanging around Jerry Rash. He was always talking about all these ideas that flew right in the face of everything my dad stood for. I liked that. I hated my dad so much then that anything that was against him seemed so cool. Jerry was so cool, and he was so nice to me. So, when he offered me a shot … of course I took it. It just made me feel so warm, and I forgot myself, and it didn't matter that my own father didn't want me. It wasn't just the blue hair. I was a handful, I know that. The hair was just … just … I can't think of it." I knew she wanted to say, "the straw that broke the camel's back," but I was under strict orders to shut the fuck up, so I kept my fucks shut up. "Anyway. The smack just made it easier, y'know? I could just lose a whole day. That was my favorite thing to do. Just … lose a day with Jerry."

She started to cry again, worse than before. Much worse. She managed to squeak out an "I'm so sorry, Zii." Zii jumped up and kneeled by the chair, taking Lisa's hands in her own like a mother warming her child's hands after they've come in from the cold.

"It's okay," said Zii. "I'm not mad at you. Don't be sorry. It's not your fault." Lisa shook her head, shook her whole body really. "Hey!" said Zii. "You listen to me. You don't *ever* apologize for *any* of this, do you understand me?" She moved her head around to meet Lisa's resistant face. Lisa twisted away, but finally gave up and looked at Zii, who repeated, slowly this time, "You don't ever apologize for any of this. Do you understand me? You have nothing to apologize for." Lisa nodded. I got the Gatorade and handed it to Lisa.

"Thank you," she said meekly. Zii looked up at me and stopped just short of smiling at me. Lisa sighed heavily, and Zii looked back to her.

"I don't remember the first time he fucked me," Lisa said. "Actually, I don't really know how many times he did before I knew he was. I came to one time but passed back out. I thought I dreamed it. I thought, *Hey, I want to fuck him. Why wouldn't I dream about it?* Y'know? Then one time I started it. I remember it. I didn't know about the other times until people told me ... because he'd told them. And I guess once or twice it was in front of other people. At a party. But I don't remember." She didn't cry. She had to take a moment, but she didn't cry. But I did.

I looked up and Rad had left the room. He was standing outside on the balcony. How tight he was squeezing the railing, I thought he would bend it. He came back in. I got my shit together. I realized then that she hadn't taken a moment for her. It was for us.

"And I don't remember making the movie," she said.

"Movie?!" I said. I looked to Zii. "What movie?"

"I didn't keep this from you, Alex. This is new to me too."

"Jerry filmed us together. Having sex. I wasn't passed out in it. But I was blacked out. I don't remember. But when I found out about it, I wasn't mad. Jerry said he was going to send a copy to my father. Jerry said it would give us power over my father. But I didn't care about any of that. I just knew that he couldn't ignore me anymore."

It was my turn to throw up. But I didn't make it to the toilet.

We took some time after that. Zii took Lisa out to eat. I stayed to clean up after my panic attack. Rad, loyal as he is, stayed with me and, practical as he is, did not help me clean up my vomit. His contribution was sitting on the edge of the second bed, shaking his head and occasionally saying, "Fuck." To which my reply was always, "Fuck."

After I'd cleaned part of my last meal off the floor, I got up to take a shower, presumably leaving Rad to say "Fuck" to himself. When I came back out, he was standing on the balcony smoking. Lisa and Zii came in the room. Lisa cringed at the sight of me in a towel, and Zii tossed me a shopping bag that contained some clothes from a nearby thrift shop. I went to catch it and dropped the fucking towel. Lisa suddenly rushed to the bathroom to throw up. Even under the circumstances, I couldn't help feeling a little hurt.

41

Lisa swore up and down that she didn't know where the film was. Given everything that she'd been through, I couldn't bring myself to push harder, which meant I was either losing my edge or growing as a person. Although it's surprising how often the two skip down the beach hand in hand. Her father had been sent a copy on Betamax. But the original film, in theory, was still out there twisting in the wind. She invoked the name of God when she swore Jerry only made one copy. She'd have been better off swearing on the life of Iggy Pop, but her guts were still splayed out on the floor, so I was inclined to believe her. Fortunately, I knew just where to start looking.

I somehow summoned the courage to go back to the "studio" that was very nearly the site of my own film debut. It helped that I had Rad with me. And, also, the new .38 that I had swiped from Cromwell's thugs' car. I still hated the fucking things. But war and principles were never exactly on speaking terms. Neither was love, for that matter. *That* bastard never got along with anybody. I also had a switchblade tucked in my coat, along with a "war chain." Which is really just a length of chain with a padlock on the end of it. I wrapped it around me like a sash. Rad had on knuckle dusters and was carrying a baseball bat. While digging this slapdash arsenal out of my trunk, I came across a short length of studded leather.

"My lucky wrist cuff," I said, slipping it on and adjusting the size. "Gonna need this."

"Thought you said you lost it," Rad said. It had been a gift from him for my twentieth.

"It always finds its way back," I said. "That's what makes it lucky." I closed the trunk. "Ready to meet a celebrity?" I grinned.

We walked up to the studio, and standing outside was John Holmes. "Welly, welly, welly, welly, welly, welly, well. If it isn't the California Gigolo himself! To what do I owe the extreme pleasure?" I proclaimed. Holmes nearly shit himself. "Aw, c'mon. You remember me, dontcha? It's Alex!" Holmes stood there, trembling like a newborn donkey trying to stand up. He stumbled backward as I walked toward him.

"Get the fuck away!" he sputtered. "I don't know you, man!"

"John! You're embarrassing me in front of my friend! I told him we were *buddies*, man!"

He tried to run, but as he turned, he smacked into a rising bollard by the loading dock and fell to the ground.

"Here, let me help you up." I grabbed him by his shirt and lifted him off the ground. "Heya, Johnny! Ya miss me? Cuz I sure missed you."

"H-hiya, Alex …"

"So, you *do* remember me?"

"Course … course I do …"

"And we're *buddies*. Right?"

"Yeah. Buddies. Right."

"Tell him." I jerked my head toward Rad, eyes still on Holmes.

"We're … we're buddies," he said to Rad.

"Cool," said Rad.

"Ya see, Rad?" I gave Holmes a little shake. "Toldja I knew John. Fucking. Holmes."

"Looks like I owe you five bucks," Rad said.

"Looks like," I said. "Now, John, I was hoping you could help me out with something. What with us bein' such *good* buddies 'n' all."

"Sure, sure, Alex. Anything. For, for a buddy …"

"Glad to hear it," I said, dropping him to the ground. "So sorry. Let me—"

"No, no, no … it's okay. I'm okay. I got it." He scrambled to his feet before I could put hands on him again. "What … uh … what do you need?"

"You remember Jerry Rash?"

"Yeah, sure. Dead punk rocker. You, you were looking for his killers!" The genuine "a-ha" in his tone made me believe that he had actually forgotten who I was. Or, at the very least, had forgotten where he knew me from. Fucking cokeheads.

"Yeah, well, apparently Jerry made his own little film. Some real sick shit. And I figured, 'Hey, who do I know in the industry that's only a degree of separation away from Jerry?' That's when I thought, John Holmes! My good buddy John, who has always been so helpful and honest …"

"Heh heh, yeah. Sure,"

"All right, Johnny, then start singing. Really *earn* that triple-threat status," I said. Holmes looked back and forth, first at me, then at Rad, then me, then Rad. Rad smacked the bat against the palm of his hand a few times. And like a conductor tapping his baton, it signaled the choir. Johnny started to sing.

"Jerry liked to do little film projects here. Sure. He worked with Seth mostly."

"Seth, huh? And where might I find Seth?"

"He's, uh … well, you're in luck. He's inside."

"Well, what are you waiting for, Johnny? Introduce us. Just because you *have* a huge dick doesn't mean you have to *be* one."

"Ha ha. Good one." Holmes laughed nervously. "Sure. Uh, this way." He walked us through the building, and I tried not to let the sights and sounds trigger any unpleasant flashbacks. My tension must have been pretty damn obvious, because Rad put his hand on my shoulder. Just for a moment. The main soundstage was now full of crates, putting it back in touch with its roots as a warehouse. Some of the crates had been opened and were full of what looked like new film equipment, sawdust, and bags of cocaine. Others remained in stacks.

"Hey, Seth!" Holmes shouted. "These guys was asking about you."

Seth turned around. He was a pale, skinny man with greasy hair and a faded AC/DC T-shirt. Crack-smoking skinny. Rad and I looked at each other.

"Oh shit," Seth said. "You're with that punk bitch, aren't you? You have any idea what that cunt did to me?"

"Probably about half of what I'll do if I don't get what I want," I said. "Y'see, she's the *nice* one."

"Look, man. I had to go to the fuckin' *hospital* after what she did to me."

"Hey! Me *too*. Look at us, finding all this common ground here. At this rate, we could be real good buddies. Ain't that right, John?"

"Yeah," said Holmes. "Good buddies. Alex is a real good buddy."

"Thanks," I said. "I sure like to think so."

"What the fuck do you want, huh? Spit it the fuck out already."

"Straight to brass tacks, eh? Yeah. We can swing it that way, sure. I'm looking for a film. Starring the late Jerry Rash."

"Yeah? Which one."

"I think you know goddamn well which one," I said.

"Yeah, yeah, yeah." Seth wiped his hands on a towel and tossed it to the floor. "I can guess."

Just then Holmes pulled a gun and pointed it at me. "Eddie! Eddie, come quick!" he shouted. A door in the hallway opened, and Eddie Nash emerged, tying his robe. His still-erect penis poking out like a hairless meerkat. "Oh, fuck me. Alex Damage. And I am guessing this is the friend who killed one of my best artists? I have seen you before, no?" Rad said nothing. "Sure. Bouncer. Starwood. You are fired. John, what is happening here?"

"These guys, they want a film of Jerry and—"

"Senator Cromwell's daughter. Of course they do. Well, you cannot have it. Cromwell is a dog. I need my leash. John, kill him."

"What?" John said.

Eddie Nash pointed at me frantically. "Kill him! Kill him!"

"Sorry, but we have to talk to him first, you Paki cunt." Rapunzel walked in holding a gun, surrounded by a pair of skins in Secret Service–looking suits. My appreciation for this unlikely calvary was short-lived, however.

"I thought you said your boys were wiped out," I said to Rapunzel.

"Yeah, well, that was a lie, innit? I tend to do that."

"You were following us, weren't you?" I said.

"Well, you've been a constant thorn in the side of my employer. You made his best inside man kill himself, and he'd like a word."

"Then why'd you help us get rid of Officer Mike?"

"The spic had to go. His appetites were ... compromising. I saw that, even if Cromwell didn't."

"Lisa? Zii?"

"Perfectly safe," Rapunzel said.

"Where are they?" I said, moving toward him, and a chorus of guns cocked.

"Wherever the fuck you left them," he said. "We weren't given any orders to bring them in. Just you. You and the film. Drop the gun, freak." That last bit was directed at Holmes, who didn't need any additional convincing. "Oh. One more thing."

Rapunzel tilted his head toward Eddie. One of the suited skins drew his gun and took aim. Eddie ducked to the side quick enough to avoid being killed. The bullet struck him in the arm, and he swore viciously in Arabic. While the skins were momentarily distracted, I drew my gun and shot at Rapunzel but hit the one who'd shot at Eddie. I cursed my handicapped aim and ducked behind a crate. The whole studio was like a coffee can full of firecrackers. Wood splintered. I just hoped this crate was filled with sturdy, high-end film equipment. Cocaine's fun, in moderation. It's not so great at stopping bullets, though. All three of the skins were packing automatics, which hardly seemed fair. I moved to the middle as bullets tore apart the edges of the crate.

"Are you hit?" Rad said. It was only then that I noticed he'd taken cover next to me. I must have looked confused. He repeated himself and pointed to a fresh bloodstain spreading out on the side of my shirt. It felt sticky and warm. Panic gripped me for a moment, and I pulled up my shirt to find a popped suture. At least it wasn't a bullet hole. Still, my sigh of relief had an asterisk.

The sound of boots moving cautiously forward snapped me back to attention, and I fired a blind shot around the corner of the crate to keep the suited skinheads from advancing.

Four shots left.

Rad was peeking around the other side of the crate.

"The one you hit earlier," Rad said, "he's leaned up against a wall, bleeding out. It's just Rapunzel and the other one. We can take 'em."

"Very glass half full. I like it," I said. "But I'm gonna need a lot more than that if we get out of here alive."

"'If,' my ass," Rad snorted. "Divide. Conquer. On three we move in opposite directions. I'll bolt for the door to our left and head outside, lure at least one out. You go right, head down that hallway toward the office. While they're chasing me, you get the film."

"That's a terri—"

"*Onetwothree!*" And he took off.

"Hey!" shouted Rapunzel's living sidekick. I moved

and fired two shots to draw their attention from Rad. Both missed, but Rad made it to the door.

Two shots left.

"Go after the spic," Rapunzel ordered. "Damage is mine!"

A chunk of wall burst just as I reached the hallway. Rapunzel fired again, and I ducked into one of the smaller sets. I heard him reach the end of the hall and curse under his breath. He hadn't seen where I'd gone, which bought me a little time. Apparently, I'd ducked into the office scene of a film noir porn parody. A door with frosted glass had the word *Privates Investigator* painted on it. Across from it was a desk that sat in front of a faux window looking out onto an admittedly competent set dressing of the Golden Gate Bridge. I ducked behind the desk and started checking for any props I could use as misdirection. Something I could use to lure him in a certain direction and take him by surprise. On the desk was a scene marker that read *The Maltese Fuckin*.

"Of course," I whispered.

"Alex," Rapunzel sang from the hallway. "Oh, Alex!" I heard him step into another set.

Marker in hand, I ducked across the hall into some kind of Egyptian tomb. It still smelled like sweat and lube. I looked for a place to take cover, but of course all the big, yellowish bricks were made of Styrofoam. I tossed the marker back into the office set, and it slapped against the ground. Rapunzel ran out in the hall again, and I ducked behind a foam rubber sphinx with a raging erection that reeked of pussy.

Lights in the hall cast Rapunzel's shadow across the tomb floor as he turned into the PI office set and snickered. Before firing three shots into the desk. I had an opening but couldn't bring myself to shoot anyone in the back. Even Rapunzel. Sticking a gun to the back of his head and making him drop his, that I could live with. I tried to move, but pain tore through my body like a hurricane. I groaned and he turned. I fired but struggled to hold my aim steady and hit the doorframe. We both ducked to the side. Him in the hall, me behind the sphinx.

One shot left.

"I've been countin', ya know," Rapunzel said with a witch-like cackle in his voice. "That was five shots."

"Looks like I underestimated you," I said. "Figured I'd have lost you at three."

"Think you're so smart?"

"Only relatively," I said. On a good day, one shot was all I needed. Day like today, I wasn't even sure an extended-clip automatic would do. From down the hall, I heard someone enter the main studio.

"Boss!" they shouted. My heart in a vice, I cursed softly but viciously. "Boss, you in here?!"

"Down here. I got Damage cornered. Did you take care of the spic?"

"I, uh, couldn't, couldn't find him ...," he stuttered. His nervousness was my own source of relief.

"Fuckin' hell, Merv. Really?!"

I poked my head out, and when there was no gunfire, I moved toward the door, slowly and quietly, doing my best to aim steady through the pain and dizzy spells.

"I'm sorry, boss," Merv said. "He, he got the drop on me."

"One move and I snap his fucking neck," came Rad's voice from down the hall.

"You dirty cunt!" Rapunzel shouted. I took my chances and came out of the door, aiming in the direction of Rapunzel's voice. His head was turned and I jammed the barrel into the lower back of his skull and pulled back the hammer. Rad was at the end of the hall, holding Merv in a choke hold with the bat. A stream of blood was trickling down Merv's face.

"Hands up or I blow your immaculately shaved head clean off," I said. "Even I won't miss at this range." He did as he was told. "Toss the gun." He tossed it about halfway between him and Rad. Right about then I noticed that the skin I'd shot before had regained consciousness. He was still trying to hold his blood in with one hand, but the other was lifting a gun and aiming it at Rad. I turned, aimed, and fired. Through some combination of will and dumb luck, I got him in the head.

And that, dear friends, was me without bullets.

I had to assume Rapunzel grinned as he elbowed me in the gut and dove for his gun. I stumbled but stayed on my feet. I dove back into the PI office set and scrambled behind the desk as he tried to get two shots off.

"You're out!" Rapunzel mocked.

"If you're so confident about that, why don't you come over here?" I shouted. I put my gun away and pulled out my switchblade, flicking it open.

"Or I could just shoot your boyfriend, innit?" he said. I cursed under my breath and closed the blade, hid it inside my sleeve, and tucked it into my lucky wrist cuff. I loosened the cuff enough that I could slip the knife into my hand with a quick motion.

"Okay!" I said as I stood up and put my hand over my head. "Okay! I'm coming out."

"Hands up. Slow like," Rapunzel said. "Count of three."

I counted off as I slowly approached the door, hands to the sky as if testifying. As I came out into the hall, I saw Rad gripping his bat like a claymore sword. Rapunzel had his gun pointed at him as Merv leaned up against a crate and attempted to catch his breath.

"Merv, grab his bat," Rapunzel said, then turned his attention and gun to me.

Rad tried to use the opportunity to strike Merv with the bat, but Merv managed to catch the bat, wrestle it from Rad's grip, and toss it away. Rad cracked him across the face with the knuckle dusters, but the guy was a brick shithouse and would not go down easy. He tackled Rad, got on top of him, and proceeded to work him over. Rad managed to deflect many blows, but it wasn't looking good. With a gun in my face, I could only watch. Rapunzel grinned with delight as he pulled back the hammer of the gun.

"I thought you needed to take us alive!" I said.

"Boss didn't say you needed to be well," he said with a smirk.

"He'll want us well enough to talk," I said. Rapunzel grunted.

"They never let me have *any* fun," he hissed. "Fine. Keep your hands up. Merv, lay off the spic. Remember this, you fuckin' poofter, I could have killed you this whole time. I was playing with you."

"Got it. Cat playin' with the mouse." I kept my hands up as I subtly twisted my wrist until I felt the switchblade in my wrist cuff start to slide.

Rad was groaning on the floor, beaten to hell. Eddie and Seth weren't in the room. They had, I assumed, slipped into one of the back rooms when the shooting started.

"Okay," Rapunzel said, "you're coming with me. Now."

"Sure," I said. "Sure." Merv went to pick up his fallen compatriot's gun and Rad sprang into action, jumping on his back. With Rapunzel momentarily distracted, I slipped the knife into my hand with a quick downward motion of my arm, flicked out the blade, and threw it at Rapunzel, hitting him in the shoulder. He got off one shot, but the shot hit a wall. I moved in and tackled him to the ground. He took a swing at me and cracked his hand on the war chain I had wrapped around me.

"Fuck!" he shouted. I headbutted him in the nose, shattering it. He clawed at me, but I held him down. I heard Rad snap Merv's neck. He picked up the gun and walked over to me.

"You okay?" he asked.

"Better than you look," I said. "Let's tie him up." We used

my chain to tie him to an exposed pipe. As we were doing so, Eddie and Seth slinked out of the office. I walked over.

"Hi, boys," I said. They both stood up.

Rad went into the office. "Okay, ladies," he said. "It's okay. Auditions are over. Go home." Three college-age girls gathered their clothes and ran out the door, averting their running mascara. Eddie stood up with his hands in the air.

"You are tough guys, yeah ..."

"We are iron," I said. "Don't fucking forget it."

"The film," Rad said.

"What about it?" said Nash.

"We want it," Rad said. "The original."

"You really think you can handle the amount of shit that will fall on you if you have it?" Nash said.

"You really want to underestimate us again?" Rad said. I hadn't seen this side of Rad in a long time. I had always known it was there. And so help me, I wouldn't have believed it myself, but Eddie Nash was taken aback.

"Basement," Nash said. "Back office on the left. Filing cabinet, bottom drawer." Rad followed his vocal treasure map and, sure enough, he walked out with a film canister. No label. I opened it, and there, resting on top of the roll of film, were the missing pages from Eddie Nash's ledger and clear-as-day photos of Senator David Cromwell soliciting prostitutes. With that, I'd also solved the mystery of who had broken into Bad Chemicals' van. How long had the fucker had it? Before he kidnapped and tortured me? After? Whatever. Irrelevant. Fuck it.

"Thanks," I said, slipping the pages and photos into my jacket's hidden pocket.

"You fuck. I will kill you for this," Nash said. His eyes seemed to foam as much as his mouth.

"Oh damn, that's right. You probably will," I said. I pulled back the hammer of Rapunzel's gun. "Thanks for the reminder." He just laughed.

"Do you realize what will happen if you kill me? Death will not stop my revenge. My men will come for you. Come for the people you love first. Beat them with hammers and pipes. Make you watch while they rape your lover. My friends in the police will throw you in jail. There you will rot. And you will wait and wait, maybe days or years, for the sword to fall, until finally you will die bleeding with a cock in your ass!"

He had me there. I had no doubt of his failsafe plan. But looking at that man, if you could even call him that, I started to think of all the things he'd done. And not just to me. I thought about the humiliation he'd subjected Brandy to when she was alive. How he'd ordered her death. The way he'd let her die. Even if it had been the act of Miguel Gonzalez, the owner of a dog is accountable for its bites. Then I started thinking about the things he had said. About the power of information. The importance of reputation. And that put a smile on my face.

But first things first. We still had our primary mission, after all. Eddie could wait. I just needed him to stay put.

I nodded to Rad, who held a gun to Seth and Eddie as I walked over to a wet bar that was set up in the corner of the "casting office." I opened the cabinet below and, just as I'd suspected, found an impressive selection of pills. I poured four drinks, mixed pills into two of them, came back out, and handed them to Seth and Eddie.

"Drink up, buttercup," I said.

"Why? Will you shoot me if I do not?" Eddie said. "Did you not hear me? You kill me and—"

"You'll still be dead," I said.

"This buys you hours," Eddie sneered before drinking, "at best."

"I only need fifteen minutes."

We tied up Eddie and Seth in a basement room before we took the film upstairs and found a door labeled *Viewing Room.*

We dragged Rapunzel in with us, his mouth taped up.

"Come on, motherfucker. I'm going to need you to verify some shit to your employer." We summoned our AV-club-geek days in high school and fired up the movie. We watched it for less than a minute. That was all it took to confirm what it was. And that was all either of us could stomach. We took it out back with some high-proof alcohol from the wet bar. We brought Rapunzel along for that too. We found an old oil drum and dumped a bunch of the booze on the film. I unraveled a bit of the film strip, set it on fire, and tossed it into the drum. We watched it burn and shared what was left of the booze before heading back inside.

Eddie Nash started to wake up, slowly at first, then all at once. He was naked and chained up, leaning over a pommel horse.

"What the ...," he stammered as he thrashed around in a vain attempt to loosen his restraints. "What the fuck?!"

He tried to take in his surroundings. At first there was a look of familiarity as he glanced around the porn set made up to look like a gym storage shed. There were bats and balls behind a section of chain-link fence, gymnastics mats, and a lightbulb hanging from the ceiling. His eyes damn near burst when he saw that a section of the ball cage served as a rack for an impressive cross-section of sex toys. Studded paddles. Paddles with holes. Whips with one tail. Whips with nine. Red-ribbed dildos. Short, fat purple ones. And one that split off into branches that showed either a deep understanding of human anatomy or a complete lack thereof.

The dots started to connect when he saw Seth, who was standing next to a camera, tears in his eyes. Eddie's eyes followed along the gun pointed at Seth's head to find Rad. With his other hand, Rad pulled a luchador mask over Seth's head. Finally, he saw me, slouched in a director's chair, an acoustic megaphone sitting next to me. I made a pyramid with my fingers and brought my hands to my face.

"We will make a film. Yes?"

It was time to talk with Rapunzel. We ripped the tape off his mouth.

"You're gonna pay for this, you dago arse-bandit. You and the spic."

"Spic? Me?" said Rad. "I'm a quarter Serrano, you limey bastard!"

"You're gonna take us to your boss," I said.

"Fuck! That's what I wanted to do in the *first place!*"

"Well, then. You should have asked nicer. *Innit?*" I said before punching him in the face.

Two punks walking into a government office with a bloodied skinhead is bound to turn heads. I get that. But screaming? Come on. The receptionist reached for the phone in a panic before Rapunzel busted out his staff ID.

"Hi. Senator Cromwell, please. We're his two o'clock," I said. She froze.

"They're with me," Rapunzel said with a touch more venom than we'd rehearsed. She just nodded.

"W-wait right here, please. W-would you like a c-coffee?"

"Yes, please," I said in my most pleasant voice. "That sounds great." But before she could ask how I take it, men in suits emerged from the office and dragged us in. "No cream and just a little sugar," I said fast as I could as they pulled me past her.

Senator Cromwell's eyes were molten lava. "Let's talk," he said. "Your friend can wait outside." Rad looked concerned, but I nodded. He hesitated a moment before he nodded back and left, but not before looking back at me just long enough to worry me. It shakes my confidence when people look at me as if they think it's the last time. Cromwell looked to Rapunzel. "Go get cleaned up."

"Employing neo-Nazis, I see?"

Cromwell just stared.

"You know he's not even American, right? It's the accent that gives him away."

Cromwell just stared.

"He calls elevators 'lifts.'"

Cromwell smacked his hands on the table.

"Where is my daughter?" he said.

"Do you really want to know where your daughter is? Or just the porn she shot with the late Jerry Rash?" I asked, helping myself to some of the M&M's in a bowl on his desk. He quickly stood up. He wanted to hit me so bad he was about to explode. "That's right, I know about the movie. We both know you know where your daughter is. And we both know you don't care. You just want to get rid of the ways she can hurt you."

"You shut your damn mouth."

"But then how can I tell you where the film is?" I said. He sat back down. He closed his eyes, and I could tell he was counting to ten.

"Very well," he said. "Talk."

"You don't have to worry about the film," I said. "I destroyed it."

"How do I know you're telling the truth? How do I know you won't use it to blackmail me?"

"Please," I said. "Kiddie porn? I don't want to have that floating around anymore than you do. Besides, your man can confirm its destruction."

"What about copies?"

"Like I said, I don't want kiddie porn out there. If you're worried about copies, take that up with your business partners."

"Business partners?" he said.

"You know goddamn well who I mean. Don't play coy. I'm your fucking constituency, after all. We respond to honesty."

"I suppose you want payment. For your ... consultant work?"

"Damn right I do," I said.

"All right, name your price. I will sign you a check."

"You can sign my ass," I said. "I don't want your money."

"It seems to me you might need it. The lifestyle you live."

"Oh, I get by just fine."

"Very well. What do you want?"

"I want you to back the fuck off me and my friends. Call off the hits."

"Hits? I'm a politician, not a gangster."

"You say 'potato' ..."

"What's to stop me from just ... doing away with you, then?"

"If that favor isn't motive enough, maybe photography is? The Moral Majority might find it interesting that you crawl for prostitutes closer to your daughter's age than your wife's. Oh, and as an added bonus, I can link you to Eddie Nash's operations in ways that will, at the very least, crucify you in the court of public opinion. If not a RICO case. I got evidence sitting in a safety deposit box. Anything happens to me or mine, it releases. I die, for any reason, and my will states its contents should be released in care of your local station and cable news providers. I've also got a few dozen newspapers from around the country listed as beneficiaries. Consider it a failsafe." His fists tightened, which made me grin. "Yeah, that's right. I have a will."

I tossed an M&M into the air but missed catching it. He watched it roll across the floor.

"I worked out a similar deal with Nash," I said, then whispered, "but yours is better." And shot him a wink.

"Fine. I suppose I *do* owe you," he said. And yet again,

I was surviving off favors. But this one made me feel dirty. Even if it did involve destroying kiddie porn. He picked up a phone.

"This is Cromwell. Cancel account 61822. Again, cancel account 61822 … Yes, thank you." He hung up and looked to me. "There. We're even. Are we done here?"

"Sweet fucking Christ, I hope so," I said. I got up and moved for the door.

"I care, you know," he said. I stopped. "Yeah. I wanted to get rid of that humiliating film. But he … humiliated my daughter. He *hurt* my daughter. *Ruined* her. I did what any father would do."

"Spare me the Father of the Year bullshit," I said. "He did, yeah. And even though I don't have kids, I *get* that the fatherly instinct to crush anyone who would hurt your child is a thing. But let's not embarrass ourselves by pretending that had anything to do with it. You killed him because he humiliated *you*, he hurt *you*, he would have ruined *you*. The fact is, your little girl wanted what every little girl wants. To be seen by the people who are supposed to love her most no matter what. But you *ignored* her. And to make matters worse, when she became inconvenient, you swept her under the rug. You want to blame someone, let me narrow down the options for you." I pointed at his reflection in the window. The night sky had turned it into a mirror.

He said nothing, just stared at me, eyes darting about.

"Oh my God," I said. "You actually believe that, don't you? You actually believe you were looking out for *her*." I shook my head and laughed. "Wow, Senator. I expect you to be really good at lying to voters. But, damn. Lying to yourself? That takes *real* talent." With that, I waved with the back of my hand as I walked out the door. "See you on the picket lines, *Senator*."

Epilogue

I was days into catching up on some long neglected sleep when I heard a knock on my door. I rolled off my shitty mattress. I didn't own a robe, so I just put my jacket on, since it was the only article of clothing within reaching distance. Of course it only goes down to the waist, so my red briefs were still on full display when I answered the door. It was Zii.

"Hi," she said.

"Hi," I said back. I gestured toward the desk. "Have a seat."

"I'm not staying long," she said. "Things got kind of intense."

"Yeah," I said.

"But, still. Thank you."

"Mmm," I grunted in acknowledgment.

"I guess I owe you some money then?" she said. "For completing the job, right?"

"That's right," I said.

"Well, here." She reached into her wallet and put far more cash on the table than she had any business walking around West Hollywood with, even if she did know how to take care of herself. It was more than we had discussed, but I wasn't going to argue. "So. Job well done." She tucked some hair behind her ear, averted her gaze, and bit her lip. Things I would normally take as a signal. But not this time. It made me wonder how many times I had read things as signals that weren't actually signals. If it were in human nature to really reflect on our past behaviors, mirrors would never have found a marketplace.

"Thanks," I said.

"I thought you should know that Lisa and I have decided to come forward about Jerry. People need to know what Jerry really was."

I nodded. "Probably," I said. "Definitely," I amended after a beat. "But it ain't my place to approve or not. That's your call to make."

"We figured you should know to expect some backlash."

"Probably," I said.

"It was really Lisa's call. I agreed and all," she said. "It's just ... I dunno. People need a leader. Where do we get one now?"

"Maybe people should just get out of the habit of following," I said. "Kill their idols."

"Maybe you're right."

"Well, thanks for the update."

"Listen," she said, and I tried to. "For what it's worth, you were so much more than a diversion."

"That's the nicest thing anyone's said to me," I said.

"I'm serious, Alex. But we've each said and done some things and, well ... I'm gonna get out of town awhile. Maybe go to college. Somewhere upstate. I just can't be ... here. Y'know?"

"Sure," I said.

"But I ... I hope I see you around again. I just need time. I think we both do."

"Yeah," I said.

"You should take a vacation," she said.

"Maybe."

"Okay, well. Bye, Alex." She leaned in like she was going to kiss my cheek, but I'm glad, for both our sakes, that she didn't.

I had a stack of cash and pent-up tension to match, so I headed to Al's. There was a gig on. I paid the cover and made straight for the bar.

"Jameson," I said as I slapped down cash. "Double. Neat." The band was really good, and I couldn't see through the crowd from the end of the bar, but I wasn't really trying either. I was just getting into the sound of it. I didn't notice that I was getting a whole room of dirty looks.

"Who's the band?" I asked the bartender when he came back to pour my drink.

"The Wire Hangers," he said.

"They new?" I asked.

"Sort of," he said. I looked to the stage and saw the former members of Bad Chemicals onstage. Reggie Reckless was singing.

He's a traitor
A Benedict Arnold
If I see that fuck
I'll run him down full throttle

Bash his skull in
It's what he deserves
Gouge out his eyes
Rip out his nerves

It was also at this time I noticed them noticing me, and when they did, the intensity of the song grew. Was this about *me?* People in the audience were nudging each other and tilting heads in my direction. My name is pretty easy to read on lips. I took my drink in one shot and ordered another.

They followed up with a cover of a Hank Williams tune that Bad Chemicals used to do, and the crowd turned its attention away from me for the two minutes it took to sing along about never getting out of this world alive.

That song apparently was their last, because by the time my drink came, they were done and Reggie was moving toward me.

"You got some nerve," he said.

Luke stepped up. "Easy now, Reggie," Luke said.

"Who the fuck do you think you are?" Reggie said to me.

"I think I'm Alex Damage," I said.

"Where do you get off dragging a dead man's name through the mud like that?"

"Hey. I'm not the one who raped a fourteen-year-old girl after getting her addicted to heroin so I could blackmail her father! You wanna be pissed at someone? Be pissed at Jerry!" At least that's what I wanted to say. I got to "raped a fourteen" before Reggie punched me in the face. I moved to retaliate, but Luke got between us. Double held Reggie back until he walked away, then focused on signaling the crowd back.

"Easy!" said Luke. "Alex, Reggie's upset."

"Yeah, I can fucking see that!" I said, checking the blood from my nose.

"Listen, man," Luke said. "It's been getting around. The stuff you, Rad, and Zii did. What you all say Jerry did. And I'm not saying that I blame you or anything. You just gotta realize that Jerry meant a lot to a lot of people. Y'know? I know he wasn't perfect. Everybody knew that, but this is a lot to process. Not everybody … *believes* it."

"What do *you* believe, Luke?" I asked.

"That doesn't matter."

"You were his bandmate. What do *you* believe?" I asked again.

"I believe you should leave."

I took my second drink in one shot, then followed Luke's advice. I stopped by Oki-Dog and got food. It was still on the house. I ate alone. It gave me a chance to think. I thought about how I could let admiration blind me to the actions of a wicked man. I thought about the darker side of having heroes and the fallacy of pedestals. And I thought about all the ways I, myself, had been guilty. I thought about all the ways I had thought about women and talked about women.

The jokes I had laughed at and the ones I had made. I thought about all the kisses I "just went for" because James Bond and Clark Gable had made me believe that was manly and romantic. I thought about how wrong I'd been about what being a man was. I had often heard that "a real man takes what he wants." But that ain't it. Babies do that. You can't learn all the things I'd learned without self-reflecting. You can't learn all the things I'd learned without taking ownership for all the times you fucked up. You can't learn all that and not change. I had to hold myself accountable for my own mistakes. I had to be better.

Once I'd finished eating, I decided I should get the fuck out of Dodge before the shows let out and the crowds showed up. I got up and started to walk down Santa Monica Boulevard.

I was waiting at a light when a white panel van pulled up, the kind bands rent to take on tour. A bunch of guys in ski masks piled out and were on me. I tried to fight them off, but even if I were fully recovered, I wouldn't have been able to take on seven guys with pipes and chains. I took blows to the arms, ribs, and face. Their steel-toed boots felt just how they looked. I want to say I've had worse. But it gets to a point where it doesn't matter. The beating hurt until I stopped feeling anything, and once you pass that point, how bad one beating is compared to another is moot.

It seemed like minutes, but I'm sure it was only seconds, because I wouldn't have walked away otherwise. Finally, some Good Samaritans shouted at them and chased them off.

"That was for Jerry, faggot!" one of the masked men shouted before he slammed the van door as they peeled out.

So much for my reputation.

The strangers helped me to my feet. "Jesus Christ! Are you okay?" My eyes were swollen, and I couldn't get a good look at them. I wasn't sure if they were punks or preps or surfers or goths or new wavers or rockabilly revivalists. Hell, they could have been cops for all the mind I paid them. I spit my blood in vain at the van as it drove off.

"It was worth it, you fucking assholes!" I shouted. But there was no way they could have heard me. So, I just laughed.

What the fuck else was I going to do?

ABOUT PM PRESS

PM Press is an independent, radical publisher
of books and media to educate, entertain, and
inspire. Founded in 2007 by a small group of
people with decades of publishing, media, and
organizing experience, PM Press amplifies the
voices of radical authors, artists, and activists.
Our aim is to deliver bold political ideas and vital stories to people from
all walks of life and arm the dreamers to demand the impossible. We
have sold millions of copies of our books, most often one at a time, face
to face. We're old enough to know what we're doing and young enough
to know what's at stake. Join us to create a better world.

PM Press
PO Box 23912
Oakland, CA 94623
www.pmpress.org

PM Press in Europe
europe@pmpress.org
www.pmpress.org.uk

FRIENDS OF PM PRESS

These are indisputably momentous times—the financial system is melting down globally and the Empire is stumbling. Now more than ever there is a vital need for radical ideas.

In the many years since its founding—and on a mere shoestring—PM Press has risen to the formidable challenge of publishing and distributing knowledge and entertainment for the struggles ahead. With hundreds of releases to date, we have published an impressive and stimulating array of literature, art, music, politics, and culture. Using every available medium, we've succeeded in connecting those hungry for ideas and information to those putting them into practice.

Friends of PM allows you to directly help impact, amplify, and revitalize the discourse and actions of radical writers, filmmakers, and artists. It provides us with a stable foundation from which we can build upon our early successes and provides a much-needed subsidy for the materials that can't necessarily pay their own way. You can help make that happen—and receive every new title automatically delivered to your door once a month—by joining as a Friend of PM Press. And, we'll throw in a free T-shirt when you sign up.

Here are your options:

- **$30 a month** Get all books and pamphlets plus a 50% discount on all webstore purchases

- **$40 a month** Get all PM Press releases (including CDs and DVDs) plus a 50% discount on all webstore purchases

- **$100 a month** Superstar—Everything plus PM merchandise, free downloads, and a 50% discount on all webstore purchases

For those who can't afford $30 or more a month, we have **Sustainer Rates** at $15, $10 and $5. Sustainers get a free PM Press T-shirt and a 50% discount on all purchases from our website.

Your Visa or Mastercard will be billed once a month, until you tell us to stop. Or until our efforts succeed in bringing the revolution around. Or the financial meltdown of Capital makes plastic redundant. Whichever comes first.

23 Shades of Black

Kenneth Wishnia
with an introduction by
Barbara D'Amato

ISBN: 978-1-60486-587-5
$17.95   300 pages

23 Shades of Black is socially conscious crime fiction. It takes place in New York City in the early 1980s, i.e., the Reagan years, and was written partly in response to the reactionary discourse of the time, when the current thirty-year assault on the rights of working people began in earnest, and the divide between rich and poor deepened with the blessing of the political and corporate elites. But it is not a political tract, it's a kick-ass novel that was nominated for the Edgar and the Anthony Awards, and made *Booklist*'s Best First Mysteries of the Year.

The heroine, Filomena Buscarsela, is an immigrant who experienced tremendous poverty and injustice in her native Ecuador, and who grew up determined to devote her life to helping others. She tells us that she really should have been a priest, but since that avenue was closed to her, she chose to become a cop instead. The problem is that as one of the first *latinas* on the NYPD, she is not just a woman in a man's world, she is a woman of color in a white man's world. And it's hell. Filomena is mistreated and betrayed by her fellow officers, which leads her to pursue a case independently in the hopes of being promoted to detective for the Rape Crisis Unit.

Along the way, she is required to enforce unjust drug laws that she disagrees with, and to betray her own community (which ostracizes her as a result) in an undercover operation to round up illegal immigrants. Several scenes are set in the East Village art and punk rock scene of the time, and the murder case eventually turns into an investigation of corporate environmental crime from a working class perspective that is all-too-rare in the genre.

And yet this thing is damn funny, too.

"Packed with enough mayhem and atmosphere for two novels."
—*Booklist*

Karl Marx Private Eye

Jim Feast

ISBN: 978-1-62963-993-2
$16.95   208 pages

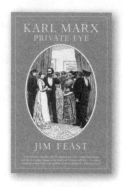

A rattling good yarn and a suspenseful
whodunit, against the backdrop of real
historical events, that brings sixteen-year-old
Sherlock Holmes together with Karl Marx
and his brilliant daughter Eleanor to solve a
cascading series of murders at a Bohemian spa.

Karl Marx Private Eye is a page-turner filled with tricky clues, colorful
detectives, and an "exotic" setting. Written in a brilliant parody of Arthur
Conan Doyle, this cozy historical mystery will keep readers guessing
until its shocking final pages.

*"'Every murder is a parable,' quips Jim Feast's Eleanor Marx. Indeed. Feast's
hyperreal historical collage manages to feel equal parts Columbo and Perec,
and to graft Nicholas Meyer's* The Seven-Per-Cent Solution *into Max
Ernst's* Une Semaine de Bonté. *I'm already greedy for another of these
ripping father-daughter whodunits."*
—Jonathan Lethem, author of *The Arrest* and *The Feral Detective*

"In Karl Marx Private Eye, *Jim Feast not only engages us intellectually, but
as the readers unravel the mysteries, there's a good laugh every few pages
and gorgeous descriptions of the hotel, the clothing, and the food of the time.
It's a very witty, fast-moving story with a terrific ending. If you like detective
fiction, you'll love this book."*
—Barbara Henning, author of *Just Like That* and *Digigram*

*"Feast writes with a poet's pen, a humorist's wit, and a Dashiell Hammett
knack for detective fiction. When a series of dastardly crimes are committed
amidst Bohemia's health spas for the rich, you don't need a Hercule Poirot
when you have the improbable team of Karl Marx and a teenage Sherlock
Holmes on the case. Luscious writing that evokes the politics and culture of
the era."*
—Peter Werbe, author of *Summer on Fire: A Detroit Novel* and member of
the *Fifth Estate* magazine editorial collective

RUIN

Cara Hoffman

ISBN: 978-1-62963-929-1 (paperback)
978-1-62963-931-4 (hardcover)
$14.95/$25.95   128 pages

A little girl who disguises herself as an old man, an addict who collects dollhouse furniture, a crime reporter confronted by a talking dog, a painter trying to prove the non-existence of god, and lovers in a penal colony who communicate through technical drawings—these are just a few of the characters who live among the ruins. Cara Hoffman's short fictions are brutal, surreal, hilarious, and transgressive, celebrating the sharp beauty of outsiders and the infinitely creative ways humans muster psychic resistance under oppressive conditions. RUIN is both bracingly timely and eerily timeless in its examination of an American state in free-fall: unsparing in its disregard for broken, ineffectual institutions, while shining with compassion for the damaged left in their wake. The ultimate effect of these ten interconnected stories is one of invigoration and a sense of possibilities—hope for a new world extracted from the rubble of the old.

Cara Hoffman is the author of three New York Times Editors' Choice novels; the most recent, *Running*, was named a Best Book of the Year by *Esquire Magazine*. She first received national attention in 2011 with the publication of *So Much Pretty* which sparked a national dialogue on violence and retribution, and was named a Best Novel of the Year by the *New York Times Book Review*. Her second novel, *Be Safe I Love You*, was nominated for a Folio Prize, named one of the Five Best Modern War Novels, and awarded a Sundance Global Filmmaking Award. A MacDowell Fellow and an Edward Albee Fellow, she has lectured at Oxford University's Rhodes Global Scholars Symposium and at the Renewing the Anarchist Tradition Conference. Her work has appeared in the *New York Times*, *Paris Review*, *BOMB*, *Bookforum*, *Rolling Stone*, *Daily Beast*, and on NPR. A founding editor of the *Anarchist Review of Books*, and part of the Athens Workshop collective, she lives in Athens, Greece, with her partner.

"RUIN *is a collection of ten jewels, each multi-faceted and glittering, to be experienced with awe and joy. Cara Hoffman has seen a secret world right next to our own, just around the corner, and written us a field guide to what she's found. I love this book.*"
—Sara Gran, author of *Infinite Blacktop* and *Claire Dewitt and the City of the Dead*

Going Underground: American Punk 1979–1989, Second Edition

George Hurchalla

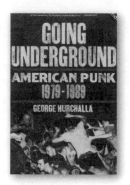

ISBN: 978-1-62963-113-4
$21.95   416 pages

The product of decades of work and multiple self-published editions, *Going Underground*, written by 1980s scene veteran George Hurchalla, is the most comprehensive look yet at America's nationwide underground punk scene.

Despite the mainstream press declarations that "punk died with Sid Vicious" or that "punk was reborn with Nirvana," author Hurchalla followed the DIY spirit of punk underground, where it not only survived but thrived nationally as a self-sustaining grassroots movement rooted in seedy clubs, rented fire halls, Xeroxed zines, and indie record shops.

Rather than dwell solely on well-documented scenes from Los Angeles, New York, and Washington, DC, Hurchalla delves deep into the counterculture, rooting out stories from Chicago, Philadelphia, Austin, Cincinnati, Miami, and elsewhere. The author seamlessly mixes his personal experiences with the oral history of dozens of band members, promoters, artists, zinesters, and scenesters. Some of the countless bands covered include Articles of Faith, Big Boys, Necros, Hüsker Dü, Bad Brains, Government Issue, and Minutemen, as well as many of the essential zines of the time such as *Big Takeover*, *Maximum RocknRoll*, *Flipside*, and *Forced Exposure*.

Going Underground features over a hundred unique photos from Marie Kanger-Born of Chicago, Dixon Coulbourn of Austin, Brian Trudell of LA, Malcolm Riviera of DC, Justina Davies of New York, Ed Arnaud of Arizona, and many others, along with flyers from across the nation.

"*Hurchalla's efforts are impressive, given the fragmented and regional nature of American hardcore in the Eighties, a time well before the Web made for a truly Punk Planet. Mimicking an Eighties-era tour, it meanders all over the place without ever fully wearing out its welcome.*"
—Marc Savlov, *Austin Chronicle*